ENEMIES TO LOVERS

USA TODAY Bestselling Author
BRITTNI CHENELLE

BROWSE YOUR OPTIONS

Welcome to the *Enemies to Lovers Collection of Series Starters!* Each story represents a different genre and heat level, all centered around the Enemies to Lovers trope. If you're not sure where to start, I recommend *The Fae & The Fallen*.

Kingdom Cold

Series: Kingdom Cold (Book 1)

YA Fantasy Romance

Heat: Low

Princess Charlotte's whole world changed one morning over breakfast. With her mother announcing a rushed arranged marriage to a humorless prince, she'll do anything to stop the wedding – including shooting him with an arrow. But after the kingdom is invaded and a sinister plot to capture her discovered, can she convince her unwanted suitor to help keep her out of enemy hands?

The Fae and The Fallen

Series: Gifted Fae Academy (Book 1)

NA Urban Fantasy

Heat: Medium

Reina Bennet won't stop believing that she'll eventually get her abilities. But when her childhood champion grows up into a smug super-powered bully, her escalating rivalry with her ex-friend gets them both kicked out of school. And after he ends up in a rebel group at their new academy, can she put aside her grudges for a chance at a fresh beginning?

Chaste Blood

Repressed Royals (Book 1)

Paranormal Romance

Heat: High

Princess Sinna of the Shadow Court fears her fated mate means certain death. So when a magical ceremony reveals him as the powerful vampire king, she's eager to prove she can be a worthy Hunter by killing him. But can she stop herself from falling hard as she tries to seduce him into a fatal embrace?

CONTENTS

KINGDOM COLD

BRITTNI CHENELLE

KINGDOM COLD

A YA Novel

USA TODAY BESTSELLING AUTHOR
BRITTNI CHENELLE

I dedicate this novel to my father—the man who saw glimpses of brilliance in me before I did.

CONTENTS

ALSO AVAILABLE
IN AUDIO

Take advantage of the
discounted price.

CHAPTER 1
PRINCESS CHARLOTTE

Dying wasn't my intention yet there I lay, ravenous—twelve hours into my hunger strike—certain I was already slipping away. The moans of my stomach begged me to submit to the various trays of food within an arm's reach. I swallowed a gulp of nectarous air, the toasty cinnamon and sweet apples making my mouth water. My mother was not relenting, but neither was I. As I lay dying, I didn't watch my life flash before my eyes. Instead, I replayed the few hours that led me to this desperate act.

She could have said, "Pass the sugar" or "Did your new ball-gown come in yet?" But "We have agreed to accept Prince Young's proposal for your hand" could have waited until after breakfast.

I pushed my plate away, the sweet crepe turning limp and unappealing. "The Eastern Statue? He never smiles! Of all people..." The full meaning of her words sunk in. "Marriage?"

She nodded, folding her napkin and placing it beside her plate, as if discussing the weather.

My head swam. I was supposed to have two more years. "You can't do this to me!"

"Oh, Charlotte. Do we have to do the dramatics? We don't have time to wait, with Drethen marching closer every day."

Sobs choked me. I never wanted to be a queen, but as their only child, there was no choice. "I-I won't say 'I do'."

Mother stood with a graceful movement, each step precisely measured. "You will do your duty, the way we all must."

She tipped my chin up and I reluctantly met her eyes. "He's only a year older than you. Without this alliance—" Her words hung in the silence, but she pursed her lips. She knew what it was to enter an arranged marriage. My father was twenty years her senior, and while they cooperated to rule Besmium, it was hardly love. I swallowed back a new wave of tears, my face hot as I melted into my chair like a wax candle at the end of a banquet. She studied my face then took her leave with poised, deliberate steps before I could respond.

I walked to my bedroom, trembling, and collapsed on the floor. Milly, my lady-in-waiting, appeared.

"Is everything—"

"Corset off. "

Milly rushed over, her small hands unlacing my corset with quick, decisive movements. From behind me, all I could see of her was an occasional wisp of summery hair. When she finished, she dropped down in front of me, as if my morbid energy was draining her.

"What happened?"

"I have to marry the Prince of Vires," I said as I buried my face in my hands.

She leaned forward, awaiting more information, as I remained motionless. Her eyes widened. "Marriage? But you're only sixteen."

I sat up and gave a hard nod, shaking a few of my dark curls from their pins. We sat there in silence. Each drape, chandelier, and ornately decorated vase screamed the same thing: my life wasn't mine.

I strained to remember him. I'd met Prince Young once. Dark hair and dark, heavy-lidded eyes that curved in at the corners... But his face—I couldn't really recall it. I could only remember the feeling of him. He'd seemed so serious and miserable, even more so than the stuffy, political vultures who circled court. I hadn't given him a single thought since we met. Now, all I could think about was his cold, heartless stature and a lifetime without laughter.

Milly wrapped her arms around me and pulled me in. She was a year younger yet I'd always gone to her for guidance. She was beautiful, the kind that could rival any well-groomed royal, but that wasn't what I envied. Even as a paid servant, she was in charge of her fate.

There was a whole world out there. Faraway kingdoms, deserts, waterfalls, mountains, all of which I'd never see. If I managed to sneak away, what skills could I offer for money or food? An escape was impractical when my only worthy attribute was my name. Without it, I wouldn't last a day. How could the name that had blessed me with such fine privileges be the one that shackled me? How could my parents trust my life and kingdom to a man we hardly knew? Should I take my chances and run away? Or try to think of a way to sabotage the wedding? Finally, I decided on a hunger strike.

Admittedly, I hadn't expected my mother to give in, but I

remained obstinate because she'd clearly expected me to. Anger welled inside me, tightening my stomach, which only emphasized its emptiness.

A fresh loaf of Sasha's wheat bread fluttered into the room on a silver tray. I sat up and stared as a servant placed the tray beside me, the corner of her mouth turned up.

I leaned into the steaming loaf and breathed in its warmth, my will sucked away like summer rain on dry soil. I was alone, for the moment. No doubt the servants were preparing to bring in the next temptation. My stomach ached for me to surrender. If I took a small bite from the bottom of the loaf, they'd never know. I lifted the loaf carefully and bit into it. My mind surged with delight and I savored the crunchy exterior and doughy flavor before carefully placing it back on the tray, bite side down.

I hesitated before I lay back down. Surely, my mother was evil for forcing me into such extremes, but my father wasn't. Why hadn't he intervened? Was the war with Drethen so dire that he was willing to sell his only daughter for a few extra soldiers?

I remembered that five years ago, when the war began, the rhythmic clop of two hundred horses reminded me of the rain. I was eleven and my father knelt before me, for kings bow to no one but the daughters they love. He urged me to hug him good-bye, but I didn't want to—I hated goodbyes. I remembered how my mother pinched the back of my arm.

"Hug your father," she rasped, coldly. "You'll regret your poor attitude if he's killed in battle."

I hugged him. The trumpets sounded as he mounted his horse—taking his place at the front. After that, we were always at war, and my father, the king, was always one goodbye away from being gone forever.

I reached over and ripped another piece of bread from the bottom of the loaf. I sighed as I popped it into my mouth.

No matter how many times my mother had prepared me for the news of my engagement, I still felt blindsided. A couple years ago, my father brought me a book called *The Dragon's Call*. At the end of the harrowing adventure, the heroine married for love and not advantage. I'd read it many times before I could even comprehend the concept, but once it was in my head, I couldn't seem to get it out. Now, as I faced my own marriage, I wondered where love was in all this. Was it just this abstract concept for novels and unspeakable inside the castle? Not even my father used the word. Maybe it was their way of protecting me from something I could never have. Marriage was the duty of every princess, and love was the cost.

I tore another piece of bread from the tray and rolled onto my stomach to avoid choking.

By the time I was fifteen, there was a party or tournament almost every month, parading me around like some trophy to be won. The other courtiers cooed over the high-standing men at court, but I never understood why. Sure, the idea of courting seemed fun enough. I could wear elaborate gowns and be whispered sonnets by handsome princes. But that's not how any of it actually happened. In the end, the choice was out of my hands. I'd marry whomever my father thought was best for the kingdom, and nothing about that seemed fun.

Throughout my early teens, I'd sneak out beyond the walls of the castle every chance I got to catch a glimpse of the world beyond. There, I saw children at play and parents home for dinner. There seemed to be a genuine warmth in the ordinary lives of Besmium's people that never existed in my world. My world was cold and structured. Every year the number of guards my father tasked to me increased. The servants seemed to be everywhere, and I could scarcely find a moment to be alone with my thoughts. Especially after my official betrothal, my mother put me under constant surveillance, and conversations about my future as a wife overtook all others. Still, I hadn't expected the day to come so quickly.

I chewed thoughtfully.

My desire to live a different life from the one I was born into remained strong. Marriage seemed like the fatal blow to my freedom. I knew it was impossible and that the consequences would be dire, but if life was different—if life was fair—the walls of the castle would fall and I'd walk out with no title and no crown. I'd be free to explore the world. Free to find out once and for all if love was only made for fiction.

Now that my engagement was official, I was certain that dream would never come to be.

I looked down at the empty platter in surprise. Did I eat the *whole thing*? I sat up, just in time to see one of the servants slip out of my room. Sure enough, minutes later, my mother strode into my chamber, her crown gleaming in the candlelight. She eyed the trays of uneaten food until her gaze landed on the empty tray beside me. Without a word she smiled, a searing and heartless grin that boiled my skin long after she'd gone. As helplessness overcame me, I scanned the room for the next tray I'd indulge in. There was no use resisting food now. I'd failed.

A week later, on the eve of the wedding, the prince was shown to my home at Hiems Castle. I could hear the distant *clip-clop* of his horse-drawn carriage as it pulled up outside. I stared into the mirror and studied my face.

It was about accepting all the things I'd never get to experience—love, freedom, happiness—but it was also about the things I wasn't ready for: a kiss, a consummation ceremony, and —above all—a husband.

CHAPTER 2
PRINCE YOUNG

I t was as if my life had finally started—an immense bolt of lightning that jolted me awake. I bowed deeply with gratitude to my father. As I headed back to my chamber, my mind played her name in a constant loop. *Princess Charlotte of Besmium*. A princess, a kingdom of my own, an adventure in a foreign land—I could hardly believe it. I barely made it inside my room when I was hit from behind and toppled to the floor. My brother, Minseo, pushed my face into the carpet.

"Brother!" He laughed, berating me with a series of playful punches. I shoved him off. "I am definitely coming along for the ride." He beamed.

I nodded, instinctively suppressing my joy.

"Aren't you excited? You'll be King of Besmium!"

I stood, dusting myself off. "Yes, brother, but this is a serious matter."

He reached out and messed up my hair. "It doesn't have to be *so* serious."

When he was gone, I allowed my mind to race with the possibilities. Minseo was right, I was happy, so I should show it, but unlike him, years of scolding and punishment had taught me to hold everything in, and it was a difficult habit to break.

As the third prince of Vires, I was destined to wed a kingdom. My father had done right by me, bartered me one of my own—a kingship. What I hadn't expected was to be matched with a western princess. I'd always assumed, based on the women they presented at court, that I'd marry an eastern princess. It seemed only obvious to join kingdoms that were closer, or at least on the same side of the Jin Sea. I'd never known anyone to marry outside of this region, and the thought that I'd someday rule as a western king thrilled me as much as it scared me. All of my traditions traded for those of another kingdom. My mind raced through my memories of their stone castles and crowded cities. I felt thrilled by the expressive attitudes and merry gatherings that I'd witnessed for a short time while visiting.

I had no time to think about the princess in the weeks that followed. I studied western culture, etiquette, political tensions, and history—it was like I was starting over. I'd been trained to handle just about any political situation that could happen in Vires or its neighboring countries, but not even my father could have predicted that King Morgan of Besmium would make such an offer. The opportunity was too good to pass up. It wasn't until I'd reached the transport ship and settled in for the long journey that my thoughts returned to Charlotte.

I remembered the first time I met her. Two years ago, I went on my first and only trip to a western kingdom. I was overwhelmed by the foreignness of all the people I saw. The women in my kingdom were mostly cut from the same mold—pale skin, red lips, and hair as long and glossy as the tail of a fully-grown stallion. But the Princess of Besmium, like many of the courtiers in her kingdom, had brown skin, which I'd only seen once as a child when the King of Besmium visited my father. I had asked to touch the king's skin only to be scolded by my father, though I was too young to understand why. Charlotte's skin was lighter, a mixture of her father and the fair-skinned queen, but it was still unmistakably brown. I could see *that* clearly across the room.

I approached for my introduction. We bowed and she looked up at me. I froze. I tried not to gape at her, but I couldn't help but notice her caramel skin which glowed a yellowish-gold in the candlelight; her black eyes, so round they made me freeze beneath their gaze; and her hair, which was curled into spirals. Then she was gone. My body pulsed. *Fascinating.* I wanted to see more of her, just to observe her features more closely, but my time had come and gone.

The swaying of the ship lulled me into a state between awake and asleep.

In my fantasy, Charlotte curtsied. I attempted to imagine how she might've changed since I last saw her—her features more defined, her body more filled out. I took her hand and slyly whisked her out of the ballroom, making sure we weren't seen. Once in the hallway, I took a knee. "Charlotte, will you be my wife?"

She beckoned me to my feet and whispered, "I am yours." I pulled her face to mine and kissed her. I wrapped my arms around her, drawing her in closer and—

"Young?"

My eyes snapped open and I lurched to a seated position. My brother hovered over me.

"I've been meaning to ask, have you given any thoughts to your duties as a husband?" He grinned.

Disoriented, I ran my hand through my hair twice before I convinced myself I was awake. "Uh, yeah. I guess," I croaked.

"Have you thought about the, you know, the wedding night?"

Heat radiated through my cheeks. *Oh, that.* I turned away from Minseo so he wouldn't see the color searing into my face.

"You don't want to disappoint your new wife," he teased.

The truth was I hadn't allowed myself to think about it. It wasn't really the type of thing you could prepare for. Although I knew the logistics of it, I'd never actually *been* with a woman. That was something male royals in my kingdom did on their nineteenth birthday, as a sort of rite of passage. Since I was eighteen, it hadn't happened yet. Minseo had turned nineteen six months ago and often requested the company of various women ever since.

"I know you're excited," he said, trying to read my expression.

Our brotherly dynamic changed when he turned nineteen. Suddenly he knew things, having experienced a world I hadn't, and he relished every moment he could remind me.

"It's no big deal," I said, stretching my arms above my head. My voice was more convincing than expected.

"Good man. I'd hate if my first time had to be in front of people. What an unusual tradition. To think I'll be there cheering you on the whole time."

My stomach tightened. "It's just a moment of discomfort."

He tilted his head back in a loud, open-mouthed laugh. "Let's hope it's more than a moment."

"All worth it for a kingdom."

His smile faded. Minseo was the second-born. Our older

brother Sumin would inherit Vires when father got too old, and Minseo would never have a kingdom of his own. I'd hurt him. And worse, he didn't deserve it.

He gave a soft, unconvincing chuckle, his shoulders relaxed. "Yeah. Good luck with that."

Before I could form an apology, he had gone on deck and left me with my guilt. What's *wrong* with me? Was I already cracking under the pressure? Honor, duty, and respect—these were the values instilled in me as a child by my father, the values he felt made a great king. Vires had proudly carried these for centuries and I was determined to do the same.

As we got closer to our destination, the nerves set in. It was like I was cycling through nervous habits, trying to find one that fit. I chewed my nails, I tapped my foot, I licked my lips. Minseo's presence calmed me. He had a joke or game ready each time he noticed signs of nerves, making me glad he had come along. The carriage ride from the port up into the forest dragged, days blurring together as if we'd slipped into purgatory. Even Minseo's spirit dimmed. With each jolt of the carriage, I felt my home slip further away. As we neared the castle, we passed through a bustling city where the rigid lines of their buildings seemed to shout instead of whisper like the gentle curves that made up Vires.

Finally I stepped out of the carriage and stretched. I hadn't expected to be this tired or this sore, but my nervousness numbed it all. Minseo patted me on the shoulder and we readied ourselves to be received.

A guard's voice rang out, "Arrow!"

The projectile hit the ground more than twenty feet away. In an instant, the guards had formed a circle around Minseo and me, searching the dusky sky. I braced myself and suddenly understood.

This whole arrangement was a trap.

CHAPTER 3
PRINCESS CHARLOTTE

The moment I let the arrow fly, I regretted it. It was as if it all happened in slow motion. I gasped and lunged to grab it from the air, but it soared beyond my reach, landing on the ground several yards from the prince. I didn't have a plan. It was an impulse when I heard his carriage wheels on the stone. Maybe I could scare him away, but then what? I could have caused another war, which would for sure ruin the kingdom. I wanted to smack my head on the stones for being so stupid. How could my parents want me to be queen when I couldn't make basic moral decisions, like don't kill my betrothed?

I leaned against the stone wall of the parapet. It cooled my skin as I slid down, and I sank my face into my hands. I heard the commotion of the guard outside—the fear in their voices. What had I done? Before I knew it, footsteps filled the corridor and I was surrounded by guards. Hot prickly tears stung my eyes. I had no intention of putting up a fight—I was cornered and guilty. They marched me into the throne room as tears spilled over my cheeks.

"This is the most shameful thing you have ever done! What were you *thinking*?" My mother's voice was as shrill as it was strained—she clearly worried her voice would carry, making the combination sound like a dying animal.

"Where's Father?" I croaked.

"He's trying to reassure your future husband that he's not under attack. This could mean *war*! How can you be so selfish?"

I gulped. "I—" The words stuck to my tongue. I was so stupid. Why couldn't I just be a normal girl? I closed my eyes, trying to remember what was going through my mind as I pulled the bow back. I was just tired of everything feeling so beyond my control.

She paced. "My daughter is a murderer. Where did I go wrong?"

"He didn't even—"

"What, Charlotte? Die?"

I swallowed to meet the bile rising in my stomach. I felt like I was going to vomit.

My father strode in, a scowl on his face. His presence weakened me. I fell to my knees and sobbed as hot tears poured from my eyes and stung my face. I wiped them furiously, taking choppy laborious breaths. I braced myself for his rage but my father pulled me to my feet. I buried my face in my arm so I wouldn't have to meet his gaze. He wrapped his arms around me and pulled me into his chest. I whimpered as he gently rubbed my back. Being hugged by my father always made me feel like a little girl.

Several minutes passed without a word as my tears slowed

and my breath evened. I pulled back. "Father—I'm so sorry. I didn't mean to—"

"I know, my dear." He dropped his arms and peered down at me.

"You do?" I sniffed.

"I trust you. Do you trust me?" he asked, the lines on his dark forehead deepening.

I nodded, a steady stream of tears still flowing.

His lips peaked at the corners. "Then trust my choice here."

I wiped snot on the sleeve of my dress and I could basically hear my mother's eyes roll across the room. I cleared my throat. "Does he still want to... I mean, will he still—"

"He will honor our agreement, but his guard and his elder brother have requested to stay here until things..." he scratched the gray stubble on his chin, "settle. I know this is difficult for you, but life is difficult, no matter your title. These trying moments show us who we are, and I'm worried about you."

"I'm sorry, Father." My chest ached with disappointment in myself, but the deepest pain was for disappointing him. "I can be better. I promise."

My mother's voice interceded, "You have five minutes to fix your face and greet your husband in the grand hall."

I turned to leave.

"Charlotte," my father called, "try to think about what he's going through."

I nodded and headed to my chamber. The more I thought about how much I must have disappointed my father, the worse I felt, but that didn't mean I was ready to hand my life over to some stranger. Not all alliances needed to be made through marriage. Perhaps I could convince Prince Young to assist in our war efforts without it. A devious plan began to gnaw at the back of my mind. If *he* canceled the wedding, surely no one could blame him. My kingdom wouldn't even suffer as a result. If I succeeded, it might even be enough to buy me a few more years. There wasn't much time—the wedding was tomorrow—so I'd have to talk him into the alliance tonight at the banquet.

In my chamber, I splashed water on my face then pinched my cheeks and pinned a few of my curls out of my face. My eyes were still red and puffy, but it was starting to get dark and, with the low lighting, I was sure no one would notice.

Minutes later, I was standing in the grand hall, face to face with a tall, dark stranger. His black eyes peered into mine. His devilish grin shot flecks of mischief into his irises. His face nearly brushed mine as he bowed, never taking his gaze off me. He'd gotten too close on purpose.

My heart fluttered and I momentarily forgot my plan, my words, my name. Heat burned the insides of my cheeks. He oozed charisma, drawing me in. My heart thudded against my ribcage. There was nothing statuesque about him, except his perfect, chiseled face. He waited for me to speak, glaring at my lips like I was a snack and he hadn't eaten in days. Electricity shot through me, shattering every cell of my body. All the determination to hate him melted away. I *wanted* him.

He cleared his throat. "Good evening, princess. I'm Prince Minseo of Vires."

CHAPTER 4
PRINCE YOUNG

The moment she turned away from my brother and looked at me, all the glitter in her eyes vanished. Her smile waned. Her posture slumped. She couldn't have been more obviously disappointed if she'd screamed it from the tallest tower.

My stomach tightened, but concealing my emotions was my specialty.

"Oh," she said, tucking a curl behind her ear. "I'm marrying *you?*"

Minseo choked, biting back his smile.

I stood paralyzed by humiliation. As I looked into her face, she did not resemble the foreign beauty I'd met once before but rather a spoiled, selfish little princess who had already crossed enough unforgivable lines in the brief time I'd been in Besmium. This marriage wasn't going to be as fun as I thought.

"I'm Prince Young of Vires," I said, bowing deeply. My mind raced.

I'll never love you.

I continued. "It's an honor to meet you."

You tried to kill me.

She said all the words she was supposed to. She even apologized for "losing control of her arrow", but it was as soulless as reciting legislation. All the while, Minseo watched over my shoulder. My lips dried. I'd expected a significant amount of discomfort from this experience, but this was public humiliation. Charlotte was to blame for all of it. What kind of princess acted like this? Why didn't Minseo let me say hello first? I was starting to think he enjoyed my discomfort.

Later that night, the banquet bustled with elegantly dressed Besmians. The royal dresser had chosen a military-style jacket with a sash and a series of multicolored pins for me to wear, and I was finding it more constricting than the loose, soft-flowing fabrics that were commonly worn in Vires. I was glad, however, that at least my clothing didn't make me stand out.

Maybe it was the way that Charlotte was still sneaking glances at my brother, but I felt like everyone in the room *knew*.

Beads of sweat prickled my neck around my collar. I hadn't been able to keep my feet under me since I'd arrived. I'd been shot at and rejected. Whatever trace amounts of bravery I was clinging to diminished the moment she sat down beside me. I speculated on what trauma she had in store for me next. Poison perhaps? I eyed my cup warily.

After our brief introduction, Minseo had given me a few pointers, but the only one I could really remember was "smile". How could I? Her presence felt unpredictable, even dangerous. I could swallow my pride and ignore that Charlotte fawned over Minseo—I mean, what did I care? But this *was* a problem. Minseo was eligible and there was no logical benefit for either king to have me marry the princess instead of him. The wedding was tomorrow and, at the rate things were going, I'd be on a ship home—shamed—and without any hope of ever being king. That would rid me of the Charlotte problem, but my father would be so disappointed. *One night.* I just had to charm her for one night. Tomorrow the marriage would be made official and my position here would be secure. Besides, I was every bit as good a man as Minseo.

Trumpets sounded, reverberating off the candlelit ballroom. Rows of servants filed in, carrying silver trays that they placed in rows before us. When the trumpets stopped, the servants lifted the covers, revealing an assortment of plain-looking food. Bowls of an unfamiliar, pale goop steamed next to platters of rubbery chicken. The pears were a ball gown shape, small up top and wide at the bottom and different from the round ones of Vires. But at least the fruit had color. Though the amount of food was immense, it didn't look very special or interesting.

The king and queen sat at the end of the table, more than twenty high-ranking members of court between us. Charlotte sat beside me but Minseo was halfway between the king and where I was. He was too far to talk to, but not too far to send him an occasional expressive glance. With the bustle of the chatting courtiers and the music from the band, they were far out of earshot, but they watched me carefully. Were they already not considering me? I turned to the princess, who was filling her plate with thick strips of chicken breast and dark purple grapes.

I summoned all my courage. "You look lovely this evening," I said.

The princess lifted her head clumsily, her mouth slightly agape. Eyes half open, her head bobbed back as a droopy smile stretched across her face. I looked into her eyes, a cloudy haze glossed over them. She picked up her silver cup and brought it to her lips, taking a long, noisy gulp before she plunged it back on the wooden table with a dull clank.

"Annnnnnnd she's drunk," I huffed under my breath. The dinner had begun maybe twenty minutes ago. How many drinks could she have possibly managed since sitting down beside me? I stared in disbelief, though she didn't seem to notice. She shoveled chicken into her mouth using her fingers. This is a *princess*? I tried focusing on my own bland meal, but Charlotte started drawing concerned glances from the courtiers across from us. She swallowed too quickly and choked. In a fit of coughs, she proceeded to wash the chicken down with more wine, before laughing at nothing, ogling my brother, and then starting the process over again. I was going to let her continue.

For all intents and purposes, this was exactly what I needed. With her so out of it and a little acting on my part, the king and queen would think we were having a good time. I could go on to marry her tomorrow, become Prince of Besmium, and eventually king, and my father would never have to know what a rough start it had been. Charlotte could drink herself into oblivion for all I cared—but then she sat up, her head swerving involuntarily. She let out a faint burp. For crying out loud, she was going to be *sick*. We hadn't stepped one foot on the dance floor and already my only option was to drag her out of here.

I stood quickly. "Miss Charlotte, would you care to accomp—"

She burped again, lowering her head to the table. I quickly picked her up and held her against my hip. There was a door at the opposite end of the table from the king. It seemed to be meant for servants, but it was my only option. She managed to get her feet under her and we were able to semi-inconspicuously slip out of the ballroom.

She led me through the dimly lit corridor, nodding in the correct direction whenever there was an option to turn. Suddenly, her knees buckled and she slumped down to the cobblestone floor.

The candles burned low, probably as a result of the servants being busy with the banquet, the cool archways a dark gray contrast to the golden-flecked columns of the ballroom.

"Come on, Charlotte," I said, kneeling. I tilted her head up to look her in the eyes. "We're almost th—" I froze. A heavy stream of tears flowed down her cheeks, dripping from the bottom of her chin.

She sobbed. "I don't want to marry you."

It wasn't news, but I'd never seen a woman cry before. She seemed so fragile it made something ache at the bottom of my stomach. This was not the girl who shot the arrow or the girl who showed her disappointment upon our first meeting. This was someone new.

I sighed. "I know." I felt fear seep into my skin before my next question manifested. "Do you want to marry my brother?"

She shook her head. "I don't want to marry *anyone*."

I nodded as her breakdown worsened. It was a terrible reality, but somehow it made me feel better. I hadn't exactly been a disappointment, she just didn't want any of this. I had a lingering urge to reach out to her, to wipe her tears, or hold her in my arms, but I didn't. I let her cry.

"I don't want to be a princess," she sobbed. "I just want to be free."

Afraid to touch her, I inched back and sat on the floor with my legs crossed.

"I'm sorry this happened to you," I said.

"Stop the wedding then!" she cried.

My body stiffened. "I too am bound to honor my father's agreement."

She wiped her face and looked me straight in the eyes, her swollen cheeks red and brimming with emotion. "What do you want?" she asked.

I shook my head.

"My kingdom? You can have it," she breathed. "Let me go."

Frozen, I begged my body to tear my gaze from hers.

Her lips parted and she breathed in like it hurt before she spoke. "Aren't you afraid of what you'll be giving up?"

My brow furrowed as I contemplated what she meant. I bit the inside of my bottom lip.

"Do you honestly think you could ever love me?"

The word "love" struck me, like an arrow masked by dusk.

She studied my face, my silence burning away her last seeds of hope. Her tears began to fall again, this time slow and sorrowful.

"I—"

"Charlotte!" a voice called.

I turned. A fair-haired girl cantered toward us and knelt in front of us, cupping Charlotte's face in her hands. A wooden emblem swayed from her neck as she attempted to calm the crying princess. The girl quickly wiped away Charlotte's tears and pulled her close. Charlotte's cries softened as the blonde girl gently rubbed her back.

I was having a day of new experiences and none were what I'd expected. Here I was, witnessing a kind of affection that wasn't shown in my kingdom. In fact, I'd never seen this kind of nurturing at all, not even from my own mother. It warmed me—entranced me.

The blonde girl lifted her chin, turning her face to me. "Your Highness!" Her voice was soft and musical. "Please pardon my rudeness."

"No—I mean, thank you. I didn't know what to do."

She nodded. "Will you help me get her to her chamber?"

I jumped to my feet and, with the help of the girl, we got Charlotte to her feet too. As we moved toward Charlotte's chamber, I felt a twinge of something stirring inside me.

The blonde girl spoke, "I'm Milly. I'm a servant here in Hiems Castle and Charlotte's friend."

"I'm Young," I said.

Milly giggled, warmth radiating from her smile. I turned to find her smiling widely.

I shook my head in confusion. "What? What's funny?"

Her laughter reached her pale, crystal-blue eyes. "*I* can't call you that."

"Oh. Well, maybe you can make an exception. Like you do for Charlotte," I said, biting down on my bottom lip.

She laughed. "Charlotte and I are close friends."

I pointed at Milly. "Exactly." For the first time since arriving in Besmium, I felt myself smile.

CHAPTER 5
PRINCESS CHARLOTTE

I awoke with an intense throbbing in my head. My limbs were noticeably heavy, and every time I moved a fraction, I felt the threat of nausea clawing at my stomach. Flashbacks of the night before came back like puzzle pieces strewn across my bed.

I don't want to marry you.

I cringed and buried my head into my pillow as if I could suffocate the embarrassment out of me. My plan was ruined. Although my behavior had been humiliating, I doubt it was enough to scare the prince away. I was out of time. Behind the door, I heard my mother's shrill voice cry out, "Open the door, you idiot."

I rolled over as the guards pushed open the door and my mother strode in.

"Get up," she said, her voice shrill and forceful. "Wash your face. Your father wants to have a word with you before the wedding."

I couldn't move. "Mom," I groaned, "I'm sick."

She sighed. "I don't care if you're dead, this wedding is happening."

Ugh. I considered sitting up quickly and throwing up on her. Then she'd have to accept that I'm sick, but based on the rigidness of her movements this morning, I decided it wouldn't change a thing—barring a smidge of personal satisfaction. I forced myself to sit up and felt the forceful pulse of a headache as the room tilted into a repetitive loop.

My dad entered, already dressed for the wedding ceremony. "Charlotte," his voice boomed, "I'd like to talk to you." He sat down at the edge of my bed while my mother headed for the door. He waited for her to leave before he spoke again. "I want to tell you why I chose Prince Young."

It was almost enough to make me sit up, but I stayed put. As my mother shut the door behind her, a strange thought came into my head: Do they even *like* each other? Why did it seem like when one came, the other left? Was I doomed to suffer a similar fate?

My father continued, jolting me from my thoughts. "King Kang-Dae and I have been friends since we were your age. He's a wise man, appeasing the countries surrounding his with fair political dealings and peace offerings." He adjusted a pin in my hair as he continued. "His military has grown quite strong while the ever-present war has left ours in tatters. Reports from the front lines say Drethen is close to breaking through. I need to make sure that doesn't happen, so the kingdom is safe and stable for your future."

I sighed. "Father, I know."

"But what you don't know—is why I chose Young specifically." He paused and waited for me to respond. I didn't move. He had my attention. That was all I had to give. "I was in Vires about ten years ago, visiting the king, when I came across his three sons playing in the garden. The eldest, Sumin, was in a scuffle with the middle boy Minseo. Young, who was no older than eight, was sitting in the grass with his eyes closed, his face turned to the sun."

I sat up slowly, resting my head in my hand.

"As I got closer, I could hear the young boys arguing about which of them would be the king in their game. *I'm taller and I'm older,* Sumin yelled. *You always get to be king!* Minseo cried. Intrigued, I walked up to the youngest boy and asked him why he didn't want to be king. He blinked in confusion, stood to face me, and said something along the lines of, 'Kingship isn't a position that you can aspire to. My father says you must be predestined or chosen. Do you see them fight?' I nodded at the boy. He continued. 'It means they haven't chosen me, so I'm not fit to lead them.' He took a seat. 'I'll enjoy this sunny weather until my time comes.'"

"What kind of eight-year-old talks like *that?*"

He tilted his head back in a wide, deep laugh that warmed me inside. "I don't recall his exact words, but the sentiment stood out in my memory. Besides, you're also a little..."

I shrunk. "Creative?"

He smiled. "Yes, creative. You just might be what each other nee—"

The door swung open and a guard rushed into the room, his face pale and covered in beads of sweat. He bowed, but not as low as usual. Out of breath, he handed my father a letter. My father opened it immediately while the guard caught his breath. My father's cheeks sunk in and his shoulders stiffened.

"What's wrong, Father?" I asked. My heart thudded,

matching the pace of the guard. Had Prince Young fled the kingdom from my drunken rampage?

"I-I have to go," he said. He jumped off my bed and headed for the door.

I stood up, feeling a surge of anxious energy rise to my chest. "Go? Go where?"

He shook off my question. "They've broken through," he blurted, half to himself. "You have to go too. To the southern castle." He mumbled something inaudible, his gaze shifting back and forth. His gaze met mine. "Quickly. You must evacuate."

"What about the wedding?"

He shook his head. "The wedding is canceled."

CHAPTER 6
PRINCE YOUNG

Everything was uncertain—my place in this kingdom, the future, and even our safety. The only two things I could really be sure of were that the kingdom was under attack and that the wedding was canceled. Drethen had broken through the front lines, and King Morgan of Besmium had gone to assist in the battle with as many Heims Castle guards as he could rally on his way out. I wasn't sure exactly how close to the castle the battle was, but I did know the castle sat only a few days on horseback from the Drethen border. Which meant, if the king's men couldn't stop them, at best, we only had a few days to escape. At worst, a few hours. I stuffed the jacket and sash, meant for the wedding ceremony, into my trunk.

"Let's just go," Minseo said, pacing around the room.

I shook my head. "We can't just leave."

"We can. They canceled your wedding and this isn't our battle."

"If this attack was a day later, it would be our battle. Besides, we don't even know how bad this attack is."

"Did you hear the king? He said canceled. Not postponed, not delayed—canceled."

I knew he was right. This was dangerous. We could get caught in the middle of a war without having any significant protection from either side. But was running away really *honorable*? If the king managed to negotiate peace, he'd likely resume the wedding. What would he think if his future king fled at the first sign of trouble?

Minseo continued, "I'll round up our guards and let them know we're heading ho—"

"I'm not going," I said, slamming my trunk closed. My words hung in the air between us.

Minseo stared at me in disbelief. His eyes narrowed and his chest puffed out. "You could *die*. We don't know how bad this is, or even how close to us the battle is."

"Why don't you go on ahead back to Vires?" I said. I stood and scanned my chamber for more of my things. "You can tell Father what's happened here and ask him if he'd be willing to send troops in support, despite the marriage contract's dissolution."

Minseo plopped down onto his bed. "You're my brother. I can't leave you behind. I'll send a message, but I'm not sure if there's enough time—"

A loud knock at the door captured our attention. Minseo leaped to his feet. We held our breath as we waited for the door to open as if about to find out that the sky had fallen. The queen strode in. Minseo and I froze. She'd hardly acknowledged us since we'd arrived, and now she barged into our chamber without introduction. It meant only one thing—bad news.

The queen's voice was forced and uneven. "Prince Young, our kingdom is not in the position to ask any favors of you. However—"

Minseo cut in. "Your Majesty, we were about to send a message to my father, asking for aid in this conflict."

A glimmer of irritation flashed across her eyes, then she softened. "That's very kind. However, the king has asked something else of you, something of a different nature. He's asked that you and your guard accompany a small group to the Cadere Castle in the south of Besmium. We can't spare our guards at the moment, and the king would like our daughter protected."

"Is the battle not going well?" I asked, trying to grab clues from her stone-like expression.

She huffed. "The king takes every precaution when it comes to his daughter." She looked me up and down and added, "Although, I can't say I agree with all of his choices."

I bowed deeply, ignoring her attempt to fluster me. "I'll do as you ask, Your Majesty." She returned the bow half-heartedly and hurried out.

I turned to Minseo. "Ready the carriage and the guard. Send the message to Father."

"Young," Minseo said.

"Make sure that everyth—"

"Young."

"What?" I asked, noticing the perplexed look spread across his face.

He chuckled. "You're not king yet."

I winced and strapped my sword to prepare for the mission ahead.

Adrenaline pulsed through me as we made our way through the castle. Servants and guards rushed about, carrying bags and weapons in every direction. I couldn't focus on the evacuation, not after the news that the wedding was canceled. I clenched my jaw in frustration. How was Charlotte taking the news? My thoughts flashed to the night before. *I don't want to marry anyone,* she'd said. I bristled at the thought that Charlotte might rejoice from this news, even if her kingdom was in danger. When my preparations had been made, finally, I had an opportunity to prove myself. I balled my hands into fists in anticipation. Only one part of this mission concerned me—the princess.

I hustled through the corridors of the castle to collect Princess Charlotte, remembering the way from last night. I knocked on the double doors, my nervousness swelling. No response. I had my fist ready to knock again when one of the doors swung open. The crystal-eyed blonde from last night clutched a wooden emblem hanging from a bare string around her neck.

"Milly..." I said, the words barely a whisper.

She curtsied. "Hello, Your Highness. The princess has asked me to accompany her on this evacuation."

A voice shot out from behind her. "Temporary safety precaution, not evacuation. My father will fix this. This is just temporary," Charlotte said, pushing the second door open.

I had to step back to avoid being hit. I nodded, my gaze darting between the women. A twinge of guilt settled at the bottom of my stomach. I turned my attention to the princess. "It is my intention to keep you safe during this evac— Forgive me, temporary safety precaution."

Minutes later, the sun was almost at its midpoint, the halls of the castle had nearly cleared. I helped the two ladies into the carriage, which already held my brother, the royal dresser— Philip, and two other men I recognized as high-ranking members of the court. I was the last to enter. As I took my seat, my stomach clenched at the way Charlotte's gaze met Minseo's so quickly.

I settled in for the long ride as the horses neared the outer gates of Hiems Castle.

We were almost to the gate when the earth shook and chaos erupted. A cannonball smashed the castle wall. Debris scattered into the air, raining down on the courtyard. The horses bucked. The carriage shook, launching seven bodies into chaos. I reached for something sturdy only to collide with pointed limbs. I glimpsed an orange orb crash beside the carriage as balls of fire rained down around us. The crackle of war sounded. The air filled with dust and smoke, filling my lungs and stinging my eyes. I choked. The world darkened as screams reverberated off every surface and rattled my bones. We scrambled to break free from the carriage just in time to see the walls of the castle crumble down around us, blocking our escape.

CHAPTER 7
PRINCESS CHARLOTTE

The crack of stone hitting stone was my only warning. The horses whinnied and shied away. The carriage jerked. We were tossed around in the cabin in a mess of limbs and colliding bones until someone pushed me out onto the cobblestoned ground. I crawled away, terrified I'd be stomped by crazed horses or crushed by giant wheels. My head throbbed. Blood trickled down my forehead. Dark masses lay in the smoke and dust, masses I didn't want to accept were bodies. The horses bucked until they snapped free from the rig. The carriage flipped as a ball of fire engulfed it. *Was anyone still inside?*

"Milly!" I screamed. I reached toward the flames. Milly took my hand, pulling me to my feet. Relief washed over me. I squeezed her hand hard, as if our locked hands could protect us from the attack like a child's blanket protects from darkness. Another flaming ball hit the ground a few yards away and I shuddered.

Young and Minseo propped Phillip between them then dragged him toward us—two Viran guards at their sides.

Minseo said, "Let's make a break for the side gate. It's closer than the castle. If we make it out—"

Another ball of fire hit a few feet away, sending dust swirling around us. Heat washed over us, and Milly let out a blood-curdling scream. She fell to her knees, covering her face with her hands. Young ran to us, then lifted Milly's chin, looking her in the eyes. "Breathe," he said. "I need you to keep your head up. You can see them coming. You can avoid them. They're aiming for the walls, so as soon as we get away from them, this will be over."

She nodded and Young helped her to her feet, tears still streaming down her face. He wrapped his arm around her, turning his attention to our group. "Let's stay together," he said.

My gaze lingered on Young, who had his arm around Milly. *Had I missed something?* I shook the thought from my mind.

Minseo led the way, still supporting Phillip who limped clumsily at his side. Behind him were the two guards from Vires. Where were the other Viran guards? Dead? Mixed up in the attack? Young and I clenched Milly's arms as we ambled toward the broken gates.

Trumpets sounded behind us as Hiems Castle guards poured out of the castle we were fleeing. I felt my heart leap. We were *saved*.

"Young, behind us!" I yelled. "The guards!"

"Should we go back?" Young called, looking over his shoulder.

Minseo shook his head. "No, we're so close."

The fire surged in front of us like an orange tidal wave. Heat licked us like slithering serpents, biting at our cheeks. We turned away. The gate was engulfed in flame. Escape was impossible. I gasped, and thick gray smoke scalded my throat.

Minseo stood in stunned silence, watching our escape burn. The crack of fireballs paused, leaving only the crackle of the burning courtyard. Minseo turned with wide eyes. "Run!" he screamed.

We dashed toward the castle and the charging Besmium guard. The flames closed in, spreading faster with each moment. My body was soaked in sweat as my lungs filled with smoke and dust, but I didn't slow down.

The northern wall collapsed, its broken stones raining into the courtyard inferno. I eyed the opening as my numb legs carried me towards the castle. Over the rubble, the silhouette of enemy soldiers entering the fray stopped my heart. Of all the years we'd been at war, I'd never actually seen an enemy soldier. They plunged into the burning arena and engaged with the Besmian soldiers. If our soldiers could hold them off a little longer, we might make it back to the castle.

The clang of metal rang through the smoky courtyard, the cries of wounded soldiers piercing my heart. Nausea threatened to overcome me. A loud crack pulled my attention back to the northern wall. I glanced over my shoulder to see a second chunk of the wall collapse, bigger than the last. Blue-suited soldiers charged in from behind us. Exhaustion and oxygen deprivation blurred my vision. My legs slowed.

Drethen soldiers closed in from the left and behind us.

Just steps ahead. I focused on our salvation—our guards. My mind raced. *We're not going to make it.* I heard the furious howls of the bloodthirsty nation behind us as they cleared the crumbled walls and charged across the far end of the courtyard. *We're not going to make it.* I glanced back. *Minseo.*

Minseo, with Phillip on his back, was several strides behind —the enemy inches away. "Young!" I screamed.

He looked back. "Take Milly and get to the castle."

He unsheathed his sword and turned toward the battle. My leg muscles shook, threatening to give out, but we were almost there now. I didn't dare look back. I ran, my hand tightly gripping Milly's arm. The front line of Hiems guards parted to clear a path for us. *We made it.* With each row of soldiers we passed, we felt safer, but we didn't slow down or catch our breath until we slipped into the castle, closing the doors behind us.

The clash of the battle outside rattled the corridors. I toppled over in exhaustion, finally looking back. There was no sign of Minseo, Young, or Phillip in the sea of soldiers.

When we caught our breath, we raced through the corridor toward a tower staircase. The tunnels beneath the castle were our only hope now. I became increasingly aware of how empty the castle felt. Every guard had joined the battle at the front. I'd never seen the entrance hall so deserted.

An unfamiliar voice filled the hall. "Aye, you reckon we'll be heroes when we return home, mate?"

"You slob, the battle's not even over! Never count your women before they've been paid for." Laughter reverberated off the ceiling.

The enemy was *inside* the castle. I pulled Milly backward, now conscious of the scratchy chuff of our shoes on the stone floor. The Drethen soldiers were blocking our only way to the tunnels, and although I wasn't sure, it could've been the path they used to get inside. They were headed our way. I pulled Milly into the closest room, a medium dining room with a grand fireplace, and closed the door, locking it behind us.

The voices in the hallway grew louder. "Now what? We found a way in, so where's the king? Bet you I'd be promoted if I was the one to take him down. No doubt hiding like a rat in this dump."

"I heard we already got him. He came out to fight the battle and one of our boys got 'im."

A dull thud sounded. "You ninny. If they'd killed the king, why are we still fighting? Honestly, it's like I'm the only man here with any brains."

I gasped as my heart crunched in on itself, feeling like my soul briefly left my body and stabbed its way back through my skin one shard at a time. Was my father *dead?*

The soldier spoke. "Whatever, mate, I'm sure some of the king's whores are still somewhere lurking around the castle. You hear that, ladies?" he called. "Your king is dead! I'm your king now." They laughed.

The other chortled, "Don't be shy!"

Trapped like a thief in my childhood home, the walls caved in around me. My father's sudden departure. Something dark tore through me.

"This kingdom belongs to us now." His voice lowered, "But I'm telling you, I'm not going to live here," the soldier said, his voice just on the other side of the door.

My body shook with rage until an alarming calm took over. No invader was going to intimidate me in my own home. I walked over to the fireplace and pulled a fire iron from the dying embers.

"Wh-what are you doing?" Milly whispered. "You can't go out there."

"Stay hidden," I said.

"You *can't* go out there," she said, squeezing my arm.

I shook her off and walked over to the door, unlocking it with a *click*.

"Yes, I can."

CHAPTER 8
PRINCE YOUNG

I ran to Minseo, who was fighting back a large Drethen soldier. With the two Viran guards covering his sides, I clashed swords with the enemy, freeing Minseo's sword. He thrust his sword into the enemy's stomach. Minseo pulled his sword free and stumbled back, bewildered. Several Besmium guards rushed over to us. In the confusion of the castle guards colliding with the Drethen soldiers, Phillip crawled toward the castle, but I didn't watch to see if he made it.

I held my sword horizontally as a bearded soldier in front of me attempted to slice me in two. With my nerves on high alert, I could feel my life hanging by a thread between inches of fatal attacks. He was slower than I was, but each strike was weighted with certainty that only came from years of experience. Though we'd made it to the Besmian guards, we were outnumbered. Drethen soldiers poured through the fallen walls. The red banners waved on either side of the castle entrance, but the Drethen soldiers continued to push forward and blue banners inched forward as one Besmian soldier fell after the other.

"We need to get back to the castle!" Minseo yelled.

He was right. Our movements were slowing. My limbs were shaking.

"Together," I called.

He nodded as we slowly inched backward, blocking the incoming attacks.

My father taught us to wield a sword from a very young age. Sumin and Minseo started when they were nine and eight and I was only six at the time. However, my father knew once their training began, I'd never be able to sit idly by and watch. My mother protested but was overruled. I'd taken to it faster than my brothers. I loved the weight of the blade and the momentum that built every time I swung it. Over the years, my brothers and I got quite good, and we sparred as often as our studies allowed. I often wondered if I would ever have a need for my sword— other than the art form it had become.

An enemy soldier on horseback approached us as Minseo and I fought off a fresh wave of blue-adorned men. The soldier on the horse yelled, the soldiers in the vicinity halted and turned, all as one, to Minseo. My stomach dropped. They're after Minseo! A group of soldiers swarmed him. My focus intensified. *Not my brother.* I lunged at the closest soldier, more determined than ever. My blade plunged into a soldier in blue.

He looked me in the eyes, the paleness of them screaming, the shock in his furrowed brow reflecting my own.

My gaze darted back to Minseo, whose sword was wrenched from his hands. Desperate, I tried to pull my bloodstained sword from the soldier's limp body, but it was stuck. "Minseo!" I screamed. Tears sprang to my eyes as adrenaline pulsed through my arms. I put my foot against the bloodstained armor and wrenched my blade from his flesh.

A group of Drethen soldiers dragged my brother, several men restraining his limbs, pulling him further from reach.

His gaze met mine with a soft and relaxed expression that whispered, "I surrender."

My stomach tightened. "No, brother." I sobbed. "Don't give up."

Crazed, I wildly swung my sword. A Viran soldier grabbed my shoulder but I shrugged him off, leaping toward the enemy. Several more allied soldiers pulled me back. I searched the crowded field for Minseo, but he was gone and there was an army between us.

My body weakened. *I'm going to die here.* I glanced back at the castle. Behind the rows of red-suited soldiers was a line of blue flags. Were they coming from the castle? The enemy is spread out, but we're *surrounded.* Dazed with grief and exhaustion, I fell to my knees. An agonizing scream tore from me. If the castle was overrun, this battle was over.

My mind jumped to Charlotte. She was inside the castle and all her soldiers were out here. Before my mind could contemplate any of the worst-case-scenarios, my body moved. I couldn't save my brother, I couldn't save myself, but maybe I could save her.

As I approached the castle, I readied my mind and blade for another fatality. A cry of pain rang out and my gaze snapped to a youthful Besmium guard with several Drethen corpses strewn in front of him. I slipped through a cloud of smoke and felt the heat of a withering fire beneath my boots. I raced toward the guard, avoiding another fight if I could help it. The guard's eyes flickered with confusion as I approached him.

"Where's the princess?" he asked as he cleared a path for me.

Out of breath, I huffed, "The castle." I glared at the blue banners. "I think the enemy is getting in the castle some other way. She's in danger." I eyed the bodies around us. "Who are you?"

"Leon."

I nodded. "Leon, get a group, as many as you can, and concentrate on reclaiming the castle. We can cut off their way in if we can drive them out. Once inside, I'll get the princess."

"Yes, sir," he said, turning back towards his unit.

"Leon!" I called.

He turned back to me, but the words stuck to the roof of my mouth before they finally emerged. "They took my brother."

Leon nodded understandingly and returned to gather his troops. Several minutes later, he had gathered four soldiers to cut through the next line of Drethens. It didn't seem like enough. Surrounded by the enemy, fighting for their lives, Leon and the other Besmium soldiers rallied, pushing their way back to their castle. Beside Leon, I fell into a rhythm, cutting through row after row of hostile enemies. I slammed my sword down, clashing it into the helmet of a Drethen. I leaped over him and hustled into the castle, knowing there would be more danger inside. I dashed through the hallway toward Charlotte's room. I didn't know where she would go, but it was one of the few places in the castle I knew.

I heard her voice in the corridor ahead. "Please don't hurt me."

My mouth dried as her fear rang through the halls.

A gravelly voice replied, "You hurt my friend, it's only fair."

I sprinted toward the voices when a metallic clang sounded. I clenched my jaw, dread seeping into me. A dull thud reverberated off the walls. She was dead. I was too late. Out of breath, I turned the corner to see two piles of flesh and blood on the floor.

The princess stood above them, unscathed, holding a blood-spattered fire poker.

CHAPTER 9
PRINCESS CHARLOTTE

The moment I saw Young, all the power I'd felt moments ago melted away. I was a blood-spattered princess standing amidst a murder scene, one I'd starred in. My gaze met his, and I searched for the horror I felt, in his dark eyes, but couldn't find it. I glanced over the gentle lines of his expression and drank in the easiness of his parted lips. He exhaled relief and I felt the sudden pull of my body towards him as I breathed it in. I couldn't understand how he could look upon me, with such reprieve, then I took a step forward. And another. He was my cage, my captor, the death of my freedom, but in one kind glance, in my darkest hour, he granted me a modicum of comfort. I ran to him and threw myself into his arms. I didn't care that he didn't embrace me. I didn't care that his body tightened with discomfort. He was *alive* and, to me, that meant that my father could be too.

"Milly's over here," I sniffed as I motioned to the door. I felt the pulse of my hand as I released the fire poker from my finger-numbing grip. It fell to the floor with a clang and I stared at my hands as they shook. Blood was everywhere. It dripped from my fingertips and pooled on the stone floor. As the adrenaline waned, the horror of what I'd just done sunk in. I bit back the urge to scream. I backed away.

"Hey," Young called, dragging my attention back to him. He shook his head. "Look at me."

My heart pounded as my mind slipped back towards the lifeless heaps on the floor, dragging my gaze to them.

"Charlotte," Young called, but he was a distant voice floating through the back of my mind. Young stepped in front of me, blocking my view of the corpses. He took a firm grip of my wrist as if to hold me to the earth. I felt the warmth of his breath on my forehead and the steady beat of his heart as his chest pressed against mine. My body numbed. My gaze crept up to his chin and stopped at his lips. My breath synchronized with his. I lifted my chin, meeting his gaze. His dark eyes peered down at me, black as a moonless night. I searched them for clues, but if he felt something, he showed nothing at all.

Feeling rushed back to my body all at once, I reached for my wrist and pried it out of his hand just in time to feel the bile rise from my stomach. I doubled over and vomited an acid more bitter than the emotions that caused it. When I caught my breath, I stood, feeling a sense of frailty in my legs that wasn't there before. I looked up at Young. "Where's—"

"He's still out there," Young replied, his voice so even and smooth it sounded like a lie.

A voice shot out from behind Young. "Prince Young, you found the princess." A brown-haired boy in a soldier's uniform approached. He couldn't have been older than me. He had a baby face, softly curved features, and not a bit of hair on his chin. He looked more like a boy in costume than a warrior.

"Leon," Young said as he walked over to shake his hand. "Yeah, thanks to you."

Young turned to me. "Charlotte, grab Milly. I'm going to... uh..." he tucked his dark hair behind his ear, "clean up."

I nodded and returned to the dining room where I knew Milly was hidden.

"Milly, it's me." I looked around. "It's safe." I said the words, but I wasn't sure how true they were.

Milly crawled out from behind a sofa. Her eyes widened. "You're covered in *blood*." She lifted her arms in front of her body and clutched the hand-carved emblem hanging from her neck.

"No, it's okay. I'm fine," I said, moving toward her.

She backed away, terror still in her eyes. "You *killed* them?"

I shook my head. "N-no. I saved us. If I hadn't done that, they would have—" Blood. So much blood. I shivered.

"Passed by," she whispered.

"Milly..." Guilt seared my skin. It was the last emotion in the world I could stomach in this situation. I clenched my jaw with rage. They'd invaded my home, they might have killed my father, they could have killed us. I'd acted in the way that I thought was right, but looking into Milly's eyes, it was obvious she felt different. Doubt started to creep in. The guilt slithered down my spine as Milly backed away. She thought I was a monster and maybe she was right.

The door swung open and Leon and Young hustled in.

"Leon has a plan," Young said. He paused, noticing the tension. His gaze moved from Milly to me. His eyebrow raised and he spoke, "That was a brave thing you did to save your friend, Charlotte." He turned to Milly, his jaw clenched. "Let's go."

I felt a warm vibration of gratitude pulse inside me. Before I could give it another thought, Young and Leon ushered Milly and myself out of the room and down the hallway. They carefully checked each corner before moving us along. I stared at Milly's back and bit down on my bottom lip. I wanted to reach out to Milly to tell her it was okay—to let her know we were in this together—but she wouldn't look at me. I saw the queasy look on her face when we passed the bodies of the two Drethen soldiers slumped into the corner in the hallway. It could take a while, but I'd get her back somehow—she was all I had left.

We rounded the corner to the staircase in the east tower. The stone platforms wrapped around the tower led up to several bedrooms, one of which I had used to access the parapet to shoot an arrow at the prince when he arrived, and another down to a tunnel below the castle that exited a mile in the opposite direction. If we could make it out, we'd have a decent chance of escaping.

I whispered, "I think they're getting in this way." Leon nodded and took the lead. Milly went next while Young took the rear. We descended the stairs into the dark tunnel. We paused at the entrance to listen for the enemy, but all we heard was the occasional drip of something leaking and the distant sounds of battle.

Leon lit a torch and signaled for us to stay quiet.

We hustled through, still on our guard. The darkness reminded me of the fear I'd felt as a child. My mind always twisted the shadows into monsters. Now, as I trudged along, the monsters took a new form. *Did my mother make it out? Was my father really dead?* We walked single-file in tense, uninterrupted silence the entire mile, expecting to hear someone shout. As we shuffled through the darkness, I picked at my hands, trying to focus on the faint light at the end as it grew nearer.

We stepped out into the sunshine. My eyes locked onto two men in blue standing nearby.

"Eh! Who the hell is that?" a scruffy Drethen soldier called.

Leon sighed with relief. "Only two."

His confidence put me at ease as the two soldiers approached us.

Young turned back to me. "Charlotte, you want to get this one or..." he trailed off.

I shook my head in disbelief. I would have missed it if I wasn't looking so closely, but unmistakably, the corners of his mouth tilted up just a smidge before he turned and readied himself for a fight. Was that a *joke*? Now? I felt something flutter inside me and quickly shook it off. I turned to Milly and pulled her into me, burying her face in my shoulder so she couldn't see. "Cover your ears," I whispered.

CHAPTER 10

PRINCE YOUNG

Every step away from the castle, I felt a little safer and a little more panicked about leaving my brother behind. There I was guiding the princess of "Oh, I'm marrying you?" to safety while my brother was being dragged into enemy territory, or worse. I glanced over at Charlotte, her arm wrapped tightly around Milly's shoulder. My gaze lingered on her blood-spattered dress. I had to admit, she wasn't exactly like my first impression of her. Even now as the glisten of fresh tears streaked her face, her strength was evident. She took sure, decisive steps as she moved away from the only home she knew. Her gaze met mine. I flinched and snapped my attention forward.

We arrived at the forest's edge. The warm green of the trees and the lush fern-covered ground was untouched by war. The crevices of the wood teemed with life, unlike the death-stained castle we'd escaped. The sounds of fighting could no longer be heard, giving us the illusion of safety, but I knew that with two dead guards outside the castle, the enemy wouldn't be far behind. The birds chirped playfully unperturbed, and for a moment I yielded to the serene environment.

Minseo.

A lump lurched to the back of my throat. My knees weakened. I clenched my jaw, biting back my tears.

We came to a slow-flowing river, its bank lined with wide trees that stretched high above us. Still battling my urge to cry, I knelt beside the river, dipped my hands in, and washed my face. I scrubbed at the dried bits of blood on my hands and drank until I was certain I'd suffocate. Leon slumped against a large tree. I could see the exhaustion in his movements, but he continued to smile, a trait that perplexed me. The girls exchanged solemn looks by the river and whispered, but I was happy to not be a part of the conversation.

After a few short minutes, Leon rose. "Follow this river," he said. "It should take you about five days on foot." He ran a bloodstained hand through his brown hair. "You can see the southern castle from this river."

I leaped up. "You're *leaving?*"

He smiled widely. "Yeah. Did you think I forgot about my *other* mission? Prince Minseo." He rested his hand on my shoulder. A rush of emotions hit me in waves. Relief, gratitude, hope. I shook his hand and he turned to leave. I wasn't sure if he was too late to help Minseo or what difference one soldier could make, but having someone like him looking for my brother gave me hope. I'd seen firsthand what he could do.

"Be careful." I suppressed my urge to bow—my kingdom's custom.

He huffed. "*You* be careful." A devious smile flickered across his face. Confused, I followed his gaze to Milly and Charlotte. Leon smirked and headed back toward the direction of the castle. I felt a pang of embarrassment. That kind of sexual joke reminded me of Minseo, though it wasn't a social norm in Vires. If Leon did rescue Minseo, they might just get along. I waited for the warmth to dispel from my cheeks before turning back to the girls.

"Is he coming back?" Milly asked as she instinctively reached for her emblem.

I shook my head. I didn't want to tell her that Leon was going to find Minseo. "We are going to the southern castle without him." Her eyes bulged. Milly was right to worry. She and the princess would be safer if Leon stayed with us. I chose to let him go for Minseo. "It'll be fine," I added. "I'll keep you both safe."

Milly's face went white. "How much farther do we have to go tonight?"

I eyed the direction we came from. "The farther, the better."

She dropped her head. She lifted her dress slightly, revealing a disproportionately swollen ankle. "I need to rest."

Charlotte gasped and rushed over. "When did it happen?"

Milly shook her head.

"Let's cool it down in the river," Charlotte said, supporting Milly's weight on her hip. "Young," Charlotte said, tucking her hair behind her ear. "I was wondering if you could give me a few minutes to help Milly and wash some of this bl—" Her gaze flickered to Milly before falling back to me, "to wash some of this dirt off my dress?"

"Ah." Leon's joke jolted into my mind, searing my cheeks with warmth. I nodded. "I'll go see if I can find anything useful in these woods. I'll be in earshot, though, so if anything happens just yell."

I turned into the woods and headed down river, debating

whether we should put more distance between us and the battle or if we should camp here so Milly could rest her ankle. Both were risky. Small bushes sprinkled the forest and were filled with black-colored berries that were familiar to me. They were also a common berry in Vires but were usually too bitter this time of year. Maybe with the slight change of climate... I popped one into my mouth and immediately crunched down on the stone-like bead. I spat it out almost immediately, but the bitterness of its skin lingered. *Fishing it is.*

I picked up a branch that split at the end and sat down beside a tree, sharpening its edges with my dagger. I'd most likely need a fire to cook the fish, but it might make us more vulnerable to attack. I clutched my stomach; we needed our strength. I'd been hunting and camping so often it felt like second nature, but it had always been for leisure, never with other people depending on me.

The sun hung low in the sky and began to set the sky ablaze with a sweltering orange. My heart weighed heavily with thoughts of home and my brother. I dusted myself off and carried my makeshift spear toward the river.

The river flickered orange as it licked its rocky banks. Tree branches stretched over it, dropping leaves and branches into the current to be swept away. I breathed in the calm of the slow-moving current. My mind drifted back to Minseo, the fear in his eyes as they pulled him away. A shadow moved in the corner of my vision, drawing my full attention. I choked. Charlotte's bare shoulders glistened in the final rays of sunlight. I ducked behind a tree to block my vision. I thought I'd gone far enough away, but the river's current must have slowly guided her in this direction. I could even hear the scratch of Milly washing Charlotte's dress in the distance, though barely. My heart raced and I struggled for breath like I'd been chased by something.

I bit down on my bottom lip, afraid she'd hear me. She hadn't screamed. I didn't think she saw me. I planted my feet firmly on the ground, determined to hold my position, and closed my eyes, leaning back against the tree. Images of her glistening shoulders and her brown skin replayed in my mind. What was I *doing*? I listened for the sound of her moving through the water but heard nothing but the steady gurgling of the river as it flowed. Then I heard a soft splash. She was getting closer.

Surely I should make sure she's okay. It was my job to get her to the southern castle safely, and that meant making sure she didn't drift too far. I reasoned with myself that I'd only look for a moment.

I knew that what I was about to do was wrong, but I couldn't find a way to talk myself out of it.

I turned to move but froze. Sharp, cold steel pricked my throat.

CHAPTER 11
PRINCESS CHARLOTTE

I hadn't bathed in a river since I was a young child. Feeling the pull of the current relaxed me. I let myself drift along and tried to bury the feeling of looming danger and my fears about my father. I clenched my jaw and promised myself that what I'd heard wasn't true and that I'd see my father again.

"Madam!" a boisterous voice called. I dropped like a stone, hiding my shoulders and my bare body beneath the water. The voice continued from the dark of the forest. "I caught this deviant trying to catch an eyeful. He is subdued. I recommend that you don your clothing so that you may thank your hero."

I waded through the water towards Milly, who was already limping in my direction, my dress in hand. She shielded my body from the direction of the voice as I slipped into the damp fabric. A soldier? Drethen? How many were there?

I cleared my throat to alert him that I was decent. "Where is Young?" I called. A broad-shouldered man walked out from the forest's edge. "Worry not, madam. You are safe." His icy blue eyes glistened under glossy blonde hair, a broad smile on his face. He was beautiful yet he set off every alarm in my body.

I thought of how I'd reacted negatively to meeting Young the night before, how I'd seen Young as the chain that would lock me in the castle forever, but the man standing in front of me was different. Each brazen move of his body whispered one thing: *predator*.

The way he puffed up his chest when he spoke reminded me of the way many high-ranking politicos carried themselves at court. My mother excelled at using her wiles to control men with inflated egos. I once asked her why she didn't yell at these kinds of men or kick them out of court to knock them down a bit. She'd warned that men's fragility was dangerous when threatened but easy to control when stroked. I didn't understand her at the time, but since that conversation I'd noticed that she handled tense situations with a smile, a complementary attitude, and an innocent but seductive gesture.

I curtsied. "Brave hero. Thank you for your assistance."

My gaze landed on Young, who rubbed his head and stumbled forward in a daze.

I turned my attention back to the stranger. "This man here is my guard, merely charged with watching over me. I am certain if he was watching, it was in my best interest."

The blonde man looked unconvinced. We gazed at each other for a moment and it dawned on me that he wasn't aware who we were. I reasoned that the more we blended in the better.

He chuckled in a manner that felt insulting. "Ah, I love the naivety of women."

I cringed. Young stepped forward but the stranger casually blocked Young's path with his sword. I gulped as Young shook his head, disoriented.

Who was this strange man? He was wearing a green tabard over his armor. Not Drethen then. His accent was unmistakably Algonian. I huffed. "Regardless, please return my guard to me so that we may resume our journey."

His eyebrows raised. "Perhaps you would benefit from keeping more moral company."

"Generous hero," I said, my voice as hard and thankless as my mother's, "have you heard that Hiems Castle is under attack by the Drethen army?"

He scoffed. "A woman shouldn't burden herself with such serious issues." Heat rushed to my face. He continued. "If you must know, I was summoned to offer my assistance as a gesture of alliance from the great kingdom of Algony."

All at once I understood. I didn't want to believe it, but he was just as the other courtiers described. Under my breath, my voice whispered, "Which means you're..."

A bright smile beamed from his dimpled cheeks. "Yes, my fortunate flower, I am Prince Emmett of Algony."

My stomach dropped. It was okay as long as he didn't know who I was. Something wasn't sitting well with me. Where were his guards? Who summoned him? How did he get here from Algony so quickly?

He continued, "I understand your shock and wonderment." Young shook his head.Emmett continued, "But it is customary for a peasant to bow to royalty once they reveal themselves."

I bit my tongue and began to curtsey.

Young's voice shot out. "Enough," he said as he knocked Emmett's sword out of his path with his own. He re-sheathed his sword. "You dare speak with the Princess of Besmium like this, you arrogant—"

His gaze caught mine, freezing him in place. *No.* Emmett's

face lit with understanding as he dropped to one knee. "My princess, if I'd but known—"

My eyes narrowed. He'd believed that rather quickly. Was he *looking* for me? "So, you see why it's imperative that we make it to the southern castle in a timely fashion?"

Emmett rose and turned to Young. "Which means that you must be..."

Young bowed. "Prince Young of Vires."

"Yes... Vires." Emmett nodded, circling Young like a vulture. "Such an unusual choice the king made to turn to a distant kingdom for military assistance, especially with Algony just to the west. Now with Hiems burning to the ground, his kingdom may fall before your Viran forces arrive." He scoffed. "To think he refused my offer to take the young princess's hand, and yet, here I am to save the day. I really am a saint." He brushed a strand of his golden hair out of his eyes.

Young's expression was neutral. If Emmett had upset him, he didn't show it. "We'll be going." Young stepped in front of me, taking my hand in his.

"Princess," Emmett said, "where's your guard?"

I said, "I could ask you the same." Emmett smiled, flashing his glistening white teeth.

"Well, good day to you," Young said with a bow and a glare. He moved me away and we began trudging through the greenery towards Milly.

Emmett scoffed as he disappeared behind a large patch of shrubbery. A moment later he reappeared, pulling the reins of a restless horse before mounting it. He turned the horse toward the Hiems Castle and I felt the tension ease.

Emmet's voice rang out, "Vires, what a joke."

Young stopped.

I could taste the tension rising. "No, Young," I whispered.

He turned back to Emmett. "I am the future prince of Besmium. I will give my life to protect it. What I don't understand is why *you* are here."

Emmett's eyes darkened as he turned his horse around with the grace of a dove. "So..." I felt the menacing nature of his words before he even finished. "What you're saying is, you're not married."

CHAPTER 12
PRINCE YOUNG

Killing was wrong. I knew that. Sure, you can defend yourself, but there had to be a better way to resolve a conflict with someone you don't like. I knew this, yet I couldn't escape the nagging voice in my head that screamed, "Find a cliff and push Emmett off of it, or better yet give my sword another go."

For one, who even was this guy? Secondly, something was off. He just happened to show up in *this* forest, all alone. Even the timing seemed too convenient. I didn't trust him. I'd doubt he was even a prince if he hadn't been barking orders at me from the moment he sucker-punched me with the hilt of his sword.

Despite a significant amount of protestation, the moment Emmett realized the throne was up for grabs, he was irrevocably tied to our quest to the southern castle, Cadere. For three days I had endured his boorish comments, his braggadocious prose, and worst of all, his attempts to court Charlotte. I'd hardly slept.

I didn't trust Emmett to be alone with the girls, and I could feel the lack of sleep putting me on edge.

The fire crackled and snapped as the sun began to set on the river's edge. I tossed some dry branches into the fire and it sparkled with dancing embers, a brief show of gratitude, before simmering back into its steady form.

"My radiant flower," Emmett called. I cringed.

"I'm here," Charlotte said, stepping into the fire's light, Milly at her side. She smiled brightly, twirling her curly hair around her finger.

Emmett approached. "It's time for the hunt." He gestured to me. "One of us must stay behind to defend you helpless women-folk while the other finds us dinner. Who do you delegate to this task?"

I didn't budge. He gave this speech every night, and every night she responded the same way. As I suspected, she smiled and said, "Surely I can put my faith in you to find us something to eat."

His dimples deepened. "Fear not, princess, I won't fail you." He smirked at me.

"Emmett," I called, the suddenness of my voice surprising myself. "Uh..." I continued zealously toward him then pulled him out of earshot of the girls. "Can I talk to you for a minute?" He eyed me warily. I sighed. "Look, maybe we got off on the wrong foot."

He grinned. "Come to your senses, have you?"

"I appreciate that you're risking your life to help us reach Castle Cadere."

He puffed up his chest. "And I appreciate you knowing your place."

I swallowed my response and the empty air hung between us.

"I'm betrothed to Charlotte and, when we reach the castle, I intend to marry her." I held his gaze, though my stomach turned from how adamantly I'd meant what I'd just said. A glimmer of firelight glinted across his eyes. He tilted his head back and laughed, open-mouthed and loud. His gaze landed heavily back on me and I felt my cheeks burn red.

"You're serious?" He wheezed. "There is no conceivable advantage you have over me."

I shifted my weight. "I-I don't see it that way."

"Your military is too far, your personality is dry, and..." He covered his mouth with his hands. "Just look at you." He grinned. "And more importantly, look at me." I blinked with disbelief. "Fair skin, eyes the color of beryl stone, golden locks."

I huffed. "So, I imagine in your world that's superior somehow?"

"In every world that's superior."

Ah. It didn't take long for his true colors to show. The valiant prince act was long gone. Was he actually trying to hurt my feelings? "You do realize that Charlotte doesn't have any of those traits, right?"

"And I'm willing to overlook that. Do you see how generous I can be?"

I leaned closer to him. "I think you're vastly overestimating yourself and underestimating me." And Charlotte, for that matter, but I didn't want to give him a reason to speak ill of her again.

"Please, you look like the stable boy who washes the weapons for the child of my sparring partner."

I smirked. *Good one.* Let me find a corner to weep in. "Want to try again?" I was almost giddy as I waited for his next insult attempt.

"Your arms are like the string on my..." He nudged a rock with his foot. "Whatever, I should get to my hunt."

If this guy was a prince of Algony, that kingdom wasn't going to last long. "Have at it," I said, heading back towards the fire.

He disappeared into the woods, but I could still hear the loud crunch of his footsteps. As soon as he was out of sight, Charlotte's demeanor changed. Her smile faded, her posture slumped, and she released the strand of hair she often twirled. Charlotte sat a few paces away from the fire and Milly made her way around it, taking a seat beside me.

I couldn't help but glare at Charlotte. Emmett had barely been gone five minutes and Charlotte was already missing him. Why was she acting like this? It was all over her face. A sliver of doubt crept in that maybe Charlotte was more attracted to him than me, plus he showered her with compliments, but it just didn't seem possible for any woman to be interested in such a deplorable man. Yet here I was, witnessing it all. She clearly liked him, reciprocating everything he threw at her. Emmett had given the same treatment to Milly until he'd realized she had no title or ranking, then he basically pretended she didn't exist for the past few days. Charlotte didn't even seem to mind. Where was her loyalty? I didn't care if Charlotte was interested in someone—even if I was obviously a better man—so why *him*?

I puffed up my chest to make myself look bigger and instantly deflated. I'm an idiot. I felt the warmth rush to my face, hotter than the heat coming off the fire. Milly's hand touched mine, jolting me back from my thoughts. "You're doing great," she said, the fire's light illuminating her yellow hair. I pulled my hand away. She continued. "Prince Emmett is difficult to tolerate."

"Yeah, he's been pretty rude to you."

She turned back to the fire. "To you too, and you've managed to stay calm. Charlotte appreciates it."

I gazed at Charlotte through the fire. I knew she couldn't possibly like Emmett, but I just needed to hear it confirmed. "I'm sure they'll be happy together."

Milly snorted. I turned to her. A bright smile spread across her lips. Her eyes searched my face for something, but when she didn't find it, her smile waned. "You're serious? Okay, you should talk to Charlotte."

"What is it? Just tell me." *Confirm it.*

She shook her head. "It doesn't seem like my place. Just go talk to her for a minute."

I let out a labored sigh and made my way over to Charlotte, my legs jellied as I neared. The fire popped and released a handful of yellow embers into the sky. I sat down beside her, suddenly hyper-aware of my hands and where I should rest them. On my knee? Should I clasp them together? She turned to me and smiled, flashing a glimpse of her pearly teeth, but there was no joy in her eyes. I felt unsettled at the bottom of my stomach and I studied her face for clues. She wrinkled her forehead for a second before returning to a smile. She was unraveling. "Charlotte," I whispered. The first few tears fell to her cheeks and she covered her face with her hands.

I froze. I didn't know how to comfort her. I didn't even know what was wrong. She seemed just fine yesterday. Not happy, but fine. Why suddenly when I sat beside her did she fall apart?

"My father," she sobbed, "my mother... the kingdom." I could barely make out what she was saying, but I understood the feeling. *My brother.* She weakened me and I swallowed back my urge to cry with her. It had been a hard few days. I wondered if that had something to do with how she was acting toward Emmett. Was it possible she was *afraid* of him?

She slumped into me, her curls falling over to tickle my cheek. I felt her sniffle against my chest, my pulse rising with each stifled breath. "Charlotte," I whispered. My heart slammed against my ribcage and I worried she could hear it. Here we were again. The wet of her tears soaked through my shirt. "Charlotte," I began again. The fire raged in front of us, suddenly heating my whole body.

My mind flashed to what I'd said to Emmett about marrying her. He was wrong about me. I was more than he knew, and as Charlotte nestled closer to my chest, I thought I might be more than I knew too. I stared in silent observation, frozen until I felt the rare urge to wrap my arms around her like Milly had that night. I lifted my arm and stopped a few inches away from her shoulder. What was I doing? I didn't know how to comfort her. She'd just lost her whole family. Panic surged through me. I leaped to my feet. Charlotte jolted back, gazing up at me with widened eyes and confusion.

"Milly," I called, "Charlotte needs you."

CHAPTER 13
PRINCESS CHARLOTTE

I was alone. That was clear to me now.

For a second, it felt like Young was an ally in all this. He had understood, he had taken my side, and he hadn't left me throughout this whole ordeal—until now. I'd let myself fall apart for a moment and he'd proven to be no more substantial than Emmett. Milly had always been a pillar of comfort, but ever since I was forced to kill those men, Milly hadn't felt like a person I could count on.

Milly rushed over to me and dutifully put her arms around me. But I could tell it was more out of habit than anything else, and I didn't need it, not out of obligation. I didn't need a servant or a prince, I needed a friend. I shouldn't have let myself cry. My parents would want me to keep going.

The orange glow of the fire seemed to suck the sunset out of the sky. Emmett returned with a carcass too fresh for me to look at. He proceeded to roast it on the fire, taking the silence as his cue to regale us with stories of his past adventures.

Normally this would annoy us, but tonight it was a welcome distraction.

"And when I was just four years old," Emmett boasted, "I climbed to the top of the tallest mountain in Algony on my own, with nothing but a small blade and the will to look down—"

I felt Young's gaze on my face across the fire.

Emmett's voice rose. "Then at the tender age of seven, I departed from my beloved kingdom in search of..."

I willed myself to continue to listen to Emmett—anything to avoid looking at Young. I didn't want to see his false sympathy. I didn't want to see him mouth an apology. I wasn't angry, just done.

"...where I pulled the sword Excalibur from a large rock."

My gaze drifted up along the fire's edge, drawn like a ship caught in the tide. I felt myself losing an internal battle against my own curiosity.

"... but I had no interest in their filthy kingdom," Emmett continued.

I surrendered. My gaze met Young's and I held it, challenging him to look away.

"I merely returned the sword back to its stone, and I've been told it's still there."

I felt my skin prickle beneath his unwavering stare. He gave nothing away. Something hot radiated from my forehead down to my chest as if my body understood his message but my brain didn't know how to translate it.

"Princess Charlotte," Emmett said, blocking my line of sight to Young and the edge of the fire. I felt cold on my face where Emmett had snuffed out the fire's light. "Weren't you listening?"

I sat up straight. "Uh... yes. The uh... mountain—"

Young interrupted. "Charlotte seemed enthralled by your

tale of Excalibur." I nodded as Young continued. "It's no wonder you've left the princess out of breath. I bet you have another fine story to tell."

Emmett beamed. "Of course she loves it." His chest puffed up and he sat back down an equal distance between Young and me and began prattling on again. I was struck by the word "princess" as it came off Young's lips. It was something I was called by most people, but Young hardly ever said it. He usually called me Charlotte, so hearing princess from his mouth sounded like an insult and not a title.

When Emmett's storytelling finally exhausted him, he walked back over, motioning to Milly to leave my side. She got up and took a seat beside Young on the other side of the fire. I knew I had to muster whatever energy I had left to keep Emmett appeased.

Emmett leaned in close. "Fair Princess, did you enjoy your dinner?"

"Very much," I said with a smile.

"Only the finest for a woman in my company."

I was worn out from playing this part, but I could feel the girl I was a week ago telling me it was exciting. I was starting to realize things were more fun before they were real. Suddenly, I was being courted. I was speaking to a handsome prince around my age. It was a scenario I'd often fantasized about while waiting for my parents to decide I was old enough to be courted. Although courting in my case was never going to be more than meeting a man my parents had already agreed to bind me to. I didn't want to be married. Not yet. But this part, the courting, seemed glamorous. I guess I never imagined it would be so much work or with someone who so severely repulsed me. There was nothing romantic about it. It was politics for the sake of survival —just like everything else in my world.

I pulled a strand of my hair out of my face. "You have quite a gift for storytelling."

I heard a laugh across the fire. Milly leaned into Young with a bright smile and tucked a strand of her summery hair behind her ear. I could hear a wisp of her voice across the fire, but I couldn't make out what they were saying.

Emmett said, "Thank you, Princess. I have quite a life."

I nodded. "So that stuff is all true?"

My eyes wandered back to Milly as she giggled again. Her laugh was so infectious it made me smile too. I wondered what was funny.

Emmett sighed. "Well, it's mostly true. Embellished in some areas, as all great stories are."

"Yes, it sounds like it takes a lot of skill," I said.

Young's laugh floated across the fire, grasping my attention. It was a sound I'd never heard before, and I realized I'd been listening out for it. The moment I heard Milly laugh, I'd been dreading it, and somehow it was worse than I expected. What did I care if Young liked Milly? But the nervous flutter in my stomach and the weight that settled into my chest told me that perhaps I cared a little. And when I couldn't stop myself from sneaking glances at them, I thought it might be possible that I cared a lot.

CHAPTER 14
PRINCE YOUNG

I knew I'd messed things up with Charlotte. It only took me a moment of her reaction for it to click. I'd tried to signal my apology to her by the fire and to assist her with Emmett, but this morning she wouldn't even look at me. Lucky for me, Milly seemed in good spirits. At least *she* didn't hate me.

Emmett watered his horse as I scouted ahead. I lumbered through the forest, the gentle rustle of the trees carrying the foggy haze of early morning. With the sun not high enough in the sky to warm the air, I felt a chill similar to stepping into the coolness of the river. The area ahead of last night's camp was not as densely wooded, and the forest floor thrived with overgrown ferns and shrubbery. I made a mental note to tell our group to step carefully through them and also noted a patch of plants I thought might be poisonous.

"Prince Young!" Milly called, a sound that snapped me out of the sereneness of the forest.

I felt my stomach tighten. I gripped my sword and turned

toward her. I mentally prepared myself for battle. I'd gone too far. My pulse rose to my throat. I sprinted but my legs couldn't carry me fast enough. Then I saw her.

She stood in a clearing by the river, her shoulders relaxed and her smile sunny.

"What's wrong?" I huffed, surveying the area.

Confusion wrinkled her forehead then dispersed into apology. "Oh, nothing's wrong. I just wanted to check on you."

I spent a moment suspended in awkward disbelief. "I'm fine," I croaked, still catching my breath. I felt a hint of relief when it sunk into my brain that nothing was wrong, but now I'd have to scout again, and I'd lost so much ground already.

"How did you sleep?" she asked.

"Oh, I uh... I didn't really sleep." The concerned look on her face said she needed more information. "Emmett. I mean, just in case."

Her smile returned. "Ah. That's very kind. You know, now that you mention it, your eyes look kind of red." She squinted and walked toward me, analyzing my face.

This whole conversation was a complete waste of time. I looked for an opening to politely escape.

"Milly!" Charlotte called, stepping into the clearing. She froze when she saw me for a moment that felt like it dragged. Her gaze crawled from me to Milly and stayed there.

This was my chance. "I should finish scouting before we get going." I turned to leave and neither of them seemed to mind.

The rest of the morning went smoothly enough. The girls kept to themselves. Emmett insisted the plant that I thought was poisonous wasn't, so he rubbed it on his chest to show us how confident he was that I was wrong. I'd only seen him scratch there twice, but I was certain the reaction would kick in soon.

We followed the river for several hours as the forest thinned around us, and then in the distance we spotted the peaked towers of Castle Cadere. Relief washed over me.

"It was so close to where we camped last night," I said. "We probably could have made it."

Charlotte looked like she was fighting the urge to sprint to it —her eyes widened and her pace quickened.

Each step up the hill revealed more of the castle, like its towers sprouted out of the grassy mound. It was unmistakable. We had made it. We hustled up the hill, the deadened thud of Emmett's horse climbing like a heartbeat rising as we neared.

As we reached the top, we could see more—a grand structure that rivaled that of Hiems, with red flags waving. Once the princess was safe inside, I'd finally return to the north and join Leon in finding my brother.

The last few strides up the hill simultaneously pushed all the air from my lungs and put my plan to find my brother on hold. When we finally saw the base of the castle, my heart sank. Cadere was surrounded by thousands of men, catapults trained at the walls. Soldiers, catapults, archers, generals, all stood ready for battle. The unmistakably green uniforms were just like Emmett's and told me three things. First, this army didn't belong to Besmium. Second, I had underestimated Emmett. Third, Charlotte had to marry him or we were all going to die.

CHAPTER 15
PRINCESS CHARLOTTE

One look at Emmett's smug expression and my recognition of the same green present on his crest was all it took to realize what was happening. Instinctively, I reached out and grabbed Milly's hand. This wasn't the haven I'd allowed myself to believe was waiting. How long had Emmett been planning this? Was he looking for *me* in the woods?

"Look, Princess," Emmett said with a sly grin, "my reinforcements have arrived. The castle is secure."

I gulped. "How did they know to come here?"

"I sent a messenger to deliver word to my general a few nights ago, during my hunt. Some of my men were a mile or so away the whole time. I told them not to be seen, so I could see your reaction," Emmett replied. He leaned forward and looked at Young's face before chuckling to himself. "Totally worth it."

I shot a look at Young. His furrowed brow and gentle frown told me he was as frightened as I was. In the back of my mind, I regretted my choice to let Emmett hunt alone. It would have been better to keep an eye on him. Despite all the posturing he displayed about how safe we were, it was clear his army was a threat. The castle was surrounded—a trap—and we were walking right into it. We could make a break for the forest, but they had horses. We wouldn't get very far. But that wasn't the only problem; something else pulled me toward the castle, the possibility that my parents had somehow made it here too. Emmett had us.

Emmett strode confidently in front of us, confirming that he too knew we had no hope of fleeing. Young's face calmed as we approached the army, but his hand rested on the hilt of his sword. Milly fiddled nervously with her emblem. As we followed Emmet past the first few rows of iron-plated men, it occurred to me that I had neither a sword nor an emblem to comfort me, and I wondered what it was I was holding onto. I approached the last major stronghold of my kingdom and felt my hope drain away as I swallowed the realization that it was already lost.

It was clear that the soldiers admired Emmett. They bowed deeply, and some cheered like they were welcoming a hero back from war. The excitement and joy was unsettling. They were victorious; their prey was surrounded, and there hadn't even been a battle. Milly squeezed my arm and leaned closer to me.

As we walked through the courtyard, now filled with Algonian soldiers, I remembered the summers I spent here with my father. Warhorses sipped water around the pond where we used to skip rocks. Besmium's forge was crawling with foreign troops, the red uniforms replaced with green. On the grassy fields where we once found pictures in the clouds, monstrous catapults were partially constructed and ominously aimed at the castle. How long had they been here? A month? Longer?

I shook with rage as the reality of how much I'd lost set in.

Just days ago I knew my father was alive, the war was just the weather and not an actual threat, and I felt safe. Now Besmium was in trouble and Algony circled it like a hawk. The doors to the castle were more than ten feet high, yet they seemed smaller than I remembered. Trumpets sounded as the doors unbarred, the way they always did, but it seemed inappropriate for prisoners to celebrate. A long line of Besmium guards stood at attention to welcome us. The castle doors closed behind us with a loud boom.

My gaze locked with Young's and in that instant I hoped we had the same crazy plan. We strode in behind Emmett, Young's gaze locked on mine. He nodded and at once I pulled the dagger he'd given me and held it against Emmett's throat. Young pulled his sword and held it at his back.

"We got him!" Young called. Milly screamed and jumped back.

I was right. He *did* have the same plan. Emmett froze. Young's gaze met mine, triumph beaming from his eyes. We'd done it. My heart swelled with gratitude as it thudded wildly in my chest. We could use Emmett as a hostage to make his troops retreat. I gazed into Emmett's face and saw nothing but a calm smile and crystal blue eyes. He reached up to his chest and scratched it. I glanced around the room to find the Besmium soldiers with their blades drawn, surrounding Young.

"W-why?" I stammered.

"Charlotte," a familiar voice said.

My heart leaped. I lowered my knife. Young's gaze burned my cheek as he kept his sword pointed at Emmett. I turned slowly to the voice. She stepped forward, her rigid features, her dark hair pinned back. Tears pricked my eyes, my body weakening. *Mother*.

Her eyes followed the dagger in my hand. "Put the knife down," she continued. I tried to slide the dagger back into my belt, but my hands were shaking. I dropped it and ran to her.

"Mom," I cried. "You made it. Is Father—"

"I don't know," she said stiffly.

I nodded, holding back tears. "We," I sniffed, "we need to take Emmett hostage. He's their prince. They'll have to leave."

The queen walked slowly toward Emmett. "Young, it's alright. You can drop your weapon." Young hesitated before lowering his sword and bowing to her.

"Apprehend him." Before the words left her mouth, the guards had Young restrained and they'd begun to shackle his arms behind him.

"No, Mom!" I called. She ignored me and bowed deeply to Emmett. He reciprocated and turned his attention to me.

"Relax, Princess," Emmett said. His voice slithered down my spine. He chuckled. "Women's minds are so cute. You seem to have the wrong impression about my soldiers. They're a wedding present."

I stumbled back. He continued. "Your mother has agreed to allow me your hand in marriage."

"Young," I said. The name suffocating me. "What about Young?"

My mother sighed. "He tried to kill the future King of Besmium."

Rage began to boil inside me as everything sunk in.

"The council will decide his fate," she said. "Don't worry, though, we can't go around hacking off princes or we'll never have peace. He'll most likely be sent back to Vires."

As they dragged Young away in chains, I felt myself detach from my mother. Tears of hate burned my eyes until I squeezed them shut and tried to picture what my father would say. *Take a deep breath.* I clenched my fists as tightly as I could manage. This was wrong. It wasn't good for Besmium and it wasn't what my father wanted. And Young—how could I let him spend the night in the dungeon? What was my mother thinking? How long had she been planning this? I scanned the Besmian guards, all in my mother's control. Emmett was untouchable. I'd have to play the part of an obedient princess until I could find another way to turn things in my favor.

CHAPTER 16
PRINCE MINSEO

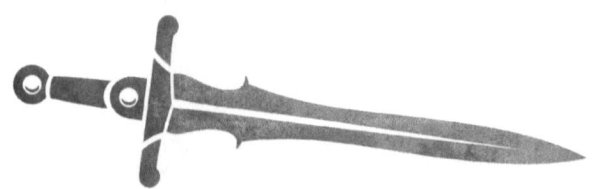

I t's my fault Young is dead.

Imprisoned, it was easy to lose track of the days. How long had it been since I was pulled away from him? Days? Weeks? The image of my brother's face remained in my mind. The fear in his eyes haunted me. When the Drethen soldiers dragged me to their camp, I'd waited up all night. If Young was still alive, the enemy would likely capture him. When he didn't arrive, I feared the worst. Still, I wanted to believe he'd escaped.

The Drethen camp was unlike any I'd seen. I'd spent some time with my father among the Viran troops and always admired their efficiency and loyalty. The Drethens were different. They were not an organized and well-led group poised for war but a drunken and obnoxious horde. The air was filled with the sound of fistfights and war songs and smelled of body odor and fiery liquor—a scent that burned my nose until I acclimated. I was chained to a tree, limited to a radius of a few feet. The iron chains dug into my wrists from their weight and blistered my skin.

Captain Trisby was in charge. A broad man with a thick beard that went down to his chest. He ordered the men not to harm me, but I didn't have much faith that they'd obey.

On the third day of my incarceration, Captain Trisby and a few of his soldiers sat down beside me, the heavy stench of booze around them. "To our honored guest," he said, raising an oversized goblet to his lips. He moved clumsily toward me, huffing as if each step drained him. He held the metallic cup in front of me. "Here, old boy," he said, pushing it against my lips.

I welcomed it. The liquid scorched my throat, a vile taste that was vastly more bitter than what I drank in Vires. I nearly choked but gulped back another burning mouthful. It was a brief distraction from my wrist pain.

"Oy. We got a real man over here!" the captain called. His soldiers burst into cheers and laughter. He pulled the goblet away but took a seat nearby. The booze hit heavily in my chest and I began to feel a dull haze creep up the back of my neck. An hour passed and, as the soldiers grew drunker, they forgot I was there and occasionally let slip information about the battle.

I felt the sting of the irons on my bare wrists as I listened to their voices in the moonlit forest.

A coarse voice I recognized as Captain Trisby floated by me. "I heard the lieutenant is transferring Besmium's king to our camp in a few days." My stomach dropped. This was *bad*. The king was my brother's only hope and a man my father trusted.

"Ain't he dead?" another soldier replied.

"Not yet. I hear he's bleeding, though. Doubt he'll live 'til he makes it here."

"Why they movin' him?"

"Because our men lost Hiems. Had to move back a few of the camps," Trisby said. A fleck of hope swirled around me. If my brother had made it back to the castle, there's a chance he survived.

"Eh. When he gets here, I'll kill him myself."

Within a few hours, most of the soldiers were asleep. Like stray dogs, they slept where they dropped. A small rotation of guards kept watch, but they were also drunk and no more aware than if they were sleeping too. I knew if I were to escape, night time would be best, but not tonight. Tonight I needed rest. I closed my eyes and leaned my head back against the tree.

"Hey," a voice whispered to me. I froze. "Are you Prince Minseo of Vires?" I didn't recognize his voice, but his accent was unmistakably Besmian. "Yes," I whispered back. "Who are you?"

"I'm Private Leon," he said. "Your brother sent me to—"

"My brother's alive?" I shouted. *Too loud.*

A soldier rolled over and tossed an empty bottle in my direction. It landed a few feet away. He rolled back, settling to sleep.

"Sorry," I whispered. There was no response. "Are you there?"

"I'm here," Leon whispered. "I'm going to get you out of here. Are you able to run?"

A wave of relief hit me. I *could* run. I could run all the way to Vires if he cut me loose. I was going to get my brother and go home.

Leon tinkered with the lock on my wrist and, with each click, I felt the hope of escape. "My battalion is only five or so miles away from here. I was scouting the enemy camp when I saw you chained to this tree," he said, his fingers working quickly. "The king is dead and your brother escorted the princess to the southern castle."

The lock clicked louder. The metal clasp released my left wrist. Adrenaline surged through me as Leon moved to work on my other wrist. "The king is only injured," I said. "I heard a soldier say he's being moved to this camp in a few days."

Leon froze, his gaze locked on mine. "The king's alive?"

"Yes." I shook my right hand to hint at him to hurry and unlock it.

"I'm sorry," he said. "If I let you go now, they won't bring the king here."

"No. No. Listen, unlock this. We'll get your army, we'll save the king."

Leon dropped my arm. The iron chain dug sharply into my raw wrist. "Just hold on a few more days."

"No!" I called. I felt my voice elevating too high. "My brother needs me," I said, closing the gap between us.

Leon backed away. "Lower your voice. Your brother is strong. He'll be fine and so will you for a few more days while I rally my troops."

He turned to leave. "No, Leon!" I called. "Don't do this! We'll find—"

"Well, well, well..." Captain Trisby stepped out of the darkness and into the moonlight. "Looks like we got ourselves an enemy soldier."

Leon drew his blade. The captain lunged forward, his sword meeting Leon's with a resounding clang. It was a noise that was likely to wake at least a few more soldiers. I shook the chain around my wrist. If I could escape I could help him, but the clasp remained tightly fastened. Once again, I found myself helplessly watching. Leon was on his own—just like my brother. But, with one hand free, I had slightly more reach.

I grabbed the chain and hustled around the tree, giving

myself an extra foot of slack. A soldier lay in undisturbed slumber a few feet away. If I lay on the ground, my legs might be long enough to reach his sword, but I'd risk waking him up. *Hang on, Leon.* I shuffled to the ground and as quietly as possible dug my heels into the ground by the sword, the clash of the battle behind me clawing for my attention.

I dragged my heels on the ground behind the sword and pulled my knees in. It moved a little. I repositioned my legs and tried again until the sword came into range of my free hand. I lifted it. The weight felt unnatural in my left hand. I positioned myself as close as I could get to the battle but was too far away to help. I considered throwing my sword, but it would be a long shot with my non-dominant hand, and I might hit Leon.

I knew I wouldn't be able to cut the chain with the sword, but perhaps I could try to pry a link apart with it instead. The blade slid along the chain with a sickening screech. I wasn't generating enough momentum. I shook my bound wrist with frustration.

"Uhh!" Leon shouted, grasping my attention. He had fallen to one knee. If I was going to save him, it had to be now. I eyed the sword and my already damaged wrist. The sword wouldn't cut the chain—but it wasn't my only way out. I lifted my sword and braced myself for pain.

CHAPTER 17
PRINCESS CHARLOTTE

I lay my head back and closed my eyes as my lady's maid for the southern castle, Glenda, poured another pail of hot water into my bath. The heat mixed in with the cooled water from previous pails, prickling my senses. I exhaled deeply. I was drowning in chaos and had no idea how to pull myself out.

My nose filled with the scent of lavender as Glenda added more oils to my bath. After spending five days in the forest, the pleasures of castle life felt good but rang hollow. Young was in danger and all he'd done since he arrived was try to protect me. I had to find a way to protect him.

A surge of guilt hit my stomach as I thought of Young. I'd only gone to the dungeons in this castle once, when I was seven. According to my father, it was dangerous and, therefore, forbidden. Regardless, one day I convinced a guard to give me a few minutes to explore. I remembered it was dark, cold, and foul-smelling—so I'd left quickly and never returned. It was hard to think about Young being kept there. We'd been through a lot in a short time. He'd taken care of me that night I drank too much, and protected Milly and me from the battle at Hiems. He'd taken my side when Milly was afraid of me and delivered us safely to Castle Cadere. My mind flashed back to his dark eyes illuminated across our campfire. I felt a nervous flutter at the pit of my stomach. Why was he doing all this? Regardless of his motives, somewhere along the way, he'd become my ally—my only ally. It was possible that my mother had good intentions—maybe she even thought she was doing what was best for the kingdom—but her scheming put us in greater danger than before. She imprisoned someone I cared about, and I needed to stop her.

"Miss?" a soft voice said. My eyes opened to Glenda sheepishly hovering above me. "Shall I heat some more water?"

I sat up quickly. "N-no. I'm just about done," I said. I was clean, but I still felt disgusting. I didn't know how to wash away the things I'd done, the blood on my hands since the Drethen attacked, or the mess that my life had become.

I opened my wardrobe and waded through the dresses that hung there, then stopped when I came to a silver chiffon one I remembered from last summer. I loved the way it flowed in the breeze, a trait that most of my dresses didn't have. I slipped into it with ease but noticed it was a bit snugger on my chest than it was a few months ago. Had I really changed so much?

"That's lovely, miss," Glenda said, fastening the clasp in the back. "I've always admired that one."

"Thank you," I said, clipping my curls back and out of my face.

The corridors of the castle were packed with soldiers. Some were Besmian and others Algonian, but all of them seemed to be under my mother's thumb. Everywhere I went, they followed.

They even waited outside of my chambers. I was not allowed outside the castle or near the dungeon, nor was I able to send letters—but that's exactly what I needed to do.

When I thought about everything at once, I shut down, so I'd planned to take it one step at a time. Today I'd write a letter to the King of Vires, and tonight I'd find a way to send it.

The day went by as a disconnected blur. I blocked out the meeting with the Besmian council and my mother's plans for the wedding. Even Emmett didn't seem to need more than an occasional nod to keep him satisfied as he droned on about his plans for "his" new kingdom.

All day, I arranged the words for the letter in my head. But when I could finally put my words to parchment, I couldn't.

Dear King, one of your sons is believed to be dead and the other imprisoned. Please send help.

No.

If you don't send troops, you'll have lost two sons for nothing.

Ugh. That was worse.

King Lee Won of Vires,
Besmium is under the attack of Algony and Drethen, our neighboring kingdoms. My father is believed to have fallen in the course of battle. The attacks interrupted the wedding agreement previously set forth by you and my father. We are surrounded by the Algonion army under the understanding that I'll wed Prince Emmett of Algony. I humbly ask your assistance in...

I crumpled the parchment and tossed it into the fire. I couldn't risk anyone finding it. I pulled out a fresh piece and quill and began again.

Besmium is under attack by Drethen, and my father, the king, is missing. I want to honor the agreement you made with my father. To do this, I need you to send as many troops as you can spare to Besmium's southern castle. These are uncertain times, and without your help I'm not sure how much time Besmium has left, but I will fight alongside your son and your kingdom until I draw my last breath.
Sincerely,
Princess Charlotte of Besmium

Satisfied, I slipped the letter into an envelope and sealed it with a few drops of wax and my family seal. Now all I needed to do was find a way to get it to Vires.

I slipped out of my dress and into my nightgown, allowing the mental exhaustion I felt to sink in. I lay in my bed and listened to the sound of Glenda's footsteps as she hustled around the room.

I couldn't trust the guards with the letter and I wasn't sure if any of the servants would be willing to disobey my mother, their queen. Not even Milly seemed like a realistic option. I couldn't risk anyone warning my mother because my plan would only work if I convinced both her and Emmett that I wanted this wedding to happen.

I sighed. "Father, I need help."

I listened for his response, half-expecting the low hum of his voice to fill the air around me, but it didn't. "Glenda?" I called, listening for her footsteps, but there was no reply. Before I could call her again, I drifted into a heavy sleep.

A loud knock at my chamber door sent a fierce panic through my body. I sat up in the darkness, the fire by my bed a glowing pile of ash, and waited for Glenda to get the door. The knock sounded again, an alarming thud, the same pace as my heartbeat, and forced my body out of bed and across the room. I opened the door. A Besmium guard with a steely expression and rigid jaw line stood at the door.

He bowed. "Your Highness, this thief claims you've given her this item. Say the word and she will be removed from this castle," he said before pulling a woman into the doorway.

"Glenda," I whispered.

Glenda heavily sobbed as her tears dripped from her chin onto the silver dress I'd worn earlier. Why had she taken it? Why was she *wearing* it? Her wet eyes pleaded with me for mercy. She slouched and winced every time the guard moved her arm.

I cleared my throat. "I apologize for this misunderstanding. I gave this dress to Glenda and asked that she contact the dresser to make another like it. This one has gotten a bit tight," I lied.

"Why is she wearing it?" he asked, unconvinced.

I laughed. "How is it you've lived in a royal castle all these years and know nothing about how women's clothing is made?" I turned to Glenda. "Glenda, if the dresser has what they need, I'll need you in here immediately to start my bath." I pulled Glenda from the guard.

"Yes, Your Majesty," she said while slipping past me into my chambers.

I turned my attention back to the guard. "Thank you for your diligence. But, there's no problem here."

I closed the door behind me. Glenda knelt on the floor, tears still pooling in her eyes. "Thank you, miss. I-I was getting it washed and I just wanted to see what it would feel like," she sniffed. "I swear I wasn't going to take it. You lied for me, Princess. I-I won't forget this."

I walked to my bed and pulled something from under my pillow. "Actually, I need something," I said.

"Anything, miss," she said, her face brightening.

"I need you to deliver a letter."

CHAPTER 18
PRINCE YOUNG

"Imprisoned in the kingdom that I was meant to rule," I huffed. "What a king I turned out to be."

My body ached as another hour in my dimly lit cell crept by. If I passed the time standing, my legs grew tired. If I sat on the damp floor for long enough, my extremities turned numb. Either way, the time in my windowless cell dragged into a timeless nightmare from which I could not escape. Luckily, the dungeons in the southern castle housed a bizarre collection of characters to entertain me. From what I gathered, the more serious criminals were sent to the prison near Hiems Castle, leaving this dungeon for people who committed petty crimes like thievery, or forgetting to bow to a high-ranking member of the council.

Despite its dark, barren appearance, the dungeon was the center of information and drama in the castle. Guards used the tunnels to share their secrets and bribed prisoners to share things they'd heard. All I had to do was wait until I heard something I could use. Most of the information was useless—a cook ran away with a guard, or the gardener hid things for people in the garden. Finally, I heard my first news about Charlotte. A servant had attempted to steal a dress from Princess Charlotte's room. It wasn't much to go on, but just hearing her name gave me hope that if anything newsworthy happened, I'd hear about it—for a price.

I crawled toward the left wall of my cell and pressed my ear to it. "Balzar," I whispered. "Do you have anything new today about the princess?"

I heard the shuffle of his feet as they dragged across the stone floor. "So eager," his weary voice rasped. "What have you to trade?"

"Nothing," I sighed.

"Then I have nothing to tell," he replied. I knew what he wanted—secrets. But the ones I knew could worsen the situation, even get me killed.

"My brother Prince Minseo of Vires was taken at the battle of the northern castle," I said.

Balzar chuckled. "That's old news, hardly worth the breath it took to spit it." He paused, waiting for a response I was reluctant to give. He went into a coughing fit and then wheezed, "What else you got, kid?"

I searched my recent memory. There was one thing that had been on my mind recently. Of course, I had no proof to support this, and worse—though it could be considered treason—it was newsworthy.

"I have something."

Without ever seeing his face, I could feel Balzar smiling on the other side of the wall. It's too big to say aloud—I'd have to whisper. I waited until I heard his breath. "Get on with it then," he spat.

"If I do this, I need you to tell me everything you know that relates to the princess from now on." I waited, unsure if he'd heard me. His voice floated through in a faint wisp. "If I decide your news is worthy," he said.

"Promise me you'll give it a fair judgment."

"You have my word," he said.

"And that you won't tell anyone I told you."

He laughed. "You don't become the center of castle news by selling out your informers," he said smugly.

"Okay," I said, being careful not to raise my voice. "In the battle at the north, we were completely surrounded. Drethen soldiers attacked the front gate before we could escape. I spotted more inside the castle. We took an underground tunnel out of the castle only to find it guarded by more Drethens. We barely made it out alive, and journeyed straight to this castle, arriving a day ahead of schedule."

"Though this story is interesting, it isn't news," he scoffed.

"Wait! Wait!" I called. "I wasn't finished." I lowered my voice. I whispered so softly that I worried he didn't hear me.

After a moment he whispered back, "You're sure she was at the northern castle that day?" he asked, his tone lit with intrigue.

"I spoke with her myself."

"Interesting," he said. His voice rang with a mischievous hum.

"Now, tell me what you know," I insisted.

He sucked in my request through his nose and pursed his lips, considering if what I offered was suitable payment.

I nervously picked at my fingernail, trying to force him into submission with my silence.

He sighed. "The princess plans to have ten thousand white roses at her wedding ceremony. Also, she's asked her betrothed to go on a hunt for the feast afterward. She plans to invite all the soldiers from Algony as well."

My mind raced. Why was she planning the wedding? What was she doing? Had I been wrong about her? "Th-this information is useless," I said, breathing out my frustration. "Guess you're not the center of information after all."

"I have more," he said, his words pulling me back to the wall. "This little tidbit cost me more than your life is worth. The maid that was caught stealing from the princess, she called in a favor to have a letter delivered."

My pulse quickened. "To where?"

"Vires."

I settled back into my cell as the hours blurred together. Charlotte sent a letter to Vires? She must be planning something.

A loud creak and a flood of light indicated someone approaching. I backed away from the wall, lay on the floor, and listened to the distinct click of jeweled shoes on the stone floor as they grew closer. The sound stopped in front of my cell. I opened my eyes and stood to see the queen. "Your Majesty," I said, bowing.

She spoke, "I'm terribly sorry for these horrid conditions. As soon as the wedding is over, I'll send you straight back to Vires where you belong."

"Thank you, Your Majesty," I said. She crossed her arms and her face darkened. "I was hoping I could get a second helping of lunch today, Your Majesty."

Her shoulders relaxed. "Ah. Certainly," she said, dropping her arms. Her gaze drifted to her right to beyond what I could see from my cell. "Balzar," she said. "Has the prince given you any information?"

My stomach tightened. Of course she knew about the information trade going on here. That's probably why she put me here to begin with. I searched my cell for something I could use as a weapon.

Balzar's voice echoed off the walls. "I don't think he said anything worthy of your time," he said.

I froze. He'd been a man of his word after all. I felt relief flush my cheeks.

"That's just it," the queen said. "It's your time I'm concerned about. I'll trade you what you know for your freedom."

Fear pulsed through me. *Did I just give the queen a reason to kill me?*

CHAPTER 19
PRINCESS CHARLOTTE

With the letter on its way to Vires, hope blossomed inside me. I was no longer marching toward my marriage to Emmett but toward freeing Young and taking back my kingdom. All I had to do was stall the wedding—an easy task that only required me to make up time-consuming requests. Emmett saw these requests as his opportunity to win my affection and my mother never got suspicious. After all, these kinds of demands were not too out of character. But one thing did weigh heavily on me: Milly. Since we'd returned to the castle, she'd disappeared from my life. I figured she'd changed her duties for a while to get some rest after our journey, but when a week went by and I still hadn't seen her, I knew something was wrong. Recent events had shown me how much we needed each other, even when we didn't see eye to eye. She'd been there through it all. She understood and I missed her.

I told my mother I was going to speak to the cook, Sasha, about the wedding day feast, but I was hoping Sasha could tell me where to find Milly. The servant's quarters were poorly lit and sparsely decorated. It was another part of the castle that royals rarely visited, but I knew them well. As a young girl, Milly would bring me here to help me hide from my mother, or skip my lessons. It was hard to believe that now Milly used these halls to hide from me.

"Your Majesty," a servant said, bowing deeply.

"I'm looking for Sasha," I said.

"Kitchen, last I saw, miss," she said, wiping her dirty hands on her apron.

I hustled down the hallway to the kitchen and turned the corner. I expected to see Sasha there, bent over the stove with permanently rosy cheeks, but instead I saw Milly washing dishes by the window. She stared out as she scrubbed her soapy hands against a metallic pot. When she didn't notice me come in, I considered turning back, leaving her in peace. I put my hand over my chest to steady my heartbeat. If I'd learned anything in the last few days, it was that friendship was more than just the good times. I stepped into the light of the kitchen.

"Hey, Milly," I said.

Her face paled. "Charlotte. What are you doing here?"

I tried to imagine her tone was welcoming. "I've missed you."

She turned back to her dishes. "Is there something you need?" The pot she was washing was clean, but she kept scrubbing it as if she hoped to wash away her problems with it.

I shivered under her cold tone then took a few steps closer. "No, I just miss my friend."

She continued to wash without speaking. I put my hand on her shoulder. "If I've done something to wrong you, please tell me."

The pot landed with a clang at the bottom of her washing pail. "Everything's wrong," she said, shrugging my hand off.

"I know. The situation is bad, but I'm trying to fix it."

She glared. "That's just it. Every decision you've made has made things worse for everyone." I stepped back as she continued. "People are killing people and you are at the center of it all."

"Yeah, but—"

"Wielding a sword, taking hostages. That isn't you. I know you. You'd never hurt anyone. You certainly wouldn't ki—" She covered her mouth with her hand. It shook. She dropped her hand and took a sharp breath. "Prince Young is in the dungeon!"

Sasha entered the room with a cheerful smile that quickly faded. She turned and hustled out. I shook my head. "Look, Milly, you're like a sister to me—"

"If only I were your sister, in truth," Milly sighed. "You could marry Emmett, and I could marry Young, and we could work together to defeat Drethen."

Marry Young? Where was this coming from? I guess I hadn't imagined things that night in the forest. The thought of it stung, but the last thing I wanted was to lash out at her. "If only I weren't being forced to marry a man I don't love. If only my father were here and safe, if only Drethen wasn't intent on conquering our land. 'If only' won't get us anywhere, Milly."

"It's always about you, isn't it?" Her eyes flashed in anger. "Just once, in your life, can you think of someone else first? You can end this war. Marry Emmett, I can't tell if you're really excited about this wedding or if you have something planned, but promise me right now you'll go through with it."

Marry Emmett? Did she really think that wouldn't have its own consequences? It wasn't just my life that would be in his hands, it was hers as well. I let out a shaky breath. "I didn't start this war."

She turned back to me, her face pink. "Yes, but you can end it. Promise me. Promise me you'll marry Emmett."

"Milly, I can't just—"

"For me," she said while wiping away her tears and moving closer. "If we are sisters, do this one thing for me."

It was a promise I knew I couldn't keep but couldn't form the words to disappoint her so I said nothing. She wrapped her arms around me and I held her for a long while. I was grateful to have her in my life and wouldn't let anything else come between us. She'd confirmed my suspicions that she had feelings for Young and I understood *exactly* how she felt. There was no use fighting over someone neither of us could ever be with. I could only lock away my feelings for Young and allow myself to think of them when alone.

After that, Milly returned to my quarters as my lady's maid. She never mentioned what passed between us, or how she felt about its resolution. But having her close put me at ease.

That night, I opted to eat my dinner in my room. Milly hurried to the kitchen to fetch it while I pondered the things she said. She had been right about a lot of it. Had all our conversations been about me? How long had she felt that way? I made the decision to prepare a royal bath for Milly as a tribute for her friendship.

A little later, Milly returned to my room before I could adequately fill the tub.

"Surprise!" I grinned. "It's for you."

Her pale face and crystal eyes glistened with horror. She spoke, her shaky voice uneven. "Prince Young has been found guilty of treason and sentenced to death."

CHAPTER 20
MILLY

Charlotte did her best to comfort me, but I knew her too well. She was as scared as I was.

I didn't even deserve her concern. I'd practically scolded her—a royal. The closer we'd grown, the deeper the discord between us crept. She could have had me beheaded for less, yet, late into the night, she wiped my tears and promised me she'd save him. But no matter what she said, one truth remained. Young was in danger.

I plopped onto my stiff bed in the servants' quarters, attempting to quell the storms that raged inside of me. My mind replayed the moments I'd shared with the prince as I prepared for my dream to be snatched away by death.

He was not the first prince I'd seen. I'd served many when they were guests at Hiems. They were needy, shallow things with no love for God or others. A visiting prince once scolded me and refused to sit because he claimed his chair was dusty. Young was different though. He looked at me with eyes that were soft and kind and saw me not as a servant, but as a girl. It was a definition with which I hardly defined myself.

After that, I prayed every night to take away the feelings I harbored. I asked God why he'd burdened me with this love if it was so *impossible*. I begged for answers.

But then, one night in the forest, Young sat beside me. I burned as hot as our campfire, yearning for what I could never have. He nodded toward Emmett and Charlotte on the other side of the fire. "Do you think she could someday love him?" he asked.

His question was so absurd that I said, "It's impossible."

Staring into the fire he said, "Nothing's *impossible*."

Even though we laughed, I couldn't help but feel like this was God's reply. There I was, despite my birth, sitting next to a prince as equals. I made a secret vow that night and pledged myself to him. I couldn't tell him now, but perhaps someday I could and maybe he could love me too.

It was obvious that Charlotte didn't feel like I did about Young. I hurt at the memory of Young being treated so poorly by her. She tried to kill him, showed interest in his brother, and hated the idea of marriage. Still, sometimes he watched her. She had a kingdom to offer him while I only had my feelings. Once the jealousy set in, I found it difficult to eradicate. Last night I found myself trying to convince Charlotte not to marry him, and this morning I was depending on her to save him. Love was maddeningly irrational. Even so, I couldn't trust Charlotte to save Young. What could she do? Did she even care? I'd have to watch him die—unless I did something myself.

I got to my knees, pushing my palms together. "Almighty Father, I have done my best to serve you graciously and thank you for your many blessings. You taught me that all life is precious, an idea I've protected even through these times of war." My heart raced as I formed the rest of my prayer. "The only thing stronger than the promises I've made to you is the vow I made to dedicate myself to love. I ask that you turn away from me now." I clutched my wooden emblem and yanked it from my neck. It landed with a clunk and slid across the stone floor. "My new God and guiding force is Young. I ask that you be merciful in your deliverance and that you consider your part in the events that led me here."

I had no choice but to kill the queen myself.

The sun peeked over the horizon, indicating that I might already be too late, but I didn't care. I had to do everything I could to save Young. I sprinted through the hallway to the servants' garden. I knew I'd find nothing useful there, but I had heard of one thing near the back of the castle: a poisonous pink flower called Owl's Bloom. I couldn't remember where I'd heard about it, nor did I know if it was really poisonous. What I did know was where pink flowers grew outside of the castle and that, for the moment, it was my only hope. I knew it was crazy. I knew there was probably a better course of action than chasing a could-be poisonous flower, but the hope of saving Young was all I had left.

I spotted the pink flowers in the leafy passage between the garden and the back of the castle. I reached for them but froze. I didn't know if they were poisonous to the touch. It seemed silly that a flower so lovely and innocent could be something other than that—proof that this flower and I were made by the same God.

I took several flowers, using my dress as a barrier between my hand and the potential poison, making sure no one was around to see me. But I was alone—not even God was watching.

I rushed to the kitchen to join Sasha in the breakfast preparation. I was late but she didn't so much as make a face in disapproval. She was kind that way. We prepared the queen's breakfast as usual. But the addition of wine with breakfast was a habit the queen had started only this year. When Sasha was far enough away, and humming along to a familiar tune, I pulled the flowers out of my pocket, being very careful not to touch them. I chopped them so finely they could have been mistaken for a bit of dust on the corner of the table. I closed my eyes, my heartbeat in my throat. I swallowed down my nerves. With the knife, I pushed the flower dust into the queen's wine. I placed the cup onto the tray, dropped the knife into the washing bucket, and turned back to collect the tray.

I froze. Sasha faced me, holding the queen's breakfast tray out for me to serve— wine and all. I studied her face, the guilt seeping in, blurring my vision. She *knew*. My breath felt strained as I pushed them out in slow, hot bursts. I took the tray and headed for the door. She didn't stop me. It must have been all in my head.

I pictured Young alone and afraid as I made my way to the queen's bedroom. I pushed open the door.

"There you are," the queen said, her voice chilling my bones. "Is it my imagination or is someone running late this morning?"

How fitting that she waits for me, her deliverer. I held the tray steady, willing my arms to stop shaking. I bowed my head. "I apologize, Your Majesty." I laid the tray before her.

"My, my, my. How lovely you've become!" She raised the cup. "I remember the first day they brought you to us in the northern castle." She sighed, bringing the cup to her lips. I froze—my attention bound to her mouth. *She sipped.* "Now you're practically a woman."

I did it. I did it. I *killed* her. I bowed and turned toward the door. "Wait," she said. "I should thank you for being such an important person to my daughter."

I wanted to run to the door—a mere ten feet from freedom.

"Have some wine."

I turned slowly. Did she *know*? Could she taste it?

"That's very kind, Your Majesty, I am but a lowly maid. I can't drink the queen's wine."

She grinned. "I insist." She took a big gulp. "It's delightful, you'll love it."

I lifted the cup from her hand and held it to my mouth. *So this was God's answer.*

CHAPTER 21
PRINCESS CHARLOTTE

The moment I woke up, I knew something was off. I must've fallen asleep while comforting Milly because I wasn't sure when she had slipped out. I rushed to get ready and hustled into the hallway. The sun was high in the sky, splashing a cheerful yellow onto the usually gray walls. Servants rushed around the hallways, carrying large white floral arrangements, no doubt preparing for the wedding which was set to begin in a week or two, depending on how quickly things came together. I headed for the servants' quarters.

"There you are, Princess."

My stomach tightened. I turned to see Emmett, an arch of white roses framing him for a moment before the servants carried it past.

He smiled brightly. "I feel I haven't been able to spend much time with my beloved since we arrived." He plucked a white rose from a passing bouquet and handed it to me. The acid in my stomach bubbled, but I feigned a smile. He continued. "Can I interest you in a walk on the grounds?"

Only a few steps from the servants' quarters, my escape, I glanced over my shoulder. "I-I... I have to—"

He moved closer. "Surely you can spare a moment, Princess."

I stepped back. "Actually, I have to—"

"I insist," he said sharply. His ocean blue eyes darkened, sending a pang of fear through me. I took it and my hands instinctively clenched, causing the thorns from the white rose to prick me. On the surface, Emmett was a handsome and charming prince, but in a moment of disagreement, the predator within glared through.

It was obvious to me that he was used to getting what he wanted, a trend I promised myself I'd break for him—but for the time being he had to believe I'd go through with the wedding. I had to play his game, but he was just a pawn and I wanted to find out if I had what it took to be a queen.

I smiled and took his arm. In an instant, the predator dispersed and the charming prince returned. *Ugh, people who are only charming when it suits them aren't charming at all.* He led me down the corridor.

"Penelope, I need that dress mended before tomorrow," I said to a passing servant. I turned to a patrolling guard nearby. "Charlie, there's this drumming sound outside my chamber at all hours. Can you investigate?" They were false requests, but I needed someone to know that Emmett was taking me. I wanted someone to know which direction we went.

"You are a busy girl, aren't you?" Emmett said. "Might I suggest you take a short break?"

I gulped, too unnerved to meet his gaze and face the beast buried inside him.

"Yes, my dear," I said as we slipped to a quieter part of the castle. If I screamed, the echo would carry. Someone would be able to hear, but then what? I needed Emmett to believe I wanted to marry him. There was no Plan B. I needed to buy enough time for Vires to respond. My muscles stiffened as Emmett pulled me into a dark stairway. We walked silently down and up to a door that was familiar, though I couldn't remember what was on the other side. Emmett opened the door and gestured for me to enter. *This was it.* No one could hear me from in there.

The door closed behind us and I stood at the edge of an overgrown atrium. The sound of running water pulled me toward the atrium's center. A small stream flowed through it, with stone bridges providing passage around the gardenesque courtyard, which was surrounded by castle walls on each side with green leafy plants crawling up each wall. The streams flowed through barred tunnels beneath the castle walls. The light came straight down from the open air above, and sunlight beaming through the long leafy branches of an overgrown willow tree. Dark purple flowers lined the stream. Why hadn't I remembered this place? It was like a dream.

In my amazement, I'd briefly forgotten the dangerous situation I was in. This garden was secluded and I didn't want to imagine the kinds of things Emmett was capable of. I spun to find Emmett kneeling before me.

"Princess," he said, grabbing my hand. "I never did get the chance to ask you officially to be my wife." He reached into his pocket and pulled out a small box. My heart repeatedly crashed into my ribs. He opened the box to reveal a pink diamond the size of his irises. Of all the horrible scenarios I'd imagined, it had never occurred to me that Emmett might actually *propose*. My mind flashed to Young, sadness clawing at my stomach.

Emmett gazed up at me with sincerity. "Will you do me the honor of becoming my bride?"

It was a beautiful proposal in a secret garden. Heat rushed to my face, filling my cheeks with a pronounced red. I couldn't help the overwhelming feeling of flattery and the way my mind continuously tripped on the word *wife*. My next move was clear —easy even. I'd simply accept his proposal and stall the wedding until the Viran troops arrived. Only I couldn't. Something about his sincerity made the lie seem unfair. I stared into his blue eyes, hoping to get a glimpse of the beast, but all I could see was the serene blue of the autumn sky on a cloudless day.

"I realize that you're in a difficult position here, Princess," he said. "But I promise to protect you and your kingdom until my dying breath."

Somehow his speech made me feel like *I* was the monster. I couldn't bring myself to form the words. I nodded. What was I *doing*? Emmett smiled brightly and slipped the ring onto my finger. He stood and pulled me into his chest, locking his arms around me. I felt a pang of guilt. I was a liar, but his embrace was comforting, the warmth of his body making me realize that I'd been cold moments ago. My thoughts returned to Young, who was sitting in a dungeon that very moment, and I wondered how I'd feel if it was he who proposed instead. My cheeks burned.

Emmett pulled away without letting go and smiled down at me. My stomach dropped. He reached his hand up and gently brushed my cheek with his thumb, his gaze drifting down to my lips. Fear tore through my body as I felt his grip on my waist tighten. Would he steal my first kiss?

He held our bodies together as he leaned in, his lips just

beyond mine. His breath was warm and sweet. My body pulsed and my head spun.

Suddenly his lips were on mine. His tongue slipped into my mouth as his body tightened.

I could've pushed him, I could have told him to stop, but I was overcome with the need to know more. The excitement thrilled me, the sensation so dangerous and new. My mind sounded with alarm, even disgust, but my curiosity got the best of me.

"Charlotte?" someone said from behind. Emmett and I leaped apart. We spun to see Milly standing in the doorway to the atrium. She bowed. "Your Grace, the queen has requested your immediate presence in her chamber."

Had she seen? The blush of her cheeks said she had. Milly's gaze surveyed our faces for clues, but not even I knew what happened. I turned to Emmett, who laughed shyly before gesturing for me to go.

I bowed and hurried away with Milly. As the door closed behind us, I wondered what story I'd tell her. My world was expanding and I hadn't yet figured out my place in it. Emmett had brought nothing but horror into my life, but somehow that didn't taint the memory of my first kiss. I blushed every time I looked down at the pink diamond on my finger.

"The date's been set," Milly said as we hurried through the corridors.

I shook my head. "The wedding?"

Tears welled in her eyes. "No, the execution." She buried her face in her hands. "They're going to kill him tomorrow." She looked up at me. "*Do something.*"

CHAPTER 22
PRINCE EMMETT

Nothing virtuous about that princess. It's possible her mother had lied. I sat in silence in the atrium for several minutes after the princess left, but even in the open air I found it difficult to catch my breath, and I couldn't regain full strength in the back of my knees. Perhaps I needed to get beyond these walls. I headed out to the back of the castle where I'd run into fewer people. I didn't feel like talking.

Behind the castle, there was a fair amount of open field, with several scattered camps packed with patrolling soldiers. Even so, the majority of the army was at the front of the castle, leaving me to roam in peace. The climate in Besmium was similar to that of Algony, but today it felt hotter somehow. Was I ill? One thing I knew for sure was that I wasn't feeling this way because of Charlotte. If I'd learned anything, it was that women were interchangeable.

I sighed and lay in the grass, the late afternoon sun casting a refreshing bit of shade. I knew that the princess wouldn't be able to resist my charms. She'd fall victim to my will eventually, just like all the simple-minded women-folk of Algony. So, what was my problem?

A soft humming sound alerted me to a nearby presence. A red-faced servant in the unappealing end of her prime dug up several patches of a soft pink flower. I watched her for a minute —it was such a shame to watch her destroy such lovely flowers that I almost felt compelled to say something. I took a deep breath, attempting to exhale the memory of my kiss with the princess. Perhaps I needed to remind myself who I was. I needed to replenish the feeling of power that came so naturally to a man of my caliber. I got to my feet and puffed up my chest before strutting toward the servant.

"You there," I called.

She looked startled, her forehead crinkling. "Your Highness," she said, curtsying. I gagged. She looked older up close, with laugh lines around her eyes and her mouth. What did she have to be happy about?

"What do they call you?"

"Sasha, Your Highness. I'm the head chef." Her hands were covered in dirt, her apron covered in grease. There was a matronly charm to her; however, I quickly concluded talking to this woman could do no good—by comparison the princess was a goddess.

"Forgive me, Your Highness. I must get back to work." She turned back to the flowers.

"Of course." I nodded while turning to leave. The scrape of Sasha's shovel stopped me. *Irritating.* I turned back. "Why is a chef out here in the gardens, murdering an innocent flower?"

"I uhm..."

Too late. Her brief hesitation was enough. She rambled on but I blocked her out and took several steps closer to the flowers. They really were beautiful. Their pointed petals had a dangerous beauty that I appreciated—appreciated but didn't recognize. For such a beautiful flower in a climate similar to that of Algony, it was strange that I'd never come across it before. My eyes widened as I recalled it.

"*Owl's Bloom,*" I whispered under my breath.

The chef's face turned porcelain white.

I smiled so big it stung my cheeks. "What an interesting kingdom this is." I waited—watched her crumble beneath my gaze. She wouldn't dare lie to me. "Who is it for?"

She visibly shook. "Your Highness, you have the wrong idea. I'm merely trying to prevent—"

"So *someone* used this flower for its purpose, then?"

She shook her head, desperation in the flare of her nostrils. "No, sire."

"So they tried? And you're out here getting rid of the evidence."

She nodded somberly. "Who took the flower, servant?" I loomed over her, using my size to intimidate her.

She lowered her head, closed her eyes, and prepared herself for pain. "Tell me!" I barked, grabbing her arm. She remained motionless. I tilted my head to the side to observe her. She was willing to die to protect someone. I respected that. I released her arm. "Will you at least tell me who it was intended for?"

She bit down on her bottom lip. A loud pop sounded from where my hand hit her cheek. I looked over my shoulder, but no one was around. She buried her face in her hands.

Her posture slumped. "The queen," she sniffed through tears, keeping her gaze from mine.

"Well, we can't have that, can we?" I said, pondering the possibilities. My tone wasn't convincing. Any idiot could see that my situation would be significantly improved if the old bat were killed off. Especially now that I've sufficiently won Charlotte's affections. Still, the flowers were a good tool to have on hand. "I'd like every single one of these flowers transported to my chambers for safe keeping."

"Yes, Your Highness."

"And servant," I added, "it's in your best interest not to mention this conversation to anyone."

I headed back into the castle, my mind reeling with excitement. Things were finally starting to get interesting. *Someone* was trying to kill the queen. I hustled into a side entrance and headed to my chambers.

"Your Grace." I turned to see Draven, my mousy advisor, standing just outside my chamber.

"Not now, Draven," I huffed, pushing past.

"The queen has requested an audience with you."

I stopped. "Fine. Where is she?"

"The throne room, sire."

Without another glance back, I headed to the throne room. I pushed through the double doors, ready to see the queen, and froze. Charlotte stood in front of me, her befuddled expression implying she was as surprised to see me as I was to see her. I bowed too deeply and too quickly. What was wrong with me? She curtsied, smiled softly, and walked past me into the hallway I'd just left.

"Welcome, Prince Emmett," the queen said from her throne. Her voice carried through the gold-lined room. She motioned to the guard, who left and pushed the heavy doors shut behind them. "Come here, we have much to discuss."

I eyed her warily. "Is this about the princess?" My throat went dry.

"Yes. Charlotte has requested to move the wedding to tomorrow," she said, brushing a pin-straight strand of hair out of her face. A wave of weakness hit my knees. I *did* leave an impression on the princess... naturally. The queen continued. "It seems she doesn't want her big day to be overshadowed by the execution."

"Yes, that makes sense," I replied lamely.

"Of course, I told her it would be impossible. You promised you'd find my husband before the wedding. That was the condition of our agreement and your betrothal to Charlotte. Have you forgotten?"

"No, Your Majesty. I sent a unit of soldiers ten days ago a little after I delivered the princess. I received word five days ago that they have the king in tow and will be arriving here tomorrow afternoon."

The queen stood, a glisten of light in the corner of her eye. "He's alive?"

"Badly wounded, Your Majesty, but yes, alive."

She slowly sat back down on her throne, the strictness of her posture melting away.

"Then the wedding will be tomorrow evening then?" I prodded, hoping she wouldn't note my eagerness. Her eyes were glazed over in a way that suggested she was more within her thoughts than in the room.

"Your Majesty," I nudged a little louder.

Her face brightened. "Yes, of course. Let the servants know. The wedding will be tomorrow."

"And the execution?" I asked.

She paused, clicking her fingertips on the armrest of her throne. "We'll let Charlotte have her special day, but rest assured, when the sun rises the morning after the wedding, Prince Young will be dead."

CHAPTER 23
PRINCESS CHARLOTTE

A fleck of scattered light tickled my eyelids, waking me like a soft whisper, welcoming me to the dawn. I traced its source to the white ball gown in the center of my bedroom. It stood erect on its own, maintaining its rigid and elaborate shape. Droves of white fabric draped in layers filling a full skirt and endless train. Tiny hand-sewn porcelain beads scattered along the bottom of each layer and across the ornately beaded bodice, with a low dipping neckline and off-the-shoulder sleeves. Beside the dress was a small table with long white gloves and a glittering tiara.

Most of the bead work hadn't yet been added during my last fitting. I circled the dress several times, leaping over the train in the back each time. It must have taken many sleepless nights to complete on time, but here it was. It was the loveliest dress I'd ever seen in any royal event. A month ago, I would have squealed and called Milly to help me put it on, but this wasn't just a fine dress, it was my wedding dress, which meant this was my last day to save Young.

I headed to the armory. The hallways of the castle were quiet and still. I must've been up earlier than I thought. Suddenly, Emmett's voice filled the hall. I stopped and hid behind a column.

Emmett's voice rang out from the castle's entrance. "Tell McCaffrey I'll need him to go with me to fetch the king. He has five minutes."

"Yes, Your Highness," a soldier responded before their retreating footsteps and the silence that followed indicated they'd gone.

I felt the strength drain from my legs. Did he mean *my* father? Tears stung my eyes. I pushed my weight against the column until I caught my breath. My father's *alive*. I took a deep breath, but I wouldn't let myself believe it until I saw him. I wiped the tears from my eyes and continued to the armory.

The royal armory was much smaller at the southern castle. Still, it was packed with enough weapons and armor to fully equip Emmett's entire army twice. The quartermaster was an elderly man with tattered hands.

"Your Highness," he said with a bright grin. His smile was pleasant, despite the fact he was missing most of his teeth. "It's been some time since you've come down here."

I smiled, straining to remember his name, but I couldn't. "Uhm, I need a sword," I said.

His smile drooped, framing his mouth with lines much akin to ripples in a lake. "What is the occasion?" he asked, looking more concerned.

"A wedding gift for my new husband," I said.

Dread filled the shopkeeper's eyes. "I hope it's not for the wedding *today*." He shook his head. "I wish you'd come sooner. I could have commissioned a sword fine enough for Prince Emmett. Surely I have nothing on hand of that caliber."

I sighed. "Please, if you had commissioned it, he would have found out about it. Will you just show me what you have?"

His smile returned. "Of course, Princess. Right this way." He led me through the rows of helmets to the swords in the back.

The collection was incredible, even to someone who didn't care much about swords. Each sword varied in size and had a unique case that complemented its design. Some were dipped in gold and displayed on a red velvet cloth, others had jeweled hilts and rested on white silk, but my gaze was immediately drawn to a huge broadsword that had a ruby-studded dragon wrapped around the top of it, acting as the hilt. Despite its size, I'd have no problem concealing it in the folds of my dress.

"That one," I said.

"Fine choice, Your Majesty," he said, lifting the glass case, placing it aside, and handing the sword to me.

The sword was even more intricate up close, with carvings and patterns all the way down the center of the blade. For my purposes, though, it was too heavy. I'd never be able to pull it out and swing it before I was stopped. I needed something lighter.

"Do you have something smaller?" I asked, feeling a wisp of sadness as the shopkeeper gently lifted the sword from my hands.

"S-smaller?" he said, "Surely the prince—"

"For me," I said flatly.

"Well, this sword comes with a matching dagger," the shop-keeper said, placing the sword gently back in its case and leading me past the swords to the daggers. He picked up the dragon dagger, a marvel—with detail equal to its larger counterpart. He handed it to me. A surge of power rushed through me, followed by a wave of fear, though I wasn't scared of Emmett. I was afraid of myself, who I was becoming, and the terrible things I was planning to do.

"Will it do?" the shopkeeper asked, regaining my attention.

"Oh, yes, it's pretty," I said.

The shopkeeper laughed, a wide-mouthed grin that exposed his bare gums. "Yes, very pretty."

"I'll take them both," I said, heading for the door. "Have them both sharpened and in my chamber by noon," I said, half calling over my shoulder.

"Would you like me to have them gift wrapped, Princess?"

I smiled. "That won't be necessary."

CHAPTER 24
PRINCE EMMETT

One little errand was all that remained between the Besmian throne and me.

I mounted my horse and trotted into the palace courtyard to meet McCaffrey. I had hundreds of soldiers at my disposal but didn't need their protection. I had ten men waiting at our destination a mile outside the castle but, more importantly, I had McCaffrey. We were unlikely to meet any Besmian soldiers as they'd all been sent to the north to recapture Hiems. I needed a calming presence, and McCaffrey was my go-to man for that.

The sun was peeking over the horizon, mixing with the morning dew to create a pink color that reminded me of the poisonous flowers I had hidden in my chamber. McCaffrey came into view as he made his way around a catapult. His hair askew, he was hunched over his horse as if he were asleep, and his droopy-eyed expression said the same.

"Morning, Your Highness," he croaked. He looked like he

hadn't been to sleep for the night, but I'd seen him in much worse shape than this. At least he wasn't vom— As if he read my mind, he leaned to the side of his horse and made a deep gargling sound. He raised a hand to me. "Just a burp," he said, his horse fidgeting nervously.

I sighed. "We're off then."

We rode away from the palace and finally into the forest where, only a few weeks ago, I'd saved Charlotte. I knew the path well and, as the sun rose in the sky, the path only became more obvious. This final task was almost too easy, just like winning Charlotte had been. She was a worthy reward for ruling over Besmium.

Once McCaffrey adjusted to the early hour, he began chatting voraciously, covering all manner of topics. Despite his constant warbling, I listened with mild interest—it was enough to distract me from the excitement of my plan coming together. An hour and a half later, when we neared the rendezvous point, not even McCaffrey could keep me calm. I wanted to burst through the wood to the clearing, collect the king, and return to my new home to claim my bride. We neared the clearing and I hurried through the surrounding bushes.

I froze. All ten of my men were tied to trees scattered across the clearing. Some were bleeding, some weren't moving—the king was gone. My stomach dropped. McCaffrey and I hopped off our horses. I hurried over to the closest soldier.

"Where's the king?" I shouted, grasping at the ropes.

"Behind," he gasped

I turned to see a single Besmian soldier holding a sword to McCaffrey's throat. A second man stepped out from behind a tree with an arrow cocked back and aimed at me. *Prince Young?* I gaped. No. It wasn't him. He was a bit taller, with longer hair—

still, the resemblance was uncanny. Must be the other Viran prince.

I cleared my throat. "I think we've gotten off on the wrong foot."

The Viran prince spoke, "I don't think we have. It seems like you and your men are trying to kidnap the King of Besmium. Whoever you are, that's an act of treason. Give me one good reason I shouldn't put this arrow in your head right now."

I spoke carefully. "I was attempting to rescue the king. I was planning to return him unharmed to his family at Castle Cadere."

The prince considered my words for a moment before gesturing to the other man. "This here is Captain Leon of Besmium. We will return the king. Just... collect your men and be on your way."

The prospect of presenting the king to the Queen of Besmium and fulfilling our deal was slipping through my fingers at an alarming rate. I didn't want to give the queen any reason to renege on our agreement. Everything I'd built in the last few weeks was on the verge of being destroyed by this man with an arrow. If I was a few feet closer, I could destroy him with one swipe of my sword, but perhaps this situation called for a more diplomatic approach. I chose my words carefully. "How about a trade. The king for your brother."

His face paled.

Leon scoffed. "We'd never consider such a deal." But it was clear from the prince's expression that he did not fully agree.

I had them. "I am Prince Emmett of Algony. I've been summoned by the queen herself to retrieve her husband the king." I focused my attention on the prince. "Prince Young of Vires has been found guilty of treason and is to be put to death tomorrow. What I am proposing is most beneficial to everyone. You release the king to my care. Me, my injured men, and both of you will all accompany the king back to safety. When we arrive, I will personally see to it that your brother is released, and you and your brother can return to Vires unharmed."

The prince turned to Captain Leon. Each moment of silence drudged on, tempting me to just draw my sword and end it. Finally, the soldier nodded. I exhaled my anxiety. The plan was back on.

"Wonderful," I said. "Now show me to the king."

CHAPTER 25
PRINCE YOUNG

I was going to die abandoned in these dungeons at this rate. Not that I wanted my death, but the waiting was going to murder me on its own. Why hadn't they come for me? After my sentencing, the other prisoners were afraid to talk to me, like my looming death was a contagion. From the moment I found out I was going to die, I hadn't been able to stop thinking about Vires—its mountainous landscape, its spring cherry blossom trees. I'd made the decision months ago that I would move to Besmium, take the crown, and spend the vast majority of my life away from my home, but now it was certain. I'd never see my kingdom again, nor my brothers, nor my father.

Maybe my ambition was to blame. If I'd been content as the third prince of Vires, if I'd never wanted to be king, I would still be in Vires and Minseo would be alive. I closed my eyes and rested my head on the cold dungeon wall. What would Minseo say?

Don't give up, Young, I imagined. *It's not your fault.*

"Brother, wake up!"

An eager voice woke me from delirium to find Emmett standing beside Minseo outside my cell. For a moment, I thought I was dreaming, but in a few short seconds, I realized my brother was actually there. My heart slammed into my ribcage. *Minseo.* Dazed, I leapt to my feet and pulled my brother into my arms, three iron bars between us. I choked back tears as I struggled to clutch him tighter through the bars. I put my forehead to his and felt the splash of his tear on my cheek, turning me into a blubbering mess.

Emmett cleared his throat.

Minseo and I jumped back, wiping our faces. Emmett stepped between us and unlocked the cell. Minseo's shoulders relaxed. He turned to Emmett. "Just like that?"

Emmett grinned widely but his gritted teeth made me believe witnessing our reunion made him uncomfortable. When the gate opened, Minseo rushed in and hugged me again, then looked me over, like a mother after her child comes home for the day. Relief surged through me. I tried to choke back another wave of tears, but it was no use, my brother was *alive.* He wasn't just alive, he was here—saving my life.

"I must ask a favor," Emmett said.

Minseo turned back to Emmett. It was hard to see in the darkness of the dungeon, but I thought I saw traces of tears still on Minseo's rigid cheeks.

Emmett continued. "You may collect your things and rest in Besmium until tomorrow, but I must ask you to not attend the event this evening."

"Event?" Minseo asked.

"My wedding to Princess Charlotte," Emmett said. Minseo's gaze darted between Emmett and me before it finally came to rest on me. Sadness spread across his face. His lips tensed, his eyebrows slightly raised. His sympathy was unsettling. He searched my face for a reaction—but this was old news to me.

I smiled, placing a reassuring hand on Minseo's shoulder. "Let's go home," I said. Minseo hesitated for a moment, like he wanted to say more but didn't. Instead, he pulled me out of the dungeon cell, notably keeping his body between Emmett's and mine.

We were given our own quarters and allowed to bathe. Minseo told me the story of how he'd nearly been forced to chop off his own hand, and I filled him in about Emmett and our time in the forest. By comparison, my last few weeks seemed uneventful though the exhaustion and hunger I felt said otherwise. I was happy to learn that Leon had assisted Minseo in his escape and I was eager to find him and thank him.

"Actually," Minseo said, "Leon refuses to leave the king's side."

"The king's *alive?*" I choked, reaching out for a chair to plop into.

Minseo tilted his head to the side as if I'd missed a crucial part of his story. "Yes, Leon and I traded the king to get you out of jail."

Excitement overflowed from within me. "Charlotte's going to be so happy." I turned to find my brother looking somber. He nodded, but I could tell that once again he was swallowing his words. "It's okay, Minseo. I'm alive. We can go home. You did that."

He feigned a smile.

"Let's get some food and find Leon. That way we can leave for Vires nice and early tomorrow." I peeked my head out the door to try and find someone to bring us lunch, but the hallways were empty.

I called over my shoulder to Minseo, "They must all be preparing for the ceremony. Hold on." I hurried into the hall and toward the servants' quarters.

"Hello?" I called, but there was no reply. I headed toward the grand hall, making sure to take the side corridor to avoid being seen by anyone going to the event.

I froze. Standing right there, on the other side of the corridor, was Charlotte. My hands began to sweat and my legs grew heavier with each endless second. I couldn't breathe. She wore a white flowing dress that cinched in her waist. Her brown skin was luminescent, her curls pinned out of her face. Suddenly, as if she felt my gaze brush her shoulder, she turned to me.

I tried to quell the electricity that tore each cell of my body apart with every step closer she took. She smiled so brightly that I almost felt myself smile back. Forgetting herself, she threw her arms around me and buried her face in my neck. My body went rigid. Instinctually, I took her by the waist and eased her away from me. Her face glittered and I wondered if she had been crying. She wiped her eyes.

"I thought you were going to be executed," she said, her white ball gown swaying with each tiny movement.

"Me too," I said, my gaze traveling around the angelic princess. "Minseo saved me."

She covered her mouth with her hands. "He's alive! That's great. My father is here in the castle. He's hurt, but he's alive."

I nodded. My gaze lifted from her waist to her chest, up to her collarbone, her neck, and finally her eyes. The sudden dread of silence sunk in. "You make a beautiful bride." My eyes widened.

She smiled softly, and all at once I could see the same sorrowful gaze that Minseo had given me. "Thank you," she said.

I prepared myself to tear my gaze away from her, trying to drink in every detail of her and capture the memory before I left, but she reached out and touched my wrist, sending sparks radiating up my arm.

"I-I..." she stammered. A faint pink blush wisped over her cheeks. She continued. "I guess I won't be needing this."

She reached under the outermost layer of her dress, digging underneath for something. She seemed to be struggling, but I wasn't sure how to help her or what she was doing. I mean, it wasn't like I could reach in there and assist her. Finally, something unhooked from her waist and from under a fold of white fabric she pulled out an ornately-decorated sheathed broadsword.

The handle of the sword was a dragon covered in red rubies. It was much too large and heavy to be concealed in a dress, or so I thought.

"I guess I don't need this anymore," she said, handing me the sword. I eyed her dress, wondering what other mysterious objects were hidden in there.

"Why do you have a sword in your dress?" I asked, unable to fight a smile.

She laughed. "I was going to save you."

"Were you going to stab him at the altar?"

She bit her bottom lip, biting back a smile.

I gaped. "*That* was your plan?" I whispered, checking the empty hallway for listeners.

She pushed my shoulder. "It wasn't Plan A."

My smile dimmed. "What were you going to do about his army after you killed him?"

"I hadn't gotten that far," she said, putting her hands on her hips.

I nodded, attaching the sword to my belt. "Well, thank you, Charlotte, for the sword and your reason for having it."

I turned to leave but glanced back one more time. "Got anything else hidden under there?" I asked.

"Matching dagger," she said with a sly smile.

With each step away, my breathing became more labored. I shook inside. How could it be unbearable to be near her and worse to walk away? It was hard to believe that this was good-bye, that after everything I had to just go on living my life in Vires as if nothing happened. As if my entire world hadn't been changed forever.

I left the corridor, heading straight back to my chamber. I wasn't hungry anymore—in fact, I felt sick. I hoped Minseo would know what to do or what to say to make my chest stop aching.

CHAPTER 26
PRINCESS CHARLOTTE

The moment Prince Young turned away from me, I felt a swirl of emotions I wasn't expecting. How could I feel this sad when everything had worked out perfectly? Young was safe, my father was home, and when I said "I do" in a few hours, Algony's army would clear out Drethen. My kingdom and everyone I loved would be out of danger. I never wanted to be a wife, certainly not Emmett's wife, but it wasn't worth losing anyone else. Besides, Emmett had given me such a beautiful proposal and that kiss... I wondered what it would have been like to kiss Young.

I shook the thought from my head. It was selfish. It couldn't happen. Everything was fine. So, why did I feel like crying?

I decided I'd given my father enough time to rest and headed to his chamber. As I approached the double doors, I noticed the guards had their ears against the door.

"What's going on?" I asked. The guards jumped back into a straightened position. "Leon!" I said rushing over. "You're alive."

He bowed and pushed a brown strand of hair out of his eyes. "I'm happy you also arrived safely."

The other guard looked like he was asleep on his feet. "That's McCaffrey of Algony," Leon said. McCaffrey slouched against the door.

I considered asking what was wrong with him, but I didn't care enough. "What's going on with my parents?" I asked.

He smirked. "Want to take a listen?"

I gasped in excitement. "Can I?" I rushed to the door and put my ear to the crack. I could barely make out the words.

"Well, what was I supposed to do?" my mother cried.

"Honor the agreement," my father said weakly.

"If I had, you'd be dead."

"I was also rescued by a prince of Vires. What kind of king backs out of an arrangement this important? Furthermore, Emmett of Algony is the worst kind of man. Are you really willing to vouch for him?" Even in anger, my father sounded much weaker than normal.

My mother's voice cracked. *"I'd stake my life on it."*

I pushed myself away from the door. I wished I didn't hear that. My corset dug into my sides. Emmett *was* the worst and Young didn't deserve how this turned out. I knew all this already, but hearing it from my father made it seem worse. I gasped for air. There was no way I was going to last in this dress until the ceremony. There were several more hours until it started. My parents had some business to work out, business I didn't want to be a part of. I'd buy myself some time to plan and marry who I had to marry. For now, I just wanted to be out of this dress. I hurried to my chambers, half expecting to see Milly there, but the room was empty. I swallowed my disappointment. Milly must be with Sasha, trying to prepare enough food for the council and nobility that would be in attendance.

I reached around my back to try and unlace my corset myself. Not even close. There was no way I was getting it off. I tried reaching one more time, but this time I wound up making myself light-headed and out of breath. A thud sounded on my door. My shoulders tensed. I hoped it was one of my maids—I needed to get out of this thing. I hurried to the door and pushed it open. Prince Young stood in my doorway.

"Charlotte," he said. I looked into the hall behind him to see if someone else was passing—anyone who could help me—but it was only him.

"Please pardon me for coming to your chamber. I wondered if I might be able to have a word with you before the—"

Grabbing him by the shirt, I pulled him into my chamber. "Get in here," I said, shutting the door behind him. I took two steps toward the center of my room and said, "Quick, untie it. Help me take this off."

"Well... this is going better than expected," he said, half under his breath.

"Hurry, I can't breathe," I shouted.

Young's hands moved clumsily over the ribbons. "Sorry, I've never done this before," he said, "Uh-uhm. I mean—"

"That's okay. Neither have I," I said without thinking. What did I even mean by that?

"How do I do this?" he whispered.

I said, "Just try to loosen it. I just need a deep breath."

He pulled at the ribbons and I felt a slight release around my waist. I exhaled. "So, what was it that you wanted to talk about?" I asked as he continued pulling aimlessly at strings. He let my question hang there. I wasn't sure if he would answer.

"I wanted to know if you're happy with Emmett."

I opened my mouth to answer. "A—"

"No, that's not what I wanted to say. I guess what I mean is, do you still want to marry me? No, I guess you never really did want to. What I'm trying to say is, I miss Vires."

My heart thudded and I felt my corset tighten.

He continued. "Now that I'm free, I can return there, but for some reason I can't—and I think that reason is that I want to marry you. Still."

My heart slammed into my ribcage. Was this a proposal? I turned to face him, holding the front of my dress up with my arm. It made no sense. "Why? There's barely a kingdom left. You know what Emmett will do if I don't go through with this."

"I don't care." He stepped closer. My eyes disobeyed me and my gaze slipped to his lips for a fraction of a second. His eyebrow raised slightly. He'd noticed. As if he was reading my curiosity, he leaned in.

The door swung open. "Brother! Emmett is headed this— Oh," Minseo said, eyeing my half-untied dress. I sprang back from Young in a panic. Minseo grinned. "Wow, that really went better than I expected." My face exploded with heat.

"Minseo, she can't breathe. How do I untie this?" Young said, gesturing to my back. With three quick fluid motions, Minseo untied my entire corset. One thing was clear: Minseo *had* done this before.

Minseo turned to Young. "Emmett is coming. Hide." The Viran princes dove behind a lounge chair on the far end of my chamber, just as a knock once again sounded on my door.

"Getting ready," I called. Emmett peeked into the room. He grinned widely at my unlaced corset. "Is this a preview? Don't worry about the audience, Princess, I'll handle everything." I'd almost forgotten about the consummation ceremony. *Ugh*. Dread pulsed through me. He stepped up behind me and tightened my corset as quickly as Minseo had loosened it. *Ah. Not his first time either.*

"You look stunning," he said, heading for the door. I felt a rush of relief because he hadn't spotted the princes. A chill went down my spine as my mind contemplated what might've happened if he'd discovered them alone in my chamber, especially since I was half-naked when he arrived.

"Oh, Princess," Emmett said, turning back to me. My stomach dropped. He continued, "I've been thinking about that kiss." He ran his hand through his hair. "I'm excited for tonight," he said, and with that he left my chamber, closing the door behind him.

Afraid to move, I concentrated on my, once again, restricted breathing.

Several still minutes passed until Young broke the silence. "You *kissed* that guy?" He stepped out from behind the velvety chair.

"Yes," I said flatly. I had no explanation. "I-I." My cheeks burned hot with guilt.

Minseo put his hand on Young's head. "It's not a big deal."

Young headed for the door. "I'm sorry to have taken up so much of your time," he said, his gaze glued to the floor. The door closed behind him.

What was *happening*? How had I lost this much control of my life? Once the parade of princes left my chamber, I tilted into my bed and cried. My corset dug in, once again too tight to breathe well. I wasn't sure what I was crying for anymore. I sobbed into my pillow until, somehow amidst the chaos, I drifted off to sleep.

CHAPTER 27
PRINCE YOUNG

"Young!" Minseo called. I kept walking straight into my chamber. "Young!" he said, grabbing me by the shoulder. "You're not seriously mad about the princess kissing Emmett, right?"

I scoffed. "Of course not."

"Good, because not twenty minutes ago, you told me she was going to kill that guy to save you. Remember that?"

I put my hands in my pockets. "I don't know."

"You don't know what? Why're you so angry, brother? You'll soon feel better once we get to Vires. Soon enough you'll turn nineteen, and after you've been with a few women, you'll forget all about the princess."

I turned away from Minseo. "I'm just not... ready. I can't just go back."

"Brother, it's over. She's marrying Emmett."

I clenched my fist and I felt something hot bubbling inside me but said nothing.

Minseo continued. "Is this about the kingdom? Father will find you an—"

"It's not," I said, unwilling to listen.

He stepped back. "So all of this is about the girl."

"It's about keeping my word."

"Brother, we're surrounded by Algonian soldiers. You think he's going to let you storm the wedding, take the throne and the girl, and walk out of here alive? This is over. We're leaving tonight."

I inhaled sharply. "You should go," I told him.

Minseo shook his head. "Don't do this. Don't die for a girl. Come home."

I couldn't look at him, so I looked down at my feet, but even without looking at him I could sense the pain I was causing him. "I'm sorry," I said. "I'm staying, but I think you should go. Now, while you still can."

We walked in silence back to our quarters. I sat on my bed examining the dragon sword Charlotte had given me. Minseo was afraid, but he knew he couldn't change my mind. I understood everything he said. I longed to see Vires, but I was tied to Besmium now. I needed to know Charlotte would be okay. I had to do whatever I could to protect her from Emmett.

My brother was going back to Vires. The only one I was putting in danger was myself. I could live with that.

Several minutes passed in frigid silence before my brother's voice broke it. "This is ridiculous! Stop being childish," he yelled. "Father would be ashamed. This kingdom is worthless and Charlotte is nothing but a pathetic, helple—" My fist collided with his jaw before I knew I'd even crossed the room. Minseo dropped his hand from his mouth, a crimson stream of blood flowing from his lip to his chin. His gaze cut into mine, a glimmer of sadness in his eyes that told me it wasn't my punch that hurt him most.

My brother packed his things without a word. It was hard knowing that he was leaving. I glued my attention to my sword until Minseo stood at the door of our chamber, a bag slung over his shoulder. He cleared his throat. "Please, Young?" he said, making my chest ache. He sighed. "I just got you back."

I wanted to go with him. To see my kingdom and my family again. I wanted to apologize to Minseo and make things right, but I couldn't leave Charlotte. She was willing to kill Emmett to save me. Now I would do the same for her. "I'm sorry, brother," I said. "I'm staying."

The door shut and the reality of my choice weighed on my shoulders. There was no escaping Besmium now.

I changed into my finest clothes. After all, I *was* going to a wedding. I tied my new broadsword to my belt and headed toward the grand hall. Leon was standing near the entrance. "Leon," I called. He grinned with his whole face. "Your Majesty," he said, bowing before looking me up and down. "I hope you're not planning on crashing the wedding." He chuckled. When I didn't respond, his smile faded. "No, Young. That's a bad idea."

"Where's Emmett?" I asked, ignoring him.

"What did your brother say about this?"

"My brother's gone back to Vires. He left a few minutes ago."

Leon shook his head, his eyes widened in understanding. "It's suicide."

"Where is he?"

Leon took a deep breath, his eyes as heavy with regret as Minseo's.

"Leon," I said, "I have to do this."

He nodded solemnly. "He's in the atrium. It's at the end of the east wing, down the stairs."

Before he could say another word, I hurried toward the atrium. I sprinted down the dimly-lit staircase, skipping stairs as I went. Finally, I stood outside a large wooden door. I pushed the door and stepped outside into a green garden courtyard.

Emmett stood on a bridge toward the middle of the atrium, seemingly enjoying the temperate weather. He turned to me, a soft smile on his face. "Ah, " he said, moving closer. "I suppose you've come to bid me farewell."

"I've come to challenge you," I said. He blinked at me dumbly. "For Charlotte's hand in marriage."

Tension closed around the atrium like a thick fog. Sweat beaded on the back of my neck. Emmett stared at me for several moments before a look of understanding flashed in his blue eyes. He threw his head back and let out a loud, breathy laugh that echoed off the walls.

"Go home, kid. You're going to get yourself killed." He chuckled, wiping tears from his eyes.

I clenched my jaw and drew my sword. "I'm a better man than you."

"Seriously," he said, still smiling. "Don't make me kill you. I have a lot on my plate. I'm getting married today." He ran his fingers through his golden hair.

He wasn't going to agree. I had to find a way to antagonize him. "It sounds to me like you're afraid."

"Afraid?" he scoffed. "I could eat you," he said, erupting into laughter. I wasn't getting anywhere.

The sun began to dip behind the castle wall, casting its final beam of light directly onto my sword. The red rubies scattered

red light around the garden, like blood splattered across a wartorn forest.

"Actually," I said, turning the sword over in my hand, " Charlotte gave me this sword about an hour ago."

Emmett's smile faded. "Shut up."

He pushed past me and headed for the door. I was losing him. If he didn't accept my challenge, I'd have no chance of stopping the wedding.

I ransacked my brain for one last bit of ammunition as he reached for the door. *Ah.* A pang of guilt hit my stomach before the words even came out. "Corsets," I huffed. "Am I right?"

Emmett stopped with his hand on the door.

I gulped, trying to keep my voice as even as possible, but my fear started to creep in. "Those things are a pain to unlace." I feigned a laugh. "You weren't even a little suspicious."

Emmett turned back to me, a fierce darkness in his eyes, like a summer storm about to break. "If you want to die so badly, I accept your challenge."

CHAPTER 28
PRINCE EMMETT

They were all lies, everything he implied. One look at him and anyone could see the man didn't have it in him. Still, the thought of him and Charlotte together made hatred surge through me. I didn't care what Young said, there was no way the princess would ever choose a man like him over a man of my caliber. Who did he think he was?

It was true that Vires had an impressive military, but the location barred them from being a threat or ally to anyone in this region. Not to mention Young himself—weak, scrawny, and barely man enough to grow facial hair. Didn't he see my sword in its sheath? As if I'd step foot in enemy territory without having it at all times. What was he thinking?

He must be so ashamed of losing his contract with Besmium that he chose suicide over returning home. This was a mercy killing—a perfect way to stab away my wedding jitters.

I glared at Young from across the atrium. He was on the bridge, a higher plane than me, but it didn't matter. I was unbeatable. I could tell by the way he held his sword that at least he'd held one before. I scoffed, unable to believe his arrogance.

He swung carelessly. I easily avoided his attack and he'd left himself open. I was going to end this with one swing. I raised my sword above my head and veered it down from above him. He blocked it with the flat of his blade. He was *fast*; it didn't matter. The sheer force of the impact knocked him down to his knees. I pressed down and he collapsed beneath the weight. I raised my sword once again and swung down for the finishing blow. He rolled to his right, off the bridge and into the water. My sword sliced into the wooden beams. I tried to pry it out but it didn't budge. Again. The wood splintered. One more, the sword dislodged, sending shreds of wood flying. Spinning around, Young charged me. I dodged his advance, his blade slicing past me, knocking me off balance.

He *was* good—I swept his leg out from under him—but *I* was better. He slammed back onto the bridge, his sword sliding out of his damp hand. I stepped on his chest as he helplessly swatted at my boot. This was the end. At worst, I'd get a little blood on my boot and have to dip it in the stream. It had been useless for him to challenge me. It was obvious before we started. He had no chance at all. I brought my sword down.

"Wait!" a voice called.

I paused, tracing the sound of the voice to the door to the castle. McCaffrey stood in the doorway, his hand outstretched, his mouth agape, and his face stark white.

"Not now, McCaffrey," I said, raising my sword.

"Don't, sire! Prince Minseo has returned..."

I shook my head. "I didn't know he'd left. This is a fair duel. Why shouldn't I finish it?"

"Prince Minseo has returned with the Viran army, sire. I feel it's in your best interest, duel or not, to let the other Viran prince live."

It was impossible. Vires was too far. They would have had to be summoned weeks ago. Minseo hadn't even arrived until this morning. Young had been in prison. That meant—*the princess*. I staggered back breathlessly. *She doesn't want me?*

"H-how many?"

McCaffrey shook his head, alarm flashing in his eyes. "More than us."

My boiling blood seared my skin from the inside. My body shook. *Charlotte.*

"Sire," McCaffrey said, "we must retreat."

"N-no. The wedding. It's—" Young got to his feet. Stunned, I stared at Young, staring back at me with fear in his eyes, so weak and helpless. Would the king just hand the throne to such a man now? Someone I could destroy this very moment. I *would* destroy him this very moment. No, I'd destroy them all. If I couldn't have Charlotte, no one could. If I didn't sit on the Besmian throne, no one would. I hustled past Young with half a mind to impale him on my way, but I had a better idea.

I returned to my quarters, out of breath, and snatched the pink flowers with a gloved hand from behind the curtains where I'd concealed them. "McCaffrey! Get the carriage ready. Start moving the troops!" I shouted.

In his contorted expression, I noticed what, to him, must have looked like a crazed, unraveling man with a fist full of pink flowers. No one would make a fool out of me. I stormed to the kitchen, ready to cut down anyone in my path. I'd find something to put the flowers in, and as they dined and celebrated their victory, I'd wipe out the entire Besmian royal family, the council, and half the nobles.

The kitchen was empty. Not a soul or a servable food in sight. The dishes were stacked high in the sink, but nothing was cooking. I must be too late. There were four large barrels at the far side of the kitchen that seemed to be pushed forward from their usual resting place. I peered in to see a black liquid. Sticking my face near one of the barrels, I sniffed. *Wine*, perfect. I ripped the pink flowers into the smallest pieces I could manage with frantic, shaky hands and dumped them into each of the barrels. I stood back, pleased with my work.

"What are you doing here?"

I looked up to see the middle-aged woman from the garden. Her face was even redder than usual. She took one look at me, and then at the wine, and realized what I had done. I clutched the hilt of my sword.

Without a second thought, I raised it and ran her through.

Blood spattered on the stone floor. She made a feeble gurgling sound and the light left her eyes. I dragged her body around the corner. Someone would find her, but it was unlikely that anyone else knew about the flowers—there was no reason to suspect the wine. I grabbed a ladle and scooped some wine from the closest barrel and poured it over the blood to make it look like the blood was just spilled wine. Happy with my work, I darted out of the castle.

I marched with my remaining men as nearly all of them were already outside of the courtyard. They must've begun retreating hours ago. I passed row after row of Viran soldiers all uniformed in yellow—with some indistinguishable symbol on their chests. I tallied the number of soldiers I saw there. I'd triple my own numbers and return. I'd slaughter every last one of them. As I passed the last row of Viran soldiers, I was greeted by Prince Minseo.

He wore a victorious grin that made me impulsively reach for my sword. Instead of drawing it, I smiled. "Enjoy the party," I said.

He waved. "Don't worry, I will. So sorry you couldn't make it."

I vowed to myself that they wouldn't get away with this. I wouldn't rest until every last person in that castle died, whether it happened tonight or tomorrow. I'd get my revenge.

How dare they humiliate Prince Emmett of Algony like this! How dare *she*.

CHAPTER 29

MILLY

I wondered where Sasha was as I scooped a spoonful of rice onto the serving plates. We'd been in the kitchen all day, but since we moved the food we'd prepared to the grand hall, I hadn't seen much of her. At first, I didn't mind her absence. She'd been especially harsh toward me since the poison incident with the queen. I was grateful to her for switching the cups and knew I deserved every bit of her anger. I would have been executed for treason if she'd told anyone, and she could be too for keeping my secret. Still, I relished the hours I was out of her company.

I never realized how many servants there actually were in Castle Cadere until today. Since I'd arrived, we stuck to our usual routines and designated areas in the castle, but today was Charlotte's wedding, and everyone was either in the grand hall or the chapel trying to get everything ready for tonight—except Sasha. Another hour passed and I still hadn't seen her; perhaps we'd forgotten some of the food.

I headed through the poorly-lit servants' quarters toward the kitchen. People rushed past carrying strings of flowers, plates, and cutlery. Droves of decorations, trays filled with candles, ribbons, and lace fabric to decorate every inch of the hall. I'd never seen an event of this magnitude.

Just as I turned the corner to the kitchen, I ran straight into a server carrying a large tray with three golden goblets. He swayed backward. The goblets wobbled, spilling a few drops of red wine onto the tray.

"Oh," I said. "I'm terribly sorry." I paused for a minute as the boy composed himself.

He exhaled. "It's alright. No harm done."

I stepped aside to let him pass. "Wait," I said, remembering what Sasha told me earlier. "We're not meant to serve wine until after the ceremony. No exceptions," I said.

"I know," he said, "but this is a special request from the king himself. Some pre-wedding toast with the groom, no doubt."

I nodded and turned into the kitchen to look for Sasha. I stood stunned in the doorway of the kitchen.

Impossible. Who could have done this? The sink was piled high with every dirty cooking utensil in the entire castle. Surely, I'd have to be the one to wash these while everyone lays down to rest tonight. But I suppose no one would miss me if I washed a few of them. I plunged my hands into the soapy water and scrubbed. I pushed myself to increase my speed with each dish, timing myself in my head. I started grabbing dishes from the countertop and tossing them into my bucket. One by one, they splashed in the water. I yanked a large pot near a bag of potatoes and tossed it into my washing barrel. The bag toppled over, sending stumpy brown potatoes rolling across the kitchen floor. *Great.* I wiped my hands on my apron and chased after the scattered spuds, grabbing as many as I could and tossing them into the sack.

One particularly ambitious potato rolled a little farther than the others toward the back door. I reached out of the dimly-lit kitchen toward the dark hallway and grabbed for the potato. It didn't move. I could tell by the weight of it I hadn't grabbed the potato, despite its similar brown color. I moved toward the object. I gasped as horror pricked into me like a thousand needles. *Sasha.* I fell to my knees, shaking her body with my hands. I struggled to roll her over only to find a look of pain frozen on her stark white face. She was covered in wine.

"Sasha, what's wrong? What happened to you?!" I screamed, but she didn't move. Her lifeless gaze chilled me. "Sasha!" I shook her but she didn't move. I pulled my wet hands back and held them towards the light. *It's not wine*, I gulped. *Blood*. I shrieked a horrible sound as the realization dawned on me. Sasha was dead. My mind reeled.

I pressed my hands together. "Oh, heavenly father, please guide Sasha safely through the gates of heaven where she—" I choked through my sobs, my ears still ringing from my scream. "...where she will be welcomed into your loving arms." I wanted to continue, but I couldn't think with the sound of a wailing girl reverberating off the walls around me. I cried for help but no one came. Half-delirious, I pulled myself away from Sasha's body, a mass now as lifeless as a sack of potatoes. I stepped into the kitchen to find myself covered in blood. Red everywhere. My vision blurred and whitened as I struggled to stay on my feet. I stumbled and caught my balance on the edge of the wine barrel. I put my weight on the barrel and rested my head on the side. Taking a deep breath, I closed my eyes.

When I opened them again, I felt my senses intensify. The

red of the wine was crisp—the smell stung my nose with an astringent aroma. I stood quickly then leaned in once again to get a closer look. Unmistakably, there were floating petals of Owl's Bloom in the wine.

Sasha knew about the flowers. She'd switched out the poisonous wine that I'd tried to serve the queen and scolded me for the attempt. She'd saved my life that day. I never told her that the queen forced me to drink it as well. However, one thing I did know was that this wine was *poisoned*. Luckily, we were instructed not to serve wine until after the ceremony, with no exceptions... except. My eyes widened. The king!

I sprinted out of the kitchen and toward the king's chamber.

"Help! Help!" I screamed. Now that I was closer to the grand hall, someone might hear me. Several servants rushed to silence me, but they stopped when they saw me—a hysterical blood-covered freak show.

"Wh-what happened, child?" another servant called as a crowd formed around me.

"Sasha's been murdered. The wine has been poisoned. The king is in danger!" I screamed.

The next hour went by in a blur—servants rushing in every which way, Sasha's body was carried out of the kitchen and the doctor was called. Everyone was asking me things, but I couldn't hear them.

Sympathetic hands removed my bloodstained clothes and washed me. Afterward, I began to hear their voices again and the truth began to reveal itself—the Viran army had arrived. Prince Young had taken Emmett's place as Charlotte's groom, and Sasha—the wine; it was all Emmett's revenge. Young was too nervous about the wedding to drink the wine, but the king and

Minseo both had. The doctor wasn't sure if either would make it through the night. I replayed the news in an endless loop until I settled on the only comforting thought I could manage—that Young was okay.

CHAPTER 30
PRINCESS CHARLOTTE

The look on the doctor's face when he entered the parlor told me everything I needed to know. His words, "The king is dead," echoed in my ears. I looked at my mother, rage filling me. "You told me to let him rest and now I'll never see him again!"

She stared at me, her eyes wet, which just added more fuel to my fire.

"I hate you," I choked. She reached out to me and I braced myself, ready to push her away. My mother wrapped her arms around me and pulled me into her chest as my limbs jellied. The wet of her tears soaked into my shoulder and I couldn't remember the last time she'd held me that way. It was the kind of hug my father gave, and in it I felt everything my mother couldn't say. *I'm hurting too. You are my only family. I love you.* But she wasn't my father. In fact, she'd stolen the last moments I could have had with him. I pushed her away and ran out of the room.

I wasn't permitted to go in the king's parlor where my father's body rested. Princesses were meant to be protected from the ugliness of the world. Instead, the doctor handed me a letter written by the king before he died. *A letter.* I held it to my chest as endless tears fell down my cheeks. It was all I had left of him, and that thought alone prevented me from opening it. All my father was—reduced to one piece of parchment.

The doctor hurried in and out of Minseo's quarters. The servants said he'd received the antidote, and while his condition was far from stable, he'd survived an hour and a half since he'd been poisoned, half an hour longer than my father. I knew Young would be there beside his brother, but I wasn't sure if it was appropriate for me to go to him. Who was I to Young anyway? I wasn't his wife yet; perhaps a friend. It didn't matter. I was all he had and I wanted to be there for him. I slipped a peek in the mirror only to find my face red and puffy from crying and then felt stupid for checking. I hastened out of my chamber.

There were two Viran guards outside Minseo's quarters, their faces stoic, their features unmistakably Viran. I lost my nerve as I approached and turned to walk away. Young stood in front of me, sending a tingling sensation that started from behind my eyes and spread to my cheeks.

He spoke, "I went to check on you."

I nodded, feeling a heaviness in my chest.

He continued. "I'm sorry about your father."

I held out the letter sealed with my father's stamp.

"He wrote you something?"

I nodded, forcing myself to break eye contact; if I hadn't, I would have begun to cry again, and once it started, it was difficult to stop. We stood in silence for a moment. I imagined he was waiting for me to say something, but I was afraid of what I'd say.

"Must be overwhelming getting that letter. Give yourself some time, Charlotte."

I sniffed. "This is all that's left of him."

"No," he said. "Every moment you've ever spent with him is what's left of him. That's just a letter."

I stared down at the crinkled paper in my hands and let my mind dance through my memories of my father. After several seconds, Young grabbed my hand.

"I have to go check on Minseo."

He lifted my hand to his lips and kissed it before sliding past the Viran guards into Minseo's chamber, closing the door behind him.

It was a kind and simple gesture of comfort, and somehow it helped a little. Had I really come here to comfort Young? Or did I come here because I knew he'd comfort me? I hadn't asked him how he was feeling, or even about his brother. More importantly, he didn't bring those things up. He wasn't thinking of himself, nor his brother. Just me.

I returned to my chamber, my mind drifting from my father to Minseo. Every time someone knocked on my chamber door, my stomach tightened. I worried for Minseo and I worried for Young. Several servants came knocking on my door to check on me, not Milly though. I'd been told that Sasha had also been killed. Milly had found her and discovered the poison in the wine. I wanted to run to her, to throw my arms around her, but everything was broken. The pieces of our friendship were too sharp to mend.

I was certain that finding Sasha the way she did had pushed her beyond what she could take. To think she had the piece of mind to report the wine afterward. I knew she needed me, but I couldn't help her—not now. Not while the news of my father's death still stung my heart with each beat.

Worse was knowing that Emmett was to blame.

Another knock sounded at my door as panic surged. *Minseo.* This time my mother strode in, a somber energy slumping her posture like I'd never seen before.

She lay beside me. "I've decided to proceed with the wedding tonight."

I sat up. "W-What? But Father—"

"I know," she said as she looked deeply into my eyes. For the first time, I noticed the age lines setting in around them. She was getting older, and she looked like she'd been crying as much as I had. She sighed. "That's why. Your father wanted this union. He trusted Prince Young."

An ache washed through me. I wasn't sure when, but things with Young had changed. I remembered what he'd said, in my chamber earlier that night about how he still wanted to marry me. I relived the flood of emotions those words unlocked. He was my ally, and like my father, I trusted him. I just wish my father could have seen it.

CHAPTER 31

PRINCE YOUNG

I put a damp cloth on Minseo's head. "Hang in there," I
whispered. What happened to him wasn't my fault—yet,
somehow, I blamed myself. He'd wanted to leave this
kingdom more than anything and now he couldn't. He must've
run into the Viran army on the way out and decided to lead
them here. Once again, he'd saved me. I knew it was Emmett
who'd poisoned the wine. I made a silent promise on my brother's life that next time I faced off with Emmett I wouldn't lose.
I'd make him pay for this.

"Sir," a voice said from behind me, "Captain Leon is here to
see you."

I nodded and the guard opened the door, allowing Leon to
pass. Leon stepped forward. "I'm sorry about your brother," he
said, anxiously shifting his weight from one foot to the other.

"Thanks," I said. "He'll be fine." I didn't believe it, but I
wanted it to be true.

"I was sent to inform you that the queen wishes to proceed with the wedding."

I stood. "But Minseo—and Charlotte's father."

He shrugged. "I think that's why. This kingdom needs stability. She didn't want to delay it anymore."

"What does Charlotte think about this?"

Leon scratched at his eyebrow. "I... have no idea."

My face reddened. Of course she was upset about her father. I guess I was just worried that this would make it worse.

Leon asked, "Uh, do you want me to go ask?"

"No," I said. "But what was her mood like when the queen told you?"

Leon bit back a smile.

I shook my head, hoping it might hide my embarrassment. "I have to look after Minseo."

"He needs to rest. You go on, I'll look after him while you're away."

I turned back to Minseo. He was breathing weakly and his skin was deathly pale. It was difficult seeing him like this. I needed him beside me to talk me through everything. I needed him to make witty comments about my marriage or my new kingdom. I needed him to antagonize me about the consummation ceremony. "Don't die," I said. "I need you, brother."

"They're waiting for you out there. Better get going," Leon said.

Two hours later, I stood in front of an altar—an ornately decorated platform dripping with golden cups, flickering candles, and velvet cushions. There were endless rows of pews with white ribbons and roses draped across them. The announcer called the names of the nobles and council members in attendance as they came in, but I'd been standing up front for over an hour, and my mind had blocked out the announcer half an hour in. The council members stood out to me as they were all wearing similar red robes. I'd heard plenty of things about them, their judgments, and their law enforcement tactics, but this was the first time I'd been able to put a face to them.

Despite the hundreds of Besmian guests that were arriving, I felt alone. On the other side of the castle, my brother was fighting for his life. My parents and my eldest brother had never planned on making the trip for the wedding. Most of my soldiers were stationed outside the castle, or, in some cases, getting settled into their new quarters. Despite the wedding, I felt defeated. I couldn't beat Emmett, I couldn't keep my brother safe, and I'd been met with trial after trial since I'd arrived. In a room full of strangers, I longed for some piece of home, or even just someone who *knew* me.

The music changed to a pleasant and flowing organ tune that I'd never heard before. The double doors swung open and Charlotte stepped through. Without her father to walk her, Charlotte walked the hundred-yard chapel on her own.

I'd loathed every moment I stood at the front of the chapel alone, but Charlotte's long walk to the altar must've been worse. Every soul in the church watched her, and why wouldn't they? Her tearful eyes glistened, her cheeks pink from crying, her curls straying free from her pins. Yet she was stunning.

She stepped up onto the altar, gifting me a small smile. The pain in her eyes was so vivid that it hurt to look at her. I wanted to tell her it would be okay. I wanted her to know I understood. I willed her to hear these messages with my gaze but had no way of knowing if she'd received them.

The ceremony was in Calvanian, a language I didn't understand. The guests stood and sat many times at the request of

Besmium's religious leader. Charlotte and I each lit a candle and fed each other bread and white wine. It all happened in a blur—slipping by like a falcon passing the mountain's peak. I tried to focus, to be in the moment, but before I could grab ahold of it, it was over.

"You may kiss the bride."

What? Oh. Looking down at Charlotte only made me more nervous. I felt the burn from the attention of three hundred people on my face, but the more I hesitated, the weirder it became. I leaned in, barely brushing her bottom lip with mine.

"I now pronounce you husband and wife," the director said.

I was flooded with relief. This time, Charlotte and I would make this walk together. I felt a surge of adrenaline as she gripped tightly onto my arm. After everything, we'd made it. I didn't know exactly what lay ahead, but I felt like it couldn't be worse than what we'd already faced. We were headed to the grand hall for a feast, although I didn't feel much like celebrating and I couldn't imagine Charlotte wanted that either. I felt drained and wanted nothing more than to lay down to rest.

Suddenly, I remembered. A nervous energy seethed through my body with alarming force. How could I possibly rest? The council members would all be there at my bedside tonight. Charlotte would be in it.

The consummation ceremony was hours away—and I could barely even kiss her.

CHAPTER 32
PRINCESS CHARLOTTE

I was allowed to change my dress before the banquet. With the ceremony over and the majority of the grand hall ready for the feast, there was plenty of help this time. As an amber-haired lady's maid unlaced my corset, I remembered how Young had struggled to unlace it earlier—and how Minseo hadn't. I stepped out of my dress and felt the drafty castle air brush my legs. I rubbed my line-printed waist with my fingers, the marks from the corset a semi-permanent design on my body, then begrudgingly slipped into my reception dress. This one was much more free-flowing, with a large ribbon that went around my waist synching in the dress and tying in a bow at the back.

My mother entered my chamber. "Daughter," she said. "Tonight you will become a full woman." *Oh God.* I turned away hoping that she'd stop, but she didn't. "The consummation ceremony is essential. It's the last step in binding the marriage—and as a woman, you have certain obligations."

"Mom, please. Stop."

"You're a wife now. You will also soon be queen."

"Mom, stop. Now."

"It's your duty to produce an heir and reestablish Besmium as—"

I couldn't take another word. "Seriously. I was going to go through with it, but now I'm reconsidering it."

She tutted at me, grabbing me by the chin and kissing my cheek. "I'm so proud of you," she said. Then she left my chamber, a grimace of pity on her face before she stepped out. I wasn't sure, though, if it was because of my father or the wedding.

I tried to push the consummation ceremony out of my head, to focus on what was ahead—the feast—but I simply couldn't.

Young sat beside me at the reception and I couldn't help but sneak glances every chance I got. Why didn't he seem nervous? Why was he eating so much? Should I eat more? What if my stomach bulged out? He was calm and at ease, his posture confident and his demeanor pleasant. It unsettled me. I considered drinking wine to relax, but it didn't feel like a safe option. Even after we had been assured that the white wine had been tested for poison and no traces were found, most people seemed to be avoiding it. Not to mention the last time I drank too much wine I'd made a fool out of myself in front of Young. It seemed unnatural that these celebrations continued as if my father were in attendance. Life just cruelly kept moving without even pausing to mourn a fallen king.

"Without further ado," the announcer called, "the Prince and Princess of Besmium will share their first dance."

Young helped me to my feet. My cheeks flushed with color as the entire room put down their cutlery and watched us take our positions at the center of the grand hall. Young pressed his body against mine, palming my right hand in his. His grip was tighter than I was used to, but once we started moving, I was grateful that I didn't have to guess where he was leading me. He swept me across the dance floor as the band filled the room with a symphony of flutes and violins. Young's steps were precise and graceful. He spun me, turning my body outward and pressing his chest against my back before continuing the dance from this position. The nobles applauded as Young strung my body around the room with long, sweeping strides. He spun me back to face him as a hint of a smile appeared at the corner of his mouth, and I felt something warm stir inside. *This isn't so bad*, I thought. Perhaps tonight wouldn't be so bad either.

When the music ended, I knew it was time for the final ceremony. The dance had quelled many of my fears, but they rushed back as I entered the royal bedchamber and had my maid slip my dress off to leave me in only an undergarment. It was a thin, loose-fitting cloth that could be easily removed. It was not like a corset, required no practice or experience, and was virtually see-through from close proximity—it was my last layer of armor, and as I stood by the bed, waiting for Young to arrive, I could feel the presence of the rest of the council chattering quietly on the outskirts of the room. The bed was already turned down and a thin white curtain, made from a material that was not unlike my undergarments was drawn, separating the bed from the rest of the room. The candles were burning low, and in this amount of light I was certain I'd only be a blurred shape to the onlookers— but Young would see everything. He'd *feel* everything. I gulped a mouthful of stale saliva.

Young entered the room, sending my pulse skyrocketing. I took a deep breath and felt tears prick my eyes. I wasn't *ready* but it was too late to back out. He entered the bed area, taking special care to fully close the sheer curtain surrounding the bed. He pulled off his shirt. A fierce wave of fear and excitement tore through my stomach as the yellow candlelight illuminated his bare chest. His muscles were defined peaks and valleys, which surprised me, but I wasn't sure what I thought a man would look like shirtless before now.

I held my breath as he grabbed my waist and pulled me close. Tears spilled from my eyes as one emotion eclipsed all the others —fear.

He pulled my body to him and I felt my chest brush against his. He put his lips to my ear and whispered softly, "It'll be okay. I promise."

I nodded but fought my instinct to flee. I wanted to lock myself in my room and never come out. I needed more time. My mother was wrong; two more years might have made a big differ-ence after all. Young took my hand and I sat down on the bed. My heart beat in pace with my thoughts. With his palm, he eased me back onto the bed. He wrapped his arm around me and moved me onto the pillows.

I pressed my knees together with all my strength. He leaned in, his body pressing on mine. A fleeting wave of relief hit me as I realized he couldn't see my body from his position on top of me.

"Trust me," he whispered.

I clenched my eyes shut as his fingers brushed down my exposed leg to my knee. I felt my body shake as I allowed my knees to separate.

He used his knees to separate them further. *This was it*, I thought as I braced myself for pain. Young slid his hand over my mouth with one hand. *What is this?* With his other hand, he ran his fingers across my ribs. It tickled, and an involuntary laugh burst from my lips. Young tightened his grip on my mouth, muffling my laugh. *What was he doing?*

He tickled me again, each time muffling my laugh into a labored groan. He increased the intensity on my ribs. I thrashed to free myself from the tickle torture but he locked my body down and continued the cycle. I felt myself begin to sweat from his unusual game. After a few short minutes, he took his hand off my mouth, he kissed me on the forehead, and lay down beside me.

He faced me, his bare shoulders under the covers of the bed. My wrinkled brow prompted him to hold his finger up in front of his lips. I didn't dare speak, catching my breath as I waited for the answers. Sure enough, in minutes, I heard the onlooking council members' footsteps as they left the room until we were finally alone.

We lay in silence for several minutes before we broke it.

I spoke first. "You faked it," I said.

He adjusted his pillow. "Yeah."

I smiled but my wrinkled brow remained. He continued, "You've been through a lot today," he said.

"But I felt you... You were ready."

His face reddened. "Yeah, sorry about that. I've never seen... I mean, you were practically naked."

I was overcome with relief and gratitude. "Thank you," I said, burying my face in his chest. He hesitated, but ultimately wrapped his arms around me. I snuggled in close, feeling the warmth and safety I'd been longing for all day. Young's body tightened.

"Woah!" I said, louder than expected. "You're still... ready."

He let go, giggling to himself. "You're still naked."

CHAPTER 33
PRINCE YOUNG

I awoke beneath a tangle of curls. I pulled a few strands out of my mouth and sat up to free myself from the rest. Charlotte lay asleep beside me with her mouth open as a steady stream of drool stretched between her cheek and her pillow. *My wife.* I felt a warm sensation in my chest. This was how I'd start every day for the rest of my life. I knew I should move, I had things to do, but instead I lay there soaking up the softness of the moment.

Last night, I'd been anxious to hear a knock at my door—afraid to hear bad news about Minseo—but with the exhaustion of the day and Charlotte's even breathing beside me, I'd drifted off to sleep.

The castle had rooms designated specifically for married couples, so I slipped out and headed to my old chambers, where my things were still kept. I'd change for the day and then head straight for Minseo's room. I swung open my wardrobe and slid out of my nightwear before reaching for my royal blue coat.

"You're meant to wear black," a voice said from behind me.

I turned to see Milly and quickly covered myself with the blue coat. "What are you doing here?" I asked.

A hint of blush pricked her cheeks. "I am to tell you to wear your black coat."

My stomach dropped. "Minseo—"

"Oh no. I'm sorry. Minseo is okay. Well, not good, but he's alive. There is a funeral for our fallen king this afternoon."

I sighed with relief but instantly regretted it. "I'm sorry, I just—"

"I understand." She tucked her golden hair behind her ear. "You were worried about your brother."

I nodded. "Exactly," I said. Today was meant to be my funeral. If my brother hadn't always shown up to save me, it very well might have. With the funeral happening later, I knew this would be a difficult day for Charlotte. I wasn't used to consoling her—or anyone. I guess I didn't know how. With my brother in his current condition, I wasn't sure if I was in a place to help anyone.

An uncomfortable silence set in. My hands grew stiff from holding the jacket over my exposed body. "Uh..." I began. "I'll wear the black one then. Is there anything else?"

Milly smiled. "Here, I'll help you," she said, hurrying toward me.

"That's not necessary," I said, but she ignored me. She pulled out my black coat and held it out for me to exchange it with the blue one. I gulped, suddenly aware of what she was trying to do. I reached for the black coat and yanked it toward me before handing her the blue one. She'd resisted handing it over but wasn't prepared for me to use so much strength and was forced to let it go without getting a look at me. She stood there, stunned.

"Charlotte is my wife," I said flatly.

"Of course," she said, bowing deeply. "If you need anything..." she took a deep breath, causing her chest to rise, drawing my attention to it, "just let me know." She smirked and left.

I shook my head. What was that? Afraid she'd return, I quickly dressed. I needed to see Minseo.

Several Viran guards stood around the room where my brother rested. They were younger than most of the other soldiers, no doubt friends of my brother, but I didn't know them well. They stood at attention as I entered, but there was a somber softness in their eyes that worried me.

Minseo hadn't so much as moved since the antidote was administered. I sat at his bedside, feeling more hopeless than last night, as I examined his pale skin and nearly lifeless body.

I looked down at my hands. The cuts from my battle with Emmett were already healing. I wondered if my brother's internal wounds were healing as well.

"Dressed in black, I see," Minseo whispered. "I'm not dead yet."

My throat tightened. Minseo's eyes were slightly open and a hint of a smirk rested on his left cheek. The guards rushed over, all laughing and greeting Minseo all at once.

"Water," he choked.

The doctor, who was waiting nearby, rushed over, a bowl of water balanced in his hands. I moved aside. The doctor lifted Minseo's shoulders and poured the water carefully into his mouth. The doctor turned to me. "He's not out of danger yet. He needs to rest."

I nodded, but my body wouldn't let me walk out of the room. I couldn't leave my brother there.

The doctor cleared his throat and the guards hurried out of the chamber. Still, I wanted to stay at my brother's side.

"It's okay, brother," he whispered. "Go." His voice was so weak his words only made it harder to go, but my brother had given me an order and, for once, I obeyed.

CHAPTER 34
PRINCESS CHARLOTTE

The morning after my wedding, we buried my father. The details about Emmett—what he'd done—were pieced together and another war seemed imminent.

I couldn't help but wonder if it had all been my fault. Maybe I'd pushed Emmett too far. I pretended. I *lied*. I made him believe I'd marry him, and all the while I was moments away from plunging a dragon-hilted sword into his chest. I was a monster, and in all my scheming, I'd forgotten something important—Emmett was a monster too.

As I slipped into the black gown laid out for me, my mind raced. I really *had* planned on marrying Emmett, hadn't I? After I knew Young was safe. I had no way of knowing that Vires received my letter, or that they'd arrive before the wedding.

My eyes felt heavy with sadness. Sasha had been killed by Emmett too. My heart ached for Milly. Sasha was family to Milly and many others, but she would not receive a grand funeral like my father. I knew she deserved one, but today I had no energy to fight for justice. My grief manifested like exhaustion and I could hardly bring myself to say my final goodbyes.

No amount of reasoning made me feel better. The church was filled with genuine sadness and the soft hum of whispered memories between the nobles who'd spent time with my father. I walked down the aisle that I'd walked the night before, this time in black—looking for a familiar face, looking for *Young*. My mother stood at the front of the church, her face covered by a black veil that ended below her shoulders.

My body numbed as I approached the casket. My limbs grew heavy with grief. My vision blurred. I needed to sit, or I might—I felt the gentle grip of a hand on my forearm.

I turned to see Young, his gaze fixed on me. "Are you okay?" he whispered.

I shook my head so he grabbed me by the waist and supported most of my weight as he gently led me to our seats near the front. As soon as I sat down, I felt better. Just a few deep breaths and the dizziness wore off.

I sighed with relief. "Thanks," I said, squeezing Young's hand. We'd been married for no more than twelve hours and he'd already saved me twice. I owed him more gratitude than just "thanks", but it was all I could muster under the circumstances.

I scanned the rows of people dressed in black. Did any of them really *know* my father? Was this just some kind of political event for them, or just an excuse to wear their fine black garments? Anger filled me. Had anyone here ever heard the sound of my father's laugh? Did they know he loved to look at constellations?

I hated the formalities of the life I was born into. It all seemed rehearsed. Fake. After the service, several nobles were selected to speak about my father. I readied myself for the politics, for the kind words meant only to gain my mother's good favor.

The first, a raven-haired woman with a sharply pointed nose, told a story about how my father had personally assisted in rebuilding a bridge in her province after a particularly bad storm destroyed it. She went on to say that my father was the kind of king who cared enough to help his subjects, even if it meant rolling up his sleeves.

I was moved to hear a new story about my father. I felt the glow of pride at the heroic deeds my father did for so many. The next speaker told a different anecdote. Again, it was a story I'd never heard, but it spoke of the many incredible traits my father possessed.

Five more speakers told their stories, each lovelier than the last. An unsettling thought weighed heavily on my mind. Maybe *I* was the one who didn't know my father. My mind tore through my memories searching for something, something he'd told me about himself. My heart tightened as the realization settled in. We'd only ever talked about *me*. Tears burst from my eyes and my body shook as panic settled in. I didn't know my father. There were a million things I wanted to ask him. I needed his advice. I wanted to hear his opinions, and now that chance would never come. I spent the precious moments of my father's life telling him about my day and complaining about my problems.

I buried my face in my hands to muffle the crying. I thought I had more time. I thought he'd always be here. Regret clouded my thoughts like a thick mist on a foggy shore just before dawn. I'd left the letter he wrote me locked away in my chamber and it took everything in me to keep from leaping up, running out of the church, and reading my father's final thoughts.

I had one more chance to know my father. It was as if I'd asked my father one question about him after all, perhaps the most important question given the circumstances. *Father, if you knew you were dying, what would you want me to know?*

CHAPTER 35
PRINCE YOUNG

Charlotte worried me. She was suffering—barely able to stand or keep from crying. The hardest part was I couldn't fix it. I could only watch her endure it, and that was dizzyingly frustrating. The funeral was arduous—an endless amount of emotional daggers continuously being hurled at Charlotte. I knew it wasn't intended to be that, but from where I sat, I worried it would be too much for her. I felt her pulse quicken with each new story. I figured Charlotte wouldn't want to fight the crowd to get to the exit, so I planned on waiting for the chapel to clear out a bit, but before I could tell her, she vanished into the crowd. I wasn't sure if I should give her space or make sure she was all right.

When I didn't see her at the banquet, I knew she'd gone back to our new chambers. I slipped out of the banquet room and followed her. As I turned down the corridor, I could hear the sniffle of a woman weeping. *Charlotte?* At the foot of Charlotte's chamber door, the queen of Besmium sat, tears and snot lining her face. I ran over, half expecting a pool of blood. Nothing but steel could take down someone so strong. As I neared, I saw no sign of pain on her face, only sadness. I knew I wasn't close enough to her to even attempt to comfort her. Physical pain was so much easier.

"Your Majesty," I said.

She waved dismissively. I turned to leave, but her voice stopped me. "It's my fault he's dead," she said, her words slurring together.

I crouched down to her eye level, the sudden aroma of stale wine hitting my nose. "I think—"

"I was the one who told Emmett to come here. If I hadn't, my husband might be alive."

"We can't know the future. We can only do our best in this moment." It was not an empathetic speech. It wouldn't mend her wounds, but those were the facts and I hoped they could at least eliminate some of her guilt.

The queen sat in silence and I eyed the door behind her, wishing I was on the other side. Finally, she got to her feet and patted me on the back. She turned away from the chamber door and headed down the hallway.

"Don't you want to talk to Charlotte?" I called.

She continued walking and called over her shoulder, "You go ahead."

"I don't know what to say," I admitted, but she was already gone.

I pushed open the chamber doors, feeling the same adrenaline as on the battlefield. Charlotte sat at the foot of our bed. *My wife.* The moment I saw her, the peaceful feeling I'd relished this morning returned. She stared down at the king's final letter, but her gaze wasn't moving. I sat down beside her and she handed it to me.

Dear Charlotte,

My time in this world is coming to an end. I feel I've lived a full life with many adventures, and you, my dear daughter, were my most precious. Since my return, your mother has filled me in on your actions since my capture, and I must say I am proud of you. It doesn't matter who you marry, I am certain you will make an incredible queen of Besmium, and with this knowledge, I can rest well.
You are my greatest accomplishment.

With love,

Your father

Charlotte leaned her head on my shoulder and cried. I put my arm around her and gently rubbed her back. She buried her face in my chest. I was grateful that I didn't have to say anything. Without thinking, I kissed the top of her head, drinking in the sweet aroma of her curls.

She leaned back, her gaze meeting mine. It startled me, but before I could say anything, she leaned in and kissed me. Her lips pressed against mine, a sharp jolt tingling violently in my chest and spreading throughout my body. I wrapped my arms around her, dizziness fogging my thoughts. Her soft lips pressed warmly into mine. Her curls tickled my cheeks, then she pulled away.

"Thank you," she said, stepping back.

I stood. "No, thank you for that. That was... I mean—"

She giggled and a rush of heat hit my face. "I mean," she said, "thank you for being there for me today. I don't know what I would have done without you."

I stopped, unable to respond.

She smiled, but it faded quickly. "I'm going to go find my mom and then get to the banquet. Meet me there, please?"

I nodded. She took the letter from my rigid fingers and then she was gone. Overwhelmed, I slumped back onto the bed. Grief was a formidable dragon to slay.

CHAPTER 36
PRINCE MINSEO

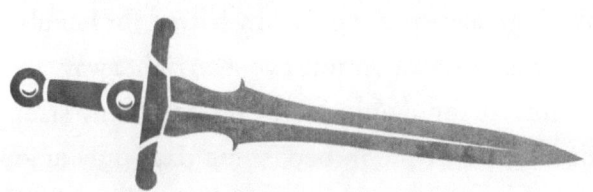

The evening after King Morgan's funeral, I was drifting in and out of consciousness when I realized Charlotte stood beside my bed. Alarmed, I sat up and glared at her. What further chaos was this woman going to bring down on me?

"Prince Minseo," she whispered.

It was strange to hear my name said with such a foreign accent—each syllable drawn out a bit more than when spoken by a Viran.

She stepped closer. "I'm sorry this happened to you."

I opened my mouth to speak but the burn of the antidote still lingered in my throat and churned my stomach. *Evil witch.*

"Don't speak," she said. "You should rest. I'm sure you're angry with me. You're stuck in Besmium because of me and you're only sick because I made things personal with Emmett. I just want you to know I'll make amends." Her eyes glistened.

"I've given this a lot of thought. I'll visit you every day until you're well again. Anything you need, I'll make sure you have it."

Don't bother. But she'd already sat down beside me and began to read a chapter of some adventure story, and before I knew it I'd drifted back into a deep sleep.

Princess of destruction, I seethed the next day, hoping she wouldn't return, but just like she'd promised, she came, with a bright smile and a book. With each passing day my hatred for her abated, and I began to see what my brother must've seen right away.

It took almost three months for me to get my strength back. I spent most of that time in bed, some days only able to get up and walk around for a short time. I'd missed my brother's first few months of marriage. Young would come by and chat with me sometimes, filling me in on things I'd missed, but Charlotte never missed a day.

It only took a week for me to realize that I looked forward to her visits and a week more to realize I needed them. She arrived each day with such a sunny disposition that I often forgot she was grieving. She must've had days where she had to find the will to get out of bed, but it never stopped her. I'd only remember in the quiet moments, when she'd chase a thought out the window and I could see the sorrow locked away in her distant gaze. Those fleeting moments were always cut short by a smile, as she forced herself to be cheerful. I didn't dare inquire, but I grew to respect her for the effort. Either I'd been wrong about her or the last few months had changed her. I suspected the latter.

Sometimes she'd read to me, sometimes she joked with me, and when I was finally able to walk, she walked with me. We had no shortage of conversation because our common ground was obvious. We both loved my brother.

Time dragged when Young spent weeks at a time away from the castle, but he had made great strides in securing Besmium in a short time. I was proud of him, happy that I'd stuck around to see him come into his own.

Charlotte glowed as she read the letter he wrote her, detailing the battle that won Hiems Castle back from Drethen and pushed back the line. He helped rebuild the northern castle and set out across the kingdom to recruit and train new troops. He seemed to be acclimating nicely to his new role and gaining the trust of the queen and the rest of the council, but it had an unexpected benefit. It gave me the opportunity to know Charlotte, the woman who had inherited my duty to protect my brother.

I had to admit she was beautiful, though, but there was a clear line between the thoughts I had about Charlotte and what I would share. My naturally flirtatious nature was on lockdown, though I suspected she'd know it was harmless if I divulged. I knew what was at stake and, therefore, always felt a little guarded. If I slipped, I'd destroy my brother.

One afternoon, Charlotte arrived waving a leatherbound book over her head.

"It's here!" she said, the brightness of her smile filling me with warmth.

I reached out to touch her face but caught myself and ran my hand through my hair instead. "Your favorite? *Dragon's Breath?*" I said, trying to match her enthusiasm.

"*The Dragon's Call*," she said, sitting beside me. "Which means that your brother could be back today or tomorrow." Her leg touched mine as she grinned, her eyes dimming as she wandered through some hidden memory. She always looked that way when she thought of my brother. I lay back on the bed. "Good. I'll finally get some peace."

"Don't act like you don't like me."

I grimaced and sighed. "Actually, I really should thank you for taking such good care of me. I know my brother appreciates it too." I stood and clumsily knelt in front of her. "I pledge, on my honor, to grant you one wish."

"Oh boy," she said, helping me back to the bed.

"Maybe I should stop reading you novels. They seem to have gone to your head."

"If you want to waste a wish, that's fine. I gave my vow, that's all I can do."

"And you won't question my wish, just blindly obey?"

I raised an eyebrow suspiciously. "Y-y—"

"You either vowed or you didn't." She grinned victoriously.

"Yes. What is it?"

She paused, her face plastered with a wicked grin. "I'm going to save it."

I sighed. "Weak." I stared up at the ceiling, my mind going blank.

Charlotte leaned over me. "Are you okay?" She put her hand to my head and a jolt of energy shot through me. Her eyes widened. "I'll fetch the doctor." She stood, but I grabbed her wrist.

"Wait! There's no need for that. I just need to rest for a moment."

She sat down again and, in a moment, the dreamy, faraway look returned to her face.

I was happy my brother was returning. In the few hours I had strength enough to move around each day, I had begun mingling with the soldiers. I'd watched a few drills and even made some suggestions. I wasn't sure if we'd resolved all of the tension that rose between us after we first arrived. I was eager to show him how differently I felt about Besmium. I liked the camaraderie of the men and the fondness in their voices as they spoke of their fallen king. I liked that they valued my input despite my age, and sought me out at meals to converse. Young had been right all along. Besmium was a kingdom worth protecting. My three-month recovery was not the prison sentence my brother worried it would be. I wanted him to know that.

I sat up and put my hand flat on top of the book. "How about we forget the book today. I think some fresh air will do me some good. Why don't we go outside and I'll show you how to use that dagger you love so much?"

"Really?" She beamed. It may have been the spell she cast on me, but I enjoyed the way she lit up about things, like she'd had a hard year and looked for any excuse to be happy.

The temperature in Besmium had dropped a lot in the last couple months. The air was crisp and refreshing—too cold if you weren't moving much. But this was combat training and, in the midday sun, I knew we'd be alright.

"Huah!" Charlotte swept the dagger through the air.

"Better, but your stance is still too weak," I said. I positioned myself behind her and kicked her left foot out, widening her stance. Then I pushed down on her waist, lowering her center of gravity.

"Ahh," she said, "I feel it. That's better."

My thoughts moved to the day she shot an arrow at us. *I hope I'm not teaching her how to kill my brother.* A practice swing of her dagger brought me back to reality.

"Yes, exactly," I said, recovering. "Remember, you'll typically be fighting someone taller than you, so swipe up at this angle," I said, thrusting my dagger upward.

I stepped away and stared down at the ground. I'd hoped to check on the rest of the soldiers, but my limbs were already growing heavy. I thought I'd be a little more recovered. I had no patience for that kind of thing.

"Is everything okay?" Charlotte asked, noting my mood change.

I nodded. "Yeah, just tired is all. Maybe I pushed myself too hard." I needed to get over this—but part of me worried I'd never really feel like myself again.

"Milly!" Charlotte called, interrupting my thoughts. Charlotte ran over to a pretty, yellow-haired servant girl and threw her arms around her.

"Prince Minseo!" Charlotte said, turning to me. "Come meet my friend Milly."

A *servant girl?* Back in Vires, I would have never even considered it, but I wanted so badly to be back on my feet, and this was the only idea I had. My time with Charlotte had me off my game. Did I even remember how to flirt? "Milly, is it?" I took her by the hand and kissed it.

CHAPTER 37
PRINCE YOUNG

The more time I spent in Besmium, the more I learned. There were still troops throughout the kingdom, but they were poorly organized. With Hiems Castle back in our control, I kept as many troops as we could spare patrolling it. We couldn't afford for them to break through again, but rumor had it that Drethen was undergoing a change in leadership, a surefire sign that they weren't stable enough to attack again. I put all my focus into rebuilding. Besmium's northern borders seemed too big for the number of available troops, and the contact between outposts was infrequent. The council delegated most of the travel work to my men and me while Charlotte stayed at Castle Cadere to watch over Minseo. In just three months, we'd begun to put the pieces of Besmium back together.

I missed Charlotte more than I can say, but I've always tended to duty before pleasure. Once her lands—our lands—were secure, I could relax.

Captain Leon dismounted his horse and tied it next to my camp near Hiems. "Your Highness, a letter came for you."

My stomach dropped. *Charlotte.* One thing I'd learned in this kingdom was that no news was good news. I tore open the letter, my fear spilling onto the wrinkled parchment.

Prince Young,

I hope this letter finds you well. The council and I are very pleased with your work around the kingdom, and as such, have decided to bring forward the coronation next week as planned. Your father, the King of Vires, has been made aware and set out early last week. He is expected to arrive in the next few days with your mother, the queen. Your eldest brother will not be in attendance.

Sincerely,

Her Royal Highness, the Queen of Besmium

I exhaled in relief. It was *good news.* I looked up from the letter to find Leon biting his bottom lip. I laughed. "It seems we've both been conditioned to expect bad news." I handed him the letter. "Worry not, my friend. There's to be a party."

Leon skimmed the letter then grinned. "Home at last."

It had been a no-brainer for me to select Leon as my right hand; he had proven himself a loyal warrior and gained my trust. However, it took several months to realize just how good a choice he'd been. With each visit to an outlying outpost, it became increasingly obvious that not all the soldiers felt comfortable being led by a foreign prince. Selecting Leon had sent two distinct messages to the kingdom. One, I didn't intend on favoring the Viran soldiers. And two, I had Besmium's best interest in mind. The council admired my political know-how, but I didn't feel I deserved their praise—I'd chosen based on trust, not politics.

It felt good to be returning. Home was the southern castle now. I'd always assumed we'd eventually return to the northern castle, but it was still undergoing repairs. After seeing it in my travels, I had a hard time believing that Charlotte or I would ever want to move back there. It was a mausoleum—littered with the memories of the massacre that still lingered within each cracked stone.

A few days later, my company arrived at the southern castle. Trumpets sounded as we rode up to a red-carpeted entrance framed by several lines of soldiers. Poised at attention, they formed a path to the palace like brightly-colored statues. It was a stark contrast from arriving here surrounded by Emmett's men.

I dismounted my horse and hastened in. I had to see Minseo. Charlotte had written me, explaining that he was doing well, but I had to see it with my own eyes. I sprang up the grand staircase and hurried straight for my brother's chamber. A Viran guard stood outside his door.

As I neared the chamber, I heard the muffled sound of a woman's cries. I gulped. It was a sound I'd heard outside Minseo's chamber before, back in Vires. Once I'd forced Charlotte to replicate it. In fact, it sounded exactly the same.

I backed away from the door as I tried to swallow the horrible thought before it manifested, but it was too late. My mind replayed the moment Charlotte first met Minseo, the glimmer in her eye. A sharp pang of fury tore through me, my temperature comparable to the sun's surface. I gripped at the air, stumbling mindlessly to my chamber. Tears stung my eyes as the wind departed from my lungs with no hope of returning. I pushed open the door with far too much force and slammed it shut behind me. *How could she?* I leaned back against the door and slid down to a seated position, burying my face in my hands.

"Young?" Charlotte's soft voice called from the other side of the chamber.

I exhaled in such sweet relief that the Viran persimmons would taste bitter in comparison. I sat frozen in a perfect world before allowing the guilt I'd earned to settle in.

"You're back!" Charlotte said, running toward me. She got to her knees and nuzzled her head under my arm, forcing it around her. "Are you okay?"

Overcome with relief, I pulled Charlotte onto my lap and hugged her. She froze as if she'd expected me to pull away, as I'd done many times while I was getting to know her.

However, today was different. I'd doubted her, and I'd doubted my brother. That thought alone meant I didn't deserve them, but for the moment it didn't matter. For once, everything was right in the world.

CHAPTER 38
PRINCE MINSEO

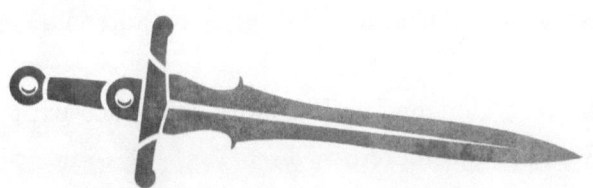

I felt disgusting. Day drinking was a terrible idea. I'd used this poor girl to cheer me up about my slow recovery—a decision I instantly regretted. Milly was so eager for my attention. I hoped she wasn't expecting it to go anywhere. She knew I wasn't free to marry her, right? It was a conversation I didn't want to have, but the way she hung on my every word and breathed truth into my every lie told me it might be impossible to avoid. I turned over, unable to look at her any longer. My body felt a little improved, but the sickness was replaced with something equally as toxic—guilt. This was not the outcome I had planned, but it hadn't been for nothing. Milly made me certain of something—I hadn't totally lost my touch with women.

I couldn't dress fast enough. Without a word, I hurried out of my chamber, leaving my mistake behind in my bed. I needed to be alone to think.

I stopped. Turned. This time headed for Charlotte's chamber. She was going to kill me when I told her what I'd done, but maybe she'd know how to handle this, without destroying Milly's feelings.

It was unlikely that she'd ever forgive me for this. I *knew* that. But I also knew that owning up to mistakes fared better than avoiding them—something Young had taught me.

My heartbeat doubled my footsteps as I pushed open the door to Charlotte's chamber. A surge of adrenaline exploded through me.

My stomach clenched as I stood face to face with a part of the plan I hadn't considered.

"Brother," Young shouted, his eyes beaming with excitement. He laughed, throwing his arms around me. "It's good to see you up on your feet again. Though I could have done without hearing... all the rest." He nudged me with his elbow, waking me from my trance-like state.

I faked a laugh, noting his mischievous smile. Ah, *Milly.* "Yes, yes. That's what the real thing sounds like." My gaze moved to Charlotte, but she'd woven her fingers between Young's, her gaze fixed on his face as if she feared he'd disappear if she looked away. The last thing I wanted to do was kill her joy or interrupt their reunion.

I'd retreat and find Charlotte another time to help me sort this out. I hoped Milly had left my chamber by now. "So, I take it you've been back for a while," I said, forcing a casual tone.

"Just a few minutes. I went to see you first, but you were busy. Glad to see you're back to your old self." I pulled nervously at my collared shirt. "Actually, brother," Young said, "you don't look that well after all." He reached out and touched my forehead with the back of his hand. "You're a bit warm. Your cheeks are flushed, and if I'm not mistaken, you're quite a bit less talk-ative than usual."

I laughed. "This is the glow of a job well done," I said with a conscious effort not to picture Milly. Charlotte's attention finally moved to me and she eyed me suspiciously. I changed the subject. "Has our father arrived yet?"

"Not yet, but any minute now."

I put my hands on my hips, hoping to relieve the heaviness that plagued my arms.

Young patted me on the back. "Well, maybe you can get some rest and not spend all night in strenuous exercise before father arrives." He turned to leave the chamber. "I'm going to bathe and rest a bit myself."

I shifted under Charlotte's unfriendly gaze. She was onto me.

I felt like a liar. But she left with Young, rather than staying to question me about what happened. Small mercies.

After they'd gone, I stood alone in my brother's chamber for a moment before springing back to life. *Parchment.* I scoured the room to find some. Now that Young had returned, it would be difficult for me to get Charlotte alone to explain myself. Young had enough to worry about, and I certainly didn't want to see him dragged into this. I'd write her a letter and slip it to her in passing. I just needed parchment. I didn't find any on the desk and started hopelessly pulling open drawers.

"Guards! Help, there's a thief in my chamber." I turned to see Charlotte standing with her hands on her hips. She smiled playfully.

My stomach dropped. This was my chance.

CHAPTER 39
PRINCESS CHARLOTTE

"Uh, hey, Princess," Minseo said, dropping something made from dark fabric into the open drawer beside him.

"Is there something I can help you find?" I asked, noting the disarray of my desk.

"Parchment," he sighed.

What was he doing here? I walked over to my cabinet and opened it, exposing four drawers inside. I peeked in the first and found nothing. I wondered what he'd say if I started going through his things. I slid open the second drawer and pulled out a blank piece of parchment. "Just one?" I called over my shoulder.

"Yes."

My heart leaped as Minseo's voice came from directly behind me. I hadn't heard him cross the room. I turned, handing him the parchment, instinctually backing up into the cabinet.

"Thank you, Princess."

I'd spent a considerable amount of time with Minseo over the last few months, enough to know something was off. I had a feeling it had something to do with Milly. I really hope he didn't do what I think he did. I closed the cabinet and slipped out from between it and Minseo.

"Is there anything else?" I asked, trying to ease the tension.

"Actually, yes," he replied while pushing his hand through his hair. "I—" He stopped. His eyes glistened like something lay hidden behind them. In a blink, it was gone. "I wondered if we were going to get the chance to finish that book. The dragon one." Maybe I misheard their conversation.

A wave of relief washed over me. "Oh, right." I wandered over to my desk and picked up the leather-bound book. "Here," I said, handing it to him.

He took the book but lingered a few seconds too long. He laughed. "I can't do this." He shook his head and traces of the Minseo I knew returned. "I'll write it then," he said. "When the words come, I'll write it." He turned and started walking toward the door.

I followed. "Minseo? Is everything—"

He closed the door between us. *Odd.*

As I straightened up the things he'd displaced, I thought about his behavior. Had he still felt ill? My heart sank. *No.* This was about Milly. I had seen him spending time with her earlier; perhaps he'd developed feelings for her. I made a mental note to gently ask Milly about it, although if it were true, I had every reason to worry. My mouth dried with anxiety. No. I knew Milly better than anyone. She'd never get involved with him.

A few hours later, I came across Milly in the hallway. "Where are you headed?" I asked, hoping to spend a little time with her.

"I..." Her hesitation worried me, but she found her words. "I have a lot of work to do."

I nodded. "I just want you to know that I'm here for you if you need to talk to someone, or if you need help with anything."

She smiled but it didn't reach her eyes. She seemed a little hollow, but my feelings might've painted her that way. Maybe part of me wanted her to want Minseo because that would make the unfairness of how things turned out a little easier to bear. Looking at her then, with her weighted gaze on me, confirmed my suspicions that three months of marriage had not altered her feelings for Young.

She turned to leave.

"Wait," I blurted. I walked over and took her hands in mine. "I'm so sorry for everything. I really did think he was the best chance Besmium had."

"So you mean you married him for the kingdom?"

"Yes."

"You don't love him."

I clenched my jaw as she slipped her hands out of mine. "I do love him, Milly. I fell in love with him, but I love you too and I'll find a way to make it right."

Her blue eyes became cloudy. "I... don't think there's anything you can do."

My heart raced as my oldest friend slipped away. "When I'm queen, I'll get a title. I'll put you out in society and you'll have your pick."

"You know my choice... And I can't change it any easier than you can. Trust me, I've *tried*."

Did she mean Minseo? "I'm sorry, Milly." I whispered, but she'd already walked out of earshot.

I had hoped she put all that behind her.

I hoped that things with us had gone back to normal—to the way they were before. On the surface, they looked normal enough, she fulfilled all her duties with a smile, but there were things we hid from each other now, topics we never discussed. I was starting to wonder if I knew her at all.

The next day, the King and Queen of Vires arrived. Young and Minseo had spent all morning and part of the afternoon with their father, and rumor had it they brought along an unexpected guest.

"She's beautiful," Glenda gushed. "A princess, all the way from Ryosun. That's even farther than Vires."

"Do you know why she's here?" I asked as Glenda laced the corset of my coronation dress. "For Minseo. The King of Vires is trying to arrange something."

My thoughts flickered to Milly.

"—the loveliest thing I've seen. Skin of porcelain and all," Glenda said as she tied the last of the ribbons.

Curiosity clawed at my belly until, at last, we were finally introduced just outside of the chapel.

I curtsied to the King of Vires. Nerves overtook me. I was used to meeting kings, but this was my father-in-law. He was a small man compared to my father. His gentle, soft-looking skin and kind eyes matched his rather pleasant demeanor. The queen remained a step behind the king, but whenever he spoke, her gaze softened. I could tell in an instant that they were more united than my parents had been. Minseo's posture was slumped with disinterest, or perhaps he hadn't slept enough. He stood several paces away from the rest of his family—and the princess.

That's when I saw her—Princess Mina of Ryosun. Creamy white skin. Black waist-length hair that shone with every tilt of her head and flowed delicately with every move. Her eyes were as dark and secret-filled as Young and Minseo's, and similar in shape.

Young leaned closer and spoke in his kingdom's language. I'd never heard him use it before, not even when conversing with Minseo. The princess smiled shyly and bowed deeply to the rest of my family.

I found it difficult to look away. She moved gently—gracefully. If she was nervous, it didn't show. Her calm disposition was that of a confident royal, and it lured in the gazes of every man who passed. Despite my best effort, I was unable to stop comparing myself to her, my opposite in nearly every feature. She made me feel like a little girl again, how I'd admired the courtiers with their pink cheeks and rose-stained lips—with one difference. The sickening ache that radiated from the bottom of my stomach to my chest every time Young spoke to her. They shared culture and language. Those were things I could never give him. I wondered if meeting the Princess of Ryosun made him regret his choice.

CHAPTER 40
PRINCE YOUNG

My family stood together outside the church, soaking in the sun, before we were forced inside by the ceremony. Everyone seemed reluctant to enter, so we remained there chatting. Charlotte and the queen had joined us, but outside of introductions, they remained quiet. I'd expected a bit of awkwardness between my parents and Charlotte's mother. But I was too excited seeing everyone together to be the bridge they needed me to be.

As I gazed into the aging faces of my parents, I realized I'd been homesick. A familiar sense of comfort consumed me, reminding me of my life in Vires. It felt nice to speak in my original language, though I didn't know I'd missed it.

My parents were *here*. I'd known they were coming and still felt surprised to see them. Was it because I thought I'd die before I saw them again? What I hadn't expected was for them to bring the Princess of Ryosun along. She was beautiful—the kind of woman Minseo and I always imagined we'd marry, but based on Minseo's lack of eye contact and cold responses, he wasn't interested.

My father must've noticed too because his posture stiffened. "At least be *polite*," he whispered to Minseo, his voice somehow dripping with daggers in his soft tone.

Minseo rolled his eyes and walked a few more steps away from the princess and the rest of us.

I pitied her. She came all this way for him to not even give her a chance. I cleared my throat. "Princess, how do you like it in Besmium?"

"It's quite beautiful," she said, her voice musical like a wind chime.

"That's wonderful. Was the journey long?"

"It was quite manageable," she said, smiling softly.

If I'd asked Charlotte a similar question, she might tell me a lengthy and dramatic tale of her misfortunes, but Princess Mina was nothing but agreeable. In minutes of small talk and replies filled with rainbows, I was bored. My gaze wandered back to Charlotte, her face riddled with befuddlement. *Had I been speaking Viran with Charlotte standing right here?*

Before I could translate, the queen of Besmium spoke. "Your Majesty," she said, gesturing to my mom, "there are some members of my council who are eager to meet you." She turned to Princess Mina. "We've also never hosted a royal from Ryosun. We would be delighted if you could squeeze a little politics in before the coronation." My mother, Mina, and Charlotte disappeared into the church—leaving us to enjoy a couple more minutes of sunlight.

I turned to my father and froze. His cold stare sent an instant chill down my spine, and for this rare moment, he looked like a king. I traced his frosted gaze to Minseo.

"Minseo. Get over here," he demanded in a tone that set my teeth on edge.

Minseo's posture straightened and I knew my father's transformation affected Minseo too. He walked over like a man condemned.

"Princess Mina of Ryosun has agreed to become your intended."

Minseo nodded. "Yes, sir."

A vein popped out of my father's temple. "Then why do you mistreat her?"

"I do not love her."

My stomach tightened. I admired my brother's courage for such an answer, but I feared for him.

My father thrust his arms into the air, causing Minseo to flinch. "How could you learn to love her if you do not give her a chance?"

"I don't want her," he admitted.

I sucked in the silence through my nose but was too afraid to exhale. My father finally shattered it. "Immediately following your brother's coronation, you will return to Vires, where I might beat some sense into your corrupted mind."

With a huff, the king turned and hurried into the church.

I turned to Minseo, feeling the heat of his pain from where I stood. Was he in love with someone? Maybe he wasn't ready to return to Vires; his feelings bound him to Besmium as mine did. He had no choice but to obey. My father was a king—in a minute's time, however, I'd be a king too.

I put my hand on Minseo's shoulder. "I'll talk to him."

He looked at me and I could swear I saw pity beaming from his sorrowful gaze. Maybe it was just sadness. One way or another, I'd find a way to help him.

As the coronation began, I contemplated all it meant to be a king. I pledged myself to Besmium, and that meant I could no longer consider Vires my home. I took Charlotte's hand as we knelt at the altar. We'd gotten into this together, and I knew we'd remain that way. She was the loveliest queen I'd ever seen. Too young, perhaps—we both were—but it was our actions that allowed Besmium to heal these last three months, and everyone, the council included, wanted to move forward.

The priest said a prayer and placed a golden crown on my head, its weight a reminder of the burden I would carry until my death. The Queen Regent of Besmium placed a crown on Charlotte.

A swell of pride filled me. I'd done it. I was finally the King of Bes—

The church door swung open and an audible gasp from the crowded pews reverberated around the vaulted ceilings as a bloody figure stumbled in.

CHAPTER 41
PRINCE MINSEO

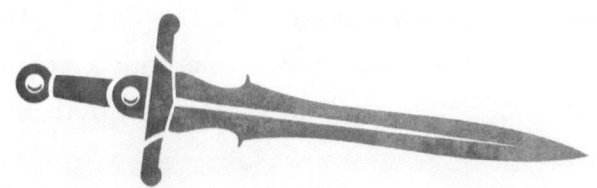

My heart ricocheted off my ribcage as I sprinted across the church to the blood-concealed figure. Each step brought me closer, his shape becoming more familiar. Pushing past the nobles all straining to get a better look, I collapsed onto my knees and cradled the fallen soldier in my arms. "Leon!"

I scanned for his injury but there was too much blood, most of it coming from his left side beneath his ribs. His pulse weakened. "What happened?" I gasped. "Wh-Who did this to you?" He opened his mouth but no words came through. Nobles crowded around as his body shook. "Who did this, Leon?" I whispered as his breathing grew more labored.

"K—" He huffed.

Tears blurred my vision, sprinkling his cheeks as I watched helplessly. Fear radiated from his body. I couldn't make myself ask again.

"It's okay, Leon. Just rest."

He turned his gaze to me, the light in his eyes fading. "K-King Emmett of Drethen," he said.

The salt of my tears lingered on my lips as I forced myself to take a deep breath. All at once, he was gone. I froze, holding the empty shell of my friend.

Whispered conversations scattered about the church. The council, adorned in their red robes, pushed their way through the assembly and stood beside me.

One of the councilmen, a thin man with a pointed nose, stepped forward. "Did he say King Emmett of Drethen?"

I nodded.

"Perhaps he meant to say Algony."

A portly noblewoman chimed in. "No, sir. Emmett's a fair few siblings away from being King of Algony."

The thin man replied, "We can't trust the accuracy of a dying man's ramblings."

"But the rumors!" someone shouted.

"His name was Leon," I said too loudly. "He used the last of his strength to deliver that message."

"Pardon me, Your Highness, I meant no disrespect," he said, shifting his weight nervously to his other foot. "Is it possible that Emmett married Princess Margaret of Drethen?"

The council went quiet. An inaudible panic filled the room.

Charlotte spoke, "They're coming for us." Before then, I hadn't noticed Charlotte and Young standing beside me. She continued, "Young, take your brother and a unit of soldiers and go find out where Leon was scouting last. If Emmett is leading his attack from Algony in the south, they could be here already. Same with Drethen in the north." Then she turned to the council. "You, write letters informing all the posts to allocate their men to either the northern or southern borders. We'll treat this as two separate wars. " She pointed at the portly councilwoman. "You evacuate the King and Queen of Vires, as well as Princess Mina."

There was so much to do, but I couldn't move. I didn't want to leave Leon. My father pulled me away, leaving Leon lifeless on the church floor and me covered in his blood.

My father turned to me. "You can still return to Vires. This is not your war."

"I'm staying," I said, unable to offer more of an explanation.

A musical voice piped up, "Then I'd like to stay as well." I turned to see Mina bow deeply to my father.

"I cannot allow that," he said, his voice stern and kingly once again.

"With all due respect, Your Majesty," she said, "my place is here beside your son."

My father's gaze stung me with a warning before a robed council member whisked him away from the crowd. Charlotte called after them, "Head northeast and you should avoid all conflicts—" Her voice broke. Her body swayed. Charlotte toppled forward, vomit erupting from her in two strong heaves. Instinctively, I reached out to her but stopped as my brother's arms were already around her.

"Call the doctor!" he shouted. A surge of fear washed over me as Charlotte's face paled. Young rubbed Charlotte's back and whispered in her ear until the doctor finally pushed his way through the crowd. The doctor put a withered hand on Charlotte's forehead then waved over his apprentices to help him move her to her chamber. I studied the doctor's face for clues of what might be wrong, but if he knew, he gave nothing away.

Young remained by Charlotte's side as she was carried back into the castle, his fingers entwined with hers.

A gentle hand rested on my shoulder and I turned to see Mina standing above me. I didn't know what to do about her. It was too late to send her off with my father, and I didn't want her to get caught in any crossfire. I stood. "Stay with Charlotte's mother."

"But I must stay beside—"

"No." I turned away. "You must do as I ask."

Without another word, she vanished into the crowd.

Young prepared for the mission ahead. Servants rushed around, prepping our horses and packing provisions, but there was still something I needed to do.

I slipped into my chamber and pulled out the parchment Charlotte had given me. I wasn't sure if any of us would survive the night. More than ever, I didn't want to die without trying to fix what I'd broken. I was in such a hurry, my thoughts came out in a jumble.

Dear Charlotte,

I wish to stay in Besmium, but I fear I've made a mistake that could impact your relationship with someone you care about. I need you. If you cannot help me reconcile these feelings, I'll return to Vires.

Minseo

It seemed vague enough that, if it fell into the wrong hands, it wouldn't hurt Milly's reputation, and surely Charlotte would know what I meant. It was all I had time for. I folded it quickly, not bothering to seal it, and headed to her chamber to check on her. I hustled through the crowded hallways. There were people rushing everywhere, but no one spoke. Fear was a thick fog that engulfed Besmium and we all disappeared into it.

I flinched as Milly stepped in front of me. I was on edge. Everyone was. "Milly, the castle could be in danger," I said, trying to pass her.

"I want you to have this," she said, holding out an embroidered handkerchief.

This was my chance to end it and I could still leave the note to see if Charlotte would be willing to smooth things over with her after. I didn't want Milly to hurt, but letting her believe this was something would hurt her more. "Milly, I don't want this."

She tucked a golden strand of hair behind her ear. "Well, what do you want?"

A guard I was familiar with from training shouted, and my attention slipped away from Milly as I answered. "It's not you. It'll never be you." Without thinking, I pushed passed her, rushing to Charlotte's chamber. I hurried in to find the doctor sitting beside her bed.

"What's wrong with her?" I asked.

He sighed. "I can't be sure just yet. She's resting. Will you stay with her while I get some more water?"

I nodded, feeling relieved to have a moment alone with her without asking. Charlotte lay sleeping with beads of sweat dotting her forehead. I brushed her cheek with the back of my hand and whispered, "I'll save your kingdom."

I slipped my letter underneath her pillow in hopes that when she woke she'd be able to clean up the mess I'd made.

CHAPTER 42

KING YOUNG

Everything fell apart at once. Leon dead, my home under attack, my parents forced to flee, and my Charlotte... that's what scared me most of all. As I stepped into the courtyard, a sharp gust of wind left the kingdom cold. Clouds masked the warm sun we basked in at the coronation.

I mounted my horse and shook with anxiety as Minseo's horse remained riderless. After several minutes, he sprinted down the stairs of the castle and mounted. We rode to the soldiers to find out which direction the attack came from. Each step felt like a betrayal to Charlotte. How could I leave her now?

I turned to one of the castle guards. "The moment you hear news of Charlotte's condition, send someone to find us straight away." Minseo paled. He must've been worried too. I secured my ruby-studded dragon blade on my belt before we set out.

After a brief interview, the courtyard soldiers agreed on the direction that Leon rode in from; we'd start there.

I clenched my jaw to suppress the fear I felt swelling inside me. Emmett was out there. It was him or me this time.

I turned to Minseo but didn't see any trace of fear in his brooding gaze. "This is a scouting mission only," I said, hoping only to comfort myself. "If we're not careful, we could easily end up like Leon. We know the enemy is close by, so we shouldn't be caught off guard." I considered taking a few more men with me, but I wanted to move quickly without being seen and needed every available man here at the castle—where Charlotte was.

Sensing my fear, Minseo smiled. "Long live the king."

I smirked, overcome with gratitude. I had my brother with me this time, and that came with a comfort I felt nowhere else.

We headed back to the forest, the mossy scent of crunchy leaves under the horses hooves filling the air. Every so often, we'd stop, hide, and listen for the sound of Emmett or his men. We rode in silence. Too much was at stake. Death hid behind every tree trunk, waiting for us to drop our guard so he could claim us.

The forest was distressingly clear. No woodcutters or animals about. No commoners out for a late afternoon stroll. It was as if the entire world had stopped to watch the battle ahead.

The *clip-clop* of horses in the distance floated around us, making my hair stand on end. We froze just to be sure it wasn't our horses we'd heard. I held my breath, hoping for silence. *Click-clop clip-shloop*. Nope. Minseo and I searched for cover but found none. Which direction was it coming from? We turned our horses around, ready to race back to the castle. The sound grew louder.

Minseo exhaled loudly. "It's one of ours," he said. Relief poured into me. Minseo ran his hand through his hair, a sure sign he was relieved too.

A Besmian soldier rode into view from the direction of Cadere. He was a guard I'd seen around, with a distinctly curved mustache that rested on his upper lip as if it could be blown away by the slightest breeze. "Sir," he said, "there's news of the queen." I dismounted my horse and Minseo followed.

My eyes widened. "What is it? How is she?" I asked. I braced myself for pain, the kind that didn't heal and had no remedy.

He shifted. "Perhaps you should read it yourself, sir." He held out the unsealed letter.

My stomach dropped. The news was too horrible for him to speak. She's *dead*. The wind pushed against me, a lump rising in the back of my throat. Unable to grab the letter, I clutched my stomach and hunched over.

Minseo snatched the letter, his gaze rapidly oscillating across the parchment. "*Impossible*," he whispered. "Th-the queen is with child." He turned to me, his eyes a cyclone of terror and confusion. He scrutinized my reaction, but I was frozen.

I inhaled a sharp gust of air, tears stinging my eyes, and laughter burst out. My cheeks stung from smiling. "She's okay," I breathed. "More than okay, she's—" I looked up at Minseo, his worried stare a monument of agony.

He spoke, "It's impossible. You said you faked the ceremony."

Tears rolled down my cheeks. "I did, but since then—I mean, I guess it's not exactly *impossible*."

Minseo swallowed a lump in his throat.

"What's wrong? Why aren't you happy?" I whispered.

He shook his head, "I... I'm sorry, brother. I'm afraid."

"Lower your voice, Emmett could hear—"

He turned away. "She's too sick to evacuate and I doubt

there's time. Which means if this Emmett situation is any worse than we think, we'll have to stay and fight."

I shot forward and reached out for his shoulder. "It was always our plan to fight."

He spun anger in his eyes. "It wasn't mine. My plan was to protect you. That's it. The baby changes things. You have more to lose—more to protect. I don't want you to die," he choked.

"I would've died to protect her before the baby if it came to it."

CHAPTER 43
QUEEN CHARLOTTE

"I'm pregnant?" I asked, rubbing my stomach in suspicion. "Yes," the doctor croaked. "Congratulations, Your Majesty."

My cheeks burned as my body filled with a flutter of nerves and excitement. My mind flashed with memories of the last few months. How I'd been so afraid of the consummation ceremony that Young faked the whole thing. How we'd grown closer each day. We rebuilt this kingdom and our lives together until one night Young returned from spending a few weeks away. I lay beside him, unable to sleep. His breath evened, so I knew he was asleep or nearly there. "Young, are you awake?" I whispered. I held my breath and waited for him to stir but he didn't. *Perfect.* There was something I wanted to say to him, but I hadn't mustered the courage when he was awake. "Young," I whispered, "lately I've been feeling like... Well, what I mean is when you're close to me like this, I feel this ache inside and I think it's because I'm in lo—" Young's palm cupped my cheek, startling me. My pulse raced as I remained frozen halfway through the word. He guided my face down to his and tasted the last two letters on my lips. It was the key that unlocked the final door between us. Without hesitation, or fear, he pulled me in for more, but the more we took, the more we craved until every unspoken word between us had been tasted or felt.

It all happened on its own.

Even the memory of it sent tingly electricity through my extremities.

I wanted to run to Young, tell him everything and see his reaction. Somehow, I thought it might help me determine what *my* reaction was.

Now felt like a terrible time for him to leave me alone. I looked down at my stomach. Only I wasn't alone—not anymore.

The doctor gave an unconvincing smile. "It's probably best if you rest a while," he said before exiting my chamber. I sat back and sighed. A *baby*.

I vaulted up. Yeah, right—*rest?* With the kingdom under attack? This was not the world I wanted to bring my—I gulped —*baby* into. Despite all the things I'd lost, I had so much to live for, so much to *fight* for. I inched up to my mirror and pinned my curls out of my face. I looked very much like the bratty teen that had protested her engagement, but in almost every way I wasn't her.

I was a queen, I was a wife, and now I was a mother. I gripped my dagger. I was battle-tested, I had killed, I had survived. The only thing that limited my abilities was my fear— and I wasn't afraid. Not of dying and certainly not of Emmett.

I headed to the courtyard fueled by a new purpose. As I neared, the commotion of a conflict hung in the air. I burst through the door to see a crowd of Besmian soldiers huddled in a circle. At the center, two men brawled, their fists colliding with each other's faces.

"Hey!" I called. The crowd turned, sending each soldier to attention. "What's going on here?" The bloody men at the center of the circle hung their heads.

An older man stepped forward. "Leon was the leader of the southern unit, but he never named a successor—or even his second in command." He scratched his thick beard. "These two men believe they should be the new leader."

I put my hands on my hips. "Listen, gentlemen," I said, projecting my voice as much as I could, though my throat was still raw from vomiting. "I can imagine why Leon didn't feel any of you were ready to lead. Here you are, fighting each other over a title, while the enemy is practically knocking down the castle door." I scanned their faces. "What good is your title when your kingdom burns to the ground? Do you want to be a hero? Then, for God's sake, act like a hero." A frost-cold wind pushed through the courtyard. "There are three outposts a reasonable distance from here with reinforcements. I need those men delivered to this castle in less than three hours. Understand? Three hours."

The old soldier finally spoke, "What happens in three hours?" The soldiers' gazes scorched my face.

My voice broke. "There might not be a castle to come back to."

He nodded, the deep lines on his face drooping. "Then I'd better let someone else take this."

"I'll do it, Your Majesty," a voice called from the crowd. A fair-haired man with a split lip stepped out of the center of the circle, blood dripping off the bottom of his chin. "I apologize for my behavior. I can make it back in time."

I eyed him warily. "Which outpost?"

"Any," he said, bowing deeply. "Let me make it up to you."

I nodded. "Make it up to your own men. It's their lives at stake if you don't make it back."

He mounted his horse. "I'm headed for Magnolia."

A tall man with several medals stepped forward, pulling another decorated soldier with him. "I'll take Begonia, and Gresham said he'd take Calla."

Instinctively, I put my hand on my stomach. "We're counting on you."

The three soldiers raced to their assigned outposts, but even if they made it back, I worried they'd miss the bulk of the battle ahead. "The rest of you, gather every soldier on the premises. We're going to back up the King and the Prince of Vires."

The old soldier pulled on his graying beard. "Excuse me, Your Majesty. Not to cause waves, but who will be leading us?"

I clutched the hilt of my dagger. "I will."

CHAPTER 44
PRINCE MINSEO

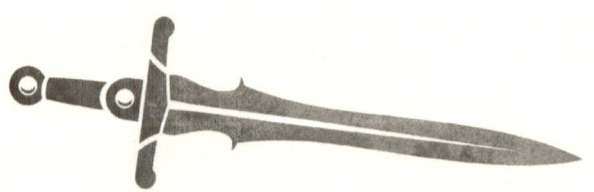

I was a mess of adrenaline and rage. My first collided with his jaw and he looked at me stunned.

"You will not die here. Do you understand. You have to survive."

Young's gaze remained transfixed on me, a glimmer of sadness in them that I'd never seen before.

The soldier who delivered the message lunged at me.

"Stay back!" Young shouted. "Don't interfere."

The guard stumbled back as if he'd been struck.

My brother's gaze returned to me.

"I'm in love with her," he swallowed. "I can't let her go."

Rage tore through me. "I'm asking you to save yourself because I can't let *you* go. Understand? You may be a king now, but you're still my baby brother."

He watched me without response.

I shook my head. Small white flakes of snow fluttered down around us.

Emmett stepped out from behind a tree. *"What a touching speech,"* he said. I clutched the hilt of my sword and my pulse raced. Of course he would show up now.

He continued, "No doubt arguing over Charlotte." Young picked up his sword and pointed it at Emmett, but he didn't seem to notice or care. Emmett sighed. "I felt something for Charlotte too, once upon a time," he said.

"Are you alone?" I called, scanning the empty woods.

He ignored me. "She has this quality about her, doesn't she? She can make you believe whatever she wants you to believe."

Young shouted, "Enough!"

Emmett continued. "She doesn't lie, exactly—she just implies things. Has she ever actually told you she loved you?"

Young clenched his jaw.

He had no idea what he was even talking about, but Young looked agitated.

Emmett huffed. "I didn't think so."

"Where's your army, Emmett?" I asked, stepping between him and Young.

He laughed. "Not three seconds ago you looked like you were about to kill him. Now you're trying to protect him? Make up your mind, Prince of Vires."

In the distance, the rhythmic clop of horses moving toward us echoed. They were *coming*. If we left now, we could make it back to the castle and our army before Emmett's men arrived— but I wasn't sure we'd get another shot at Emmett, not like this.

"Young!" I called. "Get out of here."

I clutched my blade. In my periphery, I could see Young and the castle messenger mounting their horses. Emmett smiled, amused by the prospect of battle. His confidence unnerved me. I analyzed his broad shoulders. I'd lose if this fight came down to strength alone. I needed to knock him off balance, and with Emmett's army growing closer, I had to be fast. "Young, go!" I shouted over my shoulder.

"Let him go, brother," Young ordered.

"Like he let Leon go?" My mind was already made up.

I charged toward Emmett, his army a cloud of thick dust in the forest's horizon. I tallied the number of soldiers with a glance. Forty, a hundred, perhaps more. It was about as many as we had at the southern castle. The full Algonian army must've been a bit behind. Even so, my window to defeat Emmett was closing fast.

Emmett drew his sword with a fluid motion, as if his large broadsword was an extension of his arm. It was now or never.

I lunged forward, slamming my sword down on Emmett.

He blocked, sending me stumbling back. Young rode his horse between us, holding his arm out. "Get on!" he yelled.

I spit on the ground and grabbed his hand, thrusting myself onto the back of his horse. We rode back toward the castle.

An arrow brushed my heels and landed on the frozen ground. I turned to see Emmett, another arrow already nocked on his bow—but Emmett was a swordsman through and through, and for the moment, we were out of his broadsword's range.

"You should have let me try to beat him," I told Young.

"I couldn't let you die either," he said.

"We're not going to get a better chance. With his army's support, he'll be unbeatable."

"He's already unbeatable."

"I don't see a way out of this one."

Young silently rode on. I wasn't sure if I could have defeated Emmett, but the small chance we had was gone.

Our northern army was almost equal to that of Drethen's. Emmett and one hundred of his men were here, near the southern castle. At best, we could hold them off for a good while, but when the rest of Algony's forces arrived, Besmium would fall and my brother, Charlotte, and I would fall with it.

CHAPTER 45
QUEEN CHARLOTTE

Come on, *Young*, I pleaded with the universe. Where are you? I rode my horse through the empty forest. The thud of the Besmian soldiers riding behind me soothed me. With each stride deeper into the forest and no sign of Young, I worried that Young may have met the same fate as Leon.

In the distance, a hooded figure on horseback, followed by two soldiers in green, drew nearer; their deep green uniforms an effervescent contrast to the wintery landscape. *Algonian soldiers*. I forced myself to refrain from looking back over my shoulder to my men. Though we outnumbered the three strangers thirty to one, I felt an upsurge of fear. As I approached, the hooded figure dismounted. I breathed a puff of white vapor and clutched the dagger beneath my shawl. My men drew their swords but the mysterious figures didn't draw theirs. The man threw back his hood. *Emmett*. My stomach dropped, but as I looked into the face I'd dreaded to see, I realized it wasn't Emmett's. This man was slightly taller, with similar features and a thick but light-colored beard on his wide, double-cleft chin.

"Your Highness," he said, bowing deeply. He eyed my men. "My apologies. I was not expecting to see you away from your castle." He lowered his voice. "What luck," he said, half to himself. "I am Prince Ezrah of Algony, the second son."

I eyed him warily.

"So, you're what the fuss is about?" His gaze traveled up and down, like a vulture swooping in on its prey. "I've seen prettier."

If I closed my eyes, he almost *was* Emmett.

He continued, "I've come to deliver a message from the king."

I nodded, unnerved by his likeness.

He opened a crinkled letter and read aloud. "To her royal highness, Princess Charlotte of Besmium. Algony does not support the actions of King Emmett of Drethen. Emmett is allowed to oversee a certain amount of our military forces, but when he returned to Algony to ask for military support and explained how he's been using our resources, he was refused. Some of his soldiers defected to Drethen to follow him, but this does not reflect the attitude of the Algonian council. The disgraced son of Algony is in no way associated with our king-dom. We cannot condone joining in a war and risking lives over some..." he scoffed, "romantic feud. I wish you well in your upcoming battle but cannot lend my support to either side. Sincerely, King Ethen of Algony, the first son of Jarvan."

I dismounted my horse. "How many men does he have?"

"From Algony?"

I nodded.

"A few hundred, but he claims to have a thousand coming from Drethen."

My stomach tightened. "Is that true?"

"Apologies, Your Highness, I don't know. I suggest you clear these woods before he arrives," he said, mounting his horse. "Rejoin the rest of your military. Your battle has nearly begun."

His words echoed in my head as he rode away. *The rest of my military?* It was obvious that Algony didn't know how depleted we were. If they did, they probably would have supported Emmett. The majority of Besmium's southern army was at my back, and Prince Ezrah had assumed it was a mere scouting troop. One truth was indisputable: the moment I married Young instead of Emmett, I doomed my father's kingdom.

I looked over my shoulder at my soldiers. Their somber expressions suggested the same thing: we were all going to die today.

I turned my horse around to face them. "Listen, we don't know if any of this is real. If Emmett had a thousand soldiers coming from the north, we would have been notified by now," I said. "Besides, one Besmian soldier is worth more than ten Drethen soldiers." I scanned the faces of my men and saw defeat dripping from their sunken faces.

A middle-aged soldier cleared his throat. "Maybe we haven't heard anything because everyone to the north is dead."

A weight pressed in on my chest. This was my last semblance of home and I'd die protecting it. Why wouldn't they? Was I the only one who hadn't given up? I knew we didn't have a great chance of winning, but as long as I had breath in me, I'd fight. I straightened my posture. "Emmett is near the southern castle. He's got only a few hundred men. So, we cut the head off the snake, and while the rest scrambles and dies, we hold our kingdom." I rode my horse through the soldiers, each bowing as I passed. A new surge of energy circulated the group. One drop of hope was all it took to draw the life back into Besmium's last warriors. "Let's head back to the castle," I said. "We'll have an advantage if we're ready when they come. Hopefully the king has the same idea."

CHAPTER 46

KING YOUNG

As my brother and I rode toward the castle, I felt the threat of Emmett's army behind us. They were almost here. I started to wonder if the north was really under attack again and, if so, if they were holding up against the Drethen army. Had I underestimated Drethen the way I'd underestimated Emmett? Minseo might've been right to be afraid. Every second this war seemed to slip further out of hand. If we were about to be pinched between two armies, we were already dead.

We rode through the outskirts of the castle grounds, my mind focused on making it back to Charlotte and our baby. A gust of frozen wind chilled my bones.

We'd almost made it to the castle, just in time. Emmett's men shot arrows in quick succession from the edge of the forest, falling just short. I didn't want to think about what was behind me. Charlotte was just ahead. If I could just make it to her, everything would be okay—even if these were our final hours.

Frantic energy surged through me as we made our final approach. "Archers," I breathed. "We need to get archers ready."

Before I could put together a plan for rounding up enough archers to buy us time, I saw them step forward. Row after row of bow-slung soldiers lined the top of the walls like gargoyles, ready to protect their home. *Charlotte.* Where had they all come from? How could she manage to rally so many in so little time? A glimmer of hope formed inside me. Even Minseo seemed to gain energy as we neared the walls of our salvation.

Minseo and I rode through the outer gate. The soldiers closed and fortified it behind us, thick beams crossing it at all angles. Red and yellow uniforms cut through the grayness of the sky and castle walls as Viran and Besmium soldiers joined together to defend Castle Cadere.

I dismounted and pushed through the rows of soldiers, feeling more triumphant with each one I passed, but the mood inside the castle walls didn't reflect my own. I didn't pause to observe more closely but rushed to find my wife, losing Minseo in the crowd.

I raced into the castle, ready to congratulate my queen on a job well done. I knew this new surge in troops meant Charlotte had given us a chance, and a chance was all we needed. I hurried to her chamber.

"Young," a voice called behind me.

I spun around to see Milly. "Where's Charlotte?" I asked, half out of breath. Her eyes were heavy with despair and I braced myself for an onslaught; retribution from my laxity over the past few months. We had been friends once, and now we were as disconnected as two ships passing—bound for different lands.

She held out a slip of paper and I took it. It was a vague note from Minseo to Charlotte. "I'm sorry, Your Majesty, they've been together," Milly said, twisting the message in my mind. But I had doubted Minseo and Charlotte before and I wasn't going to make that mistake again.

The danger was too great to linger.

"She's in the throne room," Milly said, sadness dripping from her lips.

"Thank you," I replied. I paused for a moment. I wanted to say more—to apologize for the way everything happened—but there was no time. Emmett's army would reach the castle in minutes, and once the fighting started, the chaos would make it difficult to find Charlotte. I headed toward the throne room, once again leaving Milly to fend for herself.

I pushed open the doors to find Charlotte sitting on the golden throne. She wore her ceremonial crown and her face was as expressionless as a stone carving. Relief poured into me. She was alive, she was carrying our child, and thanks to her fast thinking we stood a shot at winning this battle.

"You did it," I shouted as I raced toward her. "How did you manage to get so many soldiers here?" She remained frozen.

I reached her throne on the other side of the massive hall and leaned in to kiss her. Her lips brushed mine, but she didn't move. She didn't embrace me the way she'd done after each of my past missions. What spell was this?

I tried again, this time willing her back from her motionless state with my love. A single tear slipped down her cheek.

She whispered, "I'm sorry I failed you."

My stomach dropped. "Failed? No. You've done so well. Th-the soldiers—"

"They're from the north."

What did she mean? I didn't see any Drethen soldiers on my

way in. She couldn't have meant that our northern army had retreated all the way back here, could she? This was all we had left?

All at once, I understood. We'd already lost.

CHAPTER 47
QUEEN CHARLOTTE

It was the first time I'd ever sat on the throne. It was a place I'd always avoided. Maybe I'd known all along I'd fail as a leader. Now, all that was left of Besmium hid behind the castle walls, and I longed to remain here—on the throne—a little longer.

Young lifted my chin. "None of this is your fault."

I sighed. It was a beautiful lie. In the palm of his hand, I caught a glimpse of a small piece of crinkled parchment. I tightened my grip. Young reached for my hand and pulled the note from it.

"*Dear Charlotte,*" Young read, "*I wish to stay in Besmium, but I fear I've made a mistake that could impact your relationship with someone you care about.*" His voice trailed off to a whisper. "*I need you. If you cannot help me reconcile these feelings, I'll return to Vires. Minseo.*"

I sniffed. "Where did you get that?"

"Do you love him?"

The suddenness of the question threw me. It was as if we were unwittingly having two different conversations at once. I gazed into his eyes and saw fear brimming at their corners. I shook inside. *He didn't know. He didn't know how much I loved him. Young. No one else.*

My heart thudded in my chest to match the pace that my mind raced, looking for the words. How could he not know? Each breath Young took was what made my soul breathe. I collected his words. I memorized each moment we spent together so that I could relive them in his absence. Each smile was my purpose—a drop of heaven shredding every obstacle that life presented into a fine, golden dust. He didn't know. If I were to return to the moment we'd met, knowing what I stood to lose —I'd choose him again. I'd watch everyone I loved die. I'd watch my father's kingdom burn. Fueled by his motionless gaze, an electric pulse tore through me. Had I known how much I loved him before now?

This war. This life. It was not something that happened. It was my choice. No matter what lay ahead, I knew I'd choose Young every time.

I didn't have time to explain it all. I stood and leaned in. My lips brushed his, sending chills through my body. I wrapped my arms around him and slid my fingers into his hair. He stepped back in surprise, but I didn't let go. He wrapped his arms tightly around my body, pulling me off my feet. I wrapped my legs around him. He turned, walked us back to the throne, and sat, pulling me onto his lap. He deepened the kiss, separating only to kiss my neck or my jaw. I held him close, willing the ecstasy he'd given me back into his body with every delicious kiss. I needed him to know. Our child would be loved. He bit down on my shoulder, sending a gasp through my lips. My body temperature rose as Young did as he'd always done—turned the arrows and the armies outside the walls to fine, golden dust. There was no war. Only love. Just my husband, our child, and a world of glittering gold.

The doors to the throne room swung open. "Your Majesties!" a guard said, rushing into the hall. "They've penetrated the outer wall." I pulled my lips away from Young, but not my gaze. He smiled at me softly, and with that smile my life's purpose had been completed. I was ready to die. I stood, drew my dagger, and turned toward the open door. The sunlight streamed into the throne room, spilling on the floor. Young took my hand and kissed my palm. This was not goodbye. My recent losses had taught me something that I believed to my core: love was immortal.

CHAPTER 48

KING YOUNG

As I walked with Charlotte toward certain death, I'd never felt more alive or more in control of my destiny. My time was almost over, but I had two things left to accomplish before I died. One, find Minseo and say goodbye, and two, somehow sneak Charlotte out of here.

The roar of battle echoed off the walls of the corridor, along with the clang of sharpened blades against steel armor. Besmian soldiers rushed through the hallways toward the western entrance.

"They're in the castle!" a bloodied soldier cried, his eyes wide as he toppled and gasped his final breath. I drew my sword and headed in the direction he'd come from, making sure to keep Charlotte close behind me.

I heard footsteps approaching from around the corner. This was it. I raised my blade, ready to strike. A figure turned the corner, the gleam of his armor refracting light around the room.

I brought my sword down but he blocked it, leaving me vulnerable for counter strike. I braced myself.

"Brother," he gasped.

I stumbled back. "Minseo?"

He was so covered in blood that, if he hadn't spoken, I might not have known it was him. "They're in the castle," he said, out of breath. "They—" He stopped, his gaze drifting past me to Charlotte. His voice softened. "They killed Charlotte's mother. Princess Mina too."

Despite his breathlessness and the blood splattered all over him, Minseo didn't appear injured, but if the castle was as lost as he said, we had less time than I thought. There was no time for grief. My mind locked on my last remaining goal. *Charlotte.* I couldn't let her die here. I couldn't let our baby die. "Help me get her out, Minseo," I pleaded. Given what I learned the last few hours, I was certain he'd agree. I reached my hand back and felt the warmth of Charlotte's hand as she took mine.

"Where?" he asked. "The castle is overrun."

My heart ricocheted off my ribs as I ran through every possibility. Finally, the answer hit me. "The atrium."

Minseo's eyes brightened with hope and the three of us hurried through the corridors, stopping only to cut down an enemy soldier in our path. Step. Step. Step. Slice. Step. Step. Slice. As I fought in sync with my brother, I recalled how we used to imagine battles just like this. Our swords pierced a soldier's armor and the battle began to feel as make-believe as it was when Minseo and I were kids. We were untouchable. Each move created in the imaginations of innocent children practiced in adolescence and mastered at this moment.

We reached the door to the atrium, yanked on the handle, and hurled ourselves inside.

"Quick," I called to Minseo. "Help me pry loose one of the drainage bars." I leaped into the water, the current pulling at my knees. "She can swim across to the other side and escape." Minseo and I gripped the iron pole. We put our feet against the stone wall and strained to bend it. It curved slightly. "That's it," I called. "Let's go again."

As I pushed the bar, my mind turned to a memory I had from a few months ago, where I lay with Charlotte beneath the oak tree in the courtyard.

"Do you ever wish you were just normal?" Charlotte asked.

I liked the weight of her head on my arm. "What do you mean?"

"Like, not royalty. Just an ordinary person."

"I wish I was taller," I joked.

She rolled toward me, her gaze meeting mine—urging me for a real answer.

"I guess I never thought about it," I said. "It's like wishing to be a bird or a fish. You are what you are." Her gaze drifted up to the tree. I pulled her close. "I would never have met you if I wasn't born a prince."

She smiled. "If we were commoners, we could have peace. We'd only have our own lives in our hands. We could spend every day like this."

Every ounce of my life energy poured into moving that bar. *Please.* The bar gave way, bending enough for Charlotte to fit through. Relief shot through me. She was going to be alright; they both were. I turned to Charlotte but shot Minseo a quick look. He smirked and pulled himself onto the bridge, to give me a moment to say goodbye to her.

I ran my fingers through Charlotte's hair and put my forehead to hers.

Tears dripped from her chin. "If I could go back, I'd do it all again the same way," she said.

"So would I," I breathed.

She pulled away. "I-I can't leave you here."

I brushed away her tears, memorizing every detail of her face. "You have to. You need to protect our child."

She nodded, wiping her face, her dark eyelashes sprinkled with droplets. "Have you thought of a name?"

"Morgan, like your father."

She nodded. "And if it's a girl?"

I shrugged. "Morgan-a?"

She laughed and sniffled, "That's terrible."

"I kind of like it."

Minseo cleared his throat. "Young, why don't you go on ahead with her. I'll meet you later."

I smiled. "Nah, if the King of Besmium doesn't die, they'll keep looking for us. It's better if I stay."

He kicked a small stone off the bridge. "You really think they can tell us apart?" He smiled widely. "Consider it a wedding present."

The door to the atrium swung open. Out of instinct, I pushed Charlotte into the drainage tunnel, hoping to conceal her. I leaped up to the bridge beside Minseo.

Milly stood in the doorway, her icy gaze transfixed on Minseo. "Emmett," she called, "I found them."

My stomach dropped.

Minseo's eyes widened. "Wh-whose side are you on?"

She smiled. "Not yours, Minseo. It'll never be yours."

A bloody sword emerged from Milly's chest. Her face whitened. Her eyes dimmed before she even fell to the ground.

Emmett stood behind her and, with difficulty, wrenched the sword out of her fresh corpse. "Well, I hope she didn't think she was on *my* side," Emmett said with a smile.

CHAPTER 49
QUEEN CHARLOTTE

Three strides. That was how far I made it through the pipe's rushing water before I turned back. The clash of weapons echoed through the drainage pipe as I forced my way against the current back toward the atrium. *Young, stay alive*, I pleaded as if he could hear me. Baby or not, I couldn't walk away from this. I peered into the dusky atrium only to watch Minseo and Young fly back at the swing of Emmett's broadsword. They got to their feet and lunged at Emmett only to be knocked back again.

I crouched down, concealing my body in the frigid water, before venturing out of the pipe. I didn't have the courage to fully submerge; I needed to keep an eye on Emmett. The battle drew all his attention, giving me a window to reach the bridge without anyone noticing. I gripped my dagger, now wet, but I knew it would never slip from my determined grasp. Emmett was going down. He'd taken enough from me. I was going to make him pay for all of it. I waited for the fight to bring him close enough, running through the dagger training Minseo had given me.

Finally, above, I felt the heavy stomp of Emmett's boots on the bridge. *This was it.* I took a deep breath. Readied my attack. *Clang.* A cry of agony rattled my bones. It was unmistakably Young. My body shredded as if punctured by an ocean of needles. I had to get in there, now! I thrust myself onto the bridge. I rushed at Emmett, slashing at his face with my blade. He hadn't seen me but moved in time to escape the full force of the blow. He turned to me, his expression changing from surprise to amusement.

"This day just keeps getting better," he said with a smile. I wasn't in the mood to talk. I leaped forward, waiting for his blade to descend on me.

"No, Charlotte!" Young screamed.

Like clockwork, Emmett swung his blade down. Instead of jumping back to avoid it, I pushed my dagger into Emmett's chest.

In astonishment, Emmett dropped his sword and wrapped his arms gently around me. I took a slow breath, the warmth of Emmett's blood running down my frozen right arm where my dagger still remained buried in his breached chainmail. The blood dripped steadily from my elbow, but I was too afraid to let go. My gaze crept up from the bottom of Emmett's chin to his lips, and finally his pale blue eyes. He stood and held me, a warmth in his eyes as they faded. Enraged, I pulled out the dagger and plunged it into a new spot on his chest. He toppled forward, spitting blood as his weight fell on me. I snatched my dagger and jumped back, allowing Emmett's body to land with a thud. His lifeless body lay face down in front of me, but I couldn't stop. I wanted the pain he'd caused me to stop. I stabbed his corpse for my father. Again. Again. My mother. A warm hand gripped my wrist, gently pulling the dagger from my hand. I balled up my fist and punched Emmett. Again and again. Minseo kicked my dagger off the bridge and into the water then pulled me off of Emmett.

"Charlotte, it's okay," he breathed. "You saved us."

"Not yet," Young said.

I turned to see him, kneeling, both hands pressed against his leg. "Young," I called, stumbling to my feet only to fall again in front of him.

"You were so brave," he said, attempting to hide his pain. My gaze went to his leg, blood gushing through his fingers.

"Young, oh God," I cried, reaching out to help him apply pressure.

"Charlotte, listen," he said, his voice low and even, "I can't go with you."

"N-no," I sobbed. "We've done it. Emmett's gone."

"Yes, Charlotte," he said with a smile. "You made sure of that. Listen, you need to get out of here. Go through the pipe with Minseo. If I die here, they might not pursue you."

"You're crazy if you think I'm going to leave you."

Young's gaze moved to Minseo, but they didn't speak. Minseo grabbed me by the waist, pulling me toward the tunnel.

"No!" I thrashed my body around to break free, but it was no use. "Wait!" I yelled. "Wait! Young, I love you."

"I love you too," I thought I heard him say.

Minseo dragged me through the water and into the pipe. He pushed me against the wall, covering my mouth. I heard the slam of the door opening as my screams brought several soldiers to the atrium. I listened, my heart bursting from its cage, my eyes blurred with tears.

"King Emmett's dead," I heard someone say.

"Where's the Queen of Besmium?" a soldier shouted.

Minseo started pulling me down the pipe.

"Long gone," Young said.

An unfamiliar voice laughed. "She's here. Check the pipes."

Minseo pulled me faster now, trying to get us deep enough not to be seen.

A cry of pain rang through the pipes and the clash of metal echoed. "Get him!" a soldier shouted.

As Minseo pulled me farther, the sounds grew fainter.

"I said get him!"

The commotion stopped. "Good, now kill him."

"Wait, check the pipe first."

Minseo covered my mouth and stopped breathing as the soldier peered into the dark pipe.

A voice rang out so clearly through the blackness, it was as if the soldier stood beside us. "I don't see a thing, sir."

"Forget it. She probably is long gone. Why are you smiling? You're about to die."

No. I thrashed, but I couldn't get enough leverage in the water and Minseo was prepared. "Because I'm happy," Young said, his voice carrying through the pipe and to my ears like a soft whisper. With one final clang of the sword, my heart stopped. Young was gone.

Why had I survived? All the strength I'd built over my lifetime melted away. After the soldiers cleared from the atrium, Minseo carried me through the pipe to the lake where it let out.

Young was gone. Besmium had fallen. I walked beyond the walls of the castle with a title I never wanted: *widow*.

Minseo pulled me out of the tunnel and we leapt together into the lake where it let out. My body moved on instinct as we swam for our lives and, when we reached the shore, we pushed on as if our bodies could bear it. We traveled like that for days, only speaking when there was no other option. We did not look back, we couldn't. There was so much to regret, too much to process, and not a shred of comfort left in the world. The only sounds that cut deeper than my muffled cries were Minseo's. When my body began to give in, and dying seemed more enticing than pushing on, I forced myself to ask, "Where are we going?"

He could hardly look at me, but he managed to answer, "Vires."

I stopped. After everything, the prospect of stepping into another royal life saddened me, but not as much as raising my child in one. I looked around the small town as people passed by us, their gazes never lingering longer than a moment or two. Once upon a time I'd dreamed of this moment—a day then I would no longer have to be a princess, but at what cost? My family... my love? My mother was gone and I'd never gotten the chance to tell her that I'd grown to understand her. I was orphaned, for my kingdom. My family was gone, but the child growing inside me still had a chance. There was nothing I wouldn't do to keep them safe. I placed my palm on my stomach with the belief that my child's future was worth more than the pain of my past.

I didn't know what was ahead, nor how I'd make it through whatever came next, but I knew I was a survivor. I needed to believe there would be a day when I would watch Young's and my child play in the sun, free from the weight of leadership. It was the last dream I had left, and so I stopped walking.

"Do you need to rest?" Minseo asked without looking back.

I took a deep breath. "I can't go with you to Vires."

He turned slowly, his eyes vacant, his tone sharp. "You will. I can't leave you here. My brother would never forgive me."

"You're not going to understand this and we won't see eye to eye."

"I'm sorry, Charlotte. You have to come with me. I... I can't."

I straightened. "I'd like to use my wish. I wish for you to go to Vires without me."

His head drooped and, when he lifted his chin, I saw tears. "Please, don't do this."

"You made a vow."

He stared at me for so long I might've mistook him for a statue, but eventually he ran a defeated hand through his hair, shook his head, and continued on his way without another word.

My heart broke a little more with every step he took. I'd had my fair share of kingdoms and castles. My child would know a different life—a life of obscurity. Despite the odds, I would not allow myself to fail again.

My grief remained fresh and my mind became an endless cycle of the same question: *What was it all for?*

Until the day I found my answer.

CHAPTER 50
PRINCE MINSEO

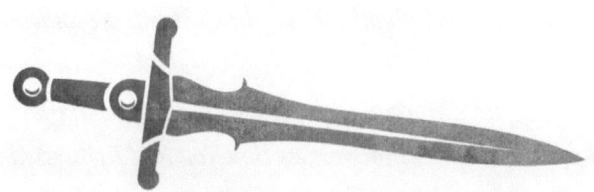

Little brother,

*It's been five years since I last saw your face and nearly the same since
I've seen your Charlotte. I know this letter is an exercise in futility, but it
helps to quell the near constant need I have to speak with you again.
I take comfort in knowing you died without regrets—a death that has
taught me much about how to appreciate life and its fleeting moments.
After I lost you, I was as broken as Charlotte and quickly realized that I
was not whole enough to console her. I offered her refuge in Vires and,
when she refused, I regrettably took my leave without regard for her
safety or the cold of the winter that followed.
When I'd finally accepted your passing, I sought her out—though I must
admit I never expected to find her. I found it difficult to gather
information about her whereabouts without revealing her former
identity. My travels brought much news. What was once the land of
Besmium had been swallowed by Drethen, only to be renamed Camelot
and ruled by a teenage tyrant named Arthur.*

After many months of fruitless searching, I finally found Charlotte. I was relieved to find that she was not the dead-eyed widow I'd abandoned but a woman of grace and silent strength. She sang while she cooked and spent long stretches of time in her garden. She picked wild flowers by the river and gazed up at the stars. When she speaks of you, she smiles to herself then looks off into the distance, as if she's waiting for you to arrive. Or perhaps she's waiting for her time to come so that she can be reunited with you in the next life. Through all the loss she suffered, she somehow became more.

Your young daughter, Morgana, glitters with all the charisma and poise of royalty and all the mischievousness that you and I possessed in youth. When Charlotte's gaze fell upon her, I saw in her eyes the glimmer of love that I'd only ever seen when she looked upon you. Though Charlotte prefers to remain tied to the simple life she's grown accustomed to, I will return to visit your daughter as often as time allows. And if Charlotte permits me, I'll bring her lavish gifts and toys from Vires. Though she was born untitled, she'll remain a princess in my eyes.

Morgana is true joy embodied, and it seems her most treasured moments are spent listening to tales of her father's adventures. Can you believe it —she has your smile.

With all my love,

Minseo

If I only knew when I wrote this letter that you were still alive, I would have done it all differently.

Read Kingdom Soul

THE FAE & THE FALLEN

Looking for something a little sexier? Check out my most popular series, *The Fae & The Fallen*.

My first kiss nearly killed me—*literally*.

When 80% of the population is gifted with touch magic, it's best to keep your hands—and your lips—to yourself. Especially if you're an ungifted serf like I am.

The problem is, the most dangerous guy at Gifted Fae Academy is the one I want to touch more than anything, even as I draw the attention of the school's most gorgeous apprentice Fae.

When my entry exam leads to the revelation that I may not be as ungifted as I previously believed... well... surviving until graduation might prove harder than I thought—particularly when a certain fatal touch may be worth the risk.

*If you love reading about childhood friends, **enemies-to-lovers**, royal and celebrity classmates, and everything Fae, then one-click today and fall into this magical new series that's* Gossip Girl *meets* My Hero Academia!

AUTHOR'S NOTE

Thank you for reading Kingdom Cold. Make sure you check out the rest of the series to see how Charlotte's story ties into the King Arthur legend. Leave a review and let me know who your favorite character was.

There are many ways to stay up to date on my new releases:

Sign up to my mailing list to get updates. I also host giveaways and free book fairs.

You can join my Facebook Group to chat with me and other readers about books and get free ARCs from a variety of authors.

Become a Patron to unlock exclusive content including early drafts, the opportunity to name characters, and swag you can't get anywhere else.

KINGDOM
SOUL

A KINGDOM COLD NOVEL

BRITTNI CHENELLE

KINGDOM SOUL - MINSEO
CHAPTER ONE

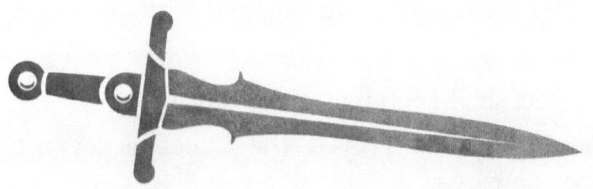

Read Kingdom Soul

Every night, when I close my eyes, it's the same. Rushing water, my body pushed against Charlotte's, my hand tightly pressed against her mouth, and the clanging of metal that ended my brother's life.

I've been drowning ever since. My screams were smothered by the waves, my movements slowed, and my tired arms unable to break the surface before another wave crashed down, tossing me through the abyss.

Year after year slips by, but the memory returns like an echo. Again and again I wonder if Charlotte hears it too, wherever she is.

I awoke to what felt like the gentle kiss of fingertips on my cheek only to discover the white petals of the cherry blossom tree had floated through my open window. The morning's golden rays granted me a moment of peace before my mind became acquainted with the world the way it was. A world without my little brother.

I dressed quickly, unwilling to break the silence, and hoped to sneak out before my attendants arrived. The sunlight seeped through the hanji walls, meaning it might already be too late to leave unnoticed, but all I could hear outside was the rustle of the cherry blossom tree.

I slid the door open and stepped onto the clay platform below.

"My prince, shall I fetch your breakfast?"

My heart leapt as I eyed the kneeling servant, Mingee. "Don't bother," I barked.

Mingee bowed and closed the door to my bedroom as I turned toward the palace. "Sir," she said, her voice breaking. She shrunk beneath my gaze. "His Majesty wishes to see you in the throne room."

I could have kicked her, and the thought lingered in my mind for several moments before I dismissed it and turned away. I needed to get out of here before she further burdened my morning. I eyed the castle walls, wondering how big of a deal my father would make if I ignored his request and went into town. But the throne room wasn't far from the front entrance, and I was in no mood to battle.

I walked past a series of buildings, each made from wooden pillars and clay-tiled roofs with elaborate, brightly-colored wood-working designs framing each pillar. The clouds hung in the sky like spun sugar, pink from the sunrise still caught in them. Beyond the palace walls, mountains reached above, like a fortress. The most striking element of Vires this season was the cherry blossoms now in full bloom. Still, the wind carried a bite of frosty air that tossed the white petals like snowflakes in a storm. I shivered as I passed the rooms of my mother and older brother Sumin, and I stopped when I reached Young's. His attendant waited outside his bedroom like he'd wake up and ask for breakfast. My father was a senseless man. Almost five years later and he can't even reassign the staff.

I stepped to the edge of the palace lake, my father's throne room platformed at the center of it. The lake, sprinkled with white petals, thrashed with a sudden gust of wind. The petals caught the morning light like stars twinkling in the night, like there was something left on Earth to celebrate. I crossed the stony gray bridge and kept my head down until I knelt at my father's feet.

"Rise, Minseo." I stood up to find my father perched on his throne in his red hanbok, with golden designs that weaved up his sleeves and a slender black hat atop his head. I bit back a smile; he looked like a great stuffed bird on a nest.

"There is a strategy session this evening. It's time you attend," he said, his gentle voice whispering around the room.

"I can't. I have plans to meet Junho at the—"

"That wasn't a request!"

I wrenched my hands, suddenly aware of the cold glares from around the throne room pricking my skin. Hanbit—the king's advisor—and a slew of guards I used to train with bristled.

I bowed. "Forgive me, Father, I only meant my presence at these meetings in the past hasn't—"

"It's time."

I clenched my jaw and bowed before turning away and making my exit, swallowing the truths I couldn't speak. He still had attendants outside my dead brother's room and somehow believed I was the one who needed to move on. I exhaled my frustration through gritted teeth and reminded myself it wasn't his fault Young died; it was mine. On my way out, I caught a flash of Jay Hyun, a soldier I'd once been close with. If he wasn't working, or if I wasn't inappropriately headed to drink first thing in the morning, I might've considered inviting him. He bowed to me as I left the throne room and stepped out onto the stone bridge.

A few hours later, I slammed down my empty ceramic cup. "More!" I bellowed, my head bobbing at the table.

Junho lay his chopsticks on his bowl of rice before reaching for a bottle of rice wine we call makkoli. "Shouldn't you sober up a bit before the big meeting?" he asked.

"More," I commanded.

Junho sighed and picked up the bottle, pouring the white liquid while his opposite hand lay politely on his chest. "You know, man, maybe he's right. Maybe it is time."

I slammed my hand on the table, rattling the dishes and sending one of my chopsticks flipping through the air and onto the floor. The clatter cut the babble of the other customers and drew their eyes to us. I raised my hand to wave away their attention and the room soon buzzed once more. Junho's face reddened, but it might have been that way from the makkoli.

"You and I both know those meetings are pointless. What is the point of having a great army if you can't use it to avenge your son's death?" I groused. "The man is a coward." I reached for my chopsticks, but one was still on the floor.

Junho nodded, his eyes flickering toward another table. "That may be true," he said, pouring himself a shot, "but how are you going to change that if you never attend the meetings?"

"Your Highness," a mousy voice whispered. A woman, who appeared to be in her late fifties, held out a new pair of chopsticks.

"Thank you," I said, trying to dismiss her with my tone. I turned back to Junho who held out his shot glass. "Gombe," I said, clashing my glass into his. Just as I was about to throw back another shot, I noticed Junho's eyes flash toward the table to our left.

I lowered my drink. "What are you looking at?" I asked.

"Oh," he said, "I think I know that guy." The corners of his mouth turned up. "Don't look."

I turned.

"Don't look!" he whispered sternly. He concealed his face in his hands.

The other table had three Viran men sharing a pot of Mayontang, a red fish soup, and drinking makkoli. Judging by the quality of their clothing, they were upper-class citizens, and the three empty makkoli bottles on their table indicated they'd likely been there as long as we had. Two of the men chatted loudly, but the youngest man on the far side of the table who seemed to be in his early twenties quietly and conspicuously stared down at a small plate of kimchi.

"Stop looking," Junho said, drawing my attention. Junho dug into the fish with his chopsticks, pulling out the meat of the jaw muscle, my favorite, and stuffing it into his mouth. "Look," he said, "it won't be as bad as when you first returned home. It was all so fresh. Nobody blames you for losing it as you did."

"You're killing my buzz."

Junho's gaze drifted to my left once more and I snapped my head to look. The three men rose from the table, scrambling for their wallets. The young man smiled shyly at Junho before his gaze met mine, and he quickly turned away and hurried out of the restaurant.

I shook my head and turned back to Junho. "Does that guy owe you money or something?"

Junho shook his head. "Should we get you some water?"

"Nah," I said, picking through fishbones to get some meat. "It doesn't matter how many meetings I go to. My father will never attack Camelot."

"What about Charlotte?"

I halted. He must have been drunker than I thought to mention *that* name. My mouth dried. "What about her?" I spat.

"She could still be out there."

Charlotte was certainly dead, and I didn't appreciate Junho's mention of her. For almost five years, I'd tried to overcome losing her. At first, I tried convincing my father to allow me to seek revenge. When he refused, I tried the company of other women, but there was no antidote to be found in my bed. No, antidotes came in bottles. Drunk, celibate, and numb, I'd drunk nearly every day to drown out those memories, and I endured headaches and nausea all so that names like hers never drifted in. The room spun, but with one mention of her name, I was transported to five years ago, when my wounds were still bleeding and her tearful eyes turned from me that final time. Anxiety pooled beneath my skin as I felt her name reverberate around the room. Surrounded, my only option was to escape the restaurant and get some air. I stood, dropping silver coins onto the table in front of Junho. "Don't be a fool."

Click HERE to keep reading.

ACKNOWLEDGMENTS

I'd like to take a moment to thank everyone who helped bring this story to life.

Thank you to my husband for being a well of inspiration and support.

EDITORS

Copy Editor: Amber Richberger
Content Editor: Jami Nord

PATRONS

Pink Conklin
Shelly Wilson
Kellie Rivera
Jeanette George
Michelle Curtis
Christopher J Canady

Click here to become a Patron! Unlock exclusive content, prizes,
and perks!

CONTENTS

THE fae AND THE
fallen

BRITTNI CHENELLE

THE fae AND THE

fallen

BOOK ONE

BRITTNI CHENELLE

For my brother, Trey.
(Even if I mostly hated him <3)

ALSO AVAILABLE
IN AUDIO

Take advantage of the
discounted price.

Reina

ONE

My first kiss nearly killed me—*literally*.

We had just entered middle school and most of our class had already received their gifts. It was the year that most people came into their abilities, and the ones who didn't—like me—were mercilessly tortured.

I wish I could say there had been strength in numbers, that by banding together, we ungifted Serfs could make it through the day in peace. The reality was that the Commons, those with useful but not extraordinary gifts, could still hurt us. The Elites were worst of all, but there were only a few of them around. They could knock all five Serfs out of school for a week with a touch, and as classmates, we were kept in frighteningly close proximity.

Still, we suffered *together*. But of the five companions I made, I grew closest to one boy in particular, Kaito. He was a transfer student from overseas, a couple of inches shorter than me and a little more than chubby, but every time it looked like I'd be targeted by the Elites, he'd do something to provoke them and draw their attention so I'd be spared their cruelty.

One day after school, we sat at our usual spot on the pier. The sun was setting, and the bright orange light splashed across the clouds.

"You didn't have to do that," I said, eyeing the sling that cradled Kai's right arm. "I could've kicked his ass."

He grinned. "If you're missing the rest of your friends, you can always just *visit* them in the infirmary."

I laughed. "It's faster just to let them knock me out." I turned away and absently watched the pink hues flicker on top of the waves.

"If only we had Fae at school."

I tilted my head. "Can you imagine the great Yemoja Roux cornering Westly in the hallway?" I laughed. "I'm sure she has bigger fish to fry than a few middle school bullies. She's out there with the rest of the Fae, holding this whole world together."

He nodded. "Things will be better once our gifts come in... *if* they come in."

I punched his shoulder, forgetting his sling. He winced.

"I'm getting my gift," I said. "And when I do, I'm going to Gifted Fae Academy just like Yemoja Roux."

I let my thoughts drift to the rhythm of the waves as I recalled my few encounters with the Fae. Sure, they were all over the news, using their powers to stop the criminal Elites from tearing society apart, but seeing them in person was like seeing the ocean for the first time. They were more than beautiful. They were infinite. Only the greatest and most morally incorruptible Gifted were selected by the government to become Fae and protect the rest of us. They were like celebrities, worshipped by the public and paid crazy amounts of money with tax dollars for their services. And from the moment I caught a glimpse of Yemoja Roux fearlessly dashing into harm's way, I knew I would follow in her footsteps someday.

"Don't move," Kai said, lifting his phone to take a picture of me. "The light is perfect." He smiled down at the screen. Without looking away from it, he said, "Don't forget about me when you go to GFA."

I tucked a curl behind my ear. "I'll never forget about you."

He looked up, his serious expression stirring a torrent of nerves and butterflies inside me. He looked down at my lips. *Is he going to kiss me?* I'd never kissed anyone before. *Had he?* I felt panicked as my mind raced my heart for top speed.

I looked down at his lips, trying to decide if I'd imagined the whole thing, but he leaned closer. I froze, squeezing my eyes shut with the hopes that he'd do the rest. His lips were soft against mine, but looking back, it was more like our lips bumped together than an actual kiss. Still, I felt a tingling sensation rush through my body and stop at the tips of my fingers. A feeling of weightlessness overcame me, like I was floating through the air.

"Reina!" Kai shouted.

My eyes snapped open to the distant voice, fear tearing through me. Stunned, I looked down—*way down* at Kai—reaching out to grab something. *Anything.* Too afraid to even scream, I floated twenty feet above the pier for twelve seconds before I plummeted down, my leg buckling under me with a snap. I was rushed to the infirmary, and after they put a cast on I was sent back home. Kai came to visit once, asking how I was, sounding very sorry. That was the last I saw of him.

It took eight weeks for the bone to heal and, by the time the cast came off, I realized Kai was no longer friends with us Serfs.

He'd unlocked his gift, a rare power that allowed him to make what he touched weightless and, in a matter of weeks, teachers and students alike were tossing around words like "genius" and "prodigy." He may not have bullied us himself, but he certainly didn't stop his new friends, either.

I was very certain my time would come someday. With eighty percent of the population possessing some uncanny ability, odds were high I would at least become a Common, but then the year passed. And the next. And the next. When the time came to begin high school and I was still a Serf, I started to lose hope.

Foolishly, my crush on Kai lingered for too many of those years before I got my head on straight. I was finally over him... At least I thought so until I returned to school for our sophomore year. In one short summer, he'd sprouted up to six feet tall, was lean and muscular, and with his high cheekbones, dark eyes, and brooding good looks, he made my heart stop. He'd gone from a genius to a high school god, and inevitably, as the last remnants of our friendship died, and the new semester began, he became a bully.

Kaito

TWO

I nearly killed the first girl I ever kissed, *literally*.

But that was the moment when my gift awakened. It was like I was suddenly someone new, someone with a gift, someone who was Elite. Reina was just a Serf and still talking about going to the Gifted Fae Academy like it was a foregone conclusion. It drove me crazy. Life wasn't fair and you couldn't get where you wanted in life by believing you would. You had to be destined for it, so I made new friends among the Elite who were more like me and when they tormented her, I just stepped back. I figured maybe that was the way for her to learn and to accept that she was never getting a gift.

But no matter how many beatings she took, she never learned. Before I knew it, I was starting to hate her. Mob mentality. Why didn't she get it? She was lesser. Lesser than Elites, lesser than Fae, lesser than me. The way she provoked us was just begging to get seriously hurt. I might've started out wanting her to accept her fate and stop pushing, to protect her and to shatter those delusions of hers. But, after awhile, I found that I enjoyed tormenting her. I had new friends, a new life. She was on her own.

It was our sophomore year and we had a little less than three years of high school left. I couldn't believe Reina was still walking around telling people that when she got her ability, she'd transfer to Gifted Fae Academy. But that was the least of my worries. I was more worried about getting myself into the Academy. If anyone at our school deserved to get in, it was me, our school's most Elite student. But I'd failed the Academy's brutal entrance exam— twice.

I strode through the hallways, feeling the pull of every female gaze I passed. It had been that way since my power had come in, but this year the look in their eyes was different. I wasn't sure if it was my sudden growth spurt, or that my private combat training had turned me lean and muscular, but the looks I got now were far more pointed than just from my power, and I planned to enjoy this level of attention. Attention was one of the reasons I wanted to become Fae. To be as respected and loved as Yemoja Roux. Bathe in the glory and wealth that came with the job. Bigger pay days for taking down high-level criminal Elites meant there was no dispute who was the strongest among them. Yemoja Roux had held the title my whole life and I wanted to be just like her. There was no other job worth having.

Across the hall, I could see Westly looming over a terrified freshman girl. I heard the crackle of ice beneath her feet, and with a gentle shove to her shoulder, her legs flew out from under her and she landed hard on her ass. I smirked, but it quickly faded as Westly stumbled back.

Reina shoved him back with two hands. "You don't have to be such a dickhead," she fumed, helping the girl to her feet. The freshman backed away and took off down the hall, leaving Reina to square off with Wes alone.

Fuck. Why did she always have to get involved?

I tried to hide my increased pace as I rushed over to them, throwing my arm around Wes before he could freeze her solid on the spot. "What do we have here?"

"The Serf is back for more," he said, pushing a handful of sandy brown hair out of his eyes. "I was just going to teach her a lesson."

I looked up at Reina. Her skin was rich and dark in color, kissed a few shades darker, from her summer exploits no doubt. Her curls had grown out to reach her lower back and today she wore a plaid skirt that stopped just above her knees. My gaze lingered over her curves. I guess I wasn't the only one who changed over the summer. I'd hoped to intimidate her with my appraisal, but she looked unfazed.

I rolled my eyes. "What, you think if we hit you enough times with magic you'll get some?"

"Reina!" a red-headed girl said, pushing through the crowd. She stepped between us and dropped forward in a deep bow. "She's very sorry," the girl said. "Please, just let it go this one time."

Wes grinned and shoved me. "Oh look, two for one." He raised his hand to attack, but I stopped him.

I spoke slowly. "If we let you go now, you'll think this kind of shit's ok."

The girl straightened, fear pooling in her eyes. She dropped to her knees. "Please," she begged, her face nearly at my feet. "That's better," I said, moving my gaze to Reina. "Your turn."

"Fuck you, Kai," she spat, helping Red to her feet.

I nodded. "Thought so." I reached out and brushed Reina's

face. She slapped my hand away, but it was too late. The moment my skin touched hers, I felt her weight slide in range of my gift. It passed through my body, mimicking the sensation just before pins and needles, and she began to rise into the air.

Wes craned to get a better look as Reina scrambled to cover herself, her skirt already rising up along with her body from my magical energy. Wes shot me a wicked look. I nodded and, with a turn of my wrist, I flipped her upside down, exposing her black lacy underwear to the crowded hallway. Within seconds, there was a huge crowd, snapping pictures and video.

I wanted her to scream, to beg me to let her down and end the humiliation, but she hung there, silently, glaring at me defiantly. So I left her there.

Reina

THREE

I dangled in the hallway for an hour and a half before Kaito's magic finally wore off and I came crashing down. Thankfully, it was during a class and there was no one to watch me cry on the floor while I waited for my body to recover. I let my limbs go limp as my blood evened out, taking deep breaths. When I was up there, all I could think about was the pressure on my lungs. I was certain I'd suffocate—a corpse suspended in the hallway as teachers and students passed below, occasionally snapping pictures of my bare ass. An unfortunate end to a ridiculous life. At least I'd saved that girl, and more importantly, I'd worn good underwear.

I didn't have long before the bell sounded and I didn't want to be in the hall when the students made their way through. I peeled myself from the floor and pushed open the front doors of the school. I was sure they wouldn't miss me, at least for my first few classes. I needed to pull myself together. There was only one place that cheered me up when I felt this bad. I headed out into the streets, my home whenever I sprung myself from the orphanage.

An elderly lady crouched on the street near the bus stop raised her tired gaze to me. "For eight dollars, I'll change your hair color to a lovely shade of orange. Lasts almost twenty minutes."

Things were getting worse. If even Commons like her were having trouble finding work, what chance did I have as an orphan Serf? Of course, orphan and Serf went hand in hand, as any kid with a gift was quickly adopted. I waited at the bus stop for the 747 bus to take me to the edge of Ancetol City. Only Serfs took the bus; there were more efficient ways for the rich and Gifted to travel, but I didn't mind it. I felt safe there, unlike at school.

An hour later, I exited the bus. When it pulled away, I found myself outside the large gated lawn of Gifted Fae Academy. This had always been my go-to place to imagine a better life, but the competition to get into GFA went from regional to international two years ago when Yemoja Roux took a first-year from GFA as her personal apprentice for the summer: a green-eyed heartthrob named Oden Gates. He appeared beside Yemoja Roux in several of her interviews that summer, and ever since, my spot had become overrun with fangirls vying to get a look at him—not that I blamed them. Regardless of your type, chances were you were into Oden Gates. He was on track to become a Gold Tier Fae, just like Yemoja Roux, and he was just a sophomore like me. Talk about putting life into perspective. Luckily, with school starting up again, the coast seemed clear.

I ran my fingers over the iron crest, the owl insignia on each side, framing the letters GFA, as I'd done so many times.

"Please," I whispered, tears springing to my eyes. I wasn't

sure if I was still upset from the incident, or if I was just worn out from fighting for my life day in and day out.

"Back again, Miss Reina?" a voice called from behind me. I spun. Professor Greene had his gray hair pulled into a bun. I wiped my face quickly. "Yes," I said. "Just getting ready for when my gift comes in."

His smile faded. "You've been crying."

"No, no, no. I just have... I just..."

"Have allergies?" He grinned. He opened his briefcase and pulled out a small bag. As he held it out, I could see there was a small piece of candy inside. "Did you know that I'm a confections professor?"

GFA was the home I'd never had. My dream of going there was the only thing I had left after my parents died last year. I'd stood outside that beautiful gate and traced the lines of it with my fingers so many times I could draw the crest with my eyes closed. I'd never been inside though—only the gifted were permitted to enter and only the staff and students who'd passed their notoriously rigorous entrance exam. But everyone knew the subjects taught in the top magic schools and the names of the retired Fae who taught there. I nodded. "Of course."

From my frequent visits, I'd met at least five of the professors, but the students rarely left campus. I'd never been fortunate enough to see Oden Gates in person.

"Give this little treat to whoever... gave you allergies."

Drug someone? I shook my head. "No thank you, professor," I said. "I don't want to hurt anyone."

He motioned to the gate. "Do you see the F on the crest? Do you know what it stands for?"

I nodded.

"Fae deliver justice. All this one does is suppress hatred for a short time."

I hesitated but, unwilling to insult him, I took the bag with the morsel. "Thank you, professor."

Whatever happened, however bad Kai made me feel, I knew I'd never give him the magic-infused confection. If anything, I would eat it to stop myself from hating him. Maybe then he'd stop being so damn... important.

The professor winked at me, and I held my breath as he squared his shoulders to the gate and it opened. I craned to see what lay behind those bars but, as usual, the image was blurred with magic. I was running out of chances to get in. Since I'd missed this year's exam, I only had my junior and senior years. If my gift didn't come by then, I'd age out of my group home and be thrust into the streets again.

Every year the likelihood I'd gain a power dropped. There was only a 7% chance left that I ever would—but that was more than enough. All I needed to do was survive until that day—the day when my life would really start and I'd finally get my chance to go to my real home, GFA.

Kaito

FOUR

I had those lace panties on my mind during every class, but I didn't see Reina again until lunch. She was chatting with the redhead at her usual lunch table, laughing. *Laughing.* What was with this girl? Why couldn't I break her? And worse, her nonchalance about the whole situation made the other students stop rubbing it in her face. I'd watched as several of them showed her pictures of her ass midair on their phones and she smiled and shrugged at them. There wasn't much fun in tormenting her if she wasn't going to be tormented. I wasn't sure if she was brave or just stupid.

Wes walked over and put our lunch trays down in front of me. "What are you looking at?"

He traced my gaze to Reina. "You still thinking about that ass? Me too, bro. I wasn't expecting all of *that.*" He laughed. "I swear the Serf girls are the biggest freaks."

I sat down, pulling my tray toward me as my table filled up with several more of the school's Elites, although I was the only

285

one at this school who could truly wear the title. Out of the corner of my eye, I saw Trevor, my number two, approach Reina's table. *He wouldn't fucking dare*. He smiled at her and her hand shot up to the charm on her necklace, the tell-tale sign she found him attractive.

My body moved, and before I knew it, I was right within earshot of their conversation. I walked up and gave Trevor a friendly pat on the back to remind him I could toss him into the air at any moment.

"Kaito," he said, "I was just telling Reina that I enjoyed her performance this morning."

I didn't like the sound of her name in his mouth. I sighed, turning my gaze to her. "I'm surprised you're back so soon. Perhaps I didn't leave you there long enough."

Reina's hand dropped from her charm. "It's actually kind of impressive that you managed to hold me up that long while you were in class. Not bad, Kai."

I hated when she did that. It was so much harder to torture her when she acted nice. I clenched my jaw to keep from smiling. "Whatever," I mumbled.

Trevor leaned closer to the redhead. "So, are you a Serf too?" he asked.

The girl nodded. Her eyes moved to me and widened. "Kaito, can I see your tattoo?"

I held my arm out to show her the black markings that snaked up from my wrist to my elbow on one side. She traced over the lines with her finger and I was surprised someone so vulnerable would be willing to touch me, knowing that she'd put herself in my magical range. It could have been a sign of surrender; after all, if I wanted to hurt her, there was nothing she could do about it.

"I had one for a year, but it wore off. I was thinking about getting another one myself because the Common in my neighborhood is pretty good at them," Trevor said. He nodded to Reina. "You going to get one?"

She shrugged, tugging on her necklace.

"But a tattoo might cover the lovely bruises." I smirked.

Reina frowned, looked up at me and asked, " What bruises?"

"The ones you got when I dropped you on your ass, of course," I laughed.

"Oh, there were no bruises. I just sort of, floated down, no problem," she lied. I knew she was lying but there was no way I could call her on it.

"Reina," I said, suddenly. "Do you ever think about that day at the pier?"

Her mouth dropped open.

A smile crept onto my face. "I do. You know, I still have the picture I took—" I snatched my arm away from Red. How *dare* she.

I leaned into her and she leaned back, fear flaring in her eyes.

"That was a huge fucking mistake," I hissed. "Who do you think you are? Yemoja Roux?"

Reina shot between us. "Wh-what happened? What's going on?"

Trevor stepped forward. "So Red's not ungifted?"

Reina shook her head. "She is. Trust me. She didn't do anything."

I crossed my arms. "Are you telling me you didn't know?"

Her gaze snapped to Red. "Emma. Tell them."

"It's true," she said, mystified. "I didn't do anything. I'm a Serf."

"Wow. That's a bald-face lie if I've ever heard one," I spat.

Reina leaned closer to Red, her voice dropping to a whisper. "If it's true, you can tell me."

She shook her head. "I didn't do anything. I swear, Reina."

She was certainly lying. I wasn't sure, but her gift seemed to purge secrets. My mind raced at the implications. It was incredible. With a single touch, she could coerce confessions out of criminals. Or gather secrets from the underground organizations that ran this city. Forget Elite, forget GFA—if I understood her gift correctly, she could have a one-way ticket to become Fae. So why was she hiding it? As the four of us looked around in confusion, I was grateful no one was asking the important question: what her gift actually was. If they did, they might think more carefully about what I'd said. I needed to make a quick exit.

I eyed the trays that lay in front of the girls. Red had a cold slice of pizza and Reina had an untouched sloppy joe which was the only option for free lunch—clearly one she didn't like much. Reina had been stuck with free lunch ever since her parents were killed, and she ended up in the group home. On the corner of her plate was something not from the cafeteria. A delicious-looking piece of candy. I tapped the trays and swiped the candy before using my gift to dump the remaining contents on the girls.

They gasped.

"Adios, ladies," I laughed, and I popped the candy into my mouth.

Reina

FIVE

I 'd be lying if I said it never got to me. If that were true, I never would have put that magical morsel on my tray for Kai to find. I'd originally planned on eating it, and I could have hidden it until I got the chance, but something dark inside me wanted him to take it, most likely the part of me that he'd scarred. I scooped a handful of sloppy joe from my lap and dropped it on the floor. "That was weird, Em," I said. "He really seemed to think you used a gift on him." I nervously picked at the food on my lap. "But what else could make him say all that stuff?"

"But, I didn't," she whispered.

"Did you see anyone else touch him?"

She scrubbed at the pizza sauce with her dry napkin, no doubt guaranteeing her a stain. "Just Trevor."

"And it couldn't be him because his gift is paralysis and that can only last a few seconds."

Emma stopped dabbing at her shirt. "Do you think someone tried to frame me?"

"Like, without touch magic? It's impossible. Yemoja Roux isn't here. Unless..."

Emma's eyes widened.

"Unless Kai was trying to frame you. I mean... maybe he was pretending." I smiled at the unlikelihood of it as I pushed more lumps of meat off my lap.

Emma nodded with a weak smile, and I scanned her face for any sign of deception. She was telling the truth, I was certain of it. Yet, somehow, I had just witnessed a gift being used on Kai.

A gasp sounded behind me and I turned to see a girl gaping at the table of Elites. Kai stood on the table, drawing the attention of the entire cafeteria. He nodded to Vinny, a muscular jock with a sound manipulation gift. Vinny opened his mouth wide and put his hand on his cell phone. Music filled the cafeteria, pouring from Vinny's mouth like amplified speakers. The lyrics rang out.

I wanna be honest, I can't hide it.

Anyway, I don't care.

My eyes are already on you.

Come to me

Let me lay my feelings bare.

That's when Kai began to move. One spin and the thrust of his hips was all it took to send every girl there into a frenzy, crowding around his table like fangirls at a concert. But Kai didn't stop there. He loosened his tie.

Down, down, let's fall

I wanna fall together.

My mind went immediately to the magical morsel. He'd eaten it and there was nothing I could do now but watch the show. I sat on my table, crossing my arms with a grin as I soaked in the glory of my victory. I had to admit, I felt the leftover shreds of my former crush stir inside me as his gaze met mine. He pointed to me and smiled—actually *smiled*—and I gulped with uneasiness as he bit his bottom lip. *I'm glad I'm over him.* I felt my daydreams mix with the spectacle, stirring feelings I'd thought long dead.

Down, down Let's fall
I'll fall only for you.

My stomach sank when Kai didn't stop there.

One by one, he popped open his buttons, his muscular chest coming into view inch by inch. Heat tore through me, but was quickly extinguished by dread when the other girls spun into near hysterics. This was getting out of hand. Before I could think about it, I was fighting through the crowd. Kai's gaze followed me as I elbowed my way through, reaching up for his hand. I had to get him out of there. I searched the cafeteria for an escape route and noted that if I could get him away from his table, we could make a break for it—preferably before his pants came off. His hand closed around mine, but instead of pulling him off the table and through the crowd, an all too familiar sensation tore through me and I rose into the air.

We ascended together, spinning slightly as if suspended on an invisible carousel.

"Oh my god, Kai. I'm so sorry."

He smiled. "Why? Don't be sorry. I'm glad I finally got your attention."

"No, you don't understand... That candy on my tray, it was gift-infused."

He tilted his head back. "Well, it feels great—"

The music cut. My hair stood on end as every person in the

room besides Kai and me were completely immobilized. They were a mausoleum of statues, timeless and horrifying. Was it some extreme form of Wes' magic? No, I saw no trace of ice. There wasn't a single student at our school who had that kind of power, or teacher. Which meant...

"Ms. Bennet, Mr. Nakamaru, to my office immediately. And put on your shirt," Principal Angora said. Her words were sharp, but they were nothing compared to the spectacle of the entire student body rooted in place.

Kai reached for my hand but I pulled it away. I wasn't used to being in trouble; in fact, no one was. In all the years I'd been bullied, I'd never seen a teacher intervene, much less the principal. I knew it was bad, but I wasn't sure why this incident in particular garnered so much attention, or what the consequences would be.

Even as we moved into the hallway, we saw more ensnared students. One girl reached for her locker but could never touch it. A guy with a contorted face looked like he'd been mid-sneeze when Principal Angora's gift hit. They were frozen in place and I shuddered that a gift so strong could live within someone I'd passed every day. A glance at my cell phone told me that time was still passing—even if it seemed like the three of us were the only ones who were able to continue our lives.

As we stepped into Principal Angora's office, I heard the slam of lockers behind me and I exhaled the relief that all had returned to normal. Even when the door closed, I could hear the chatter of nosy students that caught a glimpse of Kai and me being marched to our fate.

We sat across from Principal Angora, her dark dingy office littered with books and files, some stacks partially covering the only window at the back of the room behind her desk. The light behind her head shadowed her face, but I could see her well enough to know I hadn't given her a good look before. She had half-moon glasses that hid a beautiful face, though she was at least a decade beyond her prime.

"Excuse me," I said, without thinking. "You don't use touch magic. How'd you freeze everyone?"

She folded her hands together and I tried to ignore the way Kai's gaze was burning my cheek.

Principal Angora sighed. "I shake everyone's hand on their first day of school. Don't you remember?"

I gaped. "That's amazing. How long can you keep them frozen?"

"Just a minute or so," she said blandly. She got up and started filling a glass of water at the bubbler in the corner as a surge of questions flooded my brain.

"How long can they stay in your range after you touch them?"

She dug through her desk drawer and pulled out a small blue packet. "A few months. But I make appointments to check in with students who have fallen out of my range."

I blurted, "Why aren't you Fae? With your power, you could easily—"

"Summer vacations, holidays, home by five, not to mention this is a much safer profession than Fae. I'm not the showy type. But we're not here to discuss me," she said as she emptied the contents of the packet into the water, giving it a slight glow before it settled back to looking like ordinary water.

I eyed the glass absent-mindedly. "Sorry, yes. I know. You're just so amazing."

"I'm flattered," she said, but her dry expression said otherwise. "You," she barked at Kai, who finally tore his gaze away from me. "Drink this," she said.

He took a sip and his smile slowly faded. He turned to me, fire blazing behind his eyes. He stood. "What the fuck?" He turned to Principal Angora. "I'm sorry for the language, but...but...she fucking drugged me!"

I slouched in my chair, pulling my arms to my body to avoid letting him touch me.

"Sit down, Mr. Nakamaru."

Kaito sat slowly.

"Ms. Bennet, is this true? Did you drug Mr. Nakamaru?"

"No, ma'am." Technically, I didn't. But Kai deserved whatever happened here. After all, if he hadn't decided to throw my tray of food on me he never would have noticed the confection, and I had to admit the thought of him embarrassed for a change felt good.

"Mr. Nakamaru, how did this infused confection end up in your system? You are claiming Ms. Bennet drugged you. Would you care to elaborate?"

"She had a piece of drugged candy on her tray and I ate it. She should have stopped me! She just let me eat it knowing it was drugged!"

"Did she offer you this candy?"

"Um...no. I...um...well...I took it from her tray. But she knew! She should have stopped me! It's one hundred percent her fault!"

A big part of me wanted to laugh watching as Kai scrambled to get out of this one. I hadn't wanted any of this to happen, but I did have to admit it was funny as hell. I struggled to keep a smirk off my face.

"Mr. Nakamaru, as I see it, you saw a piece of candy on Ms. Bennet's tray, and without her permission, you took it and ate it. I'm certain Ms. Bennet knew it was drugged, but she could not have foreseen that you would steal it. The blame is entirely yours," the Principal told him. "However, Ms. Bennett, you brought drugged candy into this school which is in direct violation of our rules."

Well, I couldn't argue with that. That part was true enough. But the look on Kai's face when the Principal blamed him was worth it .

"The administration has been told to stay out of the affairs of the students. A little competition in the hallway teaches the Common or Serf students how to survive after graduation as well as encourages Elite students to improve and hone their gifts. But we have a strict policy against child pornography or drugs of any kind including infused confections, and our school has been flagged for both."

Kai looked down at his unbuttoned shirt and began to frantically button up.

Principal Angora went on. "As you know, we have a zero-tolerance policy for such extreme situations."

As if he hadn't heard a word the Principal had said about him being to blame for his being drugged, Kai nodded. "Thank you, Principal Angora. Kick her out."

I clutched the arms of my chair so tightly I felt my fingernails cut the wood. Would she really do that?

"Actually, you are both expelled."

Kai stood. "Both? What the hell did I do? She was the one with the drugs."

The principal held up her phone, my bare ass floating across the screen. I winced but was pleasantly surprised by the nice shape in the image.

Kai pressed his lips together. "But you can't expel me! I'm your best student."

"Then I imagine you'll have no trouble getting another school to take you."

Kai sputtered and spun to me. "And why are you so quiet?"

"I don't care," I said. "Besides, we *are* both guilty."

"You think that orphanage is going to pay for a private school? This is the only public school in the district. Good luck with your two-hour commute." Kai was so angry he was practically spitting. But I knew where I was going.

"You can save your concern. I'm going to GFA."

SIX

I stormed out of the school, slamming the door behind me. *Fuck this school and fuck Reina.* My stomach sank as I imagined my parents' reactions when I told them the news. It would likely be worse than when I was rejected from GFA for the second year in a row. My mom had gone into a full-on episode, screaming at me about how I'd brought shame to the family and how much I'd embarrassed her. She cried as she smashed various objects around our townhouse. But my father's reaction had been much worse. He stared at me for a long time, shook his head, and hadn't spoken a word to me since. Not that we were ever a happy family to begin with. My parents had sacrificed a lot to move us here, all to improve my chances of getting into GFA. And now I'd been thrown out of the second-rate public school that I attended.

I was so caught up going through my options that I'd reached for the door handle of my house before I realized Reina was following me.

I spun on my heel. "What the fuck do you want?"

"I've been calling your name for like five blocks, you didn't hear me?"

I sighed. "Obviously not."

"What are you going to tell your parents?" she asked. I unlocked my door and pushed it open.

"They won't be home for two more weeks." I nodded her in. "Shoes off."

She kicked off her shoes and looked around the foyer, her gaze landing on the crystal chandelier we'd added a few years after she'd last been here. "I see you're still rich," she said and her voice carried down the hallway.

She followed me to my bedroom, the muscle memory still unbroken after all these years. "Sure am. Why aren't you?"

"My parents died," she stated flatly.

"Yeah, I heard, but like... didn't they leave you money or something?"

She shrugged off my question and I wasn't about to push. I opened my bedroom door and, out of the corner of my eye, I saw Reina hesitate before crossing the threshold. The fraction of a second that she'd paused was all it took to remind me we were no longer close middle-school friends.

I scanned my room self-consciously, but when she jumped onto the foot of my bed, I relaxed. I lay in front of her and noticed she pulled her arms to her chest to avoid being touched. It was for this exact reason that most Serfs wore long sleeves and gloves. Extra protection from touch—it was also how they were so easily targeted.

"No Pokemon sheets?" she asked, trying to move the comforter to get a peek.

I smiled. "Got rid of those when I started having sex—" I

almost caught myself, but the last word came out clear as a bell. My thoughts jumped to the video clip our former principal had shown us in her office. The black lacy panties broadcasted on screen.

She pressed her lips together and a silence settled between us that set my nerves on edge.

I raised my eyebrows and she turned her face away. Even with her dark skin tone, I could see her blush.

My eyes bulged. "Are you serious? You're *still* a *virgin?*"

She covered her face with her hands.

"What about... what's his name? The Serf."

She crossed her arms over her face. "Can we talk about... anything else?"

I settled back on my bed, pleased with my investigative skills. After a few seconds, my mind returned to my parents and the fucked-up situation I found myself in. "This is all your fault," I said. "My parents... they're going to kill me."

"You started it," she said.

"No," I said, tossing a pillow at her. "You started it by getting involved in a fight that wasn't yours."

"You did the exact same thing."

I sighed. "Rei, you have no gift. You're going to get yourself killed."

She rolled onto her back and put the pillow under her head, her gaze fixed on the ceiling. "I didn't know you cared."

"I honestly don't." We lay in silence my mind wandering to why I mentioned she was going to get herself killed. I didn't care...did I?

"Kai, can I ask you something?"

I gulped, terrified of what she might ask.

"Will you come with me to GFA?"

I scoffed. "No. And I don't know why you still go there. It's pathetic."

"I'm going to convince them to let me take the entrance exam, so I need you to tell me everything you can about the test."

I rolled my eyes. "Exams are done for the year and you have no gift."

"Why do you keep telling me I don't have a gift? I know I don't have a gift! I think about it every second of every day. You don't need to remind me." She sat up. "And, honestly, it doesn't matter, Kai. Being Fae isn't about your gift. It's about being there to help people when they need you so no one dies before their time."

I knew with her last statement she meant her parents, but there wasn't the faintest sign of emotion in her voice or eyes when she said it.

"Without a gift, *you'll* die out there. I'm not going to help you get killed. If you're suicidal, there are quicker ways." I picked up a pillow and pushed her over, pressing the pillow to her face. I heard her muffled laugh as she squirmed free. "Are you dead yet?" I teased. She pushed me off, but her thumb touched a piece of my neck, yanking her into my magic range.

She stiffened.

"Relax. I'm not going to do anything."

She leaned forward. "Don't you think if anyone could pull a gift out of me, it's the greatest Fae academy on earth?"

I looked up, ready to answer—ready to shut down her delusion—but the way she looked through me told me she wasn't actually asking but trying to convince herself.

I sighed. "Ugh. Fuck... let's go," I said, hopping off my bed.

Her face lit. "Reina and Kai, back in action."

I stopped and turned to her. "Let's get this straight now. We are not friends. We're not teammates. This is a last resort because you totally fucked me over. We go to the school, we ask to get into the test, and when they say no, I go back to hating you for ruining my life."

"And if we get in?"

"*If* by some miracle they let us in, I'll continue to educate you on your place, until you learn it."

Reina

SEVEN

O h my god, what an asshole! Well, I wasn't going to let him ruin this with his nastiness. He said he'd go with me and I wasn't going to lose this chance.

I insisted to Kai that we take the bus to GFA. He, of course, was rich enough to travel through Gemini Gates, but I needed the long bus ride to formulate a plan for getting into the school and didn't want to draw any more questions about how I'd spent my inheritance or why I'd landed in a group home.

But I couldn't formulate a plan, not with my mind racing. *Holy shit. Holy shit. Holy shit.* My skin felt as if it would burst into flames the moment Kai lay beside me on his bed. I'd practically lived there in middle school, but in a few short years, everything changed. It wasn't the room where we used to sneak tastes of liquor from his parents' stash, or where we'd researched the top Fae and debated over whose gift was strongest after Yemoja Roux. Now it was the place where Kai had sex with the girls who fawned over him. I mean, of course, he wasn't a virgin. *Look at him*. Ugh. And now he knew I *was* a virgin. I chewed my lip wondering which of the girls from our school he'd been with.

"So what's the plan?" Kai asked. His gaze moved across the scattered passengers. Despite the summer heat still lingering this first week of September, many of them wore long sleeves, gloves, and scarves to prevent, as much as possible, being touched. Kai's collared shirt was rolled up and pushed behind his elbows, exposing his hands and arms—a silent warning to anyone who passed that he was a force they'd be stupid to mess with.

"I-I'm still working on it." And I was because, even if I didn't exactly have a plan for getting in, I knew I wasn't going back to my old life.

Kai grabbed my hand, setting me on edge. "You better know what you're doing."

When he let go, I could still feel his magic gripping me. It always reminded me of the feeling just after running on a treadmill when my body was moving both too quickly and slowly at the same time. Some intangible force had ensnared me and I had no gift of my own to counter it.

I gritted my teeth, resenting that I didn't have the good sense to wear gloves.

When I stepped off the bus, I felt my nerves surge with every step toward the school's front gates. I heard the scrape of Kai's shoes on the sidewalk behind me but didn't wait for him to catch up. This was my moment. But, as I neared, I could tell *something was going on*. There were at least thirty people standing in a semi-circle outside the school. I increased my pace, curiosity tearing through me. Then I saw him standing at the center of the circle—Oden Gates. My heart leapt in my chest as I craned to get a glimpse of his smile. Dark skin, green eyes, and a smile that nearly knocked my knees out from under me and sent heat straight to my face. While Kai had been a god of sorts at our school, Oden was as close to being an actual god as the world had after the Fae; an apprentice Fae and leader of the Noble Four. He wasn't even just an apprentice; he was the apprentice for none other than Yemoja Roux, the greatest Fae who ever lived.

I joined the crowd, straining to hear what Oden was saying. "No, really," he said. "She's as awesome as she seems. I swear."

I wiggled my way through the crowd, bringing my exposed hands to my chest. It was an even mix of Commons and Serfs based on who was wearing gloves and who wasn't. So I knew who would let me pass them to avoid touching me.

I got to the front, my mouth gaping at his muscular arms that were completely exposed as if he'd intentionally cut the sleeves off his uniform. I was mesmerized. As an apprentice Fae, he'd already saved people. He'd already made the world a better pla—

My thoughts were disrupted when Kai pushed passed me, reaching his hand out to shake Oden's.

The crowd gasped.

Kai smirked. "You're Oden Gates, right? I'm Kaito Nakamaru."

The entire earth seemed to freeze as if our former principal's magic lingered over us as we waited to see how Oden would react to such a blatant challenge.

I held my breath, but a moment later Oden's shocked expression dissolved back to his bright smile and he shook Kai's hand. They sized each other up, waiting to see if the other would dare use their gift, but after a few seconds of inaction, the crowd all seemed to exhale at the same time.

"Kaito Nakamaru? Yeah, it sounds familiar. You failed the

GFA entrance exam twice, right? Heh, and they say you're a genius."

"They also say the third time's the charm."

Oden shrugged, his sculpted shoulders a treat for the crowd. "Well, I definitely don't see a genius, but I don't see a coward either."

"Is that a challenge?" Kai asked.

I knew where this was going. I'd been on the wrong side of this kind of confrontation my whole life, but Kai hadn't. He hadn't been a weakling in quite some time. I had no doubt that Oden could destroy Kai. Without thinking, I sprung between them. I grabbed them both by the wrist to part their extended handshake. "Let's go, Kai," I said. But then I felt it, the dizzying magical energy of both guys at once. I sucked in a sharp breath as I released their arms and turned to Oden to beg his mercy.

"Who's your friend?" Oden asked, his green-eyed gaze burning me as it dragged down my body and back up to my face. I knew what it looked like. Like I had some kind of delusional complex where I thought I was Yemoja Roux and could challenge multiple Elites at once. The only thing I had going for me was the fact that no one knew what my gift was, or that I had none. But now that was shot to hell. It would only take a moment for him to sense the absence of my gift the same way I could sense the presence of his. I wanted to run, but the instant I touched his skin, I belonged to him just as I did to Kai.

"Leave her out of this. This is between you and me," Kai said.

Oden smirked, his dimpled cheeks sending a flutter to my gut. "I don't know. She's kinda cute."

My stomach flipped and I wasn't sure if I was going to cry or jump into his arms and tell Kai to get lost.

"She's a Serf," Kai said. "Just let her go."

I was dead. Fucking dead. Killed. Dead as fucking shit. I knew I shouldn't have trusted Kai. That was the absolute worst move. One which guaranteed me at least a beating. I dropped my gaze to the ground, ready to accept the punishment for willingly touching an Elite. And everyone knew Oden's gift. Strength. Unfathomable strength. He was going to smash me into dust right here and no one would bat an eye.

I felt Oden's gaze on my face, but I didn't dare look up. Then I heard laughter burst from him, sweet as honey. I looked up and he asked, "Are you serious?"

Kai's brow furrowed.

"You can't feel that? No, I suppose not. She's definitely gifted."

"What?" I said, drawing his attention.

He stepped closer, his green eyes burrowing into me, sending every nerve on edge.

"How do you know?" I asked. My heart raced as he smiled down at me. My legs jellied.

"I know because you feel just like she does—like Yemoja Roux."

Kaito

EIGHT

I f Reina hadn't been in range, she probably would have dropped to the ground right there. But just as she swayed back, I suspended her weight on my gift like a puppet caught in my magical strings. Oden couldn't have possibly known what a cruel prank he'd played on her, getting her hopes up like that. I'd known her for four years. She was a Serf through and through. If she'd had any hint of ability, I would've caught it.

I faked a laugh. "Whatever man, we're leaving."

But as I grabbed for Reina's wrist, Oden grabbed the other. "I'm serious," Oden said. "Headmistress Tricorn will want to meet her."

I thought exposing Reina as ungifted would force away Oden's interest in her, but I should've known he would torment her before letting her go. I flinched when Oden slung his arm around her and guided her toward the gate, but I didn't fully understand what was happening until the gate opened and Oden walked with Reina over the threshold. The threshold that no Serf had ever crossed.

"Hurry up," he called back to me, and I scrambled after them. I thought about tossing Reina into the air and holding her out of Oden's range to make a getaway, but once the gate closed behind me, the blurred image of the school cleared and I saw GFA for the first time.

The school sat at least five hundred yards back from the gate. Long stretches of green grass framed the cobblestone path that split down the center. There were several fountains that spurted clear blue water, with hedged mazes winding through the flower-arched courtyards. All those things were eclipsed by the school itself which resembled something between a mansion, a castle, and one of the wonders of the world.

I'd imagined it all wrong, the grounds and the secretive school. I couldn't have been further off. There wasn't so much as a thumbnail image of the school online. I'd hoped to catch a glimpse of it when I'd taken the test my first year, but the tests were held off-campus. Standing transfixed, I drank in the excellence.

Reina's hands moved to cover her mouth, her eyes glinting with tears. I gaped. Reina didn't cry. Not ever. Not when I bullied her, not even when I'd seen her after her parents died. As I watched her, I wasn't sure what enthralled me more, GFA or Reina crying. I couldn't let myself believe she was gifted, not after what I'd seen her go through without fighting back. Still, she'd promised me she'd get us an opportunity to take the entrance exam and she'd already gotten us much farther than I thought. If I found out that, after all this time, she'd been lying about being a Serf, I would have no reason to pull my punches.

Oden paused for a moment to let us take it all in before

leading us around a fountain and back to the main path where two staircases parted, wrapped around, and came back together in front of the large maroon double doors.

"Where are all the students?" I asked as Oden pushed the door open.

"Class," he said over his shoulder, and his hand dropped to Reina's lower back.

My throat tightened while he continued. "This building is just where the professors keep office hours, host parties, and where the headmistress's office is."

The floors were made of warm hardwood but mostly covered by the golden-trimmed maroon carpets that stretched across the foyer. At the center was the school's crest with its signature owls embroidered in jeweled tones on each side. Reina slipped her phone from her pocket and tried to snap a picture of the crest, but from over her shoulder, I could see the image come up blank on her screen.

"It's enchanted," Oden said. "One of the school's protections."

I bit back a smile. "Rei, stop being a tourist."

"Shut up," she spat.

A dull tapping sent the three of us spinning to investigate. A tall, gray-haired woman stood on the half flight of stairs. Her sleek hair twisted into a bun at the back of her neck. She looked no older than eighteen, but everyone knew that the ageless form in front of me was the very first person gifted, more than two hundred years ago. It was nice to know the internet trolls had something right. Even in her retirement from Fae, she looked formidable.

"Oden, why did you bring this riff raff in here?" she said, her voice as stern as her high-set nose.

Oden seemed to shrink several inches under the head-mistress's gaze. "It's not what you think," he said. "This girl is—"

"I know very well what *she* is. Why did you bring this Academy reject into my school?"

All the air was sucked from the room as the three of them turned to me. What kind of parallel universe had I fallen into where Reina was welcomed in GFA and I was considered a reject?

"I'd like another chance to take the test," I said.

"You failed not three months ago. Why should I give you another chance?"

Had she been there? It seemed as if she knew me before I even spoke. I wasn't sure why, but she seemed interested in Reina, so I took a shot in the dark. "I brought Reina here."

The long-legged headmistress turned to Reina. "Is that true? Are you here together?"

Reina's gaze met mine, a glimmer of the love-struck daze present as it was with all the girls in our old school.

I smirked as Reina turned to Headmistress Tricorn. She said, "I've never seen that guy in my life."

Oden snorted and my mouth dropped open. Like a reflex, I flung Reina into the air. Oden's fist collided with my ribs and I slid back across the room, catching myself with my gift. With one leap, Oden crossed the room, catching Reina before she hit the wooden floor.

Headmistress Tricorn sighed. "Enough. You may both take the exam tomorrow morning." Her gaze locked with mine. "However, if you should fail, I don't want to see your name on another test application. I don't care how much your parents donate to this school."

"What if she fails?" I said with a nod.

The headmistress's gaze moved to Oden and they exchanged a loaded smile.

"Eight AM tomorrow. If you're late, don't bother coming," she said. "And Oden," she said, her red lips pursed, "remove them from my campus."

"Yes, headmistress," he said.

Reina threw her arms around Oden. "Thank you so much."

Ms. Tricorn turned the corner and her footsteps grew fainter as she ascended the stairs.

Oden turned to me with a grin. "So I guess she's not your girlfriend then," he said.

"Fuck no," I spat as I spun and headed for the doors.

Reina's voice shot out from behind me. "Don't be such a cry baby. You got your test, just like I said you would."

"No thanks to you," I called.

"*All* thanks to me."

Even ungifted, she'd always thought she was better than me, and now I come to find she's been lying this whole time. If she thought I was hard on her before, she had another thing coming.

"You better watch your back at the test tomorrow," I said, and I meant it.

Reina

NINE

The door slammed in my face as Kaito stormed out. Revenge was kind of sweet. It was one little lie and it didn't even hurt his chances. If anything, it gave him an excuse to show off his gift in front of the headmistress. Yet out he stormed like the victim. Like he hadn't *deserved* a kick in the ass after how he'd tormented me over the years.

"Sooo... " Oden said, drawing my attention. "There's a history there, huh?"

I clutched the owl charm on my necklace. "Not really," I said, and it wasn't a lie. I would hardly describe our little rivalry as history.

"Can I walk you out?"

I nodded and, as we stepped back into the sun, I was startled by how beautiful he was. He almost looked like a sculpture, his green eyes sending waves of shivers through me.

"Got any pointers about the test?" I asked, slowing my pace. I wanted to spend every second on the school grounds that I'd attempted to imagine every day and failed so immeasurably. Rows of pink and red flowers lined the hedge mazes. The fountains filled the air with the sputter of falling water. It was as if we weren't near the city anymore, like the magical barrier that protected the school from prying eyes also blocked out the sound from beyond the walls.

"I'm afraid it's different every time."

I nodded. I heard the gate shut and wondered if Kai had used his gift to flee the school grounds so quickly. "I figured. Can you tell me about the gift you seem to think I have?"

"And rob you of the joys of figuring it out for yourself?"

Our hands bumped together and I wondered if he'd done it on purpose to renew his hold on me.

I smiled. "Obviously I'm not great at that. How'd you discover your gift?"

"One day, I broke the shit out of just about everything I touched."

I laughed, my stomach tightening. "Seriously?"

He nodded. "My parents were so proud."

I chuckled and my thoughts moved to my own parents, but no sadness came.

"Why did you and your boyfriend decide to come today?"

I slowed to a glacial pace as we neared the gate. "He's not my boyfriend. I actually come here all the time." I turned back to the school. "But I couldn't have imagined..." My breath came short.

"Take a long look, this is going to be your new home."

I turned to him, his yellow-green eyes like precious gems in the sunlight. "You seem pretty confident I'll pass. Why is that?"

"Because..." I froze as he leaned in and kissed my cheek. I

touched my hand to my cheek as if I could feel his kiss there. "That was for good luck."

It was strange to be touched and kissed, and I liked the ease with which Oden touched me. He had no fear, when all my life I'd come to know touch as the surest way to be hurt.

He smiled and turned back to the school as the gate swung open to let me out. I stumbled through, replaying the kiss in my mind again and again, my cheek tingling with the memory.

As I stepped over the threshold, Ancetol crashed down on me. Sudden flashes of piercing white light, a slew of cameras and reporters all huddled around the gate. They held microphones out with their gloved hands, hurling questions at me. The thrum of traffic assaulted, horns blared to scold the cars who crept past, craning to investigate the commotion. "Miss, can you tell us about the school?" a mousy reporter asked.

Another reporter asked, "Will you be attending?"

Overwhelmed, I backed into the already closed gate. The questions were endless. "Why did Oden Gates allow you to enter the school?"

"Will other visitors be allowed to—"

Before I could settle on one to answer, my thoughts flung back to my first kiss as my body lifted from the ground. My mind slingshotted through each memory I'd retained where I'd felt the magical pull of Kai's gift. The same strained surrender pulsing through my limbs, the energy escaping through my fingertips. I once again flailed to cover my butt from being exposed on camera as I floated over the crowd. *Fucking skirt. Never again,* I thought when I was finally able to see Kai on the other side.

"Is that Kaito Nakamaru?" I heard someone say. "Is he transferring to GFA?" Kai must've been stopped by the reporters just as I had, but they must not have known who he was until they saw his gift.

"Mr. Nakamaru!" someone yelled from behind us. I landed right behind Kai and, with a nod, we started running down the hill. We sprinted past the bus stop, along the outside of the school's walls that seemed to go on forever. We slowed to a jog and then a stroll as the footsteps behind us grew faint.

"Thanks," I said, finally. "For pulling me out of there. That was... a lot."

He smiled. "*That* was a lot?"

I looked up, confused.

"We just broke into GFA, met the world's most promising apprentice Fae, got in a fight, and won a spot in the entrance exam. Oh!" he said, his eyes widening. "And let's not forget we found out that you've been gifted this whole time."

"I'll give you that other stuff, but that last one I'll believe when I see it."

He stopped walking so I turned to face him. "You seriously didn't know?" he asked, scanning my face.

I shook my head. "Did you?"

He sighed. "No. You still seem like a Serf to me."

Kaito

TEN

Reina and I took separate ways home. I thought I could convince her to take the Gemini Gates with me, but she insisted on waiting for a bus. I popped open a soda around the corner, not so close for Reina to know that I was there but close enough for me to make sure she got on the bus safely. It wasn't that this area was any worse than the one we lived in, but a block away was a street filled with bars that sold magic-infused elixirs that often caused things to get out of hand. Alcohol and magic didn't mix well, but that never seemed to stop anyone.

As we neared happy hour, the bus stop, which was more of a multi-bus terminal, began to crowd with all manner of people. Most seemed to be arriving, no doubt headed to drown out their day with an elixir of contentment and lime or confidence gin and tonic.

There was a Gemini Gate nearby, its travelers a stark contrast to those coming by bus. For starters, the richer group wore less clothing, their gifts offering most of them adequate protection. They also seemed to have bright, multicolored hair while the bus riders mostly had their natural colors. Magical dyes wore off quickly unless you had the more expensive ones. I checked around the corner, and Reina sat unbothered, scrolling away on her phone. To pass the time, I amused myself by mentally sorting the Elites, Commons, and Serfs based on appearance alone.

Across the room, I noticed a man with blue hair and round-framed glasses smirking at me. His exposed arms were crossed over his chest and he was leaning against a vending machine. I went back to my game, but a few minutes later I noticed he was still staring.

I locked my gaze on him, narrowing my eyes in warning, but he didn't look away. The crowd rushed between our silent stand-off, and I noticed an arrow tattoo that ran across his arm in the same place where I had my own. It started at his wrist and met at a point that faced his elbow. What was this dude's problem?

He nodded toward a television screen that hung almost directly between us that, as ever, was silently playing the news. Red headlines flashed across the bottom of the screen one after the other. I thought I'd misunderstood his nod, that he might have been drawing my attention somewhere else, but an older woman stopped suddenly amidst the crowd, her gaze transfixed on the screen. She put a gloved hand over her mouth. I didn't think much of it, until one by one the other passengers stopped to read the headline. There were police gathered on the screen but I couldn't tell from the image what had happened, and the headline was too small from where I stood. I squinted, stepping closer to get a good look.

Raphael Mazarin found dead. Investigators have no leads.

Impossible. Raph was a Silver Tier Fae. No one could have taken him down. The Fae were unbeatable. I'd seen Fae get injured. I'd seen them retire early, but never had such a high profile Fae fallen in combat.

My gaze snapped to the stranger across the room and he hadn't moved a fraction. His smirk deepened as he lifted his closed fist to the side of his cheek. I swallowed hard, as in that position the arrow tattoo on his arm pointed down. I wasn't sure what it meant, but I had a sneaking suspicion he knew something about Raph's death.

I walked through the crowd and they parted like a river around a stone to avoid my touch. But the man with blue hair had vanished. I spun with the sudden realization that I might have been in the presence of someone genuinely dangerous, which meant so was Reina.

My pulse deafened me and, as I dashed around the corner back to Reina, there was a pressure in my ears and in my throat. The bench where Reina had been sitting was filled with new occupants.

Then I saw her, lifting her phone to the scanner before she stepped onto the bus. I exhaled my relief. She was safe, and it would be a quick trip through the nearest Gemini Gate for me. But no matter how hard I tried, I couldn't shake the image of the man with the downward arrow and menacing smirk.

Reina

ELEVEN

I didn't hear the news until I returned to the group home. I walked into the common area, my mind preoccupied with the possibility that I might be gifted and the sudden pressure of the test I was about to face. If I had been paying attention, I would have been alarmed by the silence coming from an area where the other orphans usually argued about whose turn it was to watch TV. As I watched the twelve others huddled around the TV in stunned silence, I felt the uneasiness in the room.

"What's wrong?" I asked, but no one responded. I moved closer and heard a sniffle coming from Jerome. He was the youngest in the home, just eight years old. I looked up at the screen and in blood red, the caption read, *Raphael Mazarin found dead.* I sat down on the edge of the armrest, the only place I could squeeze myself in without blocking someone's view. My stomach tightened as Yemoja Roux stood in the frame. I held my breath as she spoke. "I just don't know who would do such a thing. Raphael was a good man and a great Fae. And whoever did this will be found and brought to justice."

"Yemoja!" a reporter shouted. "Are there any leads?"

She leaned over to a police officer and whispered something. He nodded, handing her a slip of paper. She turned back to the camera holding up a drawing of a simple arrow. "This image was found at the scene of the crime. If anyone has information that they think could be relevant to this case, please call the authorities."

I reached out and rubbed Jerome's back as I watched the news in disbelief. My thoughts moved to what Principal Angora had said about Fae being a dangerous position. I guess I always knew it was. But only the strongest were chosen as Fae, which meant they were pretty untouchable. I shuddered to think that someone out there had a gift strong enough to take down a Fae as well known as Raphael Mazarin.

Jerome squeezed my hand, a gesture that was only safe within our home. All thirteen of us were Serfs. But it meant we could touch, in moments like this, and fight like regular siblings. My life had not thus far been kind, but I felt grateful that I'd somehow found a little peace and landed here of all places. Others had it much worse. The presence of gifts had turned the foster system into a game of roulette, for ill-intentioned people looking for helpless kids with gifts they could use, but that system collapsed long before I became an orphan.

Once we aged out, all of us would be at the mercy of the gifted for the rest of our lives. I needed to become Fae. I needed to find a way to protect the Serfs. The only way to do that was to pass tomorrow's exam, and I didn't have the faintest idea how to prepare.

The TV shut off and Alyssa, the oldest of us, held out the

remote somberly. We spun to her for an explanation. "She'll be home soon. We'd better head to our rooms and stay out of her way."

There were many things we argued about—who spent too long in the bathrooms, who ate more than their share of dinner —but one thing we all agreed on was that it was best to be in our room and out of the way when Vivian got home. She had a particularly cruel brand of touch magic and a nasty temper to match. There was a sort of electric energy that she could emit through her fingertips. It was a dull sort of pain, as she wasn't very strong, but she could hold it for long stretches, and on two at a time.

I lay awake that night thinking about Raphael. And how Yemoja Roux had, for the first time, seemed shaken. I wondered if they knew each other well, or even if she was afraid of the killer. I'd only seen her in action for a moment, many years ago. Just a flash of magenta hair and a bright smile. Of course, no one believed me, but my parents were there... *my parents*. I held their image in my mind, my mother's tender gaze and knowing smile. My father's quiet strength and optimism. They'd been gone a full year now and I felt numb to it. I'd made a huge mistake, one I couldn't take back. I learned the hard way that the only thing more dreadful than grief was indifference. And with that thought, I let myself drift to sleep.

Kaito

TWELVE

It seemed just a moment after I shut my eyes, my alarm woke me. I walked like a zombie through my empty house as I got ready. I was used to the silence, brought girls back when I felt lonely—but that morning I wanted my parents there to wish me luck. I'd almost called them to tell them about the test, but I couldn't bear the thought of disappointing them. Not for a third time, and I worried that if they knew and I didn't pass, they might stop coming home altogether.

Even though I hardly slept, my adrenaline would be enough. Surely no matter what opponent they pit me against or what they put on any written test, I could solve it. But I'd learned that this test wouldn't be like the first two, so I willed myself to push aside my expectations.

My nerves got the better of me when I arrived at the school and Reina was already there, tracing over the school's crest with her finger. "Couldn't sleep, huh?" I said.

She turned. "Hey, Kai. No, I slept just fine actually."

I clenched my jaw. I hated her tough guy act.

"How are you?" she asked as she fiddled with her necklace.

The gates to GFA crept open, the magical barrier stretching thinner until the school beyond it came into focus. It was just as striking as the first time I'd seen it, if not more so, as the grounds were covered in the silver sheen of morning dew. The top of the red-tiled roof glistened in the lazy yellow hues of the early morning sun that stretched out over the wall.

As we walked toward the school, I wondered if under her calm exterior Reina was nervous about the test. "Did you hear about Raphael Mazarin?" she asked.

I nodded.

"They have a lead. There was this arrow at the scene."

I stopped walking, my mind halting on the image of the man who'd smiled as he silently urged me to watch the news at the bus stop yesterday. "What do you mean, 'arrow?'"

She reached for my hand and turned it over, drawing the symbol on my forearm. It didn't seem like Reina was worried we'd have to face off in combat, otherwise she wouldn't have opened herself up for my attack by touching me. But as her fingers swept over my arm, I couldn't deny that it was at least similar to the man with the blue hair. *It had to be a coincidence.* "Hmm," I said dismissively. It wasn't my concern. The only thing I needed to worry about was passing the test.

We walked up the steps in silence and, just before I pushed open the door, Reina stopped me. She took my hand and took a deep breath, a warm smile on her face. "Good luck, Kai," she said.

Those were the exact words I craved that morning. I should've known she was still like this, that I couldn't beat it out of her. Not wanting to appear weak, I ripped my hand away. "Save it. You need it more than I do."

The door swung open and a large woman appeared. She was at least a hundred pounds overweight, her deep curves layered onto a wide frame, and every inch of her stunning. *Veranda Yarrow.* She was a known teacher of GFA, but there was little to no information online about what her gift actually was, only speculation. Her beauty was well known, though, undeniably so, but seeing her in person was a new experience altogether. Her blood-red hair flowed over her shoulders like lava over a volcano, her red lips plump, and her eyes had the warmth and kindness of a beloved relative. She wore thick black gloves that met her sleeves at the elbow, a rarity for Fae of her caliber. I'd rolled my eyes at the web debates about her size, but now that she stood in front of me, I knew firmly where I stood.

"You're so beautiful," Reina blurted. "Even more than your pictures online."

I bit back my smile, as she beat me to it, but it was all you could say after seeing Veranda.

"Thank you, darlin'," the red-haired goddess said, waving us through the door. "Your test will be held in exam room six. Please follow me."

We followed and my gaze was drawn to her wide hips as they swayed back and forth. *Back and forth.* Reina hit me, causing us both to chuckle.

Veranda stopped outside the door. "They want Miss Bennet first."

I nodded and the two women walked into the room, locking the door behind them with a click. I wasn't sure how long I'd be waiting outside, but every second was an eternity. Now that I'd met a few of the teachers and Fae, the stakes really sunk in.

Veranda Yarrow, I gulped. And no doubt her gloves were meant for the protection of others and not herself. I existed in a society where the amount of clothing reflected your power—where less coverage always meant more power. But now I was among Fae so Elite, their gifts so intense, they needed to protect others from them. It was almost too much to fathom. Of course, the most famous Fae, like Yemoja Roux, were not teachers. They were in the field, but the school had many gifted teachers and apprenticeships worth killing for.

My nerves flared as the lock clicked and Reina stepped out. Her gaze met mine and I wished I had the gift to know her thoughts.

"Enter," said a voice I recognized as Headmistress Tricorn. I stepped through, closing the door behind me.

My breath skipped as I walked toward the center of the room. There were five retired Fae seated at a long table— three more than either of my other two exams—and I knew every single one of them.

Veranda sat on the left, and beside her was Maxim Tuberose, a retired seer. The headmistress sat at the center with a displeased look on her face. To the right of her was the professor of confections, Mr. Greene, and finally, all the way to the right was Dr. Havier Azul who had a healing gift. Havier Azul's presence told me I could expect some form of combat in this exam as he'd also been at one of my other exams, the one where they'd tested physical combat. I shuddered at the memory—how the flat empty terrain and my quick-footed opponent had prevented me from being able to use my gift. It was a disgraceful performance that I promised myself not to repeat.

"Hello," I said, my voice cracking. "I'm Kaito Na—"

"We know who you are," Headmistress Tricorn said. "We contacted your old school, we know about your expulsion."

I swallowed hard, my throat tightening.

"So before we continue with this exam, we'd like to ask you some questions."

I nodded.

"In your own words, what was the nature of your expulsion?"

I took a deep breath. "Reina and I have a sort of..." *What word was I even looking for?* "rivalry."

She pursed her lips, pushing me to continue.

"Our pranks got out of hand."

She folded her hands. "Do you think it would cause a problem if I admit you both to my school?"

"No, ma'am," I said, too nervous to meet the gazes of the other teachers.

A strained smile touched her mouth. "If we were to select only one of you, who do you think deserves the spot. And why?"

"I do," I said. "My gift is far stronger than hers—if she even has one. I'm certain I'll have a greater chance of becoming Fae post-graduation."

The teachers exchanged glances but their faces told me I'd misspoken.

"What is it?" I demanded.

Professor Greene said, "We find it interesting because Reina also said she believed you should be given the position."

My pulse raced. "She did?"

The headmistress leaned forward. "One looking out for himself, the other striving to protect others..." She tilted her head. "Which of those sound like Fae to you?" She pressed her lips into a line and I dropped my gaze to the floor. Fuck. I was failing *again*.

Reina

THIRTEEN

The door swung open and Kai stormed through. "This is *bullshit*," he said, pushing past me.

I gripped his arm and pulled him back into the room. "Look, whatever he said, you have to read between the lines. He's not great with words."

"I don't need your help," Kai said under his breath.

Maxim Tuberose spoke, his voice velvety smooth. "He's not the type of temperament suitable for Fae in training."

"You're wrong," I said. "I know him. I've been ungifted my whole life and in middle school Kai and I were always targeted by Elites, but Kai landed in the clinic much more than me. He always did what he could to—"

"And how about after middle school?" Veranda asked. "Your former principal gave us the impression he bullied you quite regularly."

I dropped my gaze. He certainly did, and I wasn't sure if it was our past that compelled me to speak on his behalf, but we'd gotten into this mess together and I had also been to blame for our expulsion. "He doesn't want me to get hurt. That's it. It's his messed-up way of protecting me."

Headmistress Tricorn spoke, "You admit it's messed up."

"All he needs is a great teacher. That's why we're here."

The room fell silent and, after a moment, the headmistress nodded to Veranda.

She said, "Then let the exam begin. But be warned, there will be no talking your way through this time."

The teachers leaned forward with anticipation as Veranda stood in front of me. I shook, my legs going weak beneath me.

Headmistress Tricorn said, "Miss Yarrow will use her gift to determine the potential of your gifts. This was chosen mostly for Reina, as she does not yet know her gift, though we can sense a hint of its type. Kaito, if you're as strong as you think you are, you should have no problem passing the exam."

Veranda pulled off her black gloves, her perfectly manicured hands yet another show of her beauty.

"May I, baby?" she asked, holding her hands out. It was strange to see someone so powerful ask permission to touch. I nodded quickly. She had the answer I needed. She could tell me if I had any hope of becoming Fae.

I slid my hands onto hers, her head rolling back and her eyes snapping shut. I held my breath, willing any power within me to her hands, but of course I felt none. She lifted her head and opened her eyes, a deep sadness in them. She teared, putting her hand to her heart.

"What is it?" Maxim asked, but she ignored him. Instead, she looked at me, as if in search of something. "Your parents..." she said, sending my heart into a frantic race. "I know what you did," she whispered.

I felt Kai's gaze on my face and I hoped Veranda wouldn't say more.

She held her hands back out. "Let's try again."

I hesitated before putting my hands on hers. She'd uncovered my darkest secret in an instant and I was afraid of what else she might discover. Just as before, her head rolled back, her breaths became labored, and I resisted the urge to rip my hands away. Finally, she lifted her head with a gentle smile at the corners of her mouth.

"It's as we thought. Just like her."

I shook my head. "Like who?"

"Yemoja Roux," she said.

My gaze moved to Kai as a rush of emotions flooded me. I was *gifted*. I was gifted like Yemoja Roux. I clenched my teeth to suppress every emotion swirling through me because Veranda had already moved to Kai, her hands held out for him to touch.

"Your turn," she said with scarlet lips. He put his hands in hers and I found myself nearly as nervous for him as I'd been for myself. My heartbeat raced, to a new rhythm, one that echoed "Yemoja Roux, Yemoja Roux."

Veranda's breaths deepened. She began to shake, then convulse. *Something was wrong.* Her breaths grew more erratic. I gasped as blood shot from her nose and she collapsed onto the floor. Kaito stood stunned as Dr. Azul leaped over the table and ran to Veranda. Blood-red tears dripped from her eyes as the other teachers encircled her in a panic.

"What happened?" Kai asked, staring at his hands in horror.

Dr. Azul dropped to his knees and placed his hands around Veranda's throat. In seconds, her shaking stopped and the flow of blood from her ears and nose slowed. I stared down with a mix of terror and awe as Dr. Azul's gift took over, easing her convulsions.

The headmistress' gaze moved to Kai. "Maxim..."

Without another word, the gray-haired elder stood and forcefully grabbed Kai's hand. The time for asking permission had come and gone. I'd never seen a seer work in real time. But just as it looked online, his eyes lit up a radiant blue that filled the room. We all held our breath as he spoke. "The path is not set. There is greatness here, but it is not yet determined whether it will be nurtured by the Fae or their enemies."

Havier Azul looked up. "I need to get her to my office." The four teachers worked together to lift Veranda, a task Kai could have managed with a touch. But Kai was terrified. I understood why he didn't volunteer. In fact, I'd have understood if he never touched anyone again.

"Stay on campus, but speak of this to no one," the head-mistress said as they carried Veranda out of the room, her consciousness dimming as they went.

Kai stared down at his hands, his mouth open. Veranda's blood was smeared across the floor.

He turned to me. "I... I didn't—"

"It's okay, Kai. No one thinks you did."

"You know my gift. It's levitation... I... couldn't have..."

My skin prickled when a clear streak fell down his face. "Let's go get some air," I whispered. He said nothing for a long time as he continued to stare at his hands.

"It's okay, Kai." I wanted to reach out and touch him. I wanted to pull him in for a hug. But the memory of Veranda's bleeding eyes was fresh and I was afraid. I took a deep breath, thinking of something my mother used to say: *Never let fear stop you.* I reached out for him, but he hovered and slid himself back out of reach, his heels never hitting the ground.

"Let's go outside. We need some air," I said again. I opened the door and felt him follow silently behind. We burst through the front door, where we'd come in, and rushed back to the courtyard as if fleeing the school we both longed to enroll in. I turned into a hedge maze and wove through the floral labyrinth. The sun's rays warmed the top of my head, soaking into my dark curls as I turned a corner and spotted a bench that was tucked away. I didn't want anyone to see us. I didn't want Kai to feel ashamed to cry.

I sat first and Kai sat on the opposite end, taking extra care not to touch me. We didn't need words. The quiet of the morning in the garden calmed us both after a long while, and when he was ready, he spoke. "Thank you for what you did in there."

I shrugged. "It was nothing."

"Not to me."

I chewed on my lip.

"You know, none of that was really true. That stuff you said about me protecting you."

"I figured," I said, but the bite of disappointment lingered. I had, of course, made the mistake of thinking he cared. That's what I wished was true. "Can I ask you what it is that you hate about me?"

He shook his head, rubbing his hands on his knees. "I don't know. I guess I hate that it never gets to you."

"Wh—"

"You just come into school every day with a smile, as if the whole world hasn't gone to shit. I mean, all those years you thought you were ungifted. What the fuck did you have to smile about?"

I let my hand drop to the bench between us.

"I had this amazing gift and everything still hurt. So... I guess I wanted to hurt you. Or for you to, I don't know, understand." He chuckled, but it was a sad sound and the corners of his eyes glistened. He turned his confused gaze on me, "Does that sound like Fae to you?"

"Kaito." I reached out but froze before I touched him, a flare of fear halting me. "Maybe you're being a little hard on yourself." I half smiled, "I used to spend a lot of time with you, you're not so bad."

He sighed, but his expression softened. "You're too nice, Rei. You don't recognize a monster when you see one."

I grinned, "No, you're right. You're a total asshole."

His face brightened, "And yet here you are, as ever, trying to rescue me."

"Well, yeah, you're hot now so..."

He laughed and nudged my shoulder with his.

I shook my head. "It would be such a waste."

I realized we'd been inching closer, growing bold in our desire to touch.

"You've always been beautiful."

His cell phone floated from his pocket and he swiped through before holding up the image of me he took at the pier.

I took a shallow breath, "You did keep it... So why did you stop being my friend?"

He sighed, "It's complicated."

I glared.

He rolled his eyes, "Well, everything changed and..." His gaze moved to me, "I don't mean just me getting a gift. I figured the gap in our abilities would separate us eventually. Besides, at the time, I thought I'd get over it." He slipped his phone into his pocket and stared down at his hands. "I almost reached out to you when I heard about your parents, but I chickened out."

Stunned, I whispered, "I wish you had." I thoughtlessly touched his arm. We froze, staring at our touching skin, my heartbeat turbulent in my chest.

A sudden heat burned me and I wasn't sure if I would soon meet the same fate as Veranda, or if my body's reaction wasn't gift related at all.

His gaze rose to mine.

A wave of his gift pulsed through my blood and I was weightless, hovering ever so slightly off the bench. My breath caught as I felt myself move closer. My thoughts dimmed, leaving me with a burning hunger, though I wasn't sure for what. Kai reached for me, his warm palms on my cheeks. I gripped his tie, losing myself as I pulled him in. His lips were hot on mine, his tongue numbing any thoughts of stopping. His hands slid over my body as I gripped his hair. He bit down on my bottom lip and I whimpered. He pulled away slowly, his eyes wide. He stood so quickly that, if I hadn't been hanging in his gift, I would have toppled to the ground.

"I'm so sorry," he said, running his hand through his hair.

I felt myself lower to the bench, a riot still raging in my chest. "No, it's okay. I was the one who... pulled th-the..."

"No, it's me, I shouldn't have--" he pressed his lips together. "I'm sorry Reina."

I stood. "It's okay Kai. It was just a kiss."

"Was it?"

I swallowed a lump in my throat, my pulse racing. He was right. It was anything but just a kiss.

He took the silence as my response and nodded before jogging back into the maze of hedges without another word.

I sighed, was walking not fast enough? I was left alone to wonder who Kaito really was: the sweet boy from my childhood, or the bully. I was an idiot. His excuses were flimsy at best, and I spent years in pain because of him and I still went for it. Even worse, I still wanted to.

Kaito

FOURTEEN

The funny thing about momentum was, once it started, no matter if it was positive or negative, it was hard to stop. First, I practically murdered a legendary Fae, though I have no clue how. I botched my entrance exam. And worst of all, I kissed Reina.... *Again*. At least I didn't break her bones this time. I don't know what I was expecting. For her to push me away and slap me for all the things I'd done to her, I guess. But she pulled me closer, and if I hadn't suddenly remembered she was a virgin, I might've taken her right there. Why didn't she stop me? And why did it take me so long to stop myself?

I'd been horrible to her. If she felt something between us, she was an idiot too. I felt sick. I was the ultimate dickhead, *a failure*, and possibly a murderer. I understood why my parents never came home. I understood why I was always alone. Something was broken inside me. There was a darkness I couldn't seem to keep at bay. If I let myself slip up again with Reina, eventually I'd break her too—just like I'd wanted to.

My reeling thoughts were interrupted by a figure coming down the stairs. Professor Greene spotted me on the lawn. I scanned his face, half expecting to be arrested on the spot, but his shoulders were relaxed, his bun bouncing on the back of his head in time with his bow-legged gait.

"Veranda will be fine. She's resting," he said, and I felt a wave of relief crash into me.

"Do you know what happened?" I asked. I wasn't sure I wanted the answer.

He sucked in a breath, as if he were unsure if he should tell me what he knew. "We think that your potential may have been greater than her body could handle."

A pang of nervousness hit my stomach. "Does that happen a lot?"

He shook his head.

I swallowed a lump in my throat. Too much power? Was there such a thing? I knew my gift was exceptional, I'd discovered levitation had many uses, but it also had limits. I'd completely botched the physical entrance exam. I wasn't even strong enough to be admitted. My thoughts were interrupted by the professor's next words.

"The headmistress has decided to admit both of you. Pack your belongings and come at the same time tomorrow to move in and start orientation," he said, his gaze moving past me.

I spun to see Reina a few yards away. "Thank you, professor," she said, and coldly turned away without so much as a glance at me.

Professor Greene eyed me, as if he understood everything

that had transpired with our body language alone. He nodded at Reina, a gesture that to me seemed to say, *Go get her*.

I smirked and jogged after her, the news of our acceptance surging through me like a great light driving away my dark thoughts and apprehensions. I threw my arm around her. "Hey, classmate!"

"You know we were classmates before, right?"

"Not at GFA," I cooed. "Look, Reina, about earlier... I'm sorry. I-I promise I won't do that again. I was overwhelmed and just kind of lost control. Let's just pretend it never happened."

"*That's* your explanation? Seriously?"

"Let's celebrate tonight."

She raised an eyebrow and it looked like I might get the slap I was looking for earlier.

I laughed. "I mean dinner."

She moved my arm off her shoulders. "I don't know, Kaito."

"Please, let me do this. I have to thank you for getting us both in GFA."

She grinned. "So you admit I got us in?" She pulled out her phone and held it up. "Can you say that again for the camera?"

"I will. After dinner."

She sighed. "Fine."

"Great, come to my place at 8."

"You're not taking the bus home?" she asked.

I floated my cell phone out of my pocket and into my hand. "Nah, I'm going to call my parents and stuff. You know, tell them the news."

She smiled and headed for the gate.

"Don't forget, Reina," I called. "Eight o'clock."

She called back, "I'll never forget about you."

The sweetness of the memory of that day at the pier, echoed

through me. Back then, I'd been looking for the right moment to kiss her for weeks, and by the ocean that day I wanted to go for it. My nerves got the best of me and I was going to chicken out until she said those *exact* words.

Today I'd once again stolen a kiss, and it surprised me as much as it must have done her. It was a mistake I wouldn't repeat, but I was too excited to spend the night at my empty house. My "friends" would no doubt be jealous and hateful about it, and how could I explain to them that ungifted Reina and I had taken the exam together? I chuckled at the irony, that after all the years of torture I'd dished out, Reina was still all I had.

Reina

FIFTEEN

It was official. My crush on Kaito had returned with a vengeance. All I wanted was to go to GFA and leave my old life behind, but no. My stupid heart made me fight on his behalf to get him in. Kaito... the freaking master of my torment. Never mind that aneurysm or whatever happened to him earlier. Now we were going to have to live on campus together. My mind shouted in distress, but my stomach was in knots and jumbled with butterflies. My heart raced. Kaito *kissed* me... then he promised never to do it again.

My skin stung with disappointment as my mind replayed that promise on loop. Why? Didn't he want to do that again? I didn't even want it to stop that time. It was a far cry from our first kiss, and I felt... *hot*. I scrambled to crack open the bus's window, but it didn't help much. I heard the whipping of the wind but didn't feel it.

I pressed my forehead to the glass. In all the times I'd imagined what it would be like to kiss him, *really* kiss him, I'd certainly never imagined *that*. The exam, GFA, and my newly-discovered gift had taken a back seat to the kiss I could still feel on my lips.

The bus hit a sudden bump and my head slammed against the glass with a smack and, before I could react, it happened a second time. *Ouch*. That was karma one hundred percent. I took a deep breath, willing all my butterflies to drop dead. I could control my emotions. I'd gotten over Kai before, I could do it again. Instead of dwelling on the kiss, I thought of all the times Kai had humiliated or hurt me. I thought of how many nights I cried myself to sleep. And by the time the bus stopped to let me out, a few blocks from home, I had worked myself up enough to cancel our dinner plans.

Instead of going straight home, I decided to walk a few laps around the block. I found myself check-listing what I had to do rather than deal with such a weighted day. First, I had to pack my things. That would be easy enough; I hardly owned anything since I'd sold it all. Even with my inheritance, I had to sell everything to have enough for... I sighed. I hated the empty feeling that popped up when I thought about it. It was a void where something important belonged—something I'd given up. I debated whether to tell Vivian that I got into GFA and was moving out. *Fuck that*. There was no universe in which that conversation went smoothly. Finally, I needed to cancel my date. I mean *dinner*. It would only take a second to send the text, but... I could squeeze that in later. I saw something move out of the corner of my eye and spun.

I gasped. William Citrine, a Bronze Tier Fae, jutted past on the far side of the street, fire spurting from the bottom of his shoes. His trademark golden hair was almost reflective in the orange glow of the low sun, his gift blazing from his feet like he were wearing rocket boots.

"William Citrine!" I called, fumbling for my cell phone in hopes I could snap a picture, but in a flash he was gone.

It was a sign. Everything would be okay. I felt a little bit cheerful as I rounded the corner. After all, my dream of going to GFA had come true. I was finally *gifted,* and I wasn't sure how, but they said it reminded them of Yemoja Roux. I almost broke into a skip. The sun was setting and streetlights had already clicked on. I pulled open the door to my house, imagining what my roommates would say when I told them. No doubt they wouldn't believe me. I was delighted. I froze as Vivian stood at the base of the stairs. She shouldn't have been home yet. She stood with her hands on her hips, nodding as if we were having a silent conversation.

"Your school called," she said. "Why didn't you tell me you got expelled?" My gaze was drawn to movement at the top of the stairs; several of my roommates peeked around the corner.

"You don't understand. I—"

She grabbed my hand and the electric pain shot up my elbow, spreading to the rest of my body. "I got into GFA," I said through clenched teeth. "I'm *gifted.*"

She chewed loudly on her gum. "You're a fucking liar, that's what you are."

My body screamed for release. "It's true," I spat, feeling vomit rise to my throat. "I start tomorrow."

"The fuck you are," she said.

Tears swelled in my eyes, her gift twisting each cell in my body. I writhed. *I'm gifted.* Tears spilled down my cheeks. *I'm gifted.* Something snapped inside me. If I was gifted, I wouldn't take another moment of this. I gripped her second hand and pushed my gift to my hands. She stared back at me stunned, and after a moment's delay, she burst into a fit of laughter.

Veranda Yarrow was wrong. I was not gifted. Not at all. And Vivian held me in torturous pain for a full hour, but I'd already cried myself dry by then.

I splashed my face with water, my bloodshot eyes and red nose an accurate reflection of how I felt on a day that was meant to be triumphant. My cell phone buzzed in my pocket.

Kai:

My parents were so excited about the news they came home early. Reschedule?

I sent a thumbs up and felt my eyes begin to water again. Of course. I was happy for him, but the ache leftover in my chest told me how much I'd actually wanted to go.

Later that night, I was violently shaken from my sleep by one of my roommates. I sat up. "What's going on?" I asked, squinting through the dark to see who'd woken me.

"Another Fae died," she said, and I knew it was Alyssa by her voice.

"Who?" I asked, and I internally begged for her to say anything besides Yemoja Roux.

"Will Citrine."

Kaito

SIXTEEN

As I stepped out onto the fourth floor of the boy's dormitory and the smell of stale sweat hit me, I regretted my decision not to commute. My parents had encouraged me to give dorm life a try, but I couldn't remember, for the life of me, why I thought it would be a good idea. It was nice having my parents back. We'd spent the whole night discussing the circumstances of the entrance exam, all of which I fabricated and they fell back into their parental roles like they hadn't given me a debit card and abandoned me for the last two years. They were finally proud of me and I'd do just about anything not to mess that up... except live in this disgusting dorm.

I dragged my suitcases through the empty hallway, observing that the size of the rooms didn't appear to be much bigger than jail cells, but found relief that everyone appeared to be in class already. I wanted to get my bearings before I was forced to defend myself against the most Elite students in the country.

Then I heard it, the thrum of a guitar pouring out of a room at the end of the hallway. *For the love of god, please don't let that be my room.* As I read the numbers on the doors and moved closer to the end, I began to give up hope. "Fuck," I said as I arrived, double-checking that the room I'd been assigned was in fact the one with the guitar-playing douche in it.

I stepped in and my eyes were immediately drawn to the huge posters on the right side of the room, which prominently displayed a familiar pop idol. *Oh god, what the fuck?* My concern quickly changed to a cringe as my gaze lowered to the guitar slung guy with unmistakable blonde curly hair. I had to press my lips together to keep from laughing. "Carter Mason?" I asked. "Seriously?"

He brushed his curly blonde hair out of his eyes only for it to fall back into place. He grinned up at me without missing a note on his acoustic guitar. "The one and only."

Sure enough, splayed out in his desk chair with his bare feet up on the bed, was the once legendary pop star who dominated the charts in his early teens.

I turned back to the door. "I'll just get a transfer."

"Wait, bro," he said. "Listen to this part." I sighed, debating whether I should use my gift to smash his guitar. The melody switched to a slower more soulful tempo. The notes danced through the air and lulled me into a sort of involuntary calm. I gaped, but the shock I felt was instantly wiped away with every pluck of his strings.

"Chill, man. Just chill."

I pulled my luggage into the small room and sat on the empty bed to the left as my new roommate played on. A few moments later, his hands stopped and he coddled his guitar down on his bed as if it were a baby he was putting into a crib.

I ran my hand through my hair. "What was that?"

"My gift allows me to help people relax."

I swallowed. "But you didn't touch me."

"Sound waves, man."

It was unfathomable. Only Yemoja Roux could use magic without touch... This was a strange exception. "What else can you make people do?"

He shook his head. "Just relax. It may sound lame, but the last thing your opponent wants to be during an attack is relaxed. Plus the teachers allow me to use my gift outside the classrooms and training zones since I can't really cause harm with it. As your mentor, I should mention that using your gift willy-nilly is a big no-no. If you use it outside of the designated areas, you will get thrown out of here fast as shit."

I crossed my arms. "How do you know who's the strongest if you can't fight?"

"Dude, relax. You can fight all you want in the designated zones, plus there's the class ranking. I suggest you learn quickly what everyone's gift is before you go challenging people. I guarantee everyone here will know yours, although it's been impossible to get any intel on the new girl, Reina." He raised his eyebrows. "You know her, right? What can you tell me about her?"

I shrugged. "No idea. I don't think she even knows what her gift is."

"Alright, man, well get unpacked. I'm supposed to show you the campus."

I unzipped my suitcase and started pulling out my clothes. The prison cell-sized room was symmetrical with twin-sized beds pushed to the side walls. A desk and chair for each of us at the back with a window above them and an impossibly small dresser on either side of the door. My gaze drifted to the posters on the opposite walls. "Why do you have posters of yourself hung up? That's so weird."

He crawled out of his chair and lay in his bed. "Just reliving the glory days, my friend."

An odd thought popped into my head. "Wait, did you use your gift when you were on stage and stuff?"

He beamed. "You think they liked me for my pretty face?"

Reina

SEVENTEEN

When I woke up, I felt a new sense of purpose surge through me. I was finally going to begin attendance at GFA and leave my old life behind, along with my past mistakes. I found a moment to pull each of my roommates aside to say goodbye, but most of them didn't believe my story. I'd visit when I could, but I knew moving on to GFA made keeping in touch unlikely.

Considering this was my fresh start, I was certainly bringing a lot of baggage to it. I'd literally only packed a backpack full of belongings, but emotionally I carried a lifetime of expectations, along with newly-invigorated feelings for Kai.

On the bus ride, I decided to lay low at this school. I'd fly under the radar and sharpen my skills without drawing the wrath of the school's Elites. Even with all my thoughts consumed with daydreams about my new life, none of it sunk in until I was standing outside my usual place at the school's gate. I reached out to trace my fingers habitually over the crest when the doors opened.

I stepped through the magical barrier, revealing the school that sat tucked away behind it. I nearly choked with emotion, as I'd so often imagined what it would feel like when those gates opened for me. I walked through the gardens toward the front building and climbed the stairs as I'd done the day before. This time, at the top of the stairs stood a girl who looked about my age.

She had long, enviable legs, a tight blush pink ponytail, and a heavy black eyeliner that winged out from the sides of her ocean blue eyes.

"Hurry up," she groaned.

I skipped up the stairs. "Hi, I'm Reina."

She rolled her eyes. "Pleasure. I'm Miranda Callix, your mentor apparently."

Oh great. She hated me already. "Oh, well if you're busy, I'm sure I can figure it out on my own."

"And disobey Headmistress Tricorn? No, thank you. Just move quicker and don't ask me any questions. I'll tell you what you need to know. By the way, where's your shit? You were supposed to bring your stuff today."

I lifted my engorged backpack. "In here."

"That's all you have?"

I nodded. "I'm an orphan, so..."

She tossed her ponytail over her shoulder. "Luckily we wear school uniforms here, so no one will really notice you're poor. Except at the end of the term is the Winter Ball and you'll need a dress for that."

I followed her into the main hall, secretly screaming with delight as I observed the iconic maroon blazer with the school crest on the left, black gloves, collared shirt, and black, maroon, and white plaid pants. I couldn't wait to get my uniform, and I couldn't believe I was actually a student.

Instead of heading up the stairs, she led me down a different corridor. There were large portraits of high achieving Fae who had once attended the academy. I stopped at one in particular: *William Citrine*. It was hard to believe that a Fae so great he had his portrait hung in his alma mater could be dead. He wasn't even twenty-five.

"Keep up," Miranda bellowed, and I followed as she turned into an enormous ballroom. The vaulted ceilings were painted with clouds dipped in pastel colors and went up at least four stories. The entire south end of the room was made of glass that poured the light of the morning onto the hardwood floors. And just on the other side of the glass lay the rest of the campus.

"Eeeeep!" I squealed and ran to the windows to get a better look, my voice carrying through the gold-trimmed ballroom. "This is amazing!"

Miranda nudged me out of the way and pushed open what I'd previously thought were glass windows, but they must've been doors because she stepped out onto the balcony.

"Okay, left to right," she said, pointing to the closest building to us. It was a basic shape made from sand-colored stones, but had expensive looking moldings around the windows and the front door, and lush green ivy crawling up the side. "That's the girl's dorm, Pink House. You can get your room assignment and key from the security desk in the foyer. Usually you'd be assigned to a room with your mentor, but I happen to have my own room." She smiled brightly but it dimmed when she looked back at me, as if she'd only just remembered she was mentoring me.

She pointed to an identical building on the far side. "That's

Blue House. We can totally sneak in and hook up and stuff, but don't try it unless you know what you're doing. If you get caught, they'll throw you out." She looked me up and down. "Not that you'll need it. You're obviously a virgin."

My gaze bulged. "You can tell that by my face?"

She tilted her head. "I don't know, it's more about how someone carries themselves."

I started fiddling with my charm as she continued her pseudo-tour. "That big building in the back is the class hall. Obvi, it has all the classrooms."

I gulped. It looked more like a mansion, with its huge windows and ivy-covered stones, than a school. In the back right of the campus was a modern-looking building that appeared to be made of mostly iron, concrete, and glass.

"That's the student center. It's got a cafeteria, ping pong tables, a movie theater, clinic... I don't know, maybe a library. I don't spend much time there, obvi."

I wasn't sure what was supposed to be obvious about it. Or if she just liked the word.

On the far right were two massive snow globe shaped buildings that seemed to capture the sunlight and shoot it through the iridescent walls. "And what are *those*?" I asked.

"Those are the combat zones. One is for physical training, you know like weapons and stuff. It's for upperclassmen, so you won't use it this year, and the other is for gift training. At some point you can meet with Professor Cordovan to figure out how they can accommodate you in the gift training arena, since everyone is different." She put a hand on her hip, and she looked a lot like the fashion models plastered all over social media. "By the way, what *is* your gift?"

"I... I don't know."

She raised an eyebrow. "Playing it coy, I see. It's not a bad strategy except I'm fifth in our class and you don't want to make an enemy of me."

"Who's first?"

"You're so new it hurts. Oden Gates, obviously. And just so you don't do anything you might regret, he and I are kind of a thing."

I put my hands up in surrender. "Got it."

"In fact, the Noble Four are all sort of off limits to you."

I nodded. "I just came here to study."

"Atta girl," she said.

"Let's hit the Pink House first so you can drop off your little homeless lady bag. I also seriously encourage you to start wearing gloves. You wouldn't want to be seen as conceited."

I bit back a laugh. "You're right. That *would* be the worst."

"I mean, the students can use their gifts on objects and stuff around campus, but not on each other outside of the training zones. I don't mean to tell you this to make you feel safe, I just want you to know that when you step into those domes, prepare yourself for a brawl."

It was a blatant threat. So much for laying low. *Still*, as I followed Miranda down the stairs of the main building balcony, down to the GFA campus, I knew there was nothing that could mess up my day. Then, like clockwork, across the way I saw Kai.

EIGHTEEN

I saw Reina coming down the stairs from the building with the headmistress' office. Her gaze was locked on me, giving me a rush of whatever was left over from our kiss. Though Carter was on my heels and I'd practically begged him to show me the gift training arena first, I was curious how Reina was doing on her first day. That's when I noticed the bombshell showing her around.

She was all legs with pouty lips and a checklist of features that looked like they'd been strategically picked from a catalog.

"Good spot, bro. That's Miranda," Carter said. "And you already know the new girl."

We met up outside the girl's dormitory, my gaze transfixed on Miranda. Reina cleared her throat. "Hey, Kai, how's your first day going?"

"Just started," I said half-heartedly. "Who's your friend?"

Miranda interjected, "Mentor, actually."

Okay, rude. With two words she'd lost my interest. It was a clear shot at Reina, and no one messed with Reina but me.

"Rei," I said, shifting my attention, "this is my mentor slash roommate."

"Carter Mason," Reina said, her eyes bulging just as mine had when I'd first seen him, but then she touched her necklace charm and I felt a touch of jealousy flair. Carter unslung his guitar from his shoulder to give Reina a better look, but her gaze was locked on his face, like a young child meeting a mall Santa.

Miranda patted her gloved hand on the top of Reina's head. "Good girl. Stay in your lane. These are your people," she said.

I half expected Reina to jump in and defend herself, but her face beamed with suppressed amusement. I relaxed, realizing I'd felt defensive for no reason. Reina would probably be okay. Of course someone as basic as Miranda wouldn't actually get to her. Still, I was certain there was an insult for me in there and I wasn't going to let that slide.

I smirked. "I'll be one of the Nobles by the end of the day."

She rolled her eyes. "Aren't you the guy who failed the entrance exam twice?"

I gritted my teeth. "Well, it's been a pleasure," I said, hoping Miranda heard the bite in my tone.

She grinned menacingly. "Right. You better get to it if you're going to rank up by the end of the day."

Without another word, I turned away and headed for the arena while Carter slung his guitar back over his shoulder. "Man, that was intense," Carter said when the girls were out of earshot.

"She's a fucking nightmare."

Carter shrugged. "She's like some high-budget porn star mixed with a sex cosplay goddess. I don't care if she's a bitch."

"You have issues, man." But I had to admit he had a point.

"Honestly," he said, "the students here are the best in the world. The elite of the Elite. Don't let my charm fool you, I've already interviewed with a hostage negotiation Fae division and have a contract to do my apprenticeship with them next summer. Everyone here is going places, and their egos match. I suggest you get kind of used to it." He put a hand on my shoulder. "You might've been a big deal at your old school, but now that you're here, you're all the way at the bottom with a nasty rumor about failed exams to boot."

I shrugged his hand off. "Let's go," I said, dismissing him as my attention was drawn to a familiar face inside the arena—Oden Gates.

"Wait! Stop," Carter said. "I didn't realize there were students in there this period. We better come back when the area is free."

"Relax. I'm not going to do something stupid."

"That's what someone whose going to do something stupid would say." I heard him, but his words hardly processed because I was already on the move.

I pushed open the translucent door and stepped into the arena. Once inside, it reminded me of the giant greenhouse at our local zoo with panels of partially filtered light pouring through. The stadium had gift-sealed panes that were reminiscent of the seal around the school's outer wall. I recognized Oden right away, but my attention skipped over him as I sized up the three other guys in his little crew. They were the school's Nobles. I knew this because I recognized every one of them. Starting on the left was the 5'5'" prodigy from New Valand, Enzo McCain. He had slick brown hair and a smirk that insisted he was too cool to be here. He made a name for himself at the biannual World Varsity Tournament last year for possessing a gift that was hotly debated. Like most who were trying to become Fae, he never gave any direct answers about his gift in interviews, but one thing was certain; when he touched his shoes, he ran quite a bit faster than what should be humanly possible.

Next was Prince Finn Warsham, the actual fucking third prince of the four Zalmian princes, and the only of them invited to attend the academy. Like his photos online, he was a tall black man whose hair always looked like he'd just come from his barber and whose posture was so straight it made me want to loosen my tie and slouch. There was almost no information at all about his gift, but I had the feeling I would find out soon enough.

The last of Oden's stooges was Quan Levout, the legend who used his doppleganger gift to fix the Varsity Tournament. He'd been disqualified, of course, but the subsequent lime green hair trend lasted an entire year.

I was admittedly starstruck seeing them all in one place but knew what I needed to do to earn their respect.

"It's a little reckless for you to step foot in here on your first day," Oden said.

Carter grabbed my arm. "Come on, man, let's get out of here."

I yanked my arm away, steadying my nerves. "Actually, Oden, I came to challenge you."

Reina

NINETEEN

T he number of celebrities at this school was insane. I could distinctly remember swooning over Carter Mason as a middle schooler. In fact, Kaito was there for that phase. He'd seen my bedroom walls plastered with pictures of the blonde pop star. I cringed at the possibility that my little crush might find its way into the conversation.

Miranda and I headed to the girls' dorm and, besides Kai and Carter, the rest of the campus seemed deserted. It didn't seem like students skipped class around here. I almost dreaded how I might feel when the bell rang and students spilled into the court-yard. Oden Gates was somewhere around here, along with royalty and some of the most gifted people on the planet. The more I thought about it, the more I felt like an imposter.

I felt my nerves soothe when a familiar face smiled at me from outside the dorm. Professor Greene perked up. "I'll take it from here, Miranda. You may return to your morning classes."

"I haven't shown her to her dorm yet," Miranda said.

"She won't be needing it for a while."

She shot me a worried look, brushing a stray wisp of pink hair out of her eyes.

"Thank you, Miranda, for the tour and the advice."

She gave a half-smile before heading toward the back of campus where the mansion-like class hall was situated.

Professor Greene sucked in a sharp breath. "How's your first day going?" he asked.

I smiled through gritted teeth. "It's a little overwhelming. Did you know *Carter Mason* goes here?"

He nodded, but his expression didn't imply he shared my excitement. "There are many celebrities in attendance here. You'll get used to it." He shifted his weight. "I... I think we need to have a discussion."

I swallowed hard. First he stopped me from moving in and now this? "Are you kicking me out already?" I said with a smile I hoped would break his grim expression.

"That's entirely up to you." With a wave of his hand, he motioned for me to follow him back to the front building and it sent a new wave of dread beneath my skin. By the time we reached his office, I was almost in tears.

"Take a seat," he said.

I sat like a woman condemned. I felt my posture slump as I tried to disappear into the chair.

"As you must know by now, the first term for every student here at GFA is a probationary period. If you don't show significant progress on your midterm, you will be dropped from the program."

I shook my head, my throat constricting too tightly to form words. *Dropped from the program?* I shuddered at the idea of returning to the group home and how long Ms. Vivian would torture me when I returned.

"Since you and a few others have transferred this year, that means you'll need to have your skills up to par for the winter midterm."

I nodded. Three months wasn't a long time for me to pull it together, but it was a chance and that was all I needed. Still, I doubted from his tone that he was sharing the worst of the news.

I held my breath as I waited for the gavel to drop.

"I've spoken to Ms. Yarrow and she told me what you've done."

I gulped, tears pricking my eyes as they threatened to spill out.

"I'm only going to ask this once. Why did you do it?"

I straightened in my chair. I'd made many mistakes in my life, but the one Veranda Yarrow found inside me was the greatest. If I got thrown from GFA to answer for it, I'd accept it.

"My parents died a year ago. I had no one, the grief was overwhelming and I thought it was the only way to move on."

"I see," he said, lifting his nameplate and turning it over in his hands. "Ms. Yarrow thinks your gift may be tied to your emotions as a sort of way to focus and aim them. You can't reach them, let alone fully master them, if you've taken a confection to dull your feelings of loss. You need the full spectrum."

"So you're kicking me out."

He tilted his head. "I have to ask how you came to find such a rare confection. Unlike what I gave you, which might only last a few minutes, this could only be made by someone as powerful as Fae and would be expensive and extremely difficult to locate."

Despair pooled in my stomach. "I received a large inheritance."

"That's quite a sacrifice. You must've been in a great deal of pain."

"Yes, I must've." But I didn't know for sure. Even the memory of that time seemed drained of emotion.

"I can make a confection to counteract the one you took, but I need to know if that's something you'd be open to."

I stood. "Yes." I put both hands flat on his desk, leaning into him. "Please," I begged, my voice cracking. It was a miracle. A second chance at life. In less than a day, GFA was offering me everything I'd ever wanted.

Professor Greene looked down. "Before you agree, I must tell you that this will be an agonizing experience. Every emotion you've suppressed over the last year will hit you at once. You'll have to spend the week in the infirmary because the sudden burst of grief and despair often leads to thoughts of self-harm."

I sat back in my chair, but the professor didn't look at me, and I wondered if he was afraid of what he might see.

"You are not the first case I've seen. I've seen that particular confection used after a breakup or after losing a great deal of money. I fear the amount of grief you will need to process at once may be too great for you to overcome. So I'll give you the choice—leave GFA with grief suppressed, or risk your life to undo it, to unlock your full potential."

Fear tore through me so quickly that it pushed the breath from my lungs, and that's how I knew I'd already made my choice.

Kaito

TWENTY

I wasn't a fool. I knew I couldn't take GFA's top student in a fight. He was probably the most Elite teenager on earth. It may have seemed like a death wish to some, and the grin on Oden's face told me he might be of that mind, but I didn't have to beat him to earn his respect. I just had to put up a good fight.

He beamed. "Well, that's perfect because I thought I'd have to give you a few days to settle before I could kick your ass."

His goons laughed, smiling at me like I was a meal they were poised to consume.

"One on one?" I asked.

Oden stepped forward. "You think I need help to beat you?"

I shrugged.

I heard Carter mutter under his breath, "This is a bad fucking idea."

"Training zone two is open," Quan said.

Oden gestured to the back of the domed arena. "Is that cool with you?" Oden asked.

"Wherever."

The four Nobles practically squealed with excitement as I followed Oden through the greenhouse-like arena. They shook Oden's shoulders and whispered to each other as if their bodies might explode from sheer adrenaline.

The dome was separated into different zones that seemed to house a variety of environments. The one closest to where I'd entered was filled with trees and lush plant life, but as we made our way through to the neutral plane between zones, I saw that there were seven. My attention was drawn to one in particular that seemed to somehow have snow accumulating in it—the flakes falling from nothing and perfectly contained in the borders of the zone without any visible walls to contain it.

I wondered which zone was number two, and if Oden had chosen one that would play to his strengths.

The second zone from the left was a flat and empty dirt patch of land that reminded me a lot of the physical exam I'd failed. Without any materials to grab onto, I'd been unable to use my gift. However, the second zone from the right looked like a city block complete with skyscrapers and industrial construction sites. There was so much to touch there, so much to use. Oden banked left and I knew I was about to receive the ass kicking of my life. But I fought to hide it from my face. I was a great deal more gifted than I'd been a year ago. Maybe I could win.

We stopped outside the flat zone. "You go in from that side," Oden said. "The duel starts when we're both in."

I took my position, Carter following close behind me like a

puppy. "You can't be serious, man," he said. "You're going to get yourself killed." His words chipped away at my facade.

I spun to him. "I need to do this," I said. "You're either Elite or you're not."

"You're either alive or you're dead," he mocked.

I faced the zone and saw Oden near the center pacing back and forth.

Carter's voice shot out beside me in an angry whisper. "Look, man, I wish you the best. But I can't watch this. I'll be in our room if you somehow make it out of here."

I swallowed a lump of nerves and stepped through the barrier to zone two. As I entered, my heart beat like a drum marching me to war. Like I'd expected, there was nothing loose to touch, so my only option was to get close enough to touch Oden. The problem was, one touch from him and his strength gift could break every bone in my body, and the easy grin on his face told me that was his intention.

I sprinted towards Oden, the howls of his goons ringing through the zone from the other side. I was a slightly faster runner because my gift could propel me, and speed would be the way to beat him.

If I could touch him and escape his counter attack, I could drop him from a great height and his strength wouldn't be a factor.

He took a defensive stance as I charged him. I leapt into the air and used my gift to hold me. My manipulation of gravity threw him, as he incorrectly anticipated my fall. Reaching down, I swept my hand through the air to catch a piece of him. The tip of my finger hit the top of his ear. I pushed myself away with every ounce of power my gift could muster, hovering out of his powerful reach.

I have him. The onlooking Nobles went silent as I thrusted Oden into the air. Higher and higher until he bordered on the edge of my range, nearly fourteen stories up in open space. Then I dropped him.

Oden plummeted head first toward the solid dirt. I gulped, suddenly aware of the possibility that I might kill him. Still within my range, I had time to save him. I lifted my hand but froze. He cocked his arm back, ready to strike the ground with a punch.

No fucking way.

The zone exploded into a dark dusty hell as his fist collided like a bomb. The ground shredded, crunching into shards of rock and dirt that scattered through the air. *This wasn't over.* Bombarded with debris, I squinted through the dusty air, searching for my opponent.

Had I been on the ground when he'd struck, I'd be finished. Suddenly, Oden shot through the dust, nearly reaching me several yards above the rocky terrain. I shot back, barely missing his blows. How was he getting this high up? His momentum cleared some of the dust, and I saw his gift gather energy in his legs as he leapt once more, swinging his fist to kill.

I narrowly slipped it when I noticed my advantage. We were no longer in an empty zone. The shattered rock was ripe for my gift and I felt a few that had hit me in the explosion still in my range. I shot myself back toward the surface, touching as much of the surface as I could before Oden charged me. I felt some large sharp stones enter my range. Oden sprinted at me and I sent one boulder after the next at him, hoping one might slow his speed. He punched through one after the other—each crash like a bomb growing closer and closer. Dust flew, but through it I saw Oden's bloody fist blast toward me, a dark streak of blood across his face. I pulled myself back through the air, but I was too slow—his hand collided with my cheek with a crack and everything went black.

The next thing I remember was a bloodcurdling scream, but the voice was not mine, it was Reina's.

Reina

TWENTY-ONE

I clutched the sheets of my hospital bed and screamed my throat raw. Professor Greene had not exaggerated the agony. All those years of bottled up grief were coming out with a vengeance. I writhed through a cycle of screaming and vomiting, my body unable to handle the avalanche of emotion, as one memory after the next tore through me. My parents were dead. My parents were *dead*. My heart ached as I fought to come to grips with this new sensation.

I'd been there when it happened. I watched them die—their blood froze and their faces settled into this...empty expression that told me their souls had fled. It was just a touch to the backs of their necks in a crowded street. I hadn't seen who did it, just saw the life drain from them as they quietly slipped away. They were both Commons, and law enforcement officers with gifts that wouldn't have saved them even if they had seen their attacker coming. I too was helpless. I held their hands and screamed for help, too afraid to let go, and I rarely brought forth the memory since I'd taken that grief confection. I certainly hadn't felt it. Now it looped through my thoughts endlessly as if in punishment for denying the heartbreak due.

They were gone. I felt selfish as I choked on the thought that I still needed them. I still longed for their guidance, the warm sound of their voices. There were so many things I never got to ask. My shoulders shook as a wave of fresh pain cut through my chest. "I'm so alone," I whispered into my pillow.

My eyes burned from all the tears I shed, my chest so tight I couldn't breathe. The pain and loneliness were overwhelming in the intensity. Dr. Azul stood over me, trying to look encouraging. "You'll make it through this," he said, "You are *not* alone." But his healing gift did not extend to emotional pain, and all he could do was say soothing words and hope I pulled through it whole. In my haze, I heard the door slam open and another student rolled in on a gurney with a squeaky wheel. But it didn't register.

My mind was trapped on a hamster wheel. *My parents were gone. My parents were dead. I am alone.* Just when my body finally relaxed, a new wave of grief crashed over me. I curled into a tight ball as the pain swept through me in an emotional torrent so brutal that it was like a sharp electrical current shooting through me. The pain was unrelenting, draining me to a point I thought I just might die. I reached for the doctor, but Dr. Azul was no longer beside me. He had moved on to another student with injuries more pressing than mine.

Mom. Dad. I sobbed quietly into my pillow, knowing this pain was never going to end, and it was almost enough to make me regret the bitter morsel Professor Greene had given me. *Almost.*

Dr. Azul's voice cracked through the room. "Who is it?" he asked.

"Kaito Nakamaru," I heard a voice say. That seized my attention as I clenched my teeth to hold in the tears. *Why didn't he know it was Kai?* Dr. Azul *knew* Kaito. He'd seen him just yesterday. I couldn't imagine what could cause him not to recognize him.

"Is he alive?" someone asked.

"Just barely."

I held my breath, hoping to bottle up the emotional assault that awaited my next breath. But it finally broke through and my heart seized up until, inevitably, my consciousness blinked out.

I awoke slowly, my tears breaching my eyes before I could even remember why. My gaze lifted to the empty end table beside me, and then to the bed on the other side. Kaito lay bruised and bloodied on his back, his eyes open as he stared at the ceiling.

I sat up quickly, dizziness seizing hold of me. "Just like old times," I said, my throat burning with pain. It had been a few years, but back in middle school we spent a good amount of time together in an infirmary just like this one. He looked beat to hell, but that was the kind of joke he usually jumped at. He must've been in pain. "Kaito, what happened? Are you okay?"

His eyes moved to me before his head. "You were the one screaming."

I lay back down, biting my bottom lip to keep from crying.

He asked, "Are you going to tell me what happened?"

I shook my head, turning my gaze to the ceiling as I fought to suppress the sound of my sobs.

"It's about your parents, isn't it?" he asked. "I heard you call for them."

I pulled my blanket up to my shoulders as if it could somehow shield me.

"What I don't get is, you've been so calm about what happened all this time. What happened? Is it the new school?"

I took a steadying breath but it caught in my throat. "I took something," I wheezed through my sore throat. "A..." I cupped my face in my hands. "A grief-numbing confection."

Kaito was so silent I couldn't hear him breathe.

"I s-spent my inheritance," I said, the sadness overtaking my words. "So I could stop hurting."

"Veranda felt it."

I nodded and we fell into silence as I turned to muffle my cry in my pillow.

"Why did you have them undo it?"

A slew of reasons popped into my head. Because I'd be kicked out of school if I didn't. Because I regretted that decision. But only the most prominent reason came to my lips. "Because..." I sniffed, "the inability to mourn their loss felt like they were never here." I fell apart again, but as bad as the last few days had been, I was happy to finally mourn. I was happy to feel my parents' connection to me. Every wave of grief reinforced how much I loved them and, if I survived it, I'd be able to carry them forward with me.

I dared a glance at Kaito and I thought I saw his eyes get glossy. He reached out a trembling hand marred with purple flesh and lay it out across the end table. "Are you going to tell me what happened to you?" I asked. He didn't bother to answer but, knowing him, he probably picked a fight with the wrong person. His palm rested on the edge of my bed. I buried my face in it as a new wave of grief rolled over as Kai rubbed his thumb up and down the side of my face.

When I awoke again, my body felt heavy and stiff. My gaze moved to Kaito's empty bed, and a panic flashed through me before I felt his warmth along my back. My head was resting on his right arm, his left arm draped around my waist. I traced my fingers over it to find that what was purple the last I'd seen was now a blotchy yellow. I wasn't sure if I'd been sleeping for a long time or if Dr. Azul had been every bit the healer as reported by his reputation. I wondered what he'd gotten himself into to get so battered, or why the bully who tormented me relentlessly not three days before had rushed to hold me when I needed it most. I would have faked sleep for the next ten years to be held like this for a little while longer, but I had to pee. So I slipped out of bed, cupping a hand over my mouth as Professor Greene's morsel kicked back in, reminding me once again that my parents were dead and, even if Kai was here today, tomorrow I'd again be alone.

Kaito

TWENTY-TWO

I never felt more helpless in my life. Reina had always been strong. It was one of the reasons I'd been friends with her in middle school, and one of the reasons I tormented her when we got a little older. When I looked back on this past year, I suppose I always thought it was weird how casually she spoke about her parents, but I couldn't have imagined that she'd be desperate enough to blow her inheritance on a grief curber. How did she even find one that powerful? That was some deep black market shit. I shuddered to think of Reina in the kinds of places that sold that sort of thing, and all the time she was going through that, I was trying to teach her a lesson. I sighed. Now she was in the infirmary, a place I'd once taken pleasure in sending her, but I took no pleasure seeing her here now, so broken and fragile.

The infirmary was well lit and cozy with no more than ten recovery beds. I'd looked out the window to find myself across campus, somewhere in the building Carter called the student center. The past few days Dr. Azul had worked wonders on healing me, his gift like ice pushed into each cell, numbing the pain as they thawed into regenerated flesh and bone. He ran out of stamina after a while and needed long rests between treatments, but I couldn't deny that his gift was both fast and effective, so I was not surprised that Reina and I were the only patients he had. I stifled a laugh. We'd both made a hell of an impression.

I listened for the doctor's footsteps while I put together the sequence of events from the last few days. I was pretty out of it when I'd first been wheeled in and only remembered flashes of pain and voices. Enzo had rushed me here using his speed gift. I felt a pang of embarrassment about my defeat. I should have listened to Carter. I reached to search through another blurred memory, one of Oden getting his arm patched up, but I couldn't be sure if those were real or something I dreamed up in my recovery. When I came to, I found a text from my parents.

Dad:

I heard you were defeated in combat and are in the school's infirmary. This was not the kind of fresh start we were hoping for. Your mother and I have decided to leave town for a while.

I considered smashing my phone in frustration over my parents when Reina screamed out for hers. What different lives we led.

It was difficult to watch my wounds heal drastically day after day while Reina seemed to suffer to no end. I knew Reina's condition couldn't be fixed with the doctor's gift, but the worst part was his attempts to comfort her. He kept telling her that she wasn't alone which only made it more apparent that she was. She even cried when she slept, as if even her dreams wouldn't allow her peace. On my third night, there she was shaking so violently that I leapt out of bed, forgetting about the doctor's orders to rest my newly healed bones, and lay down beside her. But as I pulled her in, I found myself repeating the doctor's soothing mantra to her. "You'll make it through this," I said. "You're not alone." She calmed a little and, before I had time to think better of it, I fell asleep beside her.

I awoke to find Reina had moved to my bed on the other side of the bedside table, and I worried that my attempts to comfort her had only freaked her out. What was I *doing*? Even I had to admit I was all over the place lately. I'd bullied her so hard we got expelled from school, then I kissed her, now this. Why had she become such an obstacle all of a sudden? Reina rolled toward me and I noticed she was awake.

"You seem a little better today," I said.

"So do you. Your bruises are healing."

"Bruises." I scoffed. "I broke like fifteen bones."

Her eyes widened. "Oh my God, Kai. How are you even alive?"

Dr. Azul pushed open the curtain that separated the recovery beds from the rest of the infirmary. "That would be me."

"It's true," I said. "He's pretty strong."

Dr. Azul scoffed and froze suddenly. "Did you two switch beds?"

Heat rushed my face.

"Alright, Mr. Nakamaru, you're good to go. Focus on your classes for a while and try not to pick another fight."

I didn't like the idea of leaving Reina by herself, but if I spent any more time with her, she was going to continue to infect me with her woman magic. Still, I considered asking him to let me stay, but he'd just announced I was fine to leave, in front of her. It would look weird. I was just trying to be a good friend. Right? Fae helped people. It was nothing more than that.

I gathered my tattered clothes, grabbed my cell phone that somehow wasn't cracked, and changed from my hospital clothes to a school uniform Dr. Azul had laid out for me.

"Kai," Reina said before I could slip out. "Thanks... you know. For last night."

I half smiled. "See you around, Rei."

I felt flustered and couldn't get out of the hospital fast enough. I took an elevator to the first floor and stepped out into the hallway which passed by a bustling cafeteria with glass walls. I felt the sting of a hundred pairs of eyes on my face as I focused desperately on the door ahead. Finally, I stepped out into the cool autumn air and inhaled a mouthful of it. GFA had already proved to be a little more than I'd expected. I probably should have laid low.

"Hey," a voice shouted from behind me, drawing my attention. "Kaito Nakamaru." I turned to see Oden Gates and his three backup dancers approaching. *Fuck.* I had half a mind to flee into the infirmary until I remembered he couldn't hit me outside the combat zone.

The foursome walked over and I felt the soreness of my bruised ego flair. Behind him, I could see the prying eyes of the other students pressed against the glass.

"Have you come to gloat?" I asked.

He reached his hand out, the antiquated gesture I'd previously offered him more frightening than anything else, but I shook it without hesitation. I felt him move into my magical range and considered tossing him over the wall. It would almost be worth the expulsion. "That was one hell of a fight," he said. "I misjudged you."

I nodded, turning my face away with discomfort.

"When you get settled in, come find me. I'll show you the ropes."

Quan said, "The Noble Five. Sounds badass."

I smiled and the four guys patted me on the back before they turned back the way they came.

Reina

TWENTY-THREE

By the time I was cleared to leave the infirmary at the end of the week, I barely recognized myself. My eyes had dark circles around them, I'd grown pale, my cheeks were a little sunken in, but the biggest change was the glossy sheen of defeat in my eyes. *My parents were dead.* I couldn't bear the repetition of it. My heart ached and I clenched my stomach to keep from crying. A year of grief packed into one week had left me with an emotional hangover complete with a splitting headache. Dr. Azul had said he was proud of me for enduring it so well, but I hadn't felt proud of any of it. I was broken and I deserved every bit of it.

I put on my plaid pants, collared shirt, and blazer. I'd always imagined how I'd feel the first time I put on those burgundy uniforms, but it wasn't this. I never thought I'd feel like such an imposter. I hadn't even been strong enough to face my parents' deaths, so how could I become Fae? It felt like the entire week I'd been there was some kind of nightmare; the only reprieve from the agony was Kai. One familiar face. In the moment, I didn't care how badly he'd treated me in the past. He was there when I needed him, even if it was by pure coincidence.

As I stepped out of the elevator on the first floor, I realized I didn't know where I was or where I was going. There was a large cafeteria to the left of the hallway where students chatted and ate on maroon trays. It was separated by a glass wall that reminded me a little of a zoo or a fishbowl. Then, from inside the fishbowl, someone saw me and, like a viral disease spreading to each cluster of prying eyes, the cafeteria fell silent. I pressed my tongue on the roof of my mouth, willing myself to hold it together, when I was rescued by the person I least expected.

"Good, you're here," Miranda said. "I'm supposed to show you to your— Woah! You look like absolute shit."

"Thanks," I said, wiping my nose with the back of my hand.

Her eyes lit. "Did you hear the news?" she asked, but she didn't wait for my response before she gushed on. "Kaito Naka-maru challenged Oden Gates and, like, he lost obvi, but apparently the fight was *crazy* and like now Oden let him into his group and they're calling them the *Noble Five*." She thrust her chest out. "Gah, I can't believe I brushed him off the other day. I mean, he was obviously gorgeous but I didn't know his gift was *that* strong. I mean, didn't he fail the entrance exam twice?"

I envied her energy. "You were showing me somewhere?"

"Right," she said, flipping her rose-gold hair over her shoulder. "Your dorm." I followed her out and the students returned to their lunches.

"So," Miranda said over her shoulder, "is Kaito like *single*? You're not together or anything, right?"

My mind flickered to the past few days. *The kiss*. Waking up in Kaito's arms. He was the biggest train wreck I knew and my fractured heart was not ready to take a risk like that. Part of me wished the world was different. That my parents were still alive. That I was as gifted as Kaito so we could explore whatever was going on with us without the outside world using the gap to end it. If what Miranda said was true, and Kaito had become Elite at GFA, I could guarantee I was about to get middle school deja vu. Now that Kaito fit in again, he didn't need me to be his safety net. "No, we're not together," I said. "I don't think he's seeing anyone."

I wish I could say the pep my reply put in Miranda's step didn't bother me, or her giddy grin, or her confident gait. I wish I didn't notice her daydreaming as she twirled her silky hair around her polished finger. I wanted to lie down and forget I ever knew Kaito Nakamaru. I wanted to sleep until I remembered why I wanted to go to this stupid school to begin with.

Kaito

TWENTY-FOUR

I must've picked up my phone a hundred times to message my parents and tell them I'd turned things around, but every time I tried, I saw the last message my dad sent me, the disappointment ringing through every cold word of it. Why get their hopes up only to let them down again? Once I became Fae, they'd be proud. I was sure of it.

Since I arrived at GFA, I had no luck connecting to the internet. It seemed like all I could do was call or text and download ebooks from the library. It wasn't so bad when I was in the hospital, but now I was out and desperate to know what was going on outside the walls of the school. I made a mental note to ask Carter about it as I headed to Blue House.

I had almost made it back, while partially dreading Carter's remarks, when a very specific shade of blue caught my eye. I spun to investigate and my body pulsed. Round glasses, blue hair, and a sharply pointed nose. *The bus stop guy.* He was a few yards away, but I could have sworn it was the same guy I'd seen last week at the bus station, the one with the tattoo that matched the mark at the scene Reina described. It most likely circulated the news and internet by now, so why wasn't this creepy guy in jail? He was chatting up a girl with purple hair tied into two ponytails. *Mind your business, Kai.* I planned to hurry past, but he turned to me and shot me the same malevolent smile he'd given me the day Raphael Mazarin died.

"You," I called without thinking.

He grinned as I approached, dismissing the purple-haired girl with a wave. "Kaito Nakamaru," he said with a nod.

I gripped his gloved wrist and yanked his sleeve up to check his arm for the tattoo. He yanked his arm back in alarm, but it was too late. I'd already gotten a good look; his arm was completely blank.

"What the hell?" he spat.

"I-I-I'm sorry," I said, my mind fogged with confusion. "I thought I saw you at the bus station the other day, like a week ago."

"So what, crazy? You think I stole your lunch money or something? You have issues. Besides, I've been on campus for the last few months since I wasn't offered an internship this year," he said as he pulled his sleeve over his exposed arm. "Man, how bad did Oden rock you?"

I shook my head. "My bad, man. I'm a little off today." It was a piss poor excuse.

He nodded. "Well, no worries, bro. It happens. I'm Zane Blaque, by the way."

Zane Blaque? I hadn't heard of him, which meant it must've been true that he hadn't scored an internship worth media attention or even done well at the Varsity Tournament last year. What was wrong with me? I literally just got out of the infirmary and I was going around picking fights?

I smiled sheepishly. "Nice to meet you. I'm sorry about that."

"Not a problem. See you around," he said graciously and headed back toward the class hall.

I pulled out my phone and mindlessly tried to connect to the internet, hoping to dig up a little more information about Zane Blaque, but when I reached Blue House, I still hadn't been able to connect.

Carter stood, moving to his desk to get his guitar. "You're alive," he said, pushing a handful of blonde curls from his eyes.

"Surprise."

"I heard they're calling you a Noble now. Mission accomplished." He sat on his bed and began to strum something mellow.

"You don't seem happy about that," I said, but the calm of Carter's gift soothed me.

He shrugged.

I sat on my bed, noting how much harder the mattress was than the one in the infirmary. "By the way, how did you hear about the whole Noble thing? I can't seem to get onto the internet."

"Ah, yeah. The school barrier blocks the connection. They say it's to help us focus and keep our minds off the status and stuff and on our studies, and to keep the privacy of the school, but there was a breach using the connection like ten years back by some bum looking to cause trouble."

"Fuck, this place is like a prison."

His fingers danced over the guitar strings and I laid back on my bed.

"There are a few ways around it. You can leave campus, but

the area around the school isn't the best. There's a fort where some students go to hook up. That gets wifi, but it's slow and spotty. Or if you're friends with Briara, her gift has some kind of workaround, but she's a total psychopath—voodoo witchcraft and such."

I stared at the ceiling and let myself float in the grasp of Carter's music. I felt a rush of gratitude that I'd been assigned him as a roommate.

"Can I ask you something?" he asked, cutting through my serenity.

"Shoot."

He paused, finishing the chord progression before he timed his question with the next. "Why is being Elite so important to you?"

I sighed. He wasn't going to let this go. "Because it's a one-way ticket to a great apprenticeship and ultimately to becoming Fae. Why isn't it important to you?"

He strummed a little louder so we could still feel every note as we spoke. He looked out our window, and when his next question came, I wasn't sure it was directed at me. "Is it really heroic if they pay you a million dollars to do it?"

I opened my mouth to respond, but my answer caught. He had a point. "If you don't want to be Fae, what are you even doing here?" I asked.

"I mean, of course I do. Everyone does and everyone has their reasons. Just think about it. Have you actually thought of your reason for trying to become Fae? Is it money? Status, perhaps? I wonder why your new friends want to be Fae. How many of us are actually trying to help people?"

My fingers tapped to the rhythm. "Did those guys do something to you?"

He shook his head. "Nah, man, I think I just... don't like what they represent."

"And what I represent."

He leaned back against the wall without missing a note. "Nah, man. You're cool. I just hope they don't turn you into one of them. I hope you find a good reason before you sort of adopt one of theirs. The last thing we need is a new generation of camera-obsessed Fae."

I suppose I understood where he was coming from. Still, without the Fae, society would have collapsed ages ago. Why shouldn't they be paid well to risk their lives for us? "Don't be so naive. The system may be broken, but that's the way the world works."

He sighed his disapproval. "Personally, I think it's a Fae's job to fix what's broken in the world. Don't you?"

I didn't know what he expected me to say. "Whatever, man."

Reina

TWENTY-FIVE

Miranda stood in front of my dorm room with a smirk that said she knew something I didn't.

"I'll let you settle in," she said. "Cheer up," she added.

I forced a half smile and opened the door to find myself smack in the middle of some bizarre ritual. My nose was assaulted with a spicy aroma I couldn't place. The layout of the dorm was plain enough, but the left side of the room was draped with black webbed fabric and littered with lit candles. It looked like Halloween threw up in there. On the free bed, the one that was supposedly mine, stood a girl with two purple pigtails tied up with black ribbon. She was wearing a school uniform but her blazer was slung over her bed—a pop of red in a sea of black. It looked like she was burning scraps of paper and releasing them into the air above my mattress.

"Uh... hi," I said sheepishly.

She spun, nearly losing her balance. "Oh good, you're here," she said, "I thought I'd smudge the place for you before you got here. I thought I felt something nasty pass through earlier."

"Smudge?"

She looked more confused than I was. "Yeah. Smudge, to rid this room of evil spirits."

I nodded. "Oh. Of course," I said, too tired to inquire further. "Thank you. I'm Reina, by the way."

"Briara," she said, hopping off the bed. She threw her arms around me and held me like a long-lost relative.

"What's that smell?" I asked as a strong whiff of spice hit my nose.

She pulled away. "Sage. You have so much to learn."

I walked over to my bed, collapsing onto the bare mattress. I didn't believe any of that spirit stuff, but I wasn't going to let something so harmless bother me. One less thing to worry about. I was too tired for pleasantries and too emotionally drained from my hospital stay to put together more than a couple of words.

"Are you okay?" she asked.

I groaned. "I have to pee."

"The bathroom is at the end of the hall."

I dragged myself back up and out the door, slogging toward our floor's communal bathroom. As I walked, I sorted through my odd first impression of my new roommate. Rituals and spirits. Eh, she had her own style. Miranda's smirk insinuated I was in for a ride, but she should have considered I was a tad offbeat myself. It wasn't until I returned to my room that my opinion of Briara was cemented. While I was gone, she'd put a spare set of black sheets and blankets on my bed. I felt a wave of regret for not hugging her more sincerely the first time, but I hugged her again this time with every ounce of gratitude I could muster because my drowsy mind could not find the words.

She patted my back and watched me lay on my new bed, pleased with her work as I snuggled in, gripping my charm. I felt something hard beneath my pillow and reached under to find the smooth object. I held it up to the candlelight. It was some kind of crystal or stone. I looked over at Briara and she shrugged. I smiled as I shoved it back under my pillow. *It couldn't hurt.*

When I awoke, I felt like a new person. The bulk of the year's sea of suppressed sorrow had ebbed, I found myself feeling grateful that I'd gotten time with my parents at all and that they'd continued to guide me. Wherever they were, they must've pulled some serious strings to get me into GFA.

"Ah. You're awake." I sat up, and Briara sat on her bed, sipping a cup of tea that steamed in front of her face.

"Oh, you have a heat gift?" I asked.

She shook her head. "Hot pot." She pointed to a silver pot that had a black base and a wire that was plugged in beside her laptop. "I can mess with radio waves, you know, if I'm touching something already connectable."

My eyes widened. "Can you, like, intercept messages?"

"Really? That's where your mind goes first? Most people here call me wifi girl because I'm the only one on campus who can connect."

"Oh," I said, brushing the sleep from my eyes. "But that's so cool, though. You must be one of the most powerful students here."

She shrugged. "So glad you think so. But that's not the general consensus. Elites are chosen mostly by flash. I'll easily get an apprenticeship, but I'll likely be in some office intercepting waves instead of smashing bad guys like Oden Gates."

I moved back to lean against my wall. "Briara, right? Can I apologize for yesterday? And possibly thank you for... just everything?"

"Don't mention it," she said. "I put your class schedule on your desk, there."

I jolted forward. "Class? Fuck!" I hopped out of bed. "Oh my god, I'm going to be late on my first day."

"Uh... Reina, it's Sunday." There was a yarn spider web pinned to the wall above her bed and a sudden memory of her seance slipped through. I smiled to myself and exhaled my panic.

"Do you want to hang out today?"

She lowered her teacup. "Really? I didn't freak you out last night with all my... you know... ritual?"

I scoffed. "As far as I'm concerned, your ritual was being exceedingly kind and forgiving of my poor manners."

She walked across the room and sat at the edge of my bed, her face turned away like she was trying not to say something. "May I ask what your gift is?"

"You can, but I don't know what it is yet."

She shook her head. "What do you mean?"

"I haven't figured out what my gift is. Ms. Yarrow said—"

"You've met Ms. Yarrow?"

I nodded.

"Beautiful, right?"

I chuckled. "Stunning."

"So they let you in without knowing? I have to admit your schedule is... a little strange. Even for a sophomore, you have too many studies. They probably don't think you'll learn much in regular class without a gift. What about the new guy?"

"His gift is levitation," I said, Kai's kiss shooting back into my mind.

She spit her tea, snapping my attention back to her. "Sorry," she said with a grin. "Everyone knows his gift. I guess I was asking how well you know him."

I swallowed a lump in my throat, burying an ache in my chest. "Hardly."

TWENTY-SIX

I didn't know why, but I couldn't get Zane Blaque out of my head. The more I thought about it, the more I knew I wasn't mistaken. He was the guy I saw at the bus station, the one whose tattoo was somehow linked to the death of Raphael Mazarin. It didn't make him a killer per se, but his chilling smile had me convinced he was involved. That theory was shot to hell when a few minutes after I'd last seen him, rumors began to circulate that another Fae was found dead on the far side of Ancetol. The only teleportation gifts were through Gemini Gates. So, unless he had a twin across town, he was most certainly innocent. Still, it couldn't hurt to look into the guy.

A knock at my door halted Carter's guitar, which had become such a fixture in my life in a few short days that I felt uncomfortable in the silence. I even felt myself craving the calming effect of his gift. I opened my door to find Prince Finn Warsham. It was hard not to be starstruck. I didn't care much about his title, but last year in the Varsity Games, he'd picked up a spear and pinned his opponent to the wall, just two inches from the finish line. *Two inches.* I knew specifically because after the games they measured the exact spot. He'd swept the round but didn't fare as well in the other events. Still, that moment had always stuck with me as the most exciting of the Games that year. Now that I was at GFA, I'd get my chance to compete in next year's games which was the biggest perk GFA had to offer.

I stared blankly. "Uh... Your Highness?"

He grimaced. "Just Finn, please."

Quan Levout stepped between us, wrapping his arms around me. I froze while he gave me a tight squeeze, nearly pulling me off my feet as his lime-colored hair tickled my chin.

"Uh... okay," I mumbled.

Quan dropped me and stepped back, beaming. "Man, you were awesome in that fight. Oden's arm was pretty messed up. You were just like BAM BOOM! And he was all like whaaaa?"

Finn rolled his eyes. "Oden wanted me to check to make sure you're going to the fort this afternoon."

"I don't know what that is."

"Carter knows," he said, nodding to my seemingly uninterested roommate. "Bruh, will you show the new guy to the spot?" he said, his voice smooth and low.

"You got it, man," Carter said without looking up.

Carter was a homebody and therefore seemed a little apprehensive about leaving the dorm to help me get on the internet, so these guys were my best shot. "Do either of you know how I can get online?"

Quan nodded. "You trying to check your new status? It's all over the internet, man. You're officially one of us. No doubt you'll get a sick internship next summer."

He rattled on and I turned to Finn for help.

Finn shrugged. "There's wifi at the fort, but we don't go out there until nightfall. If you want to get online now, Quan's really the only one with a workaround for security into Pink House."

"I'll hook you up, man! It's going to be so dope. I'll, like, get you in and then you can, like, make me fly and shit in front of Miranda and you know, like, she'll be all into me and whatnot."

I rubbed my hands together, mimicking his enthusiasm. "Let's do this."

Quan's eyes lit and I followed them outside, giving Carter a quick nod before I went. Quan pulled me to the side of the girls' dorm, away from the front entrance and security desk. He pulled off his gloves and slid them into his pockets. He took a nervous breath before he reached for my hand.

"Are you afraid?" I asked, trying to read him.

He laughed. "No man. I mean, you're cool and we're friends and stuff. You wouldn't... you know, like toss me around or anything."

It amused me, but the moment he took my hand I regretted not giving his gift more thought before it was upon me. I felt my form shift along with his. My body bent and contorted in his power. I felt my hair reach my lower back and new unbalanced weight on my chest. Before my eyes, Quan changed into the girl I'd seen earlier with Zane Blaque. He now had a delicate face with purple pigtails, his skin paler, his waist smaller until there wasn't a trace left of his real self. I was suddenly wracked with anxiety when I realized he'd transformed me into Reina. This was so messed up. Panicked, I tried to yank my hand away, but he tightened his grip.

"Relax, man," he said. "It's no big deal."

"Pick someone else for me to be. Anyone else," I said, but

Reina's voice came out. "It's too weird to be Reina." I patted my new body, unable to reconcile its appearance with how I felt. "And I don't think her ass is this big."

Quan held up his phone and Reina's black lace underwear moved across the screen.

My eyes bulged. "How did you find out about that?"

He laughed. "As soon as she got in, this video went viral on campus. I'm pretty sure every guy here has it saved to their phone."

I swallowed a lump in my throat. "This is so pervy."

Quan smirked. "You have no idea."

I yanked my hand out of his and wiped it on my pant leg. "Hard no on this mission."

He grinned. "Don't act like you wouldn't do it."

I turned to head back to my dorm.

"Wait, wait, while we're on the subject, what's it like to have sex in zero G?"

I bit back a smile. It was a question I'd been asked by guys and the occasional girl a lot in the last couple of years. I sighed, leaning in so I could whisper my answer. "It's terrible."

His face lit. "Really?"

I nodded. "Gravity is one hundred percent necessary."

He shook his head. "Damn. Way to ruin the fantasy."

I shrugged.

"Look," he said, "nothing weird. We're just going to disguise ourselves as the girls, sneak past security, and ask Briara to connect you to the wifi."

I sighed in resignation and reached out for his outstretched hand. Reina's form once again formed on my body. "Kaito, you're so strong," I said with Reina's voice.

Quan snickered. "Who's the pervert now?"

Reina

TWENTY-SEVEN

I eyed my schedule warily. There were so many teachers I'd hoped to see on it, but Briara was right, it was nearly empty. I supposed you couldn't infuse confections with an ability if you had none, nor face-off with classmates in combat, but I hoped to have something.

All I saw listed on it was a general studies class with a professor I'd never heard of, a history class with a professor listed as "To Be Determined," and Gift Defense, which I immediately deemed my most interesting one. The rest of the day was a blank sea of independent studies with no professor at all broken up only by a lunch break. I was confident that GFA, with its incredible reputation, knew what they were doing. If anyone could bring out the gift in me, it was the greatest Fae academy in the world.

A knock at my door put me instantly on edge. I looked up to Briara who seemed to ask with her gaze if I'd been expecting someone. I shrugged and stood, hoping it wasn't Miranda as I reached to open the door.

I sucked in a sharp breath as I stood face to face with myself and Briara. Their hands were clasped together, a strange gesture that surely meant a gift was to blame. Stunned, I eyed my clone closely, the image slightly older than how I thought I looked. Briara's clone was spot-on accurate, which made me believe that mine must've been too.

"What the hell is this?" I said, trying unsuccessfully to cloak the uneasiness in my words. I backed away.

"Oh," Briara said. "Let them in, they're here for me." She put down her cup of tea. "Close the door."

I obeyed, but my mind seemed dead set on the possibility that we were about to be murdered and replaced with our unexpected doppelgangers.

The two silent girls stepped in and dropped their hands. Their features melted away, the deformed mixture giving way to their true forms. I nearly squealed when I saw Briara's purple hair change to the most famous green. "Holy shit," I said, practically hyperventilating. "You're Quan Levout." Duh, it was obvious. Everyone knew about his transforming ability after the stunt he pulled at the Varsity Tournament. Still, I hardly expected him to visit.

"Sup, girl," he said with a nod.

I blushed, but that was nothing compared to the heat that rushed my face when I realized that the clone of me was actually Kai, who now stood inches from my bed. I gulped. What was more horrifying, that Kaito was just in my body or that he was currently in my dorm room? With the dorms separated by gender, I'd completely let my guard down. Of course, Kai's new crew had a way into Pink House, but what were they doing *here*?

Kai watched my mental flips with a satisfied grin then turned to Briara. "Hi," he said. "I'm sorry to barge in like this. I'm Kaito Nakamaru."

My mind got foggy and Briara also seemed to lose her words until finally she uttered, "Yeah, I know. Are you here for wifi?"

Quan looked around, unsettled by Briara's spooky decor. "He's new. You know, wants to check his status and stuff. I was thinking that after you hook him up, you and I could grab lunch or something."

Briara rolled her eyes.

Kai tilted his head and gave a Prince Charming smile that turned Bri's face a deeper shade of crimson than Veranda Yarrow's hair. I couldn't help her. I was frozen, half a second from burying my face in my pillow until they left.

"No problem," Bri said. "Give me your phone."

Kai held out his phone and, even with gloves on, she hesitated to take it. Then she sat back in her chair and pulled off her gloves, resting Kai's phone on her palm.

We all waited for something to happen, but Bri's gift wasn't flashy. It hardly looked like she'd done anything at all. A moment later, she put her gloves back on and handed the phone to Kai.

"That's about twenty minutes. Use them well."

Out of the corner of my eye, I saw a weighted look pass between Kai and Quan.

Quan leaned in and began to whisper to Briara. I bit my bottom lip to stop my nerves from spilling as Kai's gaze moved across my side of the room.

Briara's voice shot out, "But she sa—" Her voice cut and Quan leaned back into her, making her giggle. She looked up at me, her eyebrows raised and her lips pressed together.

What? What was she trying to say? I unfortunately didn't

know her very well, certainly not well enough to figure out what was going on.

"Fine!" Briara said, loud enough for us all to hear. "I'll go to lunch with you." She turned to Kai. "If you stick around, I'll charge your wifi one more time when I get back."

"Wai—" Before more of my objection reached my lips, they left, or should I say Bri left with a clone of me. I turned to Kaito, my stomach knotted with butterflies, my mind screaming scenarios.

I wasn't sure if Quan was trying to get Bri alone, or if Kai was trying to get me alone, but either way I found myself alone again with Kai. My instincts told me to run, but I was too curious to obey. Kai smirked at me and lay in my bed. My breath caught in my throat.

"Oh, relax," he said, laying back. "We both knew I'd end up here eventually."

"What are you doing?"

He inhaled slowly, delighting in the torment of his delayed response. "I just came to use the internet."

I nodded, crossing my arms.

"Have a seat," he said, tapping the bed. "You've been in my bed a hundred times."

I nodded. "But this is the first time you've been in mine."

He laughed. "Your parents would have—" His smile dropped. "Sorry."

I shook my head, taking a seat at the end of the bed. "It's okay. I'm feeling a little better today."

Sensing my need to change the subject, he sat up and leaned against the wall. "Do you remember the day Raphael Mazarin died?"

"Yeah, you walked me to the bus stop."

"Yeah, well... before I left, I saw this weird guy. He had blue hair and a tattoo similar to the mark they found at the scene. He had this creepy smile and he kind of drew my attention to the news." He shook his head and looked down at his phone. "I don't know, Rei. It was like he was bragging about it or something."

"You should report that, Kai."

"Thing is, I saw him again here. His name is Zane Blaque. I confronted him and he had no tattoos and acted like he never saw me at the bus station."

"Are you sure it's the same guy?"

He nodded. "I'm at least 50% sure."

I bit back a laugh. "Well, 50% may as well be 100%."

He smiled. "Don't be a jerk, Reina."

I took a deep breath and crossed my arms. "Just admit you wanted to check out what the internet is saying about you."

He lifted his phone and the screen read *Kaito Nakamaru joins GFA Nobles after duel with Oden Gates.*

"Catchy. Maybe, just this one time, you can just chill out and enjoy your time at school. You know, be a normal high school boy for once."

He leaned closer. "Really? And what would a normal high school boy do in this situation?"

A sweet scent filled my nose as he inched closer. It reminded me of cinnamon and made my mouth water. *Deja vu.* I felt Kai about to strap me in for another go at the emotional roller-coaster. I stood breathless and flushed. Was this some kind of joke? Why was he hitting on me? It could only be a trick. "I think I prefer your old way of bullying."

"What do you mean?"

"You're confusing me," I said.

He smiled and stood. "I don't know, I like seeing you like this." As he stared down at me, I could scarcely see the boy I knew so well. This one was a mystery, a dangerous one. He was going to hurt me, and this time would be much worse than the others.

"Like what?"

"Just, the look on your face. I can't tell if you want me or if you're scared."

"Neither can I."

A knock at the door broke the silence. I opened it and my stomach dropped to find Miranda at the door. "Where's Briara? I need wifi," she said. Her gaze lifted to Kaito and her expression brightened.

"She's not here," I said, but she pushed passed me like I wasn't there.

"Are you here for wifi too, Kaito?"

"Sure am," he said. And I felt a twinge of regret that I hadn't seized my moment with him. It was like Miranda had boy radar.

"I'll wait with you," she said, pulling him to sit beside her on my bed.

She giggled and whispered something to him that made his eyebrows shoot up.

I heard him say back, "Everyone always asks that."

The urge to flee slammed into me. "I don't need wifi. I'm going to go grab some lunch," I said, moving to the door.

But instead of a response, Kaito leaned into Miranda and whispered something else.

Fickle, unreliable asses—they were perfect for each other. And that's what I told myself as I swallowed my jealousy. I went to lunch alone, reminding myself every chance I got that he wouldn't have been worth the tears.

kaito

TWENTY-EIGHT

Carter gripped the strap of his guitar as we made our way through the school's underground tunnels. He explained, "This is all within the barrier of the school, but back when Lannon Gainsboro was a student here, he cloaked the memory of this part to everyone but the students who attend here, so we can pretty much do what we want."

"Does that include him?"

He shrugged. "Probably. I mean, he hasn't returned to undo it. Maybe when he graduated his gift cloaked his memory of it too."

We'd been walking for some time and there was still no end in sight. The tunnels were well lit and cheerfully decorated with spray-painted murals of famous Fae and line art.

I stopped when I got to the image of Yemoja Roux. "Why do they call this place the fort? Do people fight there?"

"Chill, man. I hope you're not planning on starting something. I mean... didn't you prove yourself or whatever to Oden? You're not going to try and get revenge or something, right?"

I shook my head and continued walking when I noticed several more murals starred Yemoja Roux. It was no surprise that she was so popular among the other students. She was popular around the earth.

Carter continued. "Most people are just glad we have a place to hang out unsupervised that they don't risk starting anything at the fort. The combat zones are enough to keep people who need to battle it out satisfied. The fort is mostly for parties and hooking up."

"You didn't answer my question about the name," I said, but he only smirked. Thirty minutes later, when the tunnel finally let out, I understood why.

I stood before a grassy plain filled with students and music. It had huge slates of broken gray walls that rose and fell through the uneven hill. There was an inner wall with a tower and a labyrinth of open air paths which held the bulk of the forty or so students, as well as a table with bottles of liquor and rainbow-colored mixers. My gaze moved to the larger wall that ran along the edge of the ocean, where several couples sat together and gazed out at the sea. Even in their poor condition, I could tell it was made of the ruins of some forgotten coastal fort whose better days seemed long since passed. The sun had just begun to droop low, reaching out across a turbulent ocean and rigid hostile environment. I tried in vain not to notice that one of the GFA students was missing from the night's festivities.

"Carter!" We followed the voice to see a petite blonde girl in a knotted spaghetti strap top hustle over, her bare stomach and low-cut shirt a delightful alert that no one here was in uniform. I technically was wearing mine, but the way I'd rolled up my sleeves and kept it mostly unbuttoned could hardly be considered uniform. The girl grinned. "Oh my god, Carter, I can't believe you're here!" she said. "You *have* to do the music."

He turned to me and nodded with a satisfied smile that I understood completely before he followed the girl to the fort's only tower. I didn't want to wander around the party looking for someone I knew, so I turned my sights to the outer wall. I walked up the slow incline as the uneven rocks beneath me were nearly five feet wide. Even with the waves crashing against the wall, it was completely solid and, with such a wide width, it was hard to imagine someone being dumb enough to fall off. I threw a hand in my pocket as I walked easily past a couple who were so engrossed in their conversation they didn't even notice me pass. The ocean seemed alive and wild, as if in warning of a storm, but even though the clouds grew darker, no one at the party seemed to worry about rain.

I continued to the highest point on the wall, the furthest corner from where I entered, and I could see that the school's boundaries didn't extend far into the ocean. I estimated it to be about twenty feet, based on the usual movement of the ocean's waves at that exact point, on the far side of the wall. To my left, the wall turned back and sloped to the inner fort on the opposite side, where I spotted another couple who leaned in for a kiss. The salty air reminded me of the days I spent with Reina at the pier. I wished I could go back to that first kiss and redo everything, but I wasn't sure what I would do differently. Surely, if I'd protected her and made a spectacle out of her situation, she would have been targeted more. I sighed, but perhaps I didn't need to enjoy tormenting her. It was obvious she found me attractive. I could see it in her face. But lots of girls did— even Miranda. Why then did the prospect of messing around with Miranda seem so simple and easy and with Reina seem so consequential? Why did my mind linger on her, despite knowing it would be a terrible idea?

My gaze was drawn to a fleeting movement in my peripheral vision. I snapped my eyes to the water just in time to see a black object break the surface of a wave, just on the other side of the school's barrier. I leaned forward and squinted. What was it? Some kind of claw? A hand touched my shoulder. I yelled, nearly jumping from my skin. I slipped off the edge of the wall. Stunned, I caught myself in my gift and rose to face a stunned Oden who looked like he'd accidentally murdered me.

"Dude," he said. "I'm so sorry. I didn't mean to scare you. I just came to say hi."

"I saw something. There," I said, pointing to the black mass.

Oden leaned forward, squinting. "What is it?"

"I don't know."

He turned to me. "Maybe seaweed on a rock or something. In any case, it's on the outside, so don't worry about it."

I nodded, shaking the worry off my face.

"Glad you could make it," he said. "Let's get you a drink."

Reina

TWENTY-NINE

Briara clung to my arm as we walked through the party, and I didn't mind one bit. It was also my first real party, and it was nice to have someone around who shared my apprehension. It was much warmer at the fort than it should have been for the season, and I wondered if someone was somehow regulating it. More than anything, I wanted to avoid the first awkward moments of mingling, so instead, I took in the coastline and the beautiful gray structure that hosted the party.

There was a good collection of students standing around with red cups in hand. "Okay," Bri said, "if I don't leave here with a boyfriend, you've failed as a roommate."

I grinned. "Okay, so if you see a guy you want, say dibs. That way we both know he's yours and I know to help you snag him."

"Got it."

My attention snapped to a quick movement that sent my heart fluttering. "*Enzo McCain,*" I said in a daze.

At the base of the wall, Enzo zipped from one group to the

other, distributing something that was too far to see. His speed was even more impressive in person than it was when broadcasted in the Varsity Tournament. He occasionally bent down to touch his shoes to keep them in range. I sighed. If only I had a gift that special. The high I'd been riding from learning that I had a gift that was somehow similar to Yemoja Roux had worn off in the week that had passed. I still felt unremarkable—more so when in the presence of students who would certainly become Fae.

Briara laughed. "At some point, you're going to have to learn not to be so starstruck. They're ordinary boys."

I smiled, eyeing Enzo's slick hair and confident smile. "They are anything but. They are literally going to save the world."

She squeezed my arm. "Trust me. They're just boys," she said, following Enzo with her gaze. "They'll hook up with you and never speak to you again like all the rest." She turned to me, her purple eyes cutting. "Don't fall for it."

"I mean... I'll do my best, but like... just *look* at them."

In a flash, Enzo was standing beside us and I nearly choked on my breath. He held out two multicolored shots. "Sunset shots."

I lifted the shot to examine it. "What's a sunset shot?"

"Reina, right?" he said, and his eyes flickered to Briara, sending a pink tinge to her cheeks. "When the sun hits the horizon, everyone here will take the shot to kick off the party."

"The party hasn't kicked off yet?"

He put his arm around me, like we were old friends. "Not by a mile." He pointed up to the barrier that domed the entire area. "You see the protection? Notice anything different about it than back on campus?"

I eyed it. "It's see through?"

He beamed. "Yep. We can see out to the ocean, the temperature is regulated, and when it hits sunset, it'll light up in wild colors and patterns, shifting the theme of the party as it goes."

"No way."

He leaned closer. "Way. Students have been infusing this sector of the barrier for years with their gifts, kind of like the professors do with the main campus."

He had an ease about him, a confidence and familiarity I envied. I wanted to ask a question about the barrier to keep him for another minute, but before I could, he turned to the next group. "I gotta make sure everyone has a shot in hand before sunset. I'll catch up with you ladies a little later."

Briara cut in, "Hope so."

Before he left, Enzo pointed to two figures walking toward us. I gulped—Kaito and Oden Gates. Kai seemed at ease, engrossed in conversation with Oden, a halo of red cups floating around him, and one in his hand that he sipped on every few steps. *Subtle, Kai.* Oden strutted around like Kai was the finest jewel in his crown. The two of them were such a sight that I had no hope of tearing my gaze away.

Briara leaned in and whispered, "Starstruck."

"Bri... LOOK AT THEM."

We burst into laughter, nearly spilling our shots, when the two high school gods made it over to us. "What did we miss?" Oden asked.

But one exchanged glance between me and Bri and we erupted back into a fit of laughter.

I straightened, mustering as much confidence as I could. Perhaps if I mimicked Enzo's attitude, I'd feel more comfortable. "What's up guys?" I asked.

Oden's face teemed with delight. "Why are you two all the way over here?"

"We hadn't made our way in yet," I said.

Briara added, "We just got here."

Kai smirked. "First party, Rei?"

Damnit, Kai. I nodded, shyness wiping away my attempts at confidence.

Oden leaned forward. "Really? That's adorable. Okay, you girls need a drink."

I lifted the multicolored shot. "I have one."

"You can't drink that until sunset." He turned to his friend. "Kai?"

Two of the cups floating above Kai drifted down and hovered in front of Bri and me. We exchanged a glance then took the cup from the air.

"Thanks," Bri said.

Oden grinned. "Bottoms up."

I lifted the drink to my lips. After one gulp, the sting burned the back of my throat. Bewildered, I dropped my hand, but the cup remained in Kai's grasp, pouring into my mouth. It leaked from the corners of my mouth and I swallowed hard, my eyes watering until the cup was empty.

What the hell, Kai? I opened my mouth to scold him but Bri beat me to it.

"You're such a dick. I almost spilled on my shirt," Bri said.

Oden and Kai laughed. "It's all in good fun," Oden said. "Now you guys are ready to party."

Enzo rushed passed us and Briara's gaze followed. She leaned into me and whispered, "Dibs."

"Dibs?" Oden said, looking around. "On who? I was just telling Kai here that I had dibs on Reina."

I choked on nothing. My face burned with heat and I wasn't sure if it was from the drink I'd just downed or Oden's comment. I thought I'd drop dead on the spot, avoiding eye contact at all costs.

Suddenly, the barrier burst into a cascade of colors sparkling down from the top like fireworks. I gaped, half impressed and half happy to escape the awkwardness of the moment before. The color swirled around me, the alcohol hitting my stomach.

"Cheers," Oden said, and I looked up to see the three of them holding up their shots. I looked down at mine. I had no clue what was in it, nor what was in store for me that night, but just this once it didn't matter. I wanted an adventure. I deserved a night of fun. So I raised the rainbow shot and clinked it with theirs before I downed it.

Kaito

THIRTY

I awoke with a sharp pain cutting through my head and a ringing in my ears that had me disoriented. I felt a weight on my chest and peeked my eyes open, but the light slipped in and my head flared with pain. *Fuck*. After several minutes of trying to convince myself that if I was in pain, I must be alive, my headache dulled enough for me to realize how thirsty I was. My throat tightened with dryness and I waited until my desire for water overtook my pain, and ventured to open my eyes again. This time, I saw Miranda laying on my chest. She had a face full of fresh makeup and was peeking through her eyelashes to check if I was awake. *Water*. Nothing mattered but water.

I moved up to my elbows, taking it slow, and Miranda pretended to wake up. I looked around the room; we were in my dorm room, but there was no sign of Carter.

"Good morning, sleepy head," Miranda said, her chipper voice confirming my theory that she was already awake. "You were great last night. That whole thing you said about zero gravity wasn't true at all. Maybe you just haven't had the right partner before me." She dropped my blanket, exposing her chest.

I gulped. "Water."

I stepped out of bed, my memories moving back to me at a glacial pace. I stepped on a used condom and jerked my foot back, scanning the ground where I saw another. *Ugh.* I felt the alcohol slosh in my stomach and threaten to surge. I was slimy, naked, and looked down to see I was still wearing a condom. At least we were safe, though I couldn't imagine how I ended up with Miranda. Then the memory slammed into me like a truck. Oden's tongue practically down Reina's throat on the dance floor. So much from the night before was unclear—lost—but not that. That one memory rang clear as a bell. I remembered the pain that assaulted me and found no release as they spent the night holding hands and exchanging secrets.

A wave of nausea threatened to splurge out on my floor.

"Are you okay?" Miranda asked.

I stood and slipped on a pair of shorts before wordlessly moving to the hallway toward the men's bathroom. I turned the faucet and splashed a handful of cold water on my face. I hadn't been the only one grinding my teeth at the sight of them. Miranda had been too. When they approached us, hands clasped together like an actual couple, Miranda and I got the same idea. I slung my arm over her in hopes of returning the feelings of jealousy Reina had caused, and Miranda played her part splendidly for Oden. I sighed and knew exactly where that led. The running water became the background music to my thoughts as a sickening thought occurred to me. What if Reina woke up this morning in Oden's bed? I turned, desperate to reach the toilet before the vomit spewed from me. I felt a gentle hand on my back.

"Are you alright, man? Can I get you something?"

I turned to see Oden looking well-rested and composed in his unwrinkled uniform, a backpack slung over his shoulder.

I wiped my mouth, hoping I could rally what had already become an awkward morning. "I'm fine," I said.

"Quan just walked Miranda from your room. He said she was naked as shit when he knocked. Nice, bro."

I had a hundred questions of my own in regards to his night, but none I wanted the answers to.

"You better pull your shit together, though. Class starts in thirty. I'm headed to Reina's dorm to walk her."

I clenched my jaw, but it was no use; the words spilled out. "Oh yeah. I forgot you were with her. How'd that go?"

"Good, good. I'm taking it slow. You know, she's a virgin." He shrugged and I hoped he'd stop there, but he didn't. "I really like her. I think she may be the real deal. You know, like, a good person and all that. She has no idea how special she is."

I wanted to vomit on him, to douse the joy and excitement from his face, but before I could he hurried out of the bathroom, leaving me to my recovery and my thoughts. It was supposed to be my first day at GFA, which was everything I'd ever wanted. I'd spent my night having sex with the hottest girl at the school, so why did I feel so hurt?

Reina

THIRTY-ONE

I lay awake, practically holding my breath until the sun rose. What a night. What a beautiful, perfect night. The moment I entered the party, Oden did nothing but give me his full attention. He was gentle, attentive, and unfailingly kind—all the things Kai was not. How had I been so mistaken? How had I spent so many years confusing misery with love? My time with Oden had been a dream, and I lay awake all night with the fear I'd wake to a new reality. We talked, we danced, we kissed, and when the night was over, we walked hand in hand back to the dorms where he said his goodbyes. It was a perfect night. One I knew I'd relive in my imagination again and again.

I'd been so caught off guard by his attention that I asked him why he was interested. And he responded that he had been from the moment we met. Looking back, I remembered how he'd been the reason I got into GFA to begin with. How he'd kissed my cheek. He explained again, though not in any great detail, that my gift felt like Yemoja Roux and that he knew I'd be great one day.

Oden was everything good. I was crushing hard, and why not? He was so unlike Kai, who was virtually made of warning signs. Yet I found my mind continuously comparing the two.

"My fucking head hurts!" Bri said. I rolled over to see her also awake. "Last night was awesome. Thank you for making me go."

"Thank you for going. You and Enzo looked cozy."

She sat up and winced, bringing her hand to her head. "Right? I think he might like me." Her eyes bulged. "You and Oden were like... *in love*."

I smiled, turning back to the ceiling.

She continued. "Neither of you spoke to anyone else. Are you guys, like, official?"

"What do you mean?"

"Did he ask you to be his girlfriend?"

I shook my head, but inside I was delighted by the thought. "I hardly know him."

"Look, normally people like each other and then they date. Don't try to mimic whatever you had going on with Kai. I mean... like each other, and then go to war for ten years. Maybe this Oden thing will be good for you. Besides..."

"Besides what?"

She lay back. "Nevermind."

I furrowed my brow. "No, what is it?"

"I'm ninety-nine percent sure he had sex with Miranda last night."

I rolled over toward my wall and pressed my forehead against the cold surface. "Sounds about right," I said, but I swallowed a lump in my throat as fresh tears pricked my eyes.

Later that morning, I put on my school uniform, a flutter of pride and fear swirling inside me. I wondered what my parents might say to me on my first day.

This was it. My chance to see what I was made of. This was my only hope of reaching my dream, and I found myself equally afraid that they wouldn't be able to make Fae out of me, and that they would.

I walked with my arm hooked around Briara's as we made our way to the front of Pink House. I was glad to have her, an ally in an otherwise uncertain world. We stepped out into the morning air, which was cold and wet, and Briara lifted her eyebrows, dropping her arm from mine. "I'll see you later," she said, hurrying off before I could protest.

Confused, I looked up to see Oden standing with a smile. He was a solid ten on a normal day, but in his uniform, he was easily an eleven. "Can I walk you to class?" he asked.

I nodded and walked over to him. He leaned in and kissed my cheek like he had the first time we met. Any lingering thought that his affection last night had been alcohol-induced vanished. I fell into stride beside him, hooking my thumbs on my backpack straps to avoid the awkwardness of whether we would hold hands or not.

"You look nervous?" he said.

"I am. I'm shaking," I said with a smile.

"Me too."

I recoiled. "You're the top student. Why are you nervous?"

He wrapped his arm around me. "You."

I rolled my eyes. "Cute." But it *was* cute. *He* was cute and *I* was in trouble.

"Look," he said, "you're going to be great today. I know for a fact that this will be the best day of your life."

"Oh? And who's going to make it so?"

He pressed his lips together and a dimple cut through his cheek. "You'll see. When the moment comes, when you're so happy you could cry, I want you to think, 'Oden was right, I should kiss him.'"

We laughed. A throat cleared and I looked up to see a sickly Kaito leering at the pair of us. His eyes had dark circles, his cheeks were a little sunken in, and his skin was so pale that he looked like a sexy vampire. The memory of Briara's update ran through my head. Kaito and Miranda. I sighed, hoping to exhale the pain of it.

"Alright, well," Oden said, drawing my attention, "good luck today."

"Yeah, you too."

Kai passed without a word and I felt a pang of guilt that Oden's smile dimmed when he saw me looking at Kai. *Let Kaito go.*

I walked into the class hall and found it's interior looked similar to the front office building. It had wooden floors and maroon carpets, only this building was packed with students in their distinctive GFA uniforms. I would have given anything to get a picture, but I remembered the first time I tried, how nothing but a black screen showed.

Across the room, a girl with one long, yellow braid stared at me. Her arms were crossed, her face expressionless, but her demeanor was unkind. I ventured to wave, but she didn't move. I passed through the hall, my eyes searching the classroom numbers for mine, when I saw a second girl with a similar scowl. Then another and another, until it felt like every girl at GFA had a bone to pick with me. Was it in my head? Had my nerves gotten the best of me? I rushed through the hallway in hopes that my classroom would offer salvation and hurried in, although most students seemed to be chatting outside the classrooms, waiting for the bell.

The classroom was ordinary in size and shape, but had a row of large windows on one side that stretched from the floor to the incredibly high ceilings. The morning light that poured in instantly quelled my nerves. I sat at an empty desk by the window. There were four other students already seated, a girl who doodled in her notebook and three guys who seemed half asleep. My stomach dropped when the girl with the yellow braid walked in, her eyes immediately locking on me. I turned and looked out the window with the hope that she'd leave me alone, but to my dismay, she sat down beside me.

Ignoring her, I scanned the courtyard outside, watching late students jog toward the school's front steps.

"So you're Reina?" a voice said.

I turned to the girl. "Yes, and you are?"

"Not impressed."

I shook my head. "Have I offended you?"

She grinned as if she'd been hoping I'd ask. "I guess it's your sense of entitlement."

"What?"

"This school has a hierarchy, and you completely disregard it."

Oh boy. "I can actually feel myself getting dumber from this conversation."

"Oden Gates is an Elite Noble. First in our class and king of the school. You're just a Serf. If you know what's good for you, you'll back off."

"And he'll realize you're more his speed."

I could see the wicked retort brewing in her smug face.

"Actually," she said, "I feel inadequate because, even without a known gift, you've captured the attention of my crush who I know will never want me, especially when I do petty shit like this." Her eyes bulged.

What the fuck? I couldn't say I expected that, but the look on the girl's face said she wasn't expecting to say that either.

A tall figure walked into the classroom. "Please refrain from using your gift outside of the assigned zones, Ms. Bennett. Even if they're well deserved by your victim."

Kaito

THIRTY-TWO

I tapped mindlessly on my desk as my history professor droned on. It wasn't that the topic itself wasn't interesting, it was. It was boring because, as the most perplexing time in human history, it was the era that every history class always focused on. It was like the time before gifts never even happened. Everyone knew that gifts first popped up nearly two hundred years ago, that the government had been struggling ever since to reform the laws to accommodate the vast variety of them, and that gifts in highly populated areas tended to be stronger, but what irked me the most was the syllabus outlined the Fae who emerged and the enemies they faced like they weren't already such legends, that every man, woman, and child knew the stories inside out.

"Kaito Nakamaru," the professor said, drawing my attention. "Your thoughts?" I searched the screen behind her for clues, which read only Population: 8 million.

"I'm sorry?"

"Why do you think the gifts are usually stronger in areas of high population?"

"The official consensus is that there is no connection between the higher population and the gift a person receives. The higher population gives proportionally more opportunity for powerful gifts to emerge."

The class giggled.

"We've already been over the official consensus. I'm wondering if you have another theory?"

I scanned the class. "Why me?"

"Mr. Nakamaru, if you're not going to participate, I wonder why you bothered to come."

A hand shot up and I turned to see Zane Blaque in the back row. His blue hair looked brighter against the maroon of his blazer. "I think it's like a disease," he said, without waiting for the teacher's permission.

The professor raised an eyebrow. "Interesting. Do elaborate."

Zane smiled. "Although humans, and especially Fae, enjoy and benefit greatly from their gifts, they have similar properties to a disease. They develop slightly different symptoms person-to-person, not everyone catches it, and the effects are stronger in highly populated areas."

She nodded. "I see, but our bodies don't reject this 'disease', as you've called it."

"Yes, they do. They reject other people's gifts when touched."

A knock sounded at the door before the professor could respond, and Zane looked pleased with himself. I had to admit it was an interesting theory, and the approving glances of the other students seemed to suggest they agreed. A gasp and shriek make me whirl to the front of the room. My heart slammed into my chest and, without thinking, I stood as a figure entered the room. *No fucking way.* Yemoja Roux. She was tall and muscular, with her trademark magenta hair and a slitted bodysuit that left little to the imagination. Her shoulders were broad, her legs thick and muscular like vine-wrapped tree trunks. Beneath her gloves I could tell her hands were small and dainty, while the rest of her form was nothing but a show of unequaled power. Her expression was calm but I could see laugh lines around her eyes and mouth, no doubt from the smile I'd seen in every one of her advertisements and interviews since I was born. A girl in the front row began to cry with reverence and I had to will myself not to follow.

Any doubts that I had about GFA being the greatest Fae school on the planet died the moment Yemoja Roux walked in. "Good afternoon," Yemoja said. And I held my breath.

"You may sit down, Mr. Nakamaru."

Yemoja Roux's gaze met mine and I dropped into my seat.

"And what are we discussing today, Mrs. Opaline?"

"Mr. Blaque here was giving us his theory about the effect of proximity on the potency of gifts."

Yemoja Roux nodded.

"Would you care to share your theory?"

She smiled and a wave of excited whispers echoed through the room. That smile was her signature, the one you could always see on her face when in battle. Even in the face of unspeakable evil, it never wavered. Even I felt dizzy from the sight of it as I contemplated just how lethal she actually was. I could hardly fight the urge to throw myself at her feet or praise her for her deeds. But what merit would my words be to someone like her?

"Certainly," she said, turning to the students. She spoke and her gaze was directed at each student for a short time before she moved to the next. "The more I observe varying gifts in battle, the more I come to believe that all humans tap into a shared energy. Closer proximity allows those connections to strengthen the connection we have with that energy. Since we all interact with the world in our own way, we also access the energy in our own way and thus evince different abilities." I hung on her every word, drinking in the inflection in her voice, fueling my dream to become a great Fae like her.

Zane's voice shot out. "Sounds like a bunch of religious mumbo jumbo to me."

All the air sucked from the room. Had he just openly disrespected the most beloved hero of our time? Nobody dared to move.

Yemoja Roux tilted her head with a playful grimace. "And what's your name, sir?"

"Zane."

"Zane what?"

"Zane Blaque."

Her eyes narrowed. "Blaque with a Q-U-E?" It was oddly specific.

He nodded.

"What's your gift, Mr. Blaque?"

"Shield."

She lowered her chin and put a hand on her hip. "And would you say you go through life defensively?"

"You don't know me," he spat.

I laughed too loudly, drawing the attention of the room.

Yemoja winked at me. She'd made her point, though the rest of the room was too still for me to read if they found it as amusing as I did.

I tried Yemoja's theory on my own gift. I made things float... I didn't exactly float through life. In fact, I always found myself battling against my feelings. I did that with my parents, with my desire to attend GFA, to improve my rank, and now with Reina.

"It stands to reason you would battle gravity as well," Yemoja said.

What the fuck? I exhaled a shaky breath. Did she just read my mind?

"I'm not reading your mind, you're just thinking so loudly I'm sure everyone here can hear you."

My face burned, but I relished every second of attention from Yemoja Roux. I could only imagine how many lives would be lost just from her short visit.

I stood. "Sorry. Thank you. I love you. Do continue," I said. I threw my hand over my mouth. *Fuck. I just told Yemoja Roux I loved her.*

I held my breath in my seat as if that would somehow pass the moment faster.

She giggled, and I felt the sense of accomplishment that I had making my parents laugh as a kid. In those days, I would have done anything to amuse them. "Anyway," she said, "I'm here on official business as well as to speak with you about the Fae murders."

I shot a look back at Zane, half expecting to see a satisfied grin, only to find him as attentively listening like the others.

She continued. "Through anonymous tips and whispers online, we've discovered a connection between the murders—a terrorist group that are calling themselves The Fallen." She waved her hand in front of the screen, drawing a downward arrow. "This is their calling card. I would like to stress how important it is to report anything that you know to a teacher or the authorities. There are now six Fae dead."

Impossible. I had been so caught up with the party and my new status that I hadn't checked the news. Six Fae dead. It was impossible.

"Since they are targeting Fae in such close proximity to the school, and you're all such promising Fae in training, it's not out of the realm of possibility that they'll attack GFA."

"What? Are you serious?" a girl from the front row said.

Yemoja Roux nodded and continued. "There's no need to panic. We have Fae reinforcing the school's protections, but as a precaution, whether you're on campus or off, it's best you stay with a group. All of six of the deaths were from Fae who were working independently. Be vigilant and aware of your surroundings until we can take The Fallen out."

A guy at the front of the room shook his head. "That's crazy."

"One more thing. Based on the injuries found on the victims, sharp cuts and punctures, we have reason to suspect The Fallen are using non-human allies."

"Like attack dogs?" another student asked.

She shook her head. "We couldn't identify the species."

Zane leaned back in his chair. "So monsters then."

When Yemoja Roux didn't correct him, the room erupted into panicked conversation. This was a whole new kind of evil.

She only let the conversation go for a minute before she raised a hand to silence the class. "The government would rather I not share any of this information. I understand your concern, but if you're really here to become Fae, than your job is to overcome fear in order to protect those who can't protect themselves. Everyone in here is Elite gifted, but imagine being out there without the protection of a gift. Imagine the fear and helplessness of those less fortunate. I can't protect them forever, and the burden will fall to you. It is under these trying times when we learn who we really are. Only in tragedy can we rise to become great."

We sat in stunned silence as Yemoja watched us one by one. Zane Blaque clapped his hands loudly, jogging us from our daze. "Great speech. Really inspiring. Can I ask one thing?"

Our professor intervened. "Mr. Blaque, please see Headmistress Tricorn directly after class. And I'd appreciate it if you'd show Ms. Roux some respect for taking the time to speak with you today."

He looked both amused and shocked. "It was just a question. No one's allowed to question authority around here, apparently."

"Go ahead," Yemoja said, challenging him.

"How do you know The Fallen or whatever are terrorists?"

I slammed my fist down on the table, disgusted by his blatant disrespect. "She just said they killed six Fae," I barked through gritted teeth.

His glasses gleamed, and I'd never been more certain he was up to no good. Ignoring me, he turned back to Yemoja Roux, looking her dead in the eye. "So, you're saying you've never taken a life."

Silence filled the room.

I raised my hand but didn't wait to be called on. "I'd like to report a member of The Fallen," I said, pointing to Zane. "That guy."

The classroom giggled. "Settle down," the professor said. "Settle down."

Yemoja Roux shook her head, an easy smile on her face. But it didn't reach her eyes. "Unfortunately, I have a lot of class-rooms to hit before lunch. Thank you for your time, and Zane, thank you for your particularly enthusiastic participation."

She nodded to me, a gesture of gratitude, before she stepped out of the classroom.

Reina

THIRTY-THREE

The sudden shock and thrill of being reprimanded for using my own gift after a lifetime of being a Serf felt like an emotional floodgate opened. I sat in my classroom wondering what happened. I hadn't touched the girl with the braid, so why did my professor seem to believe I'd used an ability on her? And why did the girl's scowl confirm she agreed? Was it some kind of embarrassment gift? Then I remembered another misunderstanding that also occurred without touch at my old school. Kai began to say strange things before he got angry and dumped my lunch on me. At the time, I thought Emma had done something to him, since she was touching his arm when it happened. Could it have been me? Is that how my gift was like Yemoja Roux?

My thoughts were interrupted when someone came into class late exclaiming that Yemoja Roux was not only at the school but visiting each classroom. My new ability could not be overshadowed by anything except Yemoja Roux. I could think of nothing else. Yemoja Roux the Great Fae was *here*. My heart leapt whenever a student came through the door. I hoped she would grace one of my classes with her presence, but as my third class came and went, with little more than going over the syllabus, I began to think that my sparse schedule didn't give me enough chances to meet her.

I went to lunch feeling deflated. The rest of the students glowed with excitement, their presence altered by beholding the greatest of all Fae. I wondered, what would it feel like to stand in her proximity? What did it feel like to witness greatness?

I feared I'd never know beyond the glimpse I'd gotten of her so many years ago.

"Reina," Oden called, waving me over to his lunch table. I sat down, putting my tray next to his. "How were your morning classes? Did you get to meet Yemoja Roux?"

"No, she didn't come to my class. But something weird happened."

He leaned forward.

"I... I think I used my gift."

He lowered his voice. "And you had those gloves on?"

I nodded. Of course, he knew. It seemed like he knew from the first moment we met.

"What's your gift?" he whispered as if unwilling to share the news with anyone else.

"Well... I think it's—"

Oden leapt up. "You're the man!" Oden said, throwing his arm around a stunned Kai. "I heard you told Yemoja Roux you loved her. You aim high, man. I'll give you that."

I gaped. *He did what?* The thought of competing with

Miranda for his attention was one thing, but Yemoja Roux was something else entirely. Not that I was competing. *Ugh. What's wrong with me?*

Kai humored him with a smile and said, "She wants me."

"You're insane. Have a seat, man."

What? No, not here.

Oden gestured to the table and my stomach dropped when Kai's gaze fell to me. "Hey, Kai," I said sheepishly, but he couldn't have looked more eager to escape—no doubt in search of Miranda.

Kai turned back to Oden. "Sorry, guys, I promised my roommate I'd sit with him and stuff. See you around."

Phew. Dodged a bullet there.

Oden sat down across from me with a goofy grin that said he was still thinking about Kai hitting on Yemoja Roux. I was struck by how handsome he was, the green of his eyes, dizzying when he was in his uniform. It's almost like his status as king of the school and his rare gift overshadowed his looks, but not that day. Only now, as he sat eating his lunch, he wasn't a king or an apprentice Fae at all. He was just a high school boy. *A hot one.*

He took a bite of a burger. "So what did you say your gift was?"

I fiddled with the charm on my necklace. "I didn't."

"Well, you'll work it out in your independent studies."

I leaned forward. "How do you know about those?"

He lifted an eyebrow with a devious smile that was so alluring, if my virginity had been an object, I would have tossed it at him. "Still not talking, huh?"

"I can be bribed."

I leaned across the table and kissed him, taking far more

delight in his surprised and elated expression than even the kiss itself. He leaned in and groaned, "More."

I laughed. I wasn't sure how I got so lucky, or how after so much sadness and grief I could feel happy and excited for what lay ahead. Either way, if the wheel of fortune was spinning back, I wasn't going to waste it.

Kaito

THIRTY-FOUR

I grabbed my tray and made my way through the line, tossing bowls of lukewarm food onto it. I eyed the Common that stood behind the counter, Yemoja Roux's speech ringing through me. They were gifted, only enough to keep the food relatively warm. What chance would they have if The Fallen attacked? The sensor scanned my tray and I waved my school ID over the scanner which blinked red and three-dimensional letters appeared in the air in front of me that read Kaito Nakamaru before blinking out.

I appraised the tables that were half full with students engrossed so deeply in conversation, it didn't seem like anyone was eating. I looked for Zane Blaque, prepared to give him a little talk about respect, but there was no sign of him.

As I weaved between the tables, I could hear that the entire cafeteria could speak of nothing but The Fallen and Yemoja Roux.

An arm landed on my shoulders. "You're the man!" Oden

said, shaking me. "I heard you told Yemoja Roux you loved her. You aim high, man. I'll give you that."

I grinned. "She wants me."

"You're insane. Have a seat, man."

He gestured to the table and my stomach dropped when Reina was seated there. "Hey, Kai," she said. The sudden memory of my night with Miranda hit me, followed closely by the memory of Reina's kiss with Oden, and I couldn't offer her so much as a smile.

I gulped, doing a quick sweep of the cafeteria, looking for an out. The last thing I wanted was to sit through their little date. I caught a glimpse of Carter. *Perfect.*

"Sorry, guys, I promised my roommate I'd sit with him and stuff. See you around." Before they could protest, I darted through the crowd.

Carter's face lit when he saw me. "Good timing, man. I was about to have a seat outside."

"It's a little cold, isn't it?"

He tossed his blonde curls out of his face. "A little, but that just means we'll have the place to ourselves. Or do you want to look at that?" He nodded and I turned to see Reina lean in and kiss Oden across the table.

I clenched my jaw. "Good point."

We headed outside and Carter inhaled his burger in no more than three bites before he pulled out his guitar and began to play. "Bro," he said, "I hear Zane Blaque was questioned by police."

"You're kidding. I just had a class with him." I shook my head. "He was rude to Yemoja Roux."

His brow furrowed. "So she had him arrested?"

I shook my head. "No... not exactly. He sounded crazy, though. He was supporting these terrorists, or whatever."

He looked puzzled, so I recounted the conversation as closely as I remembered it.

Carter strummed thoughtfully before he spoke. "You know... he kinda had a point?"

"What do you mean?"

"Well, the Fae kill people all the time."

I nodded. "Bad people."

"Who decides who's bad? I mean, what gives one person the right to kill and not another, and who has the power to make the choice?"

My thoughts reeled. I didn't exactly know how to answer him.

He continued. "Normally, when the Commons or even Serfs are attacked, and Fae protect them, we all kind of agree that's what's fair. But now that The Fallen are attacking Fae, it seems... I don't know, like an even playing field."

"You think Yemoja Roux is a bad guy?"

"Of course not. But if you *really* think about it, without the Fae the strong would survive and maybe the weak would die out. But at the end of the day, what's more fair and just than natural selection?"

I didn't disagree. I couldn't. Carter's soothing melody extinguished any spark of rage or defense that rose. There was something to his theory, something powerful that Zane Blaque thought was worthy enough to question the great Fae Yemoja Roux.

The idea that Fae might not be all good had never occurred to me. They were the darlings of the media. Of course, they had to kill their enemies from time to time to protect the rest of us. Yet, for some reason, once the idea had found its way into my head, I couldn't get it out.

Reina

THIRTY-FIVE

I looked down at my afternoon schedule which was comprised of three hour-long independent studies. Well, this was going to be fun. All I could imagine was sitting in a training room, punching a dummy in the hopes that my gift would manifest. On top of that, it seemed like my gift made people say things—personal things. I was sure a dummy wouldn't have much to share. Under the location, it read Combat Zone One. I remembered exactly which of the two domes the combat zone was in from my tour with Miranda, and also her warning that the moment I stepped in there I could be attacked by any student. Had that girl with the yellow braid exaggerated? Were there other girls who felt slighted by me spending time with Oden? I reached out to touch the barrier around the dome. It reminded me of the one at the fort which I'd desperately wanted to touch once it started lighting up the party. This one didn't seem to have as many cool properties, but I was surprised to find the surface ribbed instead of smooth.

It took me a moment to realize I was procrastinating going in because I was afraid. I'd been a few days without a beating and already I'd become soft. I promised myself I'd never let fear stop me, but I stood frozen with my hand on the door. My heart raced. My breath became shallow. *What is happening?* My legs began to shake and buckle beneath me when I realized I was caught in someone's gift. I looked around, but the courtyard was abandoned mere seconds before the bell. No one but Oden had touched me recently, I'd even worn my gloves today to be sure. Anger tore through me. I would not be a victim, not again.

I ripped open the door to the combat zone, ready to face my attacker. When I saw her, my knees gave out and I toppled to the ground still caught in the wake of her gift.

Yemoja Roux stood at the center of the entrance, hands on hips, a victorious grin, and her unique magenta hair streaming to the side despite the virtually windless dome.

I gasped. "Yemoja Roux. I... I love you."

She winced. "I've been getting that one a lot today."

She walked over and held out her gloved hand. I took it, unable to believe my good luck that I happened to be assigned to this exact spot for my independent study.

"Good work overcoming my gift to come in here. You have spirit. I've released it now. Can you stand?"

I gawked as I scrambled to get my feet under me. "Yemoja Roux, I can't believe it's you."

"You're Reina Bennett."

I shook my head. "No. I mean yes, but it doesn't sound cool like Yemoja Roux."

She leaned in and winked. "They let you change it when you become Fae."

"Right," I sputtered, "Of course." The bell sounded and I

looked around for combat zone one. It was to the far left, a silver one above a door to a smaller dome that encased some kind of jungle.

"I'm sorry," I said. "I have an independent study that I'm late for."

She flipped her gorgeous hair. "Class is already in session, honey."

My heart stopped in my chest. "You're going to teach... me?"

She furrowed her magenta eyebrows. "They didn't put my name on your schedule? Heh, they probably didn't want this place swarming with curious students." She slapped her hands together, startling me. "Anyway, we're wasting time. Tell me about your gift."

I gulped, uneager to deliver the bad news. "I'm not sure I have one. Well... I made this one girl say weird things, I think. Veranda Yarrow seems to think we have something in common... which is crazy. I mean, obviously I don't have anything in common with you, you're like a goddess and I like—"

"I was chosen to mentor you for that exact reason. You see, both your gift and mine can be cast without touch."

My body numbed.

"It's probably why you know so little about your ability. Since it works differently than ordinary gifts, casting it by touching someone wouldn't have yielded results. Can you identify what my gift does based on what you felt before you entered?""

"Make people dizzy?"

"Want to try again?"

I took a deep breath and replayed the moment in my head. I felt weak, uneasy, and ultimately, "Fear," I said. "But... your gift can't be fear. I've seen you use it to strike an enemy, even block attacks. You can't block an attack with fear."

"You'd be surprised how crippling fear can be if you learn to understand and wield it."

I nodded. "Okay. So how do I get from here to there?"

She sat down on the ground and patted the spongy turf beside her.

I looked around. "Here?"

She closed her eyes. "We have the place to ourselves."

I sat down, mimicking her posture and closing my eyes.

"Take a deep breath," she said in a voice that was smooth like a glazed sunrise. "Meditation is essential regardless of your gift, but more so for ours. This type of ability requires an understanding of the gift itself in order to control it."

I'm off to a great start.

"Banish those negative thoughts. Now I want you to take ten deep breaths and, as you do, reach inside and differentiate your body from your gift."

"How will I know what to look for?"

"You'll find what it is you're searching for."

I cursed the school for not letting me get a selfie with Yemoja Roux, like anyone would believe this. *Focus, Reina.* I wanted to learn from the best, and who would know better about this stuff than Yemoja Roux? I took my first three breaths and felt a tingling sensation in my arms and fingertips. I wiggled my toes and took another.

"That's it," she said. "When you find it, assign it a color in your mind. Visualize it spreading through your body."

Nothing. That's what I felt, but it didn't matter. I was sitting beside my lifelong hero. I'd gotten into the school of my dreams and suddenly everything seemed possible. Then I saw it, a fleck of light in the darkness. It grew and I thought it looked like a pale purple glowing white as it ran through my body like sand over my skin. Its shape was fluid, and I saw the currents push through my extremities. It ran down my neck, shoulders, chest, stomach, legs then out the bottoms of my feet to the center of the earth, only to swirl back into my body. I blinked through closed eyes as the purple glow hung above me like luminous stars. Each breath strengthened the light, the image burning more clearly in my mind.

Excitement overtook me and I opened my eyes, whipping to Yemoja to explain what I saw. I froze. Yemoja gaped at me, her trembling hand covering her mouth, tears sliding down her beautiful face. She stood quickly and I tried to follow but lost my balance and crashed back to the floor. "Wh-what's wrong? What happened?" I asked.

"That's enough for today," she said. "You did well." Without another word, she left and all I could do was wonder if that beautiful light I saw inside me somehow hurt the world's most powerful Fae.

Kaito

THIRTY-SIX

I hung out in the hedge mazes across from the Blue House. Every now and then I peeked over a prickly hedge to see Miranda pass far too many times, no doubt hoping to run into me. I owed her an explanation, but that wasn't a conversation I was ready to have. If I was being honest, I wasn't so much as hiding from her as looking for Zane. Unless I'd somehow missed him, he'd been in the headmistress' office all day.

The sun began to hang low, giving everything an orange tint and dropping the temperature low enough for me to see my breath. Finally, I saw him headed down the stairs from the front office, no sign in his gait that he'd been the least bit shaken by the interaction. Based on his speed, I calculated how long it would take for him to get to Blue House and timed it so our paths would cross.

His glasses glinted as he turned to me, an air of delight in his charmed smile.

"I see you didn't get arrested," I said, hoping to purge a real reaction.

"No thanks to you," he said, but if he was upset, there was no sign of it on his face.

"I just said what everyone was thinking."

"Look," he said with an easy hand gesture. "You can go and be brainwashed by the media about the Fae or whatever, but don't fault me for criticizing the entire hypocritical system."

"Why are you here if you don't like or believe in the Fae?"

"To change it."

I gulped. It reminded me a bit of something Carter had said a few nights ago.

He continued. "If the only way to have my voice heard is to become Fae, so be it. I'm just not surprised that someone else discovered a way to do it."

Another way to have their voice heard? Is that what he thought these murders were? "They're killing Fae."

"And what do you think will happen to The Fallen if the Fae find them?"

"If? You honestly think the terrorists have a chance?"

He shrugged. "The Fallen are 7 and 0."

"Six."

He nodded, a half smile on his face. "My mistake."

I shuddered. This guy knew something. Why then did the headmistress let him off? Surely one of the professors had a gift that could purge it out of him. The seer, perhaps. I shook my head. "You're one of them, aren't you? The Fallen."

"Look," he said, "I feel like we got off on the wrong foot. Do you want to grab a coffee at the student center? It's cold as balls out here and I imagine you've been waiting for me for a while."

Damn. I wasn't nearly as slick as I thought. Still, it was a peaceful gesture. It couldn't hurt to hear the guy out.

Zane said very little to me on our walk to the student center. It wasn't until we grabbed coffee and took a seat in a corner away from the bulk of the foot traffic that he began to talk.

He took in a deep breath, the only sign of apprehension I'd seen him give all day. "My family's really poor," he said flatly. "My parents are both Commons and their wages are minuscule. There just aren't any options for the Commons or Serfs, no opportunity to rise up. The only people who have a shot of making something of themselves are the Elites." He exhaled slowly and I wasn't sure if he was waiting for a response.

I sipped my coffee to fill his pause.

"Somehow, my parents got it in their head that if they had enough kids, eventually one might be born Elite and be able to deliver the rest of us out of poverty. Can you imagine? The Fae's pay being so unequal that they lounge in mansions and make their talk show appearances while the rest of us starve..." The last word was a hiss through gritted teeth, his free hand balled into a fist on the arm of his chair.

I had no response. I'd always had money, a legacy of wealth left from a Fae who died five generations ago. All these years later, we still lived off his earnings, and I hadn't given much thought to the unfairness of that situation until now.

He took a sharp breath in. "I have eleven brothers and sisters. I had thirteen, but two didn't make it. I guess my parents' plan worked, though, because I was born Elite and was accepted into GFA. If I can become Fae, I can help them." He looked up to me. "Maybe I can help more than just them." He gestured to the state-of-the-art student center, his voice cracking with emotion. "There's more than enough wealth to go around."

I nodded, my thoughts racing through his story.

"Every day I lived in fear that my parents would call and tell me another one of my siblings died. And I knew when the call came, it would be my fault for not becoming Fae sooner."

"So what happened?" I asked. "How'd you make the leap from desperate to become Fae to hating them?"

His glasses glinted, hiding his eyes. "My parents called."

My stomach sank and I wasn't sure I wanted to hear the rest.

"They received a donation. The only indication of who sent it was a downward arrow. Inside the parcel was ten years of my parents' salary, clothes, and possessions, all of which were the stolen property of Will Citrine."

I gaped at him. "So you're saying the—"

"The Fallen saved my family, and who knows how many others. They kill the greedy, media-hungry Fae and help those who weren't lucky enough to be born Elite."

The lines had blurred and Zane kept talking.

"I used to use my shield gift to sneak cafeteria food to my family out through the school's barrier and a gap in the wall, but they don't need it anymore."

He looked down at his hands. "I imagined I'd be relieved, but now it's been a while since I've seen my family." He smiled at me. "Go figure."

"Zane, I... I should have known you had a good reason to—"

"Don't sweat it."

"Seriously, I misjudged you."

He sipped his coffee. "Do me a favor and don't spread any of this around. My confrontation with Yemoja Roux has given me a reputation as a badass and I'd like to uh... cash in on it for a bit."

I held out my fist and he bumped it with his. "You got it, man."

Reina

THIRTY-SEVEN

I walked back toward Pink House feeling deflated. In one day, I'd gone from Serf to gifted like Yemoja Roux, and then to someone who unintentionally attacked my most admired idol. Her face was plastered in my head. *I hurt her.* GFA was so much more intense than I imagined and, after one day of classes, I was drained. But where I expected to be physically exhausted, I found myself emotionally so. I wanted to call my parents, to tell them what happened. I wanted to hear their voices—to listen to their comforting words.

The campus seemed deserted, as everyone was still in class. I headed straight into Pink House to my room, with the thought that if I made it there, nothing else could hurt me and I couldn't hurt anyone else.

When I awoke, the sunlight that was streaming in when I'd fallen asleep was replaced with the dark of night. I was confused and disoriented, unsure how long I'd been asleep. Briara's bed was empty, but I saw a piece of paper on my desk that told me she had been to our room at some point during my nap. Her note read:

I didn't want to wake you, but I went to the library.
   -Bri

My stomach twisted. *Ugh.* I missed dinner. I couldn't think of anything worse but then my mind drifted back to my afternoon with Yemoja Roux.

How was I supposed to use my gift after that? I sighed and pulled myself out of bed and headed for the student center to see if I could grab something before the cafeteria closed.

The outside air bit my skin through my blazer. I'd vastly underestimated how cold it was. Why couldn't the rest of the campus always be warm like the fort?

The student center had groups of students clumped together. One group was playing cards and laughing so loudly that I couldn't help but smile as I passed. I spotted the fishbowl, the glass cafeteria that had a few scattered students hunched over books, half the lights on that it normally did, and no obvious staff. I walked to the buffet line and was relieved to find a few leftover burgers wrapped up like they were from a fast food restaurant. I took two and eyed the third one that was leftover in the heated tray. "Yep, doing this." I grabbed the burger and had to balance it against my chest on the other two. When I got to the scanner, I couldn't reach my student ID.

I heard a laugh behind me. "Tough day?"

My gaze snapped up to Kai who reached for the ID card that

hung from the lanyard around my neck and held it to the scanner.

"Thanks," I said shyly.

He took a burger and led me to a table. I wasn't following him, I was following my burger, and I didn't give much thought to him as he took a seat beside me.

"Do you want to talk about it?"

I unwrapped the paper around my first burger and took a huge bite. I didn't even wait to swallow it before the words flew out between chews. "There was this terrible girl and she was being mean and stuff and all of a sudden she started saying weird stuff." I took another bite, and Kai flashed an amused smirk. "And then the teacher was mad that I used my gift on her."

He leaned forward. "So you do have a gift? It makes people weird. Nice."

I shook my head. "It's not nice. Because I was sad I didn't see Yemoja Roux and then she was my mentor and my gift was purple, and she told me to use it and she cried."

"That barely made any sense at all... Wait, what? You made Yemoja Roux cry?"

"And now I don't want to use my gift ever again because I can't get her face out of my head."

He reached out and rubbed my back. "Don't feel bad. It's not like Yemoja Roux is a saint or anything."

"What do you mean?" I asked, polishing off my first burger and unwrapping my second.

"I mean, she has hurt plenty of people in her time. Not to mention, she's the richest person in the world."

What did that have to do with anything? I wanted to argue or at least ask what the connection was, but I didn't want him to stop rubbing my back with those calming circles.

"I've missed you, Rei," he said, and I froze mid-bite.

He raised his hands defensively. "I know you're with Oden and stuff, but does it mean that we can't hang out from time to time?"

"Isn't that going to freak your girlfriend out?" I asked. I was obviously fishing, but I wanted to hear him confirm or deny it himself.

"I won't tell her if you won't."

So it was true. *I knew it*. That settled that. I needed to make an escape immediately. Kai leaned in and his devilish smile brought me right back to our kiss in the courtyard. My budding romance with Oden was a spark, but whether from years of suppressed feelings or shared history, my feelings for Kaito were a raging inferno. I was a moth to the flame and I always got burned. I felt dizzy. So dizzy that I put down my burger and stared into Kai's dark eyes. Maybe if he wasn't so messed up. Maybe in a different life we could—

My thoughts were cut short as Kai put his forehead to mine. "Reina," he whispered. "I can't seem to—"

"Kaito," a voice called from across the fishbowl. We looked up to see a blue-haired boy waving him over. "Are you ready?" the boy called.

"Is that Zane Blaque?" I asked.

He nodded, his gaze dropping back to me. "Yes."

"Why are you hanging out with him?" I asked. "Didn't you say he was somehow connected to Raphael Mazarin's death?"

Kai said, "I should go. See you around?"

I nodded and, to my dismay, he grabbed my third burger off the table before following his new friend out of the cafeteria.

kaito

THIRTY-EIGHT

I leaned back in my chair, pulling on my hair in hopes that the pain might drown out the sound of Quan bouncing a tennis ball off the wall, or of Enzo trying to snatch it between bounces by running across the room at super speed. I groaned, turning to Finn. "Why does Oden even call these meetings if he never shows up?"

Finn grinned. "Give him a break, Ace, he's super into his new girlfriend."

"They're not like official or anything," I said.

Quan interrupted, "They looked pretty official to me the other night at the fort."

I shot him a glare, but he seemed not to be bothered by it. Enzo shot into my line of sight. "But let's not forget about your night with Miranda."

I shook my head. "How do you even know about that?"

Quan said, "I snuck her out, remember? Plus, she told

everyone and, by the way, I can't believe you lied to me about zero gravity."

I put my palm to my face, letting out an exasperated sigh. "I should talk to her."

Enzo zipped over to me, his hand held up for me to high five. "Yeah, you should."

"Not what I meant."

Oden rushed in the door, half out of breath. His face was red, his shirt misbuttoned, and his lips smudged in the corners. "Sorry I'm late guys, I was with Rein—"

"We know where you were," Finn said, cutting him off. I shot him a thank you with a glance. His royal highness wasn't as bad as I thought. Of the other Nobles, I'd expected to like him the least, but it was the opposite. Unlike Quan and Enzo, he sort of kept to himself, he extinguished conflict, and he seemed to communicate on my non-verbal frequency. As for Oden, I thought that guy was a dick. Green-eyed devil was right. He just took whatever he wanted. Somebody had to teach that guy a lesson.

I stood. "Actually, I was just saying to the guys that I owed Miranda a little chat."

He nodded. "Yikes."

"Do you mind if I meet up with you later?"

Oden said, "I just got here, man."

"I've been here for an hour. It's not me that's been absent lately, bro."

Finn stood. "Oden, he's right. Just let him go. He'll meet us later."

Oden stepped aside and I made my escape. I headed down the hall toward the exit when I ran into Carter. "Hey, buddy," he said, cheerfully. "Did you hear the news?"

"No, what's up?"

"They're letting me do a set at the Winter Ball."

I patted his back. "Well done, man. Congrats."

He swung his guitar around and began to play. "Where are you headed?"

"I was actually looking for Miranda."

"Good thinking, better ask her to the ball. All the hot girls get asked first. I just saw her in the cafe."

I nodded my thanks and headed to find her. When I entered the cafeteria and saw a swarm of girls hanging on her every word, I knew exactly what they were talking about. Heat burned my face as I stormed over. "Miranda."

"Hey, sweetie," she said.

"Can I talk to you..." I scanned her captivated audience. "Alone?"

She followed me across the cafe. I stopped just outside of earshot of her little crew. "I need you to stop this. Stop telling people we hooked up. You're a beautiful girl and everything, I'm just—"

I stopped as Miranda began to laugh, her eyebrows raised with pity. She bit her bottom lip. "You don't remember that this was your plan?"

"What do you mean?"

"You were upset about Reina and I was upset about Oden and we decided to date to make them jealous."

"That's ridiculous. I would never agree to it."

She shrugged. "How else would I know how into her you are?"

"I'm not into her."

She pressed her lips together, stifling a smile. "We didn't plan to hook up or anything, we just... drank a little too much I guess.

I mean you're hot and I wouldn't be opposed to another night with you at Blue House, but did you really think I liked you for your personality? No offense, but next to Oden... you're just—"

"Whatever," I said, to shut her up. Each word was colder than the last. It wasn't that I cared what she thought. It was that some of those sentiments kept me awake at night for the last few years. "I don't care about what I said when I was drunk. It stops here." I turned to leave.

"Too bad, it was working."

I stopped. "Why do you say that?"

"Well, Oden has asked me about our relationship. Has Reina asked you? Has she mentioned me in conversation to see your reaction?"

Actually, there was last night in the cafe. She'd asked me if "my girlfriend" would mind us hanging out.

Miranda leered at me, analyzing my reaction, and when she found what she was looking for she tossed her ponytail over her shoulder and said, "But if you want to stop, it's your call."

"Wait," I said, without thinking. "What do I have to do?"

"Take me to the Winter Ball."

It was a trap. Scheming wasn't going to win Reina. "Nice try, Miranda. You'll have to find someone else. Besides, I don't think this Oden and Reina thing is going to last. The ball is two months away. I'd rather be there alone just in case."

I left the cafe while Miranda headed back to her table of friends, but instead of relief, I left the conversation feeling dejected. Miranda was the most awful girl I'd ever met, and even she thought I was a monster.

Reina

THIRTY-NINE

I never thought there would be a circumstance where I would dread seeing Yemoja Roux, but as I walked toward my second day of independent study, fear spread through my bones and settled on my ribs. What if she was angry about what I did? What if she didn't show up at all? I felt so nervous that I grew increasingly suspicious that she'd already ensnared me in her gift.

I opened the door to the combat zone and felt immediate relief. Yemoja Roux stood at the center of the entrance, as she had the day before, with the same bright smile I was used to.

"Uh.. good afternoon?" I said.

"Welcome back! Let's get to work." She sat and I took my place beside her.

She looked at me, her gaze sympathetic as if to tell me she understood my apprehension.

"I won't cry again. Promise," she said with a wink.

"I'm so sorry," I said, but she raised her hand to stop me.

"It was my fault. I dropped my gift's defense in the hopes of bearing yours so I could help you understand the nature of it. I prepared myself for pain, and wasn't expecting such a unique and dangerous power to emerge from you. It's an atypical gift, and no wonder you've had so much trouble discovering it."

I shook my head. "So you know what it is?"

Her dark eyes stared solemnly into mine and I could see the glint of yesterday's memory lingering behind them as she nodded. "Your gift is truth."

Truth. I sat staring down at my hands. "I don't understand. You seemed so hurt yesterday."

"There are truths we hide from ourselves. Everyone has demons they're not ready to confront," she said, turning away, but the smile returned to her face. "Maybe we don't always trust our ability to cope." She tucked a strand of magenta hair behind her ear. "I suppose the things I've been hiding were difficult to face."

"But... you're Yemoja Roux. You can do anything."

She grinned. "And you're Reina Bennett and I have to thank you. Your gift has given me a lot to think about."

"It seemed to make you sad."

She laughed. "It's the trials in life that make us grow."

I nodded. Of course she was right. I didn't necessarily like that growth required so much pain, but I was far from the girl who once numbed her grief. I understood how important it was.

"Reina, I must urge you to be very thoughtful about when you use your gift. Unless you're in the field, you must never force the truth on someone without their consent."

The idea that I even had a gift had barely sunken in. Not to mention the obvious pain I'd caused Yemoja Roux had me far too nervous to attempt it on another person. "Of course."

"You'll be tempted. But it's just the kind of power that could corrupt even the most heroic Fae."

She took my hands in hers and said, "Promise me."

"I promise."

Her intensity softened to a gentle smile that reminded me a little of my mother and my chest ached. As I looked at her, I was surprised to see a much older woman than the posters. She appeared tired, and there was a faint scar that ran along her jawline. Despite the countless interviews and documentaries I'd seen about her, she felt like a stranger.

I spent the next few weeks fighting desperately to catch up to my peers. I'd lost so much time thinking I was ungifted, but having the greatest Fae on earth as a mentor meant my progression was swift. Yemoja Roux's presence soothed me and it pushed our training into overdrive. I'd visualized a color for my gift, but learning it was truth gave it a distinctive shape during meditation. After the first full week of private lessons, I could pull my gift out of my body at a radius of a few inches, which was more than enough to start participating in my other classes. After several failed attempts in Professor Greene's class, I successfully infused a bit of truth in a confection, but the taste was so bitter he spit it out before my gift could take effect.

By the second week, I could block a strike defensively with my gift but only in a small area and only when I could correctly predict where I would be touched. Yemoja Roux said that was the exact reason why her Fae costume had pockets of exposed skin. Her enemy always went for those areas, so they were easiest to defend. In a way, she lured them into attacking her where she wanted. If I had a thousand lifetimes to absorb all of Yemoja Roux's knowledge, it wouldn't be enough time, but I only had the luxury of training with her at my scheduled times, a minute past and she'd jet back to her patrol like Cinderella from the ball.

By the third week, I began to understand the corruption Yemoja Roux had warned me about. Before I went to sleep, I imagined things, *dark things*. Sometimes I imagined using my gift to purge the truth from my wicked orphanage guardian, Ms. Vivian. Why had she tortured me and the other orphans without remorse? Was there more to that story? I daydreamed her responses, but in my imagination, she wasn't my only victim. I wanted to know the truth of how Kai felt about me, if for nothing else than so I could put my feelings for him to rest once and for all and fully give my heart to Oden, like I wanted. Especially since things were heating up with him.

One weekend we were tucked away in one of the dark corners of the fort. A late-night picnic turned into a heavy make-out session. The friction of his jeans against mine sent chills through my body. We were both caked in sweat, our mouths unwilling to part even to breathe. Oden grabbed a handful of my shirt in frustration as I wrapped my legs tighter around him. We separated only long enough for him to move his mouth to my neck and I strained for release. "Just tell me when to stop," he whispered, sliding his hand under my shirt.

"Don't stop," I said in a stupor.

He froze. "What? Really? You want to have sex? Are you sure?"

His questions sobered my daze, but I still felt a tickle at the back of my neck that radiated down my whole body. I had no reason to hesitate. I really liked him. He was good for me. I could see myself falling in love with him. I wanted to fall in love with him, and I was sure these make-out sessions were starting to frustrate him as they were me.

Sensing my hesitation, he pulled me in for a hug. "Don't worry. There's no rush," he said, taking my hands in his.

"But I want to, it's just... I've never—"

He leaned in and kissed me. "I know. Miranda told me, or was it Kai? That's why I wanted to make it special for you."

The mention of Kai was unwelcome. Why the hell did that guy walk around telling people about my sex life anyway? I felt a pang of guilt for being here with Oden while my thoughts still lingered on Kai. Oden and I were dating. Kai was nothing. Why couldn't I get that through my head? I just needed more time with Oden. I'd known Kai since middle school. That history was already being overshadowed by my new relationship. I felt my gift press against that thought.

"Any time with you will be special," I said, and his green gaze made me melt back into his arms.

"What about the Winter Ball?"

"What do you mean?"

He looked up at me shyly, a foreign expression to his usually confident face. "Will you go with me?"

"Of course. I've never been to a dance before."

"Then maybe we can plan something special for after... you know... if you're ready."

I grabbed his shoulders and shook him. "But it's two months away."

"I know." He groaned with a smile. He kissed me softly. "But you're worth the wait."

My thoughts were consumed with the pending loss of my virginity. I knew it was a normal part of life, but I wished I had someone to talk to about it with. I wished I could ask my mom questions. I didn't know why, but I wanted permission.

I'd begun to grow closer to Briara, but that only meant I was aware that girl talk for her mostly consisted of seances with spirits and ouija board chats. We chatted about crushes a little, but when the conversation got a little more personal, she always changed the subject. Still, I thought I'd give her a try. Who else did I have in my life?

Briara's eyes bulged. "You guys haven't had sex yet?"

I shrugged. "Well actually, I haven't had sex with anyone... ever."

"You're a virgin!"

"I don't like that word."

"Not even with Kai?"

I shook my head and her posture went rigid. "I'm probably not the best person to talk with."

"Right. Of course. Sorry," I said.

"Do you want to ask the spirits?" she asked in earnest.

I shook my head. "I think I'm good. Thanks, though. I'm sure I'll... you know... figure it out."

I lay back in bed and crossed my arms over my face to block out the sensation that I was alone. I had no woman in my life that I felt comfortable enough to ask about this sort of thing. Except maybe Yemoja Roux.

Kaito

FORTY

As if the ranking of the students wasn't already a huge point of contention at GFA, the headmistress installed a giant digital board that displayed the top 100 students in every building. The class rank of the top 100 was updated in real time as the professors voted students up or down based on their performance in class. Everyone was obsessed. There was a steady camp of students around every board, and friend groups were shattered by shifting ranks among the Elites. I'd even heard the list was streamed online for the public to access. If I wasn't training to the brink of collapsing every day before the list went up, I certainly was afterward, endlessly pushing the number of objects I could hold, and their duration. Since both combat zones always seemed to be booked, I had to find creative ways to test my limits, like touching every book, pencil, backpack, or scrap of paper that crossed my path during the day and holding them in range until I fell asleep.

The Noble Five were alright because, aside from Quan

thinking he should be ranked above Finn, the rest of the rankings were as we expected. Oden on top, followed by me, Enzo, Finn and then Quan. Still, Oden and I had been tense ever since he started dating Reina.

It was no surprise that Miranda was ranked sixth, but I was shocked to see Carter in seventh. I wouldn't have thought he would even make the list, let alone the top ten. I wanted to be the type of guy who didn't care about the list, the type that only knew his rank from being congratulated by other students, but I watched it like a hawk.

I searched for Carter to congratulate him on such a great rank, but when I found him in the student center, he was playing an impromptu concert to about twenty girls all of whom looked like they were a few songs away from throwing their bras at him. He caught my eye and smiled, nodding to me. *Way to go, roomie.*

I had a meeting with the Nobles coming up, but since Oden never showed up on time, I wanted to make sure I was later than he was. Since I had time to kill, I decided to head to the library to see if I could dig up any information about life in the world before gifts and before the Fae, a topic Zane and I discussed at length that week.

I hadn't spent much time at the library since I transferred to GFA, just a few hours after I first discovered it, but I'd since made use of the database of books that I could access from Blue House with my ID card. But since I was set to meet the guys at the student center anyway, it didn't make much sense to head back.

The library was well lit and clean, like the rest of the student center. It had snack machines and nap pods tucked away on one wall. There were always a dozen or so students hanging around its various desk types and couches, which made it feel more like a cozy home than a school library.

The least popular area was the one with the stacks of books. Most students preferred the digital versions, if for no other reason than because they were much faster to find and access. But something about physical books always charmed me, so I made my way through the seemingly endless rows that stretched twenty feet up and went back further than I cared to explore. I walked through the rows of books, going deeper until I found the history section. Most appeared to be biographies of famous Fae or Fae collections from a specific time period, but I didn't immediately see anything from before. It must have been further back. I moved quickly along, the dates moving back month by month, so I picked up my pace. The shelf wrapped around the corner, like the hedge mazes in the courtyard.

I turned the corner and froze. Reina was pressed against the bookshelf by Oden, her neck craned back as his mouth devoured her neck, his hands lost beneath her shirt. Her gaze snapped to me and I spun as fast as I could to flee.

"Wait wait," I heard her whisper.

"What's wrong?" Oden asked.

What's wrong? I seethed, already reaching the end of the stacks, my feet never touching the ground. What's wrong is that bastard. I was certain when they started dating that it wouldn't last long, but this was ridiculous. I was losing her. I didn't realize things between them had gotten so serious and now it felt like every second that passed was one where Reina was slipping away from me and into the arms of Oden. To think he'd been touching her like that all this time made me sick, and I glided out the front door of the student center, hoping the cold air would numb the pain. I felt the cold reach my bones, and my teeth began to chatter. How many books had I touched on my way through the library? I pictured the tidal wave of books crashing down on Oden as he tried to scramble free from the falling tomes. I had to win her back. I couldn't lose her, *not like this*.

Carter walked by, strumming his guitar as two girls I'd never met followed him and Quan not far behind them. If Quan was being dragged into this, I knew where they were going. He caught a glimpse of me. "Oh, bro, I need you to stay out of our room for the next..." he eyed both girls who were already undressing him with their eyes, "minute and a half."

I bit back a laugh. At least someone was doing well with women. I nodded to him, and my appreciation for him lingered long after he entered Blue House with the two transformed guys and Quan, who headed back towards the student center a minute later.

Quan grinned at me. "Meeting in five," he said.

"Don't think I'll make it," I said, trying not to let my anger into my voice.

He shrugged and headed back inside. I shook as the image of Reina with Oden replayed in my head. I clenched my fists, looking for an outlet for my fury. He was a better man than me, but I wasn't ready to let her go. I wanted him to hurt.

My chance came the next day, when our combat professor, Mr. Cordovan, unwittingly paired me with Oden.

Oden grinned at me across the arena like we were friends. Like he didn't know how much danger he was in. I wasn't being overconfident either. Since he'd been dating Reina, he'd been too busy to put in extra hours of training like I had. He was slipping and this was the perfect opportunity to dethrone our school's king in front of everyone.

Zone six, where our battle was set to commence, was a city block packed with sharp metal that I was eager to make use of. I wanted nothing more than to smack the smile off his pretty boy face. A guy like this, Elite with something flashy and good looks to match, was on a one-way train to become Fae from birth. Riches and fame all showering on him along with a license to kill. There was something unjust about how his dice were loaded, and I was going to set it right.

Professor Cordovan's voice shot through the speakers, "You may begin."

I took off running away from Oden until I had no breath to spare. It wasn't a manly move, but I needed to buy some time. I leapt into the air and let my gift carry me. I slipped in and out of vacant buildings until I was sure he didn't know where I was. A crash rattled my bones as Oden smashed the glass on a building he thought I was occupying. I used every second to touch loose objects on the ground. A steel pipe, a plank of wood, anything that my gift could pull free as Oden mindlessly created more debris. One building after the next, I clouded my gift with all manner of objects which I left undisturbed in their various locations in the arena.

When I was nearing my limit, I closed my eyes to catalog my haul. It was the largest number I'd ever captured and I felt the strain of every one. It was time to make my move.

"Don't be a coward, Kaito."

Now. I propelled a shard of glass from the far side of the zone at the sound of his voice. He deflected it with ease. "Good. I was worried you weren't even going to put up a fight today," he said. "Look, man, I didn't know how much you liked Reina. But I like her too. I'm not going to mess it up."

I seethed.

"No one is forcing her to be with me. We just like each other."

I stepped out into the street and he turned to me to finish his speech. "Can't you accept that?"

I chuckled.

He smiled. "What's funny?"

"What's funny is you're out here lecturing me like some arrogant prick, and I've already won."

With a clap of my outstretched hands, I hurled every object ensnared in my gift at him, but instead of striking, I swept them into a whirlwind around him and watched as one of the pipes scraped him. I spun a thousand objects into a tornado, with him at the center. He crouched, using his gift to shield himself from the blows. The objects that struck him bounced off and it took almost no effort to yank them back to the cyclone and tighten its twirl. I walked toward him and felt the shudder of his gift as his endurance gave way. Nails, glass, metal, wood, thrashing at his skin, whittling away his strength. Then I saw the first cut draw blood. He yelled and started frantically punching the objects, but there were too many, moving too quickly, and each time he swung he left an opening for me to strike another blow.

I bared my teeth as he fell to his knees, his eyes pleading at me with terror and surrender. I pushed the objects tighter and he yelled in pain. Nearly satisfied, I walked up to him and all at once I let the objects drop from the air around him, the severity of his injuries on display for the first time. I cocked my arm back and punched him across his jaw, the pop echoing through the zone. He stared up at me with alarm as blood dribbled down his cheek.

Professor Cordovan's voice shot out through the speaker. "Congratulations, Mr. Nakamaru. That was very impressive. You didn't even get a scratch on you. I've called Dr. Azul for you, Mr. Gates. Can you stand?"

Oden never broke eye contact. Not until the zone was overrun by our fellow classmates. Only then did the weight of what I'd done settle in. Whatever kindness he'd shown me in the past, including me in the Nobles and vouching for me on the media, was gone.

By the end of the day, my name had jumped to number one in the school ranking and I had eight missed calls from my mother. Unsurprisingly, it seemed they wanted me as a son again.

I could barely move without being swarmed by students wanting to hear the story of my victory, and no one seemed more proud or supportive than Carter and Zane. The adrenaline from the battle stayed with me all day, and it was almost enough to help me forget about what I'd seen in the library.

Even Quan congratulated me before he urged me to visit Oden in the hospital. Oden would be there for a while. Today was for celebrating and tomorrow for apologies.

After a wonderful day filled with positive attention, I headed back to Blue House. I walked with my head held high as if there wouldn't be consequences. That's when I saw Reina.

"What the fuck, Kai?" she said. She had on a jacket but was shivering enough for me to guess at how long she'd waited outside Blue House. "That was messed up, even for you."

I scoffed. "I didn't break a single rule. It was a battle and he lost."

"That's not what I heard. I heard it was personal. I heard it was frightening."

I pushed past her. "You're ridiculous."

"Why are you even here?" she asked. "This school is for future Fae. You seem much more suited for The Fallen."

"Those are pretty harsh words for someone who went from a shy virgin to banging in the library in zero point two seconds."

Her mouth dropped open. "You don't know what you're talking about, Kai. We were just kissing, and it's none of your business anyway."

I ran a frustrated hand through my hair. "It didn't look like just kissing to me."

"Well, it was. We're waiting for—" She stopped herself and silence grew thick between us.

"For what?" I whispered.

She stared down at her feet, fiddling with the charm on her necklace.

"For the dance?"

She shook her head. "He wanted it to be special."

"Yeah, because that's not cliche as fuck."

"You know what, Kai," she said, her voice heavy with emotion. "You're awfully invested in my personal life. Do you want to tell me why?" She stepped toward me, her chest nearly against mine.

My breath caught. My heartbeat dashing.

"There are only two possibilities here. Whichever it is, tell me and I promise I'll believe you." A tear slipped down her face and I felt my misplaced anger break. She continued, "Either you have feelings for me or you can't stand the thought of me being happy."

I was paralyzed by her obvious pain. It seemed like no matter what I felt for her, I always ended up hurting her. I looked up to the glow of the half moon and felt the cold seep through my jacket.

I didn't want to hurt her anymore. My heart beat, *Please be with me instead.* She was only a few words away from knowing the truth, and the weight of that kept me suspended. She was right about one thing—I was no Fae. How could I ask her to choose me when I'm so unworthy? She had the chance to be with someone whole. Someone who was programmed for kindness, and I was planning on asking her to wreck it. For me. I was asking her to choose her tormentor over her savior. I clenched my fist. *Reina, I promise this is the last time.* "You're right," I said. "I don't want you to be happy. I can't stand the thought of a Serf like you sailing through life."

"You're lying," she said, tears pouring down her cheeks. "Tell the truth."

Her eyes turned angry as her gift struck me. I saw a purple glow in them and on the tips of her fingers. We hadn't even touched, yet I felt the truth surge to my lips. She was strong and everything I couldn't say to her was desperate for release. *I don't think I'm good enough for you. You're the only one who understands. Please don't go. Don't give up on me. I love you, Reina.* The urge to say the words was intolerable, but I fought it, leaning on my own gift as my final line of defense. I was losing. Tears pricked my eyes as my will gave way. Desperate for a way out, I bit down on my bottom lip hard, until it split, blood running down my chin.

I must've been a sight because Reina cupped her hands over her mouth in fear. Her gift let me go. Then, as if resigned, she wiped her face. I swallowed hard and she shook her head, her gaze slipping between sad and angry. "Okay, Kai. Message received."

Reina

FORTY-ONE

I never told Yemoja Roux that I used my gift on Kai. I was ashamed that I broke my promise and how quickly my ability corrupted me, and I knew, if she ever found out, that would be the end of my training. October gave way to November and Kai and I could barely look at each other when we passed in the halls. My anger from our last conversation burned hot without any sign of abating. He was still in the same place in my heart he'd always been, but now his presence was a dagger that on some days made it hard to breathe.

I visited Oden in the infirmary as often as he'd allow, but it took longer than Doctor Azul predicted for him to get well again. It was as if losing his rank had broken his spirit, and I missed his sunny disposition. I didn't care how long it took him to recover, I would be there for him, and not because my mind endlessly reminded me that I was responsible, because I cared. He was surprised when I first came to see him and seemed to think that his rank had anything to do with how I felt about him. Like I'd jump ship to Kai now that he was the new top student. But even the thought of Kai made me sick. I wanted nothing to do with him.

By mid-November, Yemoja Roux had me in decent fighting shape. Defense was well enough, but the day she taught me to use my gift offensively, I finally felt like I could become Fae.

"Concentrate on your arm," she urged. "Let the truth swallow it."

As the purple shade of my gift engulfed my arm, I was alarmed to discover that it felt heavy, like it was encased in metal.

"Good, now sharpen it," Yemoja Roux said, pacing around me.

I visualized its edges coming to a point. With just a few swipes of my arm, my muscles grew fatigued, but I pushed through. I slashed at the practice dummy and felt delighted when the edge of my blade sliced into it. Losing my concentration, I gaped at my ordinary hand. My troubles with Kai felt minuscule compared to the satisfaction of raw power. I whipped back to Yemoja Roux. "Let's try it again."

She smiled at me proudly. I reveled in the chance to show her my progress, or even talk about life. In a short time, she became a fixture in my life—something I hadn't had in some time. One day, when I was on a high from spreading my blade to my elbow, I worked up enough courage to ask her if she'd ever been in love. Her eyebrows rose in surprise but her expression softened, and her voice came out as a whisper. "Yes, I have, once."

I watched as her gaze turned distant and she appeared to transport to a memory she wasn't ready to share. Then she turned to me. "Why do you ask? Are you in love?"

To my dismay, my thoughts went to Kai before Oden. I

threw my hands up defensively. "No, I don't think so. I mean, how do you know exactly?"

She pulled back her hair and started to work it into a braid. "I think it's different for everyone."

My heart squeezed in my chest as the next question escaped my lips. "Do you think love is a choice? You know, something you go into with both eyes open? Willingly? Or is it something that happens to you? Like an intense feeling you get swept up in?"

She pursed her lips. "It seems you already know the answer to that, Reina."

I didn't, but it was nice to have someone to chat with, someone who never pushed me but always listened when I was ready to share. She was making me better, a guiding light brought in when I needed her most and mended things I thought broken forever.

I saw those improvements reflected in my battle skills as well, and when I could sharpen the truth into a blade and cut with it for more than a few minutes at a time, I began to excel in my defense class—a class that had deemed me helpless from the start and took turns sending me to the infirmary.

Some of the classmates who delighted in tearing me to shreds a month ago turned green in the face as I deflected the attacks of my class's best Elites, and my unplanned trips to Dr. Azul's office stopped altogether.

Then, on a cold autumn day, my name slipped to the bottom of the class rank. Reina Bennett, 100.

Ever since Kai took the number one spot, I scarcely dared a glance at the board, but a sudden rush of attention alerted me that my name had made the list. Despite my rapid progress, Yemoja Roux never reported. It wasn't until my skills started manifesting in other classes that my name rose to it, and the moment it did, I understood why Yemoja Roux had avoided putting my name up. After two days of my name on the list, moving from 100 to 94, someone discovered and leaked that I'd been training with Yemoja Roux. The combat zone was swarmed with students. I had to admit that I enjoyed the release of the secret. I was tired of it nearly slipping during conversations with Briara, and the stronger my gift grew, the more difficult it became to lie. In all the years I dreamed of becoming Fae, I imagined liking the attention that came with it, but it was so polarized between being admired and hated, I longed for the days when I was invisible. I even saw pain in Oden's eyes when he congratulated me, and I wondered if he felt I'd hijacked his spot by his mentor's side.

The one lighthouse in a stormy sea of uncertainty was that Yemoja Roux began to take me with her on actual missions in the city. I wasn't ready for combat, but was instructed to protect civilians in the vicinity when Yemoja was stopping a crime. On my first day, I had never been more excited in my life, or more nervous. The only thing that kept me going was Yemoja Roux's faith in me. Even if all I was allowed to do was guard civilians while Yemoja Roux handled anything dangerous, this was Fae work. As it turned out, I was born for it—enamored by the whole process. It was the first time I felt like Fae and even had a public stage to do good. I may have been new to my gift, but I had enough power to help and protect alongside the great Yemoja Roux. For a few short weeks, it seemed like everything would be okay. I should have known that my mentor was keeping me far from any real danger. I should have accounted for my luck running run out because, the moment I got too comfortable, everything changed.

One night, the air dropped below freezing. Yemoja Roux and I were patrolling the east side of Ancetol—covering a wide area, waiting for the local precinct to call in—when we heard the chilling scream of a young child. We exchanged a glance and tore into the direction of the sound.

We slipped down an alley when the creak of deformed limbs crackled and from behind a dumpster a black-pointed claw shot out of the darkness and slammed down onto the dumpster with a rattling crash that made my hair stand on end.

The dark mass stepped into the open alley, its body clinked as if made of shards of black glass, the pieces shifting as its form grew before us. "Go," Yemoja whispered, but my legs were locked with fear.

One pointed limb after the other sprouted from its largest heap, like barbed lances ready to impale us. I didn't know what it was, but I was certain it was responsible for killing the Fae. Without thinking, I lunged forward, sharpening the purple truth into a keen blade and slashing at the enemy. The magical edge caught and the faceless beast devoured it into itself. The glass demon thrashed, and I barely slipped out of its range before a new barb lurched forward to impale me.

I doubled over. Gasping for air. Reaching inside myself to find my gift, which felt weak and weary, like on training days when I overexerted myself.

Yemoja Roux slid in front of me. "Get out of here! Now!" she yelled.

"I won't leave you here."

"You're just a student. This is my job. Now go, or you'll put us both in danger."

With the last word, her gift filled me with such fear that I cried all the way home. I pulled out my phone, desperate for comfort.

Me:

> *Kai? I was on patrol and something happened.*

Kai:

> *Are you okay? Where are you? I'm coming.*

Me:

> *I'm almost back to campus. We were attacked by some kind of monster. Yemoja Roux made me leave. She's fighting it alone. Kai, I'm so afraid. If anything happens to her, I'll never forgive myself.*

Kai:

> *It's going to be okay, Rei. Whatever happens. We'll get through this.*

I was too panicked to respond again.

Kai:

> *Let me know when you're back.*

. . .

His words only comforted me for a second and, by the time I reached campus, I was panting as I tried to explain what happened to the headmistress.

Ms. Tricorn surprised me with her response. "You're foolish," she said.

I wiped my eyes, looking up at her in confusion.

"You think the Great Yemoja Roux will be defeated so easily?"

My stomach swirled with shame and relief and I waited eagerly in her office for nearly an hour before an exhausted Yemoja Roux limped through the door.

I ran to her, throwing my arms around her. "I'm fine," she said, rubbing my back.

The headmistress said, "I'll call Doctor Azul." She hurried back in a minute later and asked, "Did you kill it?"

Yemoja Roux nodded. "But when I broke through, it turned to ash."

I took her hand. "How did you kill it? It... absorbed my gift."

She touched my face. "By refusing to lose."

I texted Kai that I was back and that Yemoja was alright. I told him we didn't need to meet.

He replied, K. I didn't want to dwell on the fact that I'd texted Kai instead of Oden, nor did I want to explain it to Oden when Kai inevitably brought it to his attention. But Kai never mentioned it.

My independent study was suspended after that. I was moved into the classes I'd been missing, including Professor Cordovan's Combat Training with Kai and Oden. I was also allowed to visit Yemoja Roux in the private infirmary during her recovery, a privilege I took advantage of whenever I could.

"So," she said one afternoon, "things are getting pretty serious with you and Oden, huh? Are you being safe?"

Heat burned my face and I narrowly resisted the urge to flee. I'd been waiting for an opening to ask some questions and, if this wasn't it, I wasn't sure what was.

"I... uh... well. Safe?"

She smiled. "Oh my, do we need to have a talk?"

"Well, he's my first boyfriend and we haven't... you know." I fiddled with my necklace, too afraid to make eye contact. "We were thinking after the Winter Ball."

She nodded. "Big step."

"How do you know if you're ready?"

"I suppose it's different for every person, but if you care for each other and you trust him, it can be a meaningful way to express your feelings. Sex is a part of life. It can complicate and intensify things."

I tucked a curl behind my ear.

She continued. "As you grow, you face more difficult obstacles. If you think you're ready to face the ones that come when you're sexually active, and if you understand how to be safe, then it's your choice to make. However!" she said, with so much intensity I jumped. "If you can't say the word, chances are you're not ready."

I grinned. "I can say it. It's weird to say it when I'm talking to you."

She tossed a pillow. "Sure."

"You know, this is a little off topic, but there's something I always wanted to ask you."

"Shoot," she said, gesturing for me to fetch her pillow.

I handed it to her. "On our first day training together, what truth brought you to tears?"

She paused for a long time and I wasn't sure if she would answer, but then she said, "I don't want to be Fae anymore. I'm afraid my chance to have a family has passed."

"What? You can definitely have a family. You're only twenty—"

"Sixty."

I knew it, technically. She'd been saving people long before I was born. But she looked nearly identical to the images of herself when she was twenty. She was so strong and youthful it was hard to think of her as old or ready for retirement.

"Being Fae means putting others before yourself. How would they feel if I just abandoned them to pursue my own goals? Especially now."

I shook my head. "So what are you supposed to do, die in the field?" Her silence and kind gaze confirmed that theory. "You don't owe us anymore."

"I'll tell you what, train hard and take my place so I can retire."

"You got it, Roux."

Kaito

FORTY-TWO

The night of the Winter Ball arrived and I knocked back several drinks at the fort along with a ton of other students while we waited for the event to start.

I looked for Reina, but she wasn't at the pre-party. Many of the girls were still getting ready while the guys drank and bragged about their dates. However, Miranda was there, strutting around in a pink skin-tight gown that trailed behind her and left nothing to the imagination. There was some kind of furry dead animal draped over her shoulders, and her expression was pleased as she drew the lust-filled gazes of every guy there. Quan looked like he might spontaneously combust.

"You alright, buddy?" I asked.

"She's a goddess, I say. A real live goddess."

I patted his back and took a swig from my cup.

I had kept my distance from Reina over the last few months because I knew I'd have a chance to see her at the midterm exam that marked the end of our first term at GFA, but since

Reina and I both ended the term ranked in the top ten, Headmistress Tricorn waived it.

My suit didn't feel much different from my school uniform, except thank god it was a nice charcoal gray instead of that horrible maroon color.

The only one who seemed more nervous about the dance than I was, was Carter. How could a famous pop star be so wary about performing at a small high school function?

On the other side of the fort, Zane caught my eye. He raised his cup and took a sip. He was a good guy and I felt guilty for being virtually a shut-in this past month while I tried to let go of Reina.

The ballroom glowed with lights that hung mid-air like snow, and everyone looked so different than how they normally looked in their uniforms. Even Carter had taken the time to slick back his hair, though his shirt was just a long-sleeved mesh monstrosity that proudly showed his nipples. I thought he might've been wearing eyeliner too, but I didn't get a good enough look at him to know for sure.

He took his place on stage and I held my breath as I shared in his nervousness. The moment he began to play, the party boomed to life and his voice sailed through the arched ceilings strong and angelic. My chest warmed. Even though I lost Reina, I'd been more than fortunate to leave this term with some new friends. Carter, Zane, Finn, even Quan. If I got nothing else from GFA, I got them. Things weren't so bad.

When Reina arrived at the top of the stairs, my breath caught and my mouth fell open as she glided down the steps in a dress that glimmered the same iridescent purple that I saw when she used her gift.

Fuck. I was not over her.

The world crashed back to me as Oden took her hand and led her onto the dance floor. Why had I even come tonight? For Carter? With the number of crazed women who reached for him at the bottom of the stage, I was sure he'd be just fine. Wait. Why were the women crazed when they should have felt relaxed by his music? In fact, even I felt a sort of involuntary mania coursing through me. Was Carter's music causing it? He could only calm, right? Unless he lied.

Reina and Oden danced into my line of sight, Oden's hands running up and down her body.

I turned away. Reina was with Oden. I had to let her go, and I refused to stay here and risk wrecking her special night.

I'd wrestled with the idea and finally made my mind up to leave. Then I heard her voice behind me. "Kai."

I spun. "Oh, hey, Reina. You... you look beautiful. I mean, obviously... like for Oden, because you're his girlfriend and not mine." *Oh god. Shut up. Shut up.*

She smiled. "Thanks." She reached up and started fiddling with her necklace. "I uh... I just wanted to thank you for being there for me that day, when Yemoja Roux and I—"

"It's no problem. I'll always be around if you need me." I gulped. "I'm so sorry about everything I said. It's your life and I've been terrible."

"It's really okay."

"Can I ask a favor?" I asked before I panicked and turned away. Across the hall, I could see Oden carrying two glasses of punch and scanning the crowd for Reina. "Uh, never mind, it's stupid."

She tucked a curl behind her ear. "What is it?" She grabbed my arm and turned me back to her.

"I wanted you to use your gift on me one more time, so... you know I'm not a monster."

She took a step closer. "I know you're not a monster, Kai."

"Please?"

She smiled. "You're not going to make yourself bleed again, are you?"

I felt the blush sting hot on my cheeks but, before I could respond, her eyes flashed purple and I felt her gift take hold.

Reina

FORTY-THREE

Kai looked down at me, the truth on his lips. I felt wracked with nerves. What could he possibly say? I knew whatever was coming would hurt, even if that wasn't his intention, yet I couldn't walk away. I was sure Oden would be looking for me now, but when I saw Kai across the dance floor alone, I knew the least I could do was come over to thank him. A moment ago I believed myself to be completely over him, but now, as he stood in front of me, I wasn't so sure.

"Reina, I know I'm not good enough for you."

"That's my choice to make."

"But you won't. You never do. No matter how I hurt you, you always end up back here. Choose better. I mess up everything in your life and most days I can't see any good in myself. I'm afraid I'll never meet anyone else who can believe in me like you do, but you're wrong about me." His eyes began to tear and mine mirrored them. "I think I might be in love with you, which is why I'm going to let you go be happy. Even if that means being with Oden."

My heart raced, and I wanted nothing more than to touch him, but I didn't. "Kai, I—"

A shrill scream filled the air as the glass wall separating the ballroom from the balcony shattered and rained down on us all. My gaze snapped up and three shadowy figures crept into the room. *Glass demons.* The students scattered into a panic. A sharp whistle shot out and in an instant Oden, Enzo, Quan, and Finn were assembled in formation.

"Run, Reina," Kai said, and he dashed to Oden's side.

Oh, fuck no. I sprang into action behind the guys, taking licks at the creature from a safe distance as the guys tried wounding it from close range. Behind me, Professor Greene and Professor Cordovan took on a glass demon of their own, its barbs shooting out and retracting with no predictable pattern. The shrill screech of glass on glass echoed through the ballroom while most of the students sprinted for the exit.

The third demon was headed for Carter, whose expression showed no trace of fear as he strummed his guitar, no doubt lending his assistance in our battle. Kai shot audio equipment from the stage at the demon, and it seemed to hardly affect the faceless creature at all. Oden was slower than usual, no doubt from his injuries, but still kept his body in front of his team as they slung their attacks futilely at the monster. But the demon absorbed Oden's punches and his fists had already begun to bleed. He slipped. A barb flew toward him. I slashed at the monster to deter it, but it was no use. Quan leapt between Oden and the glass demon, only to be run through his chest with black demonic glass. Stunned, Quan turned back to us before he collapsed on the floor in a pool of his own blood.

I screamed with horror as the boys charged in recklessly. We were all going to die here. A flash of magenta shot through. With an arm encased in magic shaped like a sword, Yemoja Roux sliced through the demon. It burst to ash and smoke so I sprinted to Quan, pulling him onto my lap and pressing his wound. Kai grabbed my shoulder and slid Quan and me out of the way as a second demon attacked. As if thirsty for more of Quan's blood, the demon charged me, and my gaze moved to Yemoja Roux who was busy blocking attacks from the third demon. Too far to help. I dropped Quan and stood to block the attack, but its powerful limbs broke through my gift. The demon's talon slammed into my head as Kai's gift yanked me back and tossed me into the air.

My ears rang as my vision blurred. I hung suspended over Quan as he bled out, but the darkness stole the scream from my throat and everything went black.

Reina

FORTY-FOUR

I awoke in a haze, feeling the warmth and familiarity of Kai's gift wrapped around me. It had been some time since I was held by him, like this. The memory of the attack on the school dance slammed into me, jogging me fully into consciousness. Suspended above a shattered ballroom, I resisted my urge to scream. Below I saw Yemoja Roux, Headmistress Tricorn, Veranda Yarrow, and some police officers standing around a body-shaped lump under a black blanket. They whispered sharply and their voices carried just enough for me to catch bits of their conversation.

Ms. Tricorn said, "I understand, Yemoja, but a student is dead."

Yemoja Roux shook her head. "I know how it looks, I just think we should take a moment to consider other possibilities."

Veranda Yarrow held out a large screen, but the headmistress blocked my view of it. Veranda said, "This was obviously orchestrated by The Fallen. But how did these students get involved? And what was their end game?"

Yemoja shook her head. "If he wanted to betray us, why did he try and rescue Reina? Why is he still holding her?"

The three turned, noticing that I was awake. Yemoja walked over and I felt her gift slip between me and Kai's gift. It broke and she caught me like I weighed nothing at all.

"Are you okay?" she asked, and she reached out and touched my forehead where a sharp sting flared beneath her touch. "We'll get you to Dr. Azul," she said.

I looked at the lump on the floor, tears springing to my eyes. "Is that Quan?"

Yemoja Roux nodded, putting me down before pulling me into her shoulder.

"W-why did they attack here?" I said, my voice breaking. I reached instinctively to touch my necklace charm for comfort, but it was gone. I must've lost it in the battle.

Veranda Yarrow stepped forward, a harsh look on her beautiful face. "We think it was a recruiting mission. A message to the students to pick a side." She turned to Headmistress Tricorn, who nodded at her, before returning her gaze to me.

Yemoja Roux said, "I'm not sure this is a good time—"

"This is a crime scene. I'm sure for Mr. Levout's sake, Reina would like to help in any way she can," Ms. Tricorn said, her words pin sharp.

"I do," I said, and Veranda Yarrow held out the screen. I held my breath as a video played. Zane Blaque stood at the school's barrier. He cast his gift, a shield that seemed to be concentrated on his left arm. He reached out and held it to the barrier, the glossy wall bending around his gift like a crowd of Serfs around an Elite. My pulse rose as one demon creature after another crept through the gate.

"Oh my god. Zane Blaque let them in," I said.

Veranda Yarrow said, "Just wait." She swept her finger over the screen and the video sped up. She slowed it as two figures approached Zane's gap in the wall. My heart stopped as Carter walked cheerfully toward Zane, his ever-present guitar slung on his back. Beside him was Kai. *My Kai.* The guy who had apparently saved my life. No. *It was impossible.* Kai didn't have anything to do with it. He and Carter fought with us. Carter stepped through the barrier and Kai looked back at the school dance as if reconsidering his choice. Then, of his own free will, he walked through the gap in the barrier—and Zane followed before closing it for good.

"It's a mistake," I said. "Kai isn't involved."

"You never saw him spend time with Carter or Zane?"

"I... I mean of course. Carter was his roommate."

"And Zane?" the headmistress asked.

"He..." My breath skipped as I exhaled. "He's not involved."

Kai seemed to become more unhinged these last few months. Was it possible I'd missed the signs? Was I so blinded by our history and his pretty words to know he was saying good-bye? No. *I knew him.* I balled my hands into fists, grinding my teeth. I knew with certainty that someone had set Kai up.

The evidence was damning. Which left me with only one option: find him and clear his name. There was no one left to believe in Kaito Nakamaru but me.

Read The Brave & The Broken

GIFTED FAE ACADEMY

THE brave AND THE
broken

BOOK TWO

USA TODAY BESTSELLING AUTHOR
BRITTNI CHENELLE

THE BRAVE & THE BROKEN

REINA

Lightning crackled through the courtyard as the last of the students filed into the auditorium. Though midday, the clouds blocked the sun's rays and threatened a storm like a knife at our throats. The thick mossy smell of the impending rain filled my nose as I stepped out of the cool air and into the auditorium, only to regret it a moment later. The sobs of the broken-hearted students reverberated off the domed ceilings, and the air was so thick I thought we might suffocate in each other's grief. Dressed in black attire, the room was guarded by a host of Fae ready to jump into action at a moment's notice. We were no longer safe. The walls of Gifted Fae Academy had been breached, and with them fell one of our most beloved students.

I took my seat beside Briara, my head pounding from a night spent crying, but unlike her I had no more tears to shed. It was as if I cried myself dry. My roommate, however, seemed to have an endless supply. I wanted to reach out and hold her hand, but she was so fragile I worried she'd shatter at my touch. I traced her gaze past the rows of students to the stage where a large portrait of Quan Levout sat, grinning brightly. Bri choked on her tears, and I turned my face away, clenching my jaw to the point of pain at the sound of her agony. I reached for the owl charm on my necklace only to remember that it, too, was gone.

There is nothing so senseless as a murdered kid, and at a school filled with aspiring Fae where we should feel safe, we instead felt helpless in the aftermath of his death. As I replayed the night of the winter ball in my head, I kept coming back to the same thought. *What was all this training for if I couldn't even save a friend?*

The big screen above the stage lit, and a close-up of Veranda Yarrow filled the space. Although I could see her on stage just fine, the live feed intensified her expression. Her wide hips and fierce red hair swayed as she stepped behind the podium, her eyes glistening with pain. "Quan Levout was kind and brave," she said, her words slicing into the crowd. "He died defending his friends and his school, an act worthy of the title Fae." Her voice broke and she stepped away from the mic while Yemoja Roux took the stage.

I leaned forward at the sight of my mentor. Her magenta hair was dulled, her skin ashy and her eyes sunken in and dark. When her gaze flicked up to the crowd, I saw in her vacant expression that she'd been asking herself the same questions I had. Her slumped posture made it evident that she blamed herself. She lifted the mic. "I'd like to present the honorary title of Fae to Quan Levout for his heroic actions during the recent attack."

A flare of sniffles and sobs filled the air, and my vision began to blur. I was no stranger to funerals. I'd been to my parents' just over a year ago. The only thing that got me through back then was the hope that I would one day get into GFA, and things would be better. Only now, behind the walls of the institution I had admired all my life, I found myself walking toward the same despair, but without that comforting vision of a better future.

I snapped back to attention when the next speaker took the stage. Oden Gates, my boyfriend, and Quan's closest friend, stepped behind the podium looking much worse than Miss Yarrow or Yemoja Roux.

He hadn't returned a single call or text since the attack, and I'd imagined he was in bad shape. I just wanted to be there for him if he needed me. Dread flared inside me at the sight of him. Unlike Yemoja's dulled appearance, Oden's eyes blazed such a vivid green that he hardly looked human. His skin was waxy, his plump lips chapped. Rather than broken, he looked frightening, dangerous, ready to kill at the slightest provocation. Just from looking at him, and everyone else for that matter, I feared, if the school and the local Fae could be so defeated by a decimated spirit alone, the Fallen had already won. Robbed of my usual nervous habit, I smoothed out the folds in the black fabric of my dress as I waited for Oden's first words.

Finally, Oden tapped on the microphone, his green eyes glazed over like he forgot the whole school was watching.

"I can't believe he's gone. Just like that." He snapped his fingers as he shook his head. "Quan didn't deserve to die." He gritted his teeth, his jaw clenching. "What's the point of these Gifts if we can't protect the people we care about? What's the use of all this training?" he asked, a low growl in his voice.

I swallowed; there it was. I bit my bottom lip and shut my eyes. Oden was unraveling, and it was painful to watch. Professor Greene and Veranda Yarrow exchanged a look, as if debating whether to put an end to his speech. I hoped they would, but I supposed they were giving him leeway since he knew Quan best.

Oden sputtered, "When I find Kaito Nakamaru, I'll make him fucking *pay* for what he did!"

Veranda snatched the microphone away and the room sat in stunned silence.

I dropped my head, the heat of fresh tears streaking my face. *Kai.* I placed my hand flat on my chest where my owl charm used to rest. My heartbeat raced against it as I swallowed the urge to defend him. Miss Yarrow spoke, "Emotions are running high. There will be grief counselors available to any who feel the need to talk. Please join us in the cafeteria for refreshments, if you wish."

The screen above the stage flipped to static. Taking it as a sign that the ceremony was over, some eager students stood and prepared to move to the cafeteria. I didn't blame them. The sorrow in the auditorium was palpable. Thunder crackled outside as the first few students filed out, then the screen lit up again. My stomach dropped, my heartbeat racing as I gaped at the screen. Kaito Nakamaru stared back and, before he spoke his first words, I feared trusting him had been a terrible mistake.

Read The Brave & The Broken

AUTHOR'S NOTE

Thank you for reading The Fae & The Fallen. The sequel, *The Brave & The Broken,* is available for pre-order.

If you enjoyed this story, don't forget to leave a review and let me know what you thought. Reviews are an author's best friend. A simple, "I liked it." makes a huge impact and it's a key factor in deciding whether or not I'll continue writing a series.

Thank you for your support.

Happy reading,

Brittni Chenelle

CONTENTS

CHASTE BLOOD

BRITTNI CHENELLE

REPRESSED 1 ROYALS

USA TODAY BESTSELLING AUTHOR
BRITTNI CHENELLE

CHASTE
BLOOD

CONTENTS

ONE

— MADDOX —

I jolted awake with the sharp, white pain of steel plunged into my chest. Nova's long, jet-black hair did little to hide the tears that fell down her cheeks. Her arms shook, driving the dagger deeper as sobs shook her body. The urge to cry out in pain, to wrestle the blade out of me and end the agonizing ache, was outweighed by my desire to watch her. The desire to understand.

"I'm sorry," she said, sobbing, but her grip never weakened.

Moonlight poured through my window, haloing her head and glinting off the top of the hilt as she held it firmly in place.

Why? Why are you doing this? I wanted to ask, but the blade had pierced my lung.

Am I dying?

My immortality fought to regrow the flesh around the wound, but the blade halted the regeneration. My thoughts moved to the night before, when Nova's body shook beneath my fingertips as she tightened to orgasm. I remembered how she sighed and kissed me, only to work herself up for another round. My thoughts raced through every second we'd spent together, desperate to find the moment that led her to this.

I had known she was special the first time we met. Herod had presented another batch of tributes and my eyes went straight to Nova. The same blue eyes that now willed my life to end, had lit when she first saw me, as if taken by surprise, just as they did now as she tightened her grip.

Nova lifted the dagger from my chest and plunged it in again, this time cutting into my heart. I coughed, wracked with pain as my immortality started to mend the first wound.

The adjustment was considerably more painful, but my lung was free. "Why?" I whispered.

She clamped her eyes shut, unrelenting.

My heart writhed, and each beat shredded the muscle against the blade. *You look so beautiful when you cry.* I wanted to reach out and wipe her tears, to tell her not to hurt, but I was frozen, confused, and in pain.

Then I understood this nightmare. *I am a fool.* I closed my eyes as laughter began to rise through the pain. I'd defended my actions to Ronan, assuring him that Nova was not my mate and that she meant nothing to me while, in reality, I was sure I was falling for her. Then, last night Nova whispered those three forbidden words, and they filled me with so much warmth that I was prepared to accept the consequences. Prepared to lose everything. My throne, my immortality, my life, just as my parents had, all for the one thing immortals couldn't have.

I suppressed my laughter, pressing my lips together to hold

back my smile. The pain made me delirious, but my thoughts and memories were crystal clear.

I planned to stop accepting tributes from the other courts, a move that would publicly declare that I was in love, and therefore mortal. How long would we have before the Moon and Arrow Courts attacked? Or would it be the greedy gaze of my own people that led to my early end? I thought any measure of time where I could give myself fully to Nova would have sufficed and that the swell of release when I said those words aloud was worth letting the immortal world burn, but I could never have guessed that the girl who had stolen my heart might be the most eager to stop it from beating.

Everything we had was a lie, a ploy to make me fall in love so that my immortality would break and she could take my life. Laughter burst through my lips. The malice radiating through her blue eyes gave way to fear. I wasn't sure who sent her or if she'd made the plan on her own, but it didn't matter. She was the only one in the world I trusted, and she was a liar.

I wasn't sure what was funnier, that she never loved me or that I had thought I loved her. My immortality was strong and intact, a sure indication that I'd only felt a shadow of the real thing. As she watched me regain my strength, I realized how wrong I had been.

Her chest rose and fell so quickly that I could almost taste her fear. I grinned at her, pushing her deeper into despair.

She pulled the dagger from my chest. "Mad," she breathed, "I'm sorry."

I could see the war raging behind her eyes. I could see the dots connecting as she swallowed her failure, one breath at a time.

I leaned in and put my forehead to hers. "It seems that neither of us are capable of love."

"I-I do love you."

"We're beyond that game now, aren't we?"

Her sobs grew heavy. "Please," she begged, "Make me immortal, and I'll faithfully serve you forever. I promise, Mad."

"I don't believe you," I growled, my words dripping with malicious intent.

She grabbed my jaw, kissing me fiercely, and smearing tears onto my face. I allowed it, waiting for whatever I'd felt to come rushing to the surface, but whatever that feeling was, she'd struck it dead with that dagger.

Feeling my indifference, she pulled away. "Please, let me prove it. Tell me what I have to do. I'll do anything you want. I'll be anything you want me to be."

I lifted the dagger from my bed, handing it back to her. "I need you to be proof that the Blood King has no heart."

"Wh-what?"

"Stab yourself with this to prove your allegiance, and before you die, I'll make you immortal."

She swiped at her eyes with her free hand. "How can I trust you?"

"You can't, just as I can't trust you."

She tucked a strand of hair behind her ear, but her gaze was glued on the dagger as she considered her options.

"Are you going to save me?" she asked.

I brushed her cheek with my thumb and smiled softly. "We'll see."

"And if I don't do it?"

"We'll see."

She lifted the dagger, her shaking hands fragmenting moonlight off the blade and splashing it across the room. She lifted her chin, and her blue eyes bored into mine.

"Maddox," she whispered. "Don't forget about me."

I swallowed a lump in my throat, and with a sudden jerk of her hands, she plunged the dagger into her chest. Her eyes widened. She held my gaze until hers began to droop. I looked within myself for a memory, a feeling strong enough to push me to lean forward and bite her throat. A touch of venom was all it would take, but I felt nothing, not even as her life-blood spilled out of who I thought was my only ally, and on to my sheets.

"Please," she said, surprising me. "I love you."

A twinge of something stirred then. Like a wave, it engulfed me, overrunning my thoughts and pushing my body into action. I lunged forward, sinking my fangs into her neck.

She wrapped a limp arm around me and whispered, "thank you," through gasps, but it was not love that I felt in that moment.

It was hatred.

Instead of pushing the venom through my fangs, I sucked, draining away her life before she knew she was going to die.

Her corpse lay still in my bed, and if I ignored the potent smell of blood on my sheets, she looked like she was just sleeping. Death was a mercy I regretted granting her, and I had to look away to stop myself from mutilating what was left. Ronan might grow suspicious. I wasn't fit to lead the Blood Court to absolute dominance. Not if I could be so easily fooled and manipulated.

I pulled off my torn shirt, tossing it into the fire. The less evidence Ronan could gather, the better. I called for a maid, and they promptly cleared the body away, changing my sheets as they routinely did with the tributes I'd grown tired of. I sat on my windowsill and stared mindlessly at the full moon.

I didn't care about Nova.

My wounds had already healed, but as the anger began to wear off, sadness took its place. I was grateful for it. Only Nova could have taught to trust no one, ever. For the first time, I understood what Ronan had fought to teach me all my life. That love was nothing but a weakness designed to usurp immortal thrones. If I had been capable of feeling it, Nova would have succeeded in killing me. Whether she'd been my mate or not, I'd never know, and there was no use in dwelling on it. All that mattered was that I would never fall for it again.

Or so I thought.

TWO

— SINNA —

I strained for breath, but the corset dug deeper into my sides. Of all nights, the royal dressers chose my divination ceremony to exact revenge. Years of snide remarks regarding their broken fashion sense went unaddressed, and tonight they were somewhere in the castle snickering about making my dress too small. I cursed under my breath, but whichever dark corner of the castle they'd slunk into was too far out of my range to retaliate with a spell. I tried one anyway. Several, in fact. It was birthright as a princess of the Shadow Court to wield magic and although I wasn't studious enough to conjure anything as flashy as a divination spell, nor skilled enough to fully shadow walk without a Hunter, I could certainly muster enough magic to ruin someone's day.

Ezra smiled to herself. "And who are we cursing today?"

But I was too invested in finishing my enchantment to respond.

She looked pleased and carried herself with a dignified grace I couldn't mimic. Her crown gleamed as she slid a pin through my hair to secure mine. Her golden skin and hair contrasted her charcoal lipstick and smokey eyes. She was radiant, but my sister hardly needed enhancements to look regal. She wore it that way because the color black was as bound to our history as the shadows that made up our home.

She reached for another pin. I wondered if she was going to start shoving random objects in there when she ran out. Still, I was happy to have some alone time with her before the ceremony. She had a calming presence that my sanity greatly relied on. The Queen of The Shadow Court didn't have to help me with my hair; we had people for that, but Ezra never missed an opportunity to be a good sister. I was lucky to have her. She was the only family I had left. She'd stepped into the role of Queen when our parents died, despite being only two years older. She was identical to our mother. I looked more like our mortal father, and I had the blemishes to prove it.

She was the superior beauty, as she had the superior heart.

I pulled down on my corset, hoping to move it enough to take a decent-sized breath, but Ezra's next pin dug straight through my elegant updo and into my skull. I swatted her hand away.

"I'm pretty sure it would stay on, even if someone punched me in the face."

She reared her arm back, balling her hand into a fist. "Should we test it?"

"I can't breathe. Can we have the dressmaker killed?"

She stepped back, giving me a once over. "I would, but you've never looked better," she teased. "Your face looks so pretty in that shade of purple."

She moved to my back and pulled at the strings until the corset popped open.

"Thank god," I said, gulping in air.

"If I loosen it, there will be a gap between the two sides. It might look. . . I don't know, sloppy?"

My ribs ached in response. "That's fine. I'll probably start a new trend."

She re-tied it looser than before and then grabbed another handful of pins. Instead of picking up where she left off, she stepped back, her honey-colored eyes narrowing as she scanned me. "I thought it was the dress, but you seem kind of nervous."

"No, of course not," I said too quickly. "What's there to be nervous about?"

She began circling me in search of a place to put her next pin. "Exactly. I changed the law specifically, so no choice needs to be made."

I wasn't about to let her feel sorry about this. She was too kind. I spun to her, grabbing her by her forearms since her hands were occupied with pins.

"You don't have to explain anything to me. I will always be on your side."

Her gaze dropped to the floor as she exhaled, but I could see some tension release from her shoulders. "I know. I just wanted to check with you since it's finally your turn. . . you know, in case that changed things."

I watched her, wondering how a person could be so delicate and so resolute at the same time.

"Tell me, if you still had the choice, what would it be?"

"Hunters. Easy choice."

"We'll see if you still feel that way after the tether takes hold."

"I know what I'm talk—" I stopped myself. "Tether?"

She stared at the granite ceilings, caught in her own memory. "When you see him..." She looked at me and raised an eyebrow. "Her?"

I shrugged noncommittally.

"When you see your mate for the first time, the connection comes to life. It's like an invisible string that ties you together."

I snorted. *As if this ceremony could get any more ridiculous.* But she'd piqued my interest, and I didn't want to miss whatever came next.

"You'll feel the pull of them until one of our Hunters takes them out. After that, it'll go back to normal."

I must've looked worried, because she smiled victoriously. "It usually only takes a day or two. You can handle it."

"Of course I can. You're working yourself up over nothing."

She smiled, dismissing her concern as she returned to her task. If the roles had been reversed and I had become Queen, I could not have handled it with half her grace. Yet, in typical Ezra fashion, she was worried about how her decisions affected me. When Ezra first changed the law to exclude the choice, I'd given her decision a lot of thought. My feelings were mixed at first. On the one hand, if our mother hadn't made the choice to seek out her fated mate, Ezra and I wouldn't even exist.

On the other hand, that choice was to blame for her death.

No, I was certain that even with a choice, I wouldn't be so reckless as to seek out my mate. Sending the Hunters to kill them was the best option, both for me and the rest of the Shadow Court.

I could tell that Ezra's decree weighed heavily on her, but I wasn't sure why. Our court would be extinct if not for that law. We'd seen the choice whittle our court away to almost nothing. Immortality was too important to toss away for a few short years of love.

So when the divination ceremony commences, and I steal a look at my mate, it will be my last. I will gladly send the Hunters to exterminate him and rule at my sister's side forever.

THREE

—— M A D D O X ——

My throat tightened as the scent of mortal blood drifted into my quarters. Thirst choked me, and my mind fell into a haze. I might be a glutton for punishment, but I've always liked to delay feeding. I liked the unhinged feeling, the utter desperation, just before I gave in. That need was how I imagined mortals might feel in their final moments, desperate to cling on to one more shred of life before their bodies forced them into submission.

I could hear the scrape of Ronan's boots in the hallway growing louder as he moved toward my quarters to deliver the news, but there was no need. I could already smell what was standing in my throne room.

A knock sounded, and the door swung open. I stifled a laugh. His curly hair was ruffled, but his leather armor was neat and clean. I was amused by how little he did to hide his irritation. He had once been a well-respected Hunter for the Blood Court, but that was before the war ended, leaving a new set of royals to look after the Three Immortal Courts.

I didn't care much for Herod, the King of the Moon Court, or Delton, The King of the Arrow Court, but none of us wanted another outright war. We'd settled on the subtler battle of wills.

"Your Highness," Ronan said. "Herod has sent you some new tributes. They're waiting for you in the throne room."

My mouth watered as I stood, heading for the door.

"Should I have them drained for you?"

I stopped, giving him a sideways glance as I raised my brow. "No, I can manage."

"I just think you're playing a dangerous game. If one of them was to be your mate, you could risk—"

"I am not weak like my father."

My thoughts turned to the night Nova died, almost two years ago, as I stoked my fire with extra fuel.

"If I were to find my mate, I'd murder her without a second thought."

Silence was his disagreement. When Ronan found out I'd killed Nova, he seemed relieved, but since then I'd indulged in a parade of tributes for extended stays at the castle to prove my indifference when I drained them. That had the opposite effect on Ronan.

His eyes narrowed, so I glared back at him. He might've been an old friend of my parents, but I didn't trust him or anyone else as far as I could throw them.

"Don't pretend like you're concerned for my immortality," I said, straightening my tie.

"I am. You have no heir. If your immortality is lost, the court will be lost as well."

Heir. I scoffed. Becoming mortal enough to produce an heir required finding my mate, but since he was vehemently against that, I was sure he was alluding to the second way. Naming one. I could choose a mortal successor and turn them into a vampire, but the number of times an heir dismembered and scattered the king to get the throne practically guaranteed that outcome. I could name someone who was already a vampire, but every one of them would see it overrun with new, greedy vampires who killed mortals for sport and would clear our town of the small pieces of civilization we were allowed.

I put my hand on his shoulder and he flinched. "I think you're bored. With all these tributes, there's plenty of blood to go around, and your position is practically obsolete."

His gaze dropped to the floor. "Before they died, your parents charged me with your protection."

I raised an eyebrow. "Then perhaps you should have given them this lecture."

I stalked out, refusing to let his irritation worm its way into me. I followed the sweet scent of mortal blood through the halls. I wasn't going to lose face with Herod just so Ronan could sleep better at night. The gifts that the other kings and I exchanged were supposed to be temptations, fulfill our lust, or in my case, thirst, but the chance of actually finding someone's mate was, well, zero. It was impossible. All immortals knew that, so our tradition was nothing but a harmless game, not to mention an endless supply of free meals for the Blood Court.

Two guards opened the doors to my throne room, and the warm, blood-scented air slammed into me. My tongue tingled as

I focused on my throne, denying myself a view of the lovely tributes until I took a seat.

Herod stood at the foot of my throne, blocking my view with one of my guards at his side. Even using hushed tones, I heard my guard warning him not to shift. Not that there was any real danger for us if he did. The shifters generally couldn't defeat vampires in combat one-on-one. They moved in packs for that reason, but we outnumbered them five to one, and tonight, Herod seemed to be alone. The warning was unnecessary. He wouldn't dare shift in my territory anyway and risk losing twenty years of peace. I just enjoyed wasting his time. His gaze locked on me as my guard finished giving him the rundown. Herod's blue body paint looked purple in the dim reddish light of my throne room and I got a twinge of pride to see my court's customary color start to consume his. Not that I'd ever admit it, but I admired the shifter look--shirtless, free, and painted like warriors. I had once smeared blood down my lips and across my cheeks in a similar fashion, only to wash it off before anyone from the Blood Court saw.

I gestured to the guards. "Can we get Herod a shirt?"

He snorted, crossing his arms over his muscular chest. "A hundred years, and you're still not tired of that joke."

Of course, I knew that the members of the Moon Court dressed sparsely to accommodate shifting, but I'd never pass up an opportunity to give Herod a hard time, especially since this was technically an assassination attempt--a gift given with the intention of eventually finding my mate to make me vulnerable to death. The Moon and Arrow Courts sent me tributes more often than I sent them, but as the largest, strongest, and most influential court, they were right to target me. Ronan didn't understand that every tribute that was sent was confirmation of the Blood Court's dominance.

The tributes moved behind Herod, and I was tempted to sneak a peek at them, especially since the scent of the warm pulsing blood was so strong. The edges of my vision turned to a distinct crimson.

Herod cleared his throat. "Your Highness, please accept these lovely tributes as a token of the Moon Court's respect."

He moved aside and I nodded in appreciation before allowing myself to appraise the tributes.

Five women stood in the center of my throne room, donning white gowns that differed slightly, complementing their unique features. Like delicious morsels wrapped in shiny foil, each was lovelier than the last. They'd all end up the same way, a bloodless corpse, but from their confident and seductive smiles, it was obvious they each believed themselves to be the exception.

Herod smirked and nodded to one of the girls. She was an inch or two taller than the rest, with jet black hair, blue eyes, and a smoldering presence. I knew exactly why he thought I'd like her. She looked a lot like Nova. I wasn't surprised that word had gotten to other courts that I had kept Nova for so long, but I was surprised how frequently his tributes resembled her, even years later.

Each time I took to a tribute for an extended period, Ronan would be convinced that I'd found my mate and that we were all in grave danger. He'd check for signs of my immortality waning, but Herod had continued to bring me a specific type as if he knew she had been different from the others. His opinion hardly mattered.

I was more concerned with Ronan as his nagging affected my daily routine. I hoped as the years passed, Ronan would come to learn what I knew all along. Regardless of their beauty, it always ended the same way, with a bloodless corpse in my bed.

I took a long look at each tribute and saw the same hopeful expression plastered onto each of their faces. Their gazes all screamed the same two things.

Make me immortal. Make me a queen.

If they had any sense at all, they'd know that royalty would never beg to become so, not even with their eyes. If they really knew what I suffered, they wouldn't wish for it.

There were so many at my disposal. So many who would murder me if I let my guard down.

Everyone wanted a bite of my throne.

One of the girls shifted slightly, drawing my attention. Her hair was chin-length and light in color. Her bangs hid her eyes, and although I couldn't see her well, she set off an alarm in my body. I felt my fangs sharpen as heat tore through me and I sprung from my throne. I stalked over to the girl. She was a few inches shorter than the rest and far less curvy.

The girl wilted beneath my stare. I pushed her bangs out of her eyes to get a clear look at her face, and she winced. I was horrified by what I saw in her softly curved features.

Herod came up beside me. "Good choice, Sire, this is—"

I spun with bared teeth, the pulse of his neck pulling in my full attention. He growled, which intensified his appearance, as if his body was itching to shift.

"What's wrong?" Herod asked, crouching defensively.

My legs shook. "Return this tribute to wherever you found her."

Ronan stepped between us. "What is it, Sire?"

The words sickened me before I said them. My stomach churned with unease.

"The tribute..." I said through bared teeth. "She's not fully grown."

Herod's eyes widened "My apologies. She said she was—"

"Look at her!"

Herod's gaze dropped to the ground. I headed for the door, my appetite soured, as Herod called after me, his words lost in the torrent of my rage.

FOUR

SINNA

I held my head high as I entered the dark hall and stepped out onto the black carpet that stretched out in front of me. Our court's Hunters stood at attention on either side; their solemn expressions breathing intensity into the sound of the drums as I approached. The Hunters were dressed in black armor that looked similar to their usual set; only tonight they had silver swirls embroidered into the collars and around the seams. I scanned them for one in particular but didn't see him.

The lethally trained men and women were muscular, and stood unnervingly still, which seemed to grate on my confidence, but once I recognized a few of them from various nights of indulgence, the intimidating formality of the ceremony lifted in my mind. I eyed each one as I passed, admiring their strength and versatility. If I had one regret in life, it was that I was born royal and, therefore, could not become a Hunter myself. They might've had to kill innocents, but their brave actions ensured our court's immortality, not to mention they were able to roam above ground with the mortals as long as they reported back on time. They had our lives in their hands and they seemed incapable of failure, never before missing a mark they'd been assigned to eliminate. The closest I could get to being a Hunter was the occasional night time interlude, a glimpse or two at their vicious training regime, or a nugget of information gleaned from Finn in exchange for sexual favors.

My attention snapped to Finn when he finally came into view. Despite keeping his eyes trained directly ahead, he bit back a smile. His shaggy hair was messy, his clothing wrinkled, and unlike the other Hunters and their neutral expression, he seemed more than a little inappropriately amused. I spent my nights with various Hunters for variety, but I called on Finn most due to both his adequacy in the bedroom as well as his aloofness and discretion outside of it. We'd made a deal that I'd select him for the honor of eliminating my mate, and in exchange, he'd regale me with the play-by-play of my mate's death, as well as a detailed description of the world above ground. I wasn't sure why, but I felt embarrassed by the possibility that my mate might beg for his life in the end. A mate was in some ways a reflection of oneself, and while the other Hunters would hide a detail like that from their report, Finn would tell it to me straight.

Ahead, I spotted the pool of foresight, a beacon of shimmering light in a comfortably dark world. As I neared, my thoughts moved to my sister's ceremony.

I remember the anxious energy that hung in the air as she took a silent moment to look into the face of the man reflected in those magical waters. I remembered how carefully the Alpha

Mages watched her as she drank in the visage of the only person she could truly love. Knowing what my sister would choose, I promised myself I wouldn't look. After all, he was unwittingly in his last few days alive, but when the glowing ripples settled and my sister leaned forward, I caved and gaped at the man who looked back at her. He was pleasant looking, but ordinary as all mortals were. He didn't have the divine beauty of immortality like my sister, but his youthful energy shone through his warm brown eyes.

As expected, Ezra ordered a Hunter to eliminate the visage without hesitation, and we hadn't spoken about it since. I could barely recall the man's face in my mind's eye, but I could never forget the kindness in his smile. Every now and then, I saw it reflected in my sister.

I was fortunate not to have the choice. Fortunate I'd never have to wonder about the person I saw reflected in the magical waters. The drums echoed through the darkness, synching up with my heartbeat as I prepared to glimpse one of the few experiences I'd ever be denied. Like becoming a Hunter or visiting the world above, I'd learn to live without this. Without my mate.

Ezra cleared her throat. I jolted to attention, lost in my own thoughts. My sister stood at the far edge of the circular pool, and the glow of the water splashed onto her beautiful face. The Shadow Court's Alpha Mages all grasped the granite edge of the basin, their eyes transfixed on the water as they focused on their forthcoming task.

Ezra's eyebrows rose slightly and she shot me a wondering look. I forced a grin. When she reciprocated, I felt mine grow into a genuine smile. *This is just my first of many.* I knew a new mate would surface for me every hundred years or so, so this ceremony would become a tired routine eventually. I just had to get out the jitters of the first one.

I stepped up to the edge of the granite pool and could see that the water was only a foot or two deep. I squinted as they adjusted to the light, which flickered whenever one of the mages moved their hands through the liquid. I was proud of our court's unique ability to divine mates, though I was grateful not to have to endure this procedure daily for each member of the court. The Alpha Mages, or Diviners, as they were sometimes called, were well respected in our society, but the labor they did was intensive and endless.

Ezra raised her hands, and the drums silenced. "Today is a very special divination ceremony as it is the first for Princess Sinna. Our court was nearly eliminated by the temptation to abandon life for fleeting and meaningless moments of affection, but now that our court has chosen life over defeat, we need not burden ourselves. I ask that we all reflect on today as a celebration of life and prosperity for the Shadow Court and all who belong to it."

Applause filled the dark hall, and for the first time I could feel how vast our audience was. I took a steadying breath as I prepared to look into the face of my mortality.

"Have no fear,"Ezra said. "Our Hunters will not fail to protect you."

"I am not afraid."

Her expression softened as she watched me. "Then let the ceremony commence."

FIVE

—— H E R O D ——

My nostrils flared as I stepped back into the moon's light, the wolf within tore through my human skin like a child unwrapping their first Christmas gift. The cobblestones cooled my paws as I slunk through the shadows towards the wood. *How dare he?* I'd vetted each of the tributes. Knowing the Blood King's sensitivity to age, I'd triple-checked each one. The girl was admittedly a bit underdeveloped for her age, but for him to insinuate that I'd violated the terms of our treaty was a testament to his arrogance. I stepped through the tree-line, but my wolf was too enraged to allow me to move any farther away. I wanted nothing more than to topple his reign and rid the world of those blood-sucking monsters that considered themselves superior. I turned back and glared at the cathedral they called home. The metallic scent of blood was bearable in my human form, but as a wolf, it burned my nose, stretching further than a mile radius around their base. If I moved any closer I would struggle not to gag from the smell.

I watched as shadows passed in front of the stained-glass windows, digging my claws into the leafy terrain at the edge of the city. The futility of my desire to retaliate kept me from returning home. Even if the Blood King was dumb enough to step outside alone, I wouldn't be able to do more than injure him. Instead, I paced in the shadow of the tree-line, imagining what it would feel like to hear King Maddox cry. A branch snapped, and I bared my teeth at the sound.

Ronan stepped into view, cradling the unconscious tribute in his arms like she weighed nothing. My father's favorite pastime was recounting tales about the war that caused this pyramid system and won the Blood Court its position on top. Ronan was a key player in every story, a brawler through and through.

He didn't look like much to me, but the way he so casually approached me while I was in wolf form spoke volumes of his lethality. The girl in his arms was so still that I thought she might be dead, but I could still hear the pulse of her beating heart. King Maddox trusts this guy to return her unharmed? I eyed her warily. Ronan moved closer, so I bared my teeth, but instead of fear, he spoke casually.

"The king is in a mood tonight. I'm ever so sorry for his outburst." The unmistakably metallic scent wafted from his breath.

I growled as I decided whether it would be worth the trouble to tear his limbs off.

"Perhaps it's time to give up your search. These tributes never yield results, and I'm sure it's been exhausting collecting them to no avail."

This time when he spoke, the moonlight shone off of his red

teeth. My gaze moved back to my failed tribute, and I shuddered as I listened more carefully. Sure enough, the heartbeat I'd heard coming from the tribute had tripled in speed. It began to skip beats and her body jerked in Ronan's arms. He did not so much as look down at her. Instead, he stepped into the tree-line, as if the woods were safe and not a blatant disregard for my court's territory.

I felt a new consciousness slip into my head as one of my fellow wolves neared us, then another, and another, but Ronan turned away and stared at the moon as if lost in thought. A collective growl echoed through the wood as a handful of wolves surrounded us. Ronan's dinner went still as her heart beat one final time. The lone vampire snapped from his daze. He looked up at my pack, his attention moving from the moon-white fur of one pack-mate to the other in detached appraisal.

Finally, he sighed deeply. "It seems my meal's gone stale."

Ronan tossed the corpse, and it landed with an empty thud at the feet of my pack. Tren leaned in and sniffed at it before his gaze moved to me.

His thoughts rang in my head. "What are you going to do?" he said through the link. "You going to let this bloodsucker disrespect us like this?"

"Fall back."

"You can't be serious."

Kay's voice cut through. "Tren, he's right. That's Ronan the Brutal."

She glared at Tren. She was my number two, and the only voice I didn't mind having in my head.

Ronan turned his back to us, and Tren lowered to the ground.

"Well," Ronan said, "I'll get going. I suppose I'll see you at your next offering. Make sure you're conscious of their ages. She did taste a little young."

I gritted my teeth.

"Now, Herod! While his back is turned." Tren said, but his voice was less sure than a moment ago. "He can't take all five of us."

Kay's voice was harsh. "You can't smell how many of them are around? Your alpha said fall back, so fall the fuck back."

Tren's head lowered as we all watched Ronan walk down the hill to the chapel. It was a gut punch to us all.

As a new alpha, I didn't have the benefit of having ever fought a vampire, but I wasn't willing to risk the lives of our people by underestimating one. Especially not one known for his exceptional combat skills. The Blood Court had the unique ability to bite and turn mortals, increasing their numbers, but they did so with caution. One should always be cautious when giving the gift of immortality to any mortal being. Even so, that advantage had won them the war. The Moon Court's ability to shift, communicate with our pack telepathically, and hunt anything as long as we had a scent, wasn't enough to change the status quo.

Before he passed, my father had taught me how to choose my battles. It might've seemed too passive to Tren and some of the others, but there was only one way to eliminate the Blood Court, and that was finding King Maddox's mate.

SIX

— SINNA —

The Diviners lowered their hands to the bottom of the glowing water and began to hum. The even tone swelled through the hall as I locked my gaze on the center of the glowing pool. My heart beat so quickly that it pushed the air from my lungs, and I clenched my jaw to steady my body from shaking. No matter what I felt when the image appeared, attraction, lust, sadness, fear, humiliation. . . I'd only need to endure it for a moment. *I can endure anything that long.* Finn was waiting to erase my mate from existence, to spare me one hundred years of wondering or a few blissful years of knowing before an abrupt and eternal end.

The pool's light brightened as the Diviners poured their magic into it. During my sister's ceremony, I'd seen the way the white of the Diviners' eyes overtook their irises and pupils. I'd watched the granite basin glow like the moon, filling every crevice of the hall with cold, white light, but now that it was my turn, I could not enjoy the splendor of the event. Curiosity clawed at my mind, rendering me incapable of looking anywhere but the center of the pool for fear I'd blink and miss it.

A red hue brushed the surface of the pool, and I leaned in as the blurred image took form.

All went still.

Dark wavy hair covered his face, obscuring all but plump red lips. Every nerve in my body writhed against the sensation. The urge to turn away was maddening, like leaning too close to a campfire in order to fully savor the relief of cold air on your cheeks when you turned away, but I didn't dare to move. Paralyzed by the instantaneous tethering of my life to his, I longed for relief. I longed to feel the lines cut and the release of his hold on my existence. The pull was immediate and powerful. I hadn't even seen his face. My body pulsed. *Please. Look at me.* As if I'd said the words aloud and they'd somehow carried to him, he lifted his chin, his gaze lifting to meet mine.

I felt naked, swallowed by the charcoal black of his eyes. One glance and I knew something had gone terribly wrong. This was no blemished mortal threatening my existence but a divine entity. His dark eyes were rimmed with red, and his jawline was sharp and smooth as polished stone. The tether tightened, fortifying itself with his details as I drank him in. Emotions overran me, filling my body with their toxic mixture until I landed on the only one that mattered, a dark and intense hatred.

My jaw ached, but I didn't dare unclench it. As if he'd sensed the fire he'd lit inside me, his red lips stretched, turning up the corners of his wicked mouth. Joy filled his whole face, but even that couldn't light the pitch blackness of his eyes. Then his lips parted and the nightmare I didn't dare to imagine slipped into reality. Two gleaming white fangs revealed themselves, plunging the Shadow Court into utter chaos.

The light of the pool was snuffed out and the image along with it, but it was burned into my mind as the shrieks and screams of everyone in attendance reached me, jolting me from my silent stasis. The sound rattled my bones as the shadows closed in and my legs buckled. I felt strong hands close around my arms, as a thousand people rushed the pool.

"Finn!" I screamed, but my voice was engulfed by the others.

I screamed again, the only indication a fresh scrape of soreness against my throat.

Then I felt the soft brush of lips against my neck. A chill ran through my body. The lips moved against my neck again, and this time I was sure they belonged to Finn. Bodies barreled into us as Finn grabbed my hand and led me through the crowd towards the exit. I lifted my free hand with every intention of casting something, anything, but before I could, a light cut through the shadows and silence fell on the hall.

Ezra held her hand above her head, light beaming from her palm.

Her voice was amplified and strong. "We will consider our next move carefully. This situation will be dealt with appropriately. I assure you, the Shadow Court's survival is of the utmost importance."

But Finn didn't stop to listen. He pulled me out of the hall, through the tunnels, and didn't stop until we were alone, panting in my quarters with the doors locked behind us.

"The Blood King," I said, fighting to catch my breath.

"I know."

"It's the Blood King!" I turned away, trying to settle my thoughts.

An immortal mate? It wasn't possible, yet the pull of the tether on my chest was unmistakable. Why hadn't anyone prepared me for this possibility? Our Hunters were lethal, but they had no chance in hell of killing an immortal, let alone the leader of the most powerful immortal court in the world. Did that mean I had to suffer the tether forever? The Blood King. The fucking Blood King. He was a ruthless killer; everyone at the Blood Court was. I hated him. I hated every disgusting monster in his demonic court. What did it say about me if I was mated to one?

"Calm down."

"You promised you'd kill him. I'm going to be stuck like this. . . with this feeling."

Tears sprung to my eyes. Reeling, a new mouthful of despair filled me with each breath.

"Calm down." He inched toward me.

"Don't tell me to fucking calm down. Fix it, Finn! Make it not hurt."

Without hesitation, he unsheathed his knife. My bedroom's light caught the edge of the sharpened blade. I watched with detached curiosity as he closed the gap between us with his weapon drawn. He claimed my mouth, his tongue sliding between my lips. Stunned, I forgot about his knife until my body was jerked upwards along with the slice of his blade. I broke the kiss, and the small space allowed my dress to fall to the floor, its strings frayed where Finn had cut them.

I heard a zip, and he peeled off his armor and tossed it aside. A valiant effort, but my situation was hopeless. My heart seized as my thoughts returned to the ceremony, and I took a defeated step back.

"It's not going to work, Finn."

He shoved me back hard and I scrambled to keep my balance, only for my bed to hit the back of my knees, sending me toppling backwards. Finn stepped out of his pants, his body sculpted to perfection, his honey-colored eyes ablaze with desire. *Stay in the moment. Be present.* I closed my eyes and felt the flat of Finn's blade press against my stomach. My breath pushed my body against it, and I liked the coldness of the steel as much as the danger. It lifted, and my bra popped open, spilling tiny glass beads across my bed.

The lips that had found me in the chaos now trailed down to my lace panties, which he tugged with his teeth. I covered my face with my hands, so I could wipe away any tears that dared to slip out. Finn would fix this, just like he fixed everything else. I just had to trust him.

"Faster," I begged.

"Yes, Princess," he said, as he straightened and cut them off with two fluid moves of his blade.

His hands were hot as they tightened around my waist from where he stood at the foot of the bed. Before I had time to brace myself, he drove into me, pleasure bursting between my legs. My back arched to deepen the pleasure with each powerful thrust of his hips.

"Yes," I breathed. "Hurt me."

His fingertips pressed into my sides as he gritted his teeth and pushed deeper to obey. Pleasure crawled up from the bottom of my spine and escaped in a moan that made Finn's pace increase. He dropped his chin, his focus waning as his body's instincts took over.

"Don't you fucking dare!" I said through gasps.

He grunted a reply. I wasn't done yet, not by a long shot. Not until my body gave out. Finn's hair slipped forward, casting shadows across his eyes. My heartbeat stuttered. They looked charcoal black. A flicker of pleasure sent sparks onto the fuse.

Focus Sin, stay present. "Harder!" I cried, hoping Finn could pull me out of my head.

His muscles flexed, but I had already returned to the ceremony in my mind's eye. Charcoal eyes. A wave of pleasure slammed into me. Bloodstained lips. My body bucked, straining for release. A smile stretched across a statuesque face, revealing the sheen of pointed fangs. I closed my eyes, desperate to make the memory stop, but that only strengthened the image. Finn was gone, and in his place, the Blood King smiled wickedly down at me, pushing me to orgasm.

SEVEN

I doubled over the pristine porcelain as fresh, blood-stained bile shot from my mouth. I hated the red splatter almost as much as the sick feeling that claimed my focus.

I could hear Ronan's voice through the door. "The King is ill. Don't return until morning."

I wiped my mouth and stood upright to get a look at myself in the mirror. Blood dribbled from my chin, but otherwise I looked normal, and not nearly as sick as I felt. I splashed my face with water. *Fucking Herod.* The gag-inducing sensation rose up so quickly. I'd barely held it in until I made it to the bathroom, despite only being a few yards away.

He had fucking poisoned me. The last thing I needed was to appear weak, not while the literal wolves were circling, and whispers of my own people were second-guessing my every move. If Herod was bold enough to try a move like this, perhaps Ronan was right about how casual our relations with the other courts had become. I'd always considered the war to be foolish. It resulted in the dismemberment of all of the monarchs of the immortal courts and the total elimination of the Shadow Court. I thought the tribute system would allow us to compete with a battle of wills, without resorting to the violence that orphaned us all, but Herod had gone a step too far.

Even as the nausea subsided, the weight on my chest remained. What the hell had he slipped me? If I could find the smallest shred of evidence, I'd have grounds for war, and my court would only praise my ruthlessness.

I flushed the regurgitated blood and cracked open the door. "I want you to test the tributes for poison."

"Sire, they've all been tested. I sampled each one before delivering a single drop to your chamber."

"He poisoned it. I'm certain."

"Perhaps you just need some rest."

I grabbed a towel and wiped my face with it before I followed him into my chamber. I flashed my fangs. "I want them retested."

"Yes, Sire."

I took a seat on my bed. "And what of the young girl? Did you return her?"

"Yes. She was heartbroken that you didn't allow her to join the court and make her immortal."

"See to it that Herod stops promising them that. It only makes the tributes more irritating."

He bowed. "Will that be all?"

The pressure in my chest flared, so I waved him out. I took a steadying breath. It was odd how mortals craved eternal life, like immortality was the opposite of death. But a true immortal knew better. The opposite of death was life and immortals were barred from both. Ever since my parents died, I had resented their decision to surrender their immortality. I always assumed they knew something about what it meant to live that I couldn't understand. Only now, as I lay with my hand pressed to my chest, I could feel Death's presence. He was not nearby, but I felt his existence on the edges of my illness. I savored the feeling, like a fine wine washing over my tongue.

I closed my eyes until the sensation passed, but a fragment of the feeling lingered, like the memory of a dream. My thoughts moved to Nova, her blue eyes, and the tribute who vaguely resembled her. Perhaps I was too eager to feed on tonight's tributes, too stubborn to admit to Herod that he was right about Nova. Regardless of their similarities, and how they dulled the ache of her absence, I didn't want him to fill my throne room with blue-eyed imitations of her. I'd barely even looked at the others, and in the silence, my thoughts drifted to places I tended to avoid. It would have been nice if, just for tonight, I had someone begging for immortality if, for no other reason, to remind myself it was mine to give.

The sun was setting when I woke, but I could still feel the frigid glare in the last of the sun's light, through my red, stained glass window. I liked to wake after it dipped below the horizon, but based on how low it hung on the horizon line, I'd only risen a few minutes early.

I made quick work of my nightly routine, and as expected, Ronan waited for me outside my door.

"How are you feeling, Sire?"

"Fine." We walked together through the hallway. The portraits of my ancestors glared at me as I passed.

"I've retested the tributes and couldn't find a trace of poison in any of them. Perhaps you overindulged?"

I glared at him but didn't slow my pace. "Or perhaps it was you who tried to poison me."

He sighed. "Seems rather pointless, wouldn't you say?"

"Send thirty of our soldiers to the Moon Court to tell Herod we won't be accepting tributes for the next month, pending an investigation of his recruitment methods."

"Thirty, sire? Surely the Moon King will consider it a threat to—"

"It is.

"Perhaps a more diplomatic—"

I flicked my hand, stopping him short without so much as looking in his direction.

He cleared his throat. "The Clan is assembled in the study."

I turned in a huff and headed back up the corridor. "Lead with that next time."

The study was by far the stuffiest room in the refurbished cathedral. The drapes were black, the furnishings jewel-tone velvet and the fireplace always filled with ashes, though it was never lit.

As ever, the Clan was seated on one side of a long table, with my vacant throne at the center. The set up resembled depictions of the Last Supper, but with a few important differences. Each of the vampires in the Clan was blessed with ageless beauty. They were less like companions and more like a company of betrayers, and instead of The Messiah, Satan himself sat on the throne. This was not a court of round tables and equality. The highest-ranking Clan members sat at the center, and the lowest sat further toward the edges.

It was the ideal arrangement for reviewing candidates for immortality.

I took a seat at my throne beside Aiko, who had been my right hand since I was crowned. She bowed her head in greeting. Peng sat to my left. He was next to inherit my throne if I didn't choose an heir, and therefore my biggest threat. He grinned at me, not for kindness' sake but to flash his fangs. I reciprocated, and a moment later, the double doors opened and a mortal was ushered in.

EIGHT

—— S I N N A ——

Even as I buttoned my jeans and straightened myself up in my bedroom mirror, Finn lay sprawled naked across my bed. I thought he might be asleep, but when a knock sounded at my door, his head jerked up. Without thinking, I yanked open the door. Ezra looked deeply into my eyes as if she'd be able to see the pain in them.

"Hey, what's going on?"

Her eye-contact broke, and her gaze flitted to Finn. I looked over my shoulder and Finn made no efforts to cover himself. He smiled and waved proudly, donning his limp member like a participation trophy.

I sighed. "I was just—"

"It's okay," she said, taking my hands in hers.

She pulled me into the hallway and I looked around the abandoned area, curious.

"Are you okay? I sent everyone to their quarters while we get things sorted."

I swallowed a lump in my throat as the last hour replayed in my head in fast motion, ending with the Blood King triggering an orgasm. "I'll be fine."

She pulled me in for a hug and I wanted to wiggle free. I couldn't stand feeling so exposed. Every single person I knew was suddenly privy to my potential feelings, but if I panicked, I'd scare the shit out of Ezra.

I backed away slowly, making sure to keep my tone analytical. "So, we can't send the Hunters after him, right?"

Her gaze dropped and an expression I knew very well came over her face. She had looked the same when she'd asked me if I would choose to send the Hunters.

Guilt.

"What is it?"

She glanced around the deserted hallway. "I need to know if you can bear this."

"You mean, do nothing?" The words came out sharper than I meant them to.

She took me by the wrist and silently led me through the tunnels to her chambers. The Hunters outside her door separated and let us through. She closed the door behind us.

Her voice was low. "I need you to be very honest with me."

I felt my emotions swell as tears threatened to spill from my eyes. "Okay," was all I managed.

I thought she was going to ask a question, but instead, she took a seat in a chair beside her bed. "Take your time. Tell me how you feel."

"Angry. Humiliated." I shook my head. "Disgusted."

"This is not your fault."

"How can you say that? My mate is a bloodthirsty murderer."

She pulled her knees to her chest. "He's hot, though."

"Fuck you."

She looked up at me slowly. Guilt swirled inside me. I shouldn't have taken any of this out on her. She was just trying to lighten the mood. Luckily, sisterhood proved to be durable. There was virtually nothing that I could do or say to truly damage it.

She walked over to me. I considered apologizing, but I didn't.

"What about the tether?"

You mean the ache in my chest that's fighting to find him? "If it's there, I want it cut."

She wrung her hands. "There's one way. The elders are putting pressure on me to push you into it, but I refused."

"What? Why would you do that? Ezra, I want this done."

"Because if things go wrong, I won't be able to save you."

"Just tell me."

She exhaled slowly before she spoke. "They want you to infiltrate the Blood Court as a spy and seduce the King."

I turned away, stunned, as my thoughts diverged into two paths. The first, born of the tether, was a powerful desire to meet the Blood King face to face. The second was the sudden realization that I was going to die. My mind shot through the stages of grief in a matter of seconds, before restarting. My immortality, they'd have me lose my immortality.

"All you'd have to do is make him fall in love with you, before you fall in love with him. Once you're sure his immortality is broken, you'll signal us. Our mages and Hunters will do the rest. The elders believe this is our opportunity to return to power. We could topple the Blood Court if we play this right."

"I'm going to die."

"Not if you remember who he is. Not if you hold onto who you are. But say the word, and I'll fight the elders on this. We won't do it."

It was an impossible task. I don't think anyone had ever met their mate and lived longer than a mortal life afterward, and they were thinking about sending me directly to our enemy's court? There were only two ways I could see this going, and neither ended with me alive. Either they drained my blood immediately, discovering I couldn't die, torturing me for eternity. Or I'd trick them long enough to fall in love with my mate, and then when they drained me, I'd die. I didn't like those options.

"If he's my mate, how would I even stop myself from wanting him?"

She stood with her hands on her hips, watching me like our mother used to. "We could cast some protections, but it would ultimately come down to you. You'd need to find something stronger than the tether. Something you want more. I wasn't even going to ask, but you seemed so detached that I thought maybe the tether wasn't that strong."

If only she knew about that imaginary rendezvous. *No.* I'm definitely going to die. "I can't."

"Right," she said quickly. "Of course." She smiled. "You don't give this another thought. Your big sister is going to handle this."

I bowed icily and headed back to my room. I hated to disappoint her, but almost seemed relieved by my decision. My bedroom was empty when I got there, and I figured Finn had rushed off to meet up with the other Hunters.

How long had I dreamed of leaving these caves? How long

had I wanted to become a Hunter? Ezra's mission would grant me both, but the cost was far too high.

I was glad for the opportunity to be left alone with my thoughts, but once I lay down and the world became quiet, I realized that until this was over, I would never truly be alone. I was bound to the tether. Tied 'til death to an immortal monster.

NINE

—— MADDOX ——

Peng's fist slammed down on the table, and I snickered in response.

"Our army can't grow if you never allow anyone to join our court. They're mortals; of course they're imperfect. You can't be so selective."

I yawned. "Believe me, if I'd been King when you were presented to this Clan, you wouldn't have made the cut."

A chortle burst from Aiko, and she covered it with a fake coughing fit.

I propped my elbows on the table and rested my head in my hands.

"Sire," someone said from across the room. "You should take this more seriously."

Irritation burned hot in my throat, but I exhaled it and leaned back in my chair. "Ignorance is rampant in our court." I pulled my hair back securing it with a band. The bottom strands were too short to stay and I felt the tickle of them as they slipped out and came to rest at the back of my neck. I stood, slowly walking toward the front door. I stopped when I got midway across the room and turned back to the table and eyed each member of the clan. "You'd imbue all mortals if you got the chance."

Peng said, "If we did, we could wipe out the other courts."

"And to what end? The Blood Court is already the highest court. Greed will be our undoing."

Another Clan member chimed in. "Are we to understand that you never intend on exterminating the other courts?"

Peng grinned. "He's leaving us open to attack. If we don't bolster our numbers, the other courts will catch up and the courtiers agree."

I sighed. "Your lack of understanding astounds me." I was met with a row of blank stares. *This is why you don't grant immortality to whoever presents a decent case.* "Each mortal who turns is one less to feed on and one more to feed. The courtiers depend on us to supply them with sustenance as does everyone in this room. You've been provided for for far too long and don't remember how it feels to be thirsty. You seek power and plot against me, riling the spoiled courtiers into rebellion-- waiting for a moment to take my throne-- completely oblivious to the fact that you're marching your own court to extinction," I scoffed. "You'd invite unworthy scum into our court for all of eternity without a second thought, yet you claim that I'm the one who isn't taking the task seriously." I smiled and headed toward the door, but said over my shoulder, "If you go looking for trouble, you'll find it. Just ask my father."

I only made it halfway to my chamber when Ronan found me. "I heard what happened."

"I'm not in the mood for a lecture."

"I agree with what you said."

My ears pricked.

"Increasing our numbers too quickly and thoughtlessly will most certainly lead to a loss of power."

I nodded to the guards outside my quarters and they opened the doors. I moved to make my escape, but Ronan followed me.

"Just spit it out."

He tugged at his collar nervously and I caught a glimpse of a scar.

"Sire, nothing good is going to come from alienating the rest of your court."

"How did you get that scar?" I asked.

He slipped two fingers under his collar as if he could feel the memory in its rigid edges, and his voice came out softly. "War."

"No shit."

He moved over to the couches and had a seat, as if in preparation for a long story. I felt a flare of excitement as I went to the bench on my windowsill where I did my best processing.

"It was one of the last days of the war. The Shadow Mages had already been wiped out, the Shifters were on their last legs and the Fae were the last real threat left fighting. I was in tough shape after taking an arrow to the shoulder. My vision blurred, and my immortality strained against the arrow's venom. I stumbled back toward our base, but a small pack of Shifters caught me out alone and chased past the tree line. I was outnumbered, exhausted, and sure they'd scatter my limbs and use them for chew toys for eternity."

I would have given anything to participate in the war, but I wasn't yet of age, and my immortality hadn't fully set in. The members of my court who had participated or thrived, carried an unspoken badge of honor that I could not wear. It held enough weight that even those below my rank could question my decisions—a king eclipsed by his own soldiers—I didn't know our enemies like they did. I'd never witnessed the unique carnage of each immortal element in its rawest form.

Ronan turned to the window as he continued. "The disgusting beasts growled, and I saw in their beady eyes that they still thought they had a chance, they still thought themselves better than the Blood Court. I was overtaken with rage, and I put those mutts down one by one. Their fight dimmed with each ally lost. I stood victorious over twitching limbs."

I nodded with the assumption that he'd reached the end. The tale was entertaining enough, but didn't answer the question at the back of my mind. Why hadn't his immortality healed him? Vampires, Shifters, and Fae had gotten into small skirmishes since my reign--but as far as I knew, none yielded scars, or at least, none that couldn't be healed with immortality over time. But before I could ask, Ronan continued.

"I was badly injured, claw and teeth marks reached down to my bones. My consciousness dimmed as I stumbled for the tree line. Just as I made it to the light, I fell, and my shadow stretched out in front of me."

Shadow Mage.

"A figure rose from the darkness, muttering an enchantment that engulfed her hands in darkness. She reached out for me." When his gaze moved to me I saw a flicker of fire in them. "That's the last thing I remember."

"My father had slew her, the last Shadow Mage."

He stood. "He saved my life, but I wasn't able to save him.

His legacy as a Shadow Mage killer lives on. They were a great threat, even to themselves."

He headed for the door, but I needed no more information. Shadow Mages had always sounded powerful in stories, but if the bulk of their court had died of old age from divining their mates, they were hardly worthy of their power.

TEN

—— S I N N A ——

I jolted awake as someone burst through my door. Finn stormed in, glaring at me.

He didn't bother closing the door behind him, but another Hunter poked her head in and said, "Make it fast," before closing the doors.

I groaned. "Aren't you all supposed to be guarding me?"

Finn's expression was rigid and determined as he stormed to my bedside. He was usually so easygoing. I'd never seen him look so severe, but as a Hunter, I knew he must have a killer instinct somewhere inside. I just never expected him to turn it on me, his Princess. I eyed my clock; it was 8:00AM.

His words cut like knives. "What the hell is wrong with you?"

I slid out of bed and stood, annoyed that I wasn't a few inches taller. "Excuse me, *servant?*"

"Ferah is threatening to overthrow your sister, and you're just going to let her do it?"

I'd barely woken up, and he had the audacity to not only drop that bomb, but to blame me for it?

"What are you talking about?"

There was no way Ferah would do something so treasonous.

"If you can't stoop to care about the Shadow Court or your sister, do it for you."

"Do what? March to my death?" *How dare he?* I was so angry I could barely pull together responses without spitting.

"You're immortal."

"Not if I fall in love with him."

"Then don't."

I crossed my arms, but when his gaze flickered to the gesture I threw my arms out and shoved him. "You have no business attacking me like this. You know it won't be as simple as 'Don't do it.' He's a killer. He eats people. "

"You're scared. I get that, but there's too much on the line here, Sin."

The mention of my name disarmed me.

Finn's voice softened. "You wanted to be a Hunter? This is your chance. Hunters don't choose their missions, taking whichever ones sound safest."

I tried to respond, but the words got lodged in my throat.

"I know you, Sin. You're not going to let them overthrow your sister."

Inside I was screaming, as flashes of fangs cutting into my flesh dashed across my imagination. Finn walked towards me, his expression softening. He rubbed my arms, and I pulled away.

"I could come with you. Be your shadow."

Is he insane? If they discovered him, we'd both be killed. "That's twice as dangerous."

"And yet, still worth the risk. Our court doesn't belong underground," he said, his gaze burning into me. "The bigger the light, the stronger the shadow. If you make him mortal and kill him, you'll be the greatest Hunter that ever lived."

"Don't try and play on my ego. That won't work."

"Really? Because you look terrified and I think it's because you've already made up your mind."

I paused, then let out an exhale of surrender. "Where is she?"

"The Queen? She's at the drop with Ferah and the other elders."

I chewed on my bottom lip. "Leave, I need to change before I go."

"It's nothing I haven't seen before," he said, his excitement over his victory slipping into his voice.

"I said, get out."

A few minutes later I readied myself and swung my doors open, but Finn wasn't there. I forgot I'd sent him away. Now I needed him to come along if not for emotional support, for the simple fact that I was going to pitch him as my shadow for the mission. But I understood his reluctance. Ferah was the leader of the Hunters and his direct superior. The tension between Ferah and my sister was not one he could get in the middle of, but I could.

There was no way to mentally prepare for what I was about to do, and worse, I doubted Ezra would let me take such a risk on her behalf. However, Finn had been right about one thing: this was my only chance to become a Hunter.

The Hunters parted, allowing me passage onto the top of the granite spiral staircase which stretched around the drop. I could see my sister on the center platform, standing with her head held high and her crown glimmering with darkness. On the far side of the platform, Ferah stood with several of the elders, huddled in a semi-circle as they whispered to each other.

My shoes scraped the ground, echoing down the drop into the seemingly endless pit. I compiled my list of demands, as I wanted to do it on my terms. I wanted as many protections as I could get. Finn would be my shadow, and I wanted an official position as a Hunter. But most of all, I wanted to be the one to take the Blood King's life.

I made my way down, but quieted my steps to listen as Ferah turned away from the elders to my sister. Ferah's movements and appearance were smooth and pointed like a snake, as was her unpleasant demeanor, but her killer instinct when backed into a corner had turned our broken survivors into formidable Hunters.

She hissed. "You've let your personal feelings cloud your judgement on what's best for our people."

My sister held her ground. "I won't make her do it and what you're preparing to do is treason. I was the one who took away the choice and revived this court."

"And you will see it destroyed as well. You are unfit to lead us."

Something in me snapped. Who the hell did she think she was speaking to her Queen like that? Ezra had banned execution to bolster our numbers, but this was the first time I'd seen a lack of respect from any of our subjects, even since then. Finn was right, this was serious, but I had the power, and thanks to Ferah's little outburst, my terms shifted.

"Enough," I called as I made my final descent to the highest platform. All six women watched me expectantly, except for

Ezra, whose concern was marked by a wrinkle between her brows. "I will accept the mission, but I have conditions."

The elders, who looked no older than twenty mortal years, immediately brightened and Ferah bowed her head respectfully.

"A wise decision," Ferah said. "I'm sure we can accommodate your terms. Please," she said, gesturing for me to come closer, "Name your terms."

My sister interjected. "You don't have to do this." Ferah's face tightened and I could practically hear her tail rattling.

I held my hands out, palm down. "I've made my choice."

"Excellent," Ferah said. "Now, the terms."

"I shall be granted all resistance protections from our best casters."

"Of course, your Highness," Ferah said with a smile.

"I shall select a Hunter to shadow me for the duration of my mission."

Ferah straightened. "Lerant is skilled enough to—"

"I want Finn."

She threaded her fingers together. "Perhaps someone with more experience?"

"I want Finn."

She bowed her head. "As you wish."

I could feel my sister's gaze burning into the side of my face.

"I want to kill the Blood King myself."

Ferah slithered toward me, her eyes black slits through glassy yellow bulbs. She forced a laugh. "When an opportunity arises, you may make the first attempt on his life. However, if you should fail, my Hunter will finish the job. Sound fair?"

I grinned wickedly, my gaze shifting to my sister for a fraction of a moment before I delivered my finishing blow. "Funny you should mention, 'your Hunters' because that's my final request."

Ferah raised an eyebrow.

"On the completion of this mission I will be granted your position as the Head Hunter and you'll be demoted to my underling."

She looked amused. "You?"

"Those are my terms."

"Impossible, but I might consider making you a Hunter."

"I was going to ask for that, but then I saw how you disrespected your Queen. I think you need to be reminded who you serve."

Ferah's voice was casual but her gaze shifted nervously to the four elders. "The elders will never agree to this."

Instead of their confirmation, their judgmental gazes sent Ferah coiling into a panic, her movements twitchy and her eyes unblinking.

Time to finish her. "Sounds like you've let your personal feelings get in the way of what's best for our people."

ELEVEN

—— D E L T O N ——

T he greenhouse sprouted to life, with fronds reaching out as I passed a row of potted Geraniums. The air was wet and fragrant with mist teeming off the waterfall, and filling the garden with thick cloud-like plumes just below the top of the hundred and twenty foot glass ceilings.

I circled the mossy mountain structure at the center, climbing the staggered floor plates that wrapped around the internal core. I closed my eyes to listen more closely to the hum of the garden. My ears twitched and I rounded the corner where a spore drooped. The bulb weighed on its delicate stem, split, and threatened to snap. I knelt and touched a hand to the spongy wall and felt its life energy flicker weakly within the vibrant web of life. I touched it gently, bowing my head and sending my life force, first to my fingers, then to the wounded stem. The sound of footsteps approaching disrupted the bridge, but I forced more energy into the struggling plant. It straightened, its cells thickening and its bulb lifting until it was secure once again against the wall.

A man cleared his throat. "King Delton, you have a visitor."

I stood, drinking in my Chamberlain. He was pristine as ever, the medallions on his armor freshly shined, the greenery woven through his hair secure, his eyes rested and alert, but his stiff posture and the way his fingers twitched warned me that something was amiss. "Cadmus, you look unwell."

"I am perfectly well, your Highness, but you have a visitor."

"I will see them when I have finished tending to the greenhouse."

I turned away, prepared to resume my work when I felt Cadmus' energy shift. It rose in intensity, but instead of peace and balance, I felt twinges of apprehension and fear.

I turned. "What is it, Cadmus?"

His nostrils flared and he tucked a loose strand of icy-white hair behind his pointed ear. "There's a woman here, your Highness. I think you'll want to meet her."

A vague answer from the most direct person I knew meant he wasn't sure of what we were dealing with yet. He only withheld information when he wasn't certain of the truth. I followed him to my throne room, as the canopy spilled light onto the potted foliage at the base of the Redwoods. The mother tree separated her branches, revealing my vine-woven throne. Mother tree rustled as if in an indistinguishable breeze and in the hush of it, I felt her calming presence calling out in support.

I nodded to Cadmus and he signaled the Obstinacy at the door. The doors opened and several Obstinacies marched in with their bows, slung over their shoulders. I could feel the dark energy sapping away the greenery behind them. A buck lowered its horns. *What is this?*

The Obstinacy split and, reverting to tradition, took a knee beside the stranger. I observed the woman that scowled up at me, too intrigued to have her thrown out until I had confirmation of what I already suspected. Why come to the Arrow Court alone, and with ill intent? Her brow furrowed. It wasn't a scowl on her marble-like face, but she merely squinted at the errant beams of light that forced their way through the trees. She had the poised elegance of royalty, the calm nature of an assassin, and such levels of beauty that I hadn't seen in so long, I thought I'd imagined it all. Even her dark, dusty cloak didn't give her away, yet my mind wrestled with the improbability.

Impossible.

"Speak!" I demanded, impatiently. "Why have you come here?"

She blinked against the light, her discomfort as seemingly uncomfortable as it was to watch.

"Step closer," I said, gesturing to the bottom of my throne.

The limbs of the mother tree moved to block the light and the woman stepped forward, and her piercing gaze met mine for the first time.

My breath caught. "Shadow demon, why have you crawled from your shame? To throw yourself at our mercy?

"The shame belongs to all defeated parties, your Highness."

Heat flashed across my neck and the hall filled with the rustle of the trees, sensing my unease.

"Begone. Or I shall squash you and any other roaches from your court."

"I am the lone survivor. I hold no ill will to you or your court."

I clenched my jaw. *Nothing good can come of this.* "Then why have you come?"

She crossed her hands behind her back and a small smile moved onto her face. "The extinction of my court had much to do with our own weakness. Our nature was our undoing. I suppose war is also a part of nature, sussing out the dominant court to reign above the rest."

My grip on the armrests of my throne tightened, and I felt the bark threaten to give way beneath my nails. Vampires were a disgusting prideful breed, unworthy of their position. They used no logic, no sense, just brute force and hubris. They were no more fit to rule the immortals than the dogs of the Moon Court who now cowed to their every whim.

A wave of energy pulsed through my arms from the mother tree, a warning.

"Leave my court, witch, or you'll learn firsthand what a Fae Obstinacy's arrow tastes like."

Out of the corner of my eye, I could see Cadmus' body relax.

"I will take the arrow if you do not accept the gift I have prepared for you."

I raised my fingertips and the Obstinacies each knocked their arrows and aimed at the dark mage.

"Are you certain?"

She smiled and the only trace of fear that I felt in the room's energy web was my own.

I nodded.

"Since the extinction of my Court, I've longed for companionship, desperate to share my time with another. In my despair,

I disregarded the dangers of my heritage and attempted to divine my mate."

A veil of unease settled through the room and the woman paused to savor it. We dared not speak of such dangerous things in the Arrow Court, and our attention was irrevocably arrested. Finally the mage spoke again, "I was unable to locate my mate and instead divined something with the power to defy nature. I found the mate of a king."

My eyes widened, fear pulsing into my body, as my life slipped into her hands. *My mate?*

Cadmus yanked the bow off his shoulder and rushed the yellow-eyed woman, pressing the tip of his arrow to her cheek. "How dare you bring such information here!" he shouted and the mage leaned away from the arrow. "I will not allow you to reveal it and risk the life of the Fae King."

I was frozen, terrified that if I spoke, I might disagree. That curiosity would pull me to my demise and put my entire court at risk. But even with Cadmus' poisonous arrow pressed to the mage's cheek, she showed no sign of fear. Her gaze met mine with pleased resolve.

Her lips parted.

"Say one word and you die."

"Cadmus!" The name shot out like a reflex. "Let her speak."

Cadmus backed away slowly and a bright smile slipped onto the stranger's face. "I assure you, I mean you no harm. The king I was referring to was King Maddox of the Blood Court."

Silence fell on the room like a thick fog and we each breathed in the toxic temptations of our own devices. Just when I thought it wouldn't end, Cadmus broke it. "What is your name?"

Her gaze slithered to me as she said, "Ferah."

Finding my voice, I stood and descended the stairs to meet her at the bottom of my throne. "And what is it that you ask in exchange for such intriguing information?"

"I wish to serve you, your Highness. I wish for refuge in your court."

TWELVE

──── S I N N A ────

Ezra chewed her thumb nail as we waited for Ferah's signal, but she looked less like a queen and more like a worried older sister. I leaned back in Ezra's granite throne, my own thoughts occupied by my imminent demise.

I felt the tug of Finn moving inside my shadow like a puppet on strings, but I swallowed the urge to lean in the opposite direction to counterbalance it. It was not the glamorous Hunter training I'd longed for all of my life. Not the furious lethal strikes nor the weeklong rock climbing courses over the dark empty pits. I need only to be still and ignore Finn's presence as I would when I stood before the Vampire King. If I let any indication that Finn hid within my shadow we'd surely be dismembered and tortured for all eternity.

But even that would have been favorable compared to the alternative. If I somehow allowed myself to be seduced by the

Blood King, my immortality would wane and I'd throw away my infinite birthright, expose my court, and likely lead them all to extinction. Those fears were evident in Ezra's distant gaze but when she finally spoke, her words surprised me.

"Do you think Ferah will betray us?"

"I don't. And neither do you. She may have wanted the throne but only with the intent to lift our court."

She shook her head. "You didn't have to antagonize her with your conditions."

I shrugged. "Didn't I?"

Finn yanked at my shadow and I bit back a smile. His form sprung from darkness, a thick black cloud that dissipated into a Hunter. "You smiled. You can't do that," he said flatly.

"People smile, you know. Sometimes for no reason."

Ezra spun to us. "You're not taking this seriously. Are you not worried what that monster is going to do to you?"

Her glare was hateful, but behind it was only concern for my safety. I swallowed a lump in my throat. She was overruled, even by me, tossing her only family into the heart of the enemy for the sake of our Court. If the roles were reversed, I doubted I could have done the same, but it was that deficit of character that made the subjects in our court glad that she was first in line.

"You are not forcing this task on me. This is what I want. The choice has been made."

As I spoke, I realized this was not so different from the choice Ezra had worked so hard to eliminate, only I had every intention of being my own Hunter, regardless of if Finn seemed to think he'd be the one to take the Vampire King's life.

She eyed me, her voice lowering to a pained whisper. "I wish I could take your place."

"I'm stronger than you think. I'll come back a hero. You'll make me a Hunter yet."

She smiled, but it didn't reach her eyes. "As long as you come back safely, we'll sort out the rest."

Finn's voice broke our attention. "Have the enchantments settled in yet? We should get moving to the surface soon."

"I don't know what they're supposed to feel like." It was alarming how much of our plan relied on Ferah and Ezra was right to doubt her, but only in the confines of our own court. At the end of the day Ferah was a member of the Shadow Court, and her allegiance was as tied to it as her immortality.

Before she left to convince the Arrow Court to offer me to the Blood King as tribute, she had cast enchantments on me. One spell accentuated my mortal features, but I had to avoid mirrors. There was also one that acted like a block on the tether, but when Ferah cast it, she warned me not to become reliant on it, because its effects would fade quickly over time.

But even with a ticking clock, I had many advantages. Civilizations were always toppled by the women in the shadows of history. In my vast experience with men, I'd come to know them as the greatly inferior sex. Easily manipulated, controlled, prideful, quick to anger, and often oblivious to the social currencies that women traded right in front of them. Not to mention fragile, hyper-sensitive, vulnerable, and emotionally stunted. And of all men who shared these traits, royal men had no equal for folly or ignorance.

Ezra watched me carefully, as if trying to read my thoughts. "I think you should alter your persona."

"No," Finn said. "She's his mate, she should act normally. Besides, our spies confirm the king prefers. . ." he looked me up and down, "confident women."

"She'll need to stand out. The tether should take away some of the work, but if she were chaste and innocent, she might stand out from the other tributes. She could even avoid being bitten or touched for a while."

Finn pressed his lips together to suppress a laugh. "Chaste? Sinna? No one is going to believe her."

I slapped him upside the back of the head. "Enough. I'm the Shadow Court's only hope at redemption, and none of you have a shred of faith in me."

"I'm sorry, Sin," Ezra said. "This is just a lot to process."

"Then let's be glad I'm the one who's taking it on."

The throne room lights dimmed, and we plummeted into total darkness for a few moments before they returned to their normal, dull glow.

My gaze locked with Ezra's. "That's Ferah. It's time."

I should have felt more apprehension, but one of my dreams was so close. My head rushed with the whispered memories the Hunter's shared about the mortal world above. Finn and I would begin our trek to the surface where I'd hide among the living until King Delton came calling.

THIRTEEN

— M A D D O X —

Ronan crossed his arms over his chest, and the soft glow of the blazing fireplace haloed his head.

"I don't think it's wise to leave the Blood Court, not while things are so tense with the council."

I narrowed my eyes. "I wasn't asking."

Embers popped in the fireplace behind him. I saw a flicker of the fire's light behind his brown eyes that hinted at his annoyance.

He leaned in. "Maddox, don't push them."

I exhaled through my nose. "Fine, I'll approve three of their choices for the Blood Court. Now accompany me to the town before I think better of it and bring along someone I actually like."

"It's a full moon, Sire."

"I won't hunt. I just need to get away from this place, and I wager you do, too."

His face brightened, and his features softened. "The pub then?"

"Where else?"

Ronan and I didn't agree on much, not about politics, not about how to rule the Blood Court, but we both appreciated a night at the local pub. Intoxication purged all manner of fascinating truths from the lips of otherwise dull mortals.

We bundled up. The autumn air was colder than normal for the season, or perhaps it felt that way since we had moved away from the fire, but I'd never had a night in the pub that wasn't unbearably sweaty and full of lush, red-cheeked patrons. Plumes of mist burst from my lips with each breath as Ronan and I made our way down the winding hills that sheltered the cathedral. The walk was a short fifteen minutes from the town, but it was the long, drunken trudge back up the steep pathway that I usually forgot to consider.

Compared to the cathedral, the rest of the town was plain and lacking in the refinements that come with a thousand years of generational wealth. It only functioned at a basic level, yet it had charming buildings, and cobblestone roads that discouraged travelers from driving through. In comparison, the cathedral which had once housed the worship of mortal gods, and now housed immortal demons, looked as out of place, and it truly was. I saw a jewel being swarmed by roaches. I supposed our wealth was one of the reasons why so many were eager to volunteer to join our court, even given the high risk. We paid a small sum to the governor to allow us to continue, with the understanding that we could only drain volunteers.

Of course, we didn't always follow that rule, but there was no breach that money couldn't easily resolve. Ronan's pace increased when we were close enough to hear laughter and could see the yellow light pouring from the pub's foggy windows. I bit back a laugh as he practically sprinted the last few feet. The cold bit at my knuckles as Ronan pulled open the door, and a wave of heat greeted us along with the thick and saliva-inducing scent of fresh blood. Ronan stopped in his tracks and turned to me, pausing before we entered the blood-scented building.

I had to admit it was much stronger than I remembered. Perhaps the cramped pub was more packed than usual, but there was nothing that enticed me more than a battle of wills. Ronan's teeth were still a little red from his last meal, so I was certain he'd be able to behave himself.

I nodded to him, and we began our unlikely search for an empty seat. I could feel stolen glances from the fifty or so mortals, but they all appeared to know better than to be caught staring outright. The bulk of them crowded around tables littered with glasses filled with pale hued liquids that ranged from clear to honey brown., but there were a fair few that were standing around the bar where an exhausted bartender rushed back and forth like he was on skates.

I grinned. These were not the polished beauties that Delton or Herod sent as tribute, though their thick, supple forms seemed more appetizing, and their boisterous, exuberant exclamations seemed more appealing. My appraisal of the crowd halted when I noticed two divine forms glaring at me from the corner. The wolfish blue gaze of King Herod, and the green-eyed pointy-eared King Delton.

A grin stretched onto my face as I patted Ronan on the back

to get his attention over the noisy crowd. I nodded to the corner and we wove our way through the scattered tables. Herod lifted his cup and downed the remainder of his beer before standing. He was wearing a shirt for once, if the shredded material that was slung over his shoulder could even be considered a shirt. I was preparing to tease him about it, when I realized he was leaving.

Was he sore about our last interaction? "Leaving so soon?"

He bowed his head respectfully. "Afraid so."

I turned to Delton, but the Fae King seemed unfazed by my presence. His arms were slung lazily up on the top of his booth, and his drooped head and hollow eyes indicated that he'd had quite a few drinks already.

Ronan patted me on the back before taking Herod's seat. "Don't worry about it. It's me he hates."

Delton snorted. "You must be quite used to it by now."

I cleared my throat and Ronan jumped back up. "So sorry. Another round Delt?"

He nodded, and Ronan hustled back to the bar where the crowd immediately parted to let him through.

"I haven't seen you here in some time," I said. "Tending to your flowers?"

He smirked. "Something like that." He finished his beer. "I've heard you've been a shut in as well. That council of yours not giving you trouble?"

I glared at him and Ronan placed three beers between us. "Gentlemen, let's not waste a perfectly good night at the pub on politics."

We raised our glasses and toasted the pub, not as immortals but as three men looking for a bit of amusement. By the thir-

teenth drink, we each had a woman or two on our laps entertaining us with offers of the eternal sexual favors they'd provide
if we made them immortal. My vision blurred, but I'd been
swept up in the euphoric energy of the night. I was thoroughly
enjoying the alcohol-induced bond between Delton, Ronan, and
me, even if it would only last until the ale stopped flowing.

FOURTEEN

Finn squeezed my hand in the dark as we climbed our way up the tunnels towards the surface. I knew the gesture was meant to ease any anxiety, but I refused to let that be the case. If the Vampire King was going to capture every waking thought once the tether grew stronger, I wanted to savor every second of sanity I had left. My thoughts were consumed with the surface. I'd dreamed of visiting for even longer than I'd wanted to be a Hunter. Although I'd seen it before we went underground, those memories had all been replaced with the dark and safe tunnels that made up my life. With each step of the long, ten-hour trek, the air felt colder and more pure, until I could feel the bite of winter nipping through my fur coat. Finn smirked. "Why couldn't we have been sent on a lovely summertime mission?"

I stopped as a tiny whistling sound echoed through the caves.

"We're nearly there," Finn said, turning to face me. "You know the plan?"

I nodded.

"Then I'm going to shadow you. Assume there are spies from the other courts watching at all times, and don't acknowledge me, but," he said, brushing my chin, "remember. I'm with you always."

He leaned in but I turned my cheek to meet his lips. The corners of his mouth drooped a fraction before he began to melt into the floor, his body darkening into a charcoal black pool, before disappearing beneath my feet and blending with my barely visible shadow.

I didn't like the finality of a kiss. It felt too much like good-bye. This was a mission, plain and simple. Not only was I coming back, but I was coming back as a Hunter. A fraction of Finn's weight tugged at my shadow, and the already strenuous walk wore on my tired legs. I knew I'd have to acclimate to the added weight, and quickly, but after several minutes passed in dark silence, I missed Finn's conversation.

I was about to insist that he come out of shadow form, at least until we got a little closer, but something in my peripheral vision caught my eye. A thin, crescent moon-shaped glow stretched across the rocky terrain in front of me, and a second brighter version of the same shape beamed on the edge of the cave. *This is it.* The added weight on my shadow was buried by my enthusiasm as I raced toward the light. I knelt, dipping my fingertips in the beams that spilled onto the floor of the tunnels, wishing there was a way to bottle the glow and keep it.

I followed the trail of light to the exit, the bite of winter entangled with the moon's light as I peered through the opening. I lay my hands flat on the bolder that blocked the path and pushed. It didn't budge, so I pressed my shoulder against it, lowered my stance and drove into it all of my weight. The massive stone didn't even stutter. I peered through the opening, my eyes clamping shut as the moon's light shot straight into my eyes. The other side was littered with snow covered trees that glistened with white moon dust.

What am I supposed to do? I'm too close to the surface to ask Finn, someone might hear and I can't shadow through the gap, without the risk of being seen. The crunch of footsteps in the snow outside the cave sent a chill through my body. I ducked away from the opening, putting my back to the stone and stifling my breaths. The crunching sound drew closer, then multiplied, until I could no longer detect how many mortals were on the other side. I swallowed a lump in my throat, my heart racing as I listened with keen interest.

A familiar voice floated through the gap. "I've imprisoned her here."

Ferah. I thought I'd have an hour or two to explore the mortal town before she was to come find me, but the trek to the surface must've taken us longer than expected. I peered through the gap, and the moonlight snuffed out. A green-eyed figure glared at me. His white hair practically glowed in the moonlight, his ageless face and beauty reeked of immortality and I wondered if my half-mortal blood would be enough to mask my own immortality. I was paralyzed under his stare until he moved away from the gap, and I was able to see how bulky his frame was. I wouldn't have thought it possible but he made Finn and the other Hunters look weak by comparison.

"If this is a trick, witch, you'll die first."

I couldn't see Ferah from my limited view, and I waited for the hiss of her quick witted response, but she said nothing.

"Cadmus," his voice boomed. "You and the other Obstinacies push from this side. And you three, arrows at the ready in case our guest is foolish enough to run."

Run? I scoffed. Arrogant of him to believe me to be intimidated. This must be King Delton of the Arrow Court. I'd sooner spit in his face than run. My shadow tugged slightly, snapping me from my intrigued analysis back to the plan we'd pored over again and again the last few days. While I might've wanted to stand up, to knock the Fae King down a peg, I was supposed to be a shy and vulnerable mortal girl. I sat on the ground and pulled my knees to my chest, suppressing the groan that threatened to burst out as I pretended to cower. I heard a grunt, and silver moonlight spilled onto the cave floor, drenching my shoulders as I peeked through my hair.

"Please don't hurt me," I whispered, as the King strode to my side. He took my arm and forced me to my feet and I fought to break eye contact. The stories of the Fae's beauty, which I assumed to be exaggerated, now hardly seemed to live up to reality at all. He took my chin and tilted his head to let the moonlight fall on my face. The seconds dragged for so long as his gaze skimmed over my face, that I wondered if my cover was blown. Another Fae grabbed his shoulder snapping him from his thoughts. He dropped my chin and turned to his companion.

"Is it true?" the man asked. "Is this really the one?"

King Delton's eyes narrowed. "I'm not sure."

FIFTEEN

— DELTON —

A gentle breeze sent white flakes drifting into the rocky cave as I observed the girl. Her teeth chattered and she bundled her fur coat tighter, staring at me with her honey-brown eyes. I was startled by the soft lines of her features. As I studied her, I saw that the moonlight lit up the golden tones within her skin, highlighting her lightly freckled cheeks. She was beautiful enough to halt me in a crowded street, and nothing less would have convinced me that she was in fact, the Blood King's mate, but it still didn't feel right. She was not the smoldering temptress that Maddox preferred, but a terrified and fragile blossom, wilting from being held too close to my immortal sun. She was far more suited for me than him. It was that thought that struck me motionless as I lost myself in the ocean of her tear-filled eyes..

My curiosity and imagination had been working full time to

create an image of Maddox's mate from the moment I agreed to this plan, but I had greatly missed the mark. I had expected to meet the woman who would topple the Blood Court. I'd expected this to be an easy task. I'd gleefully ship her off to the blood drinkers where she no doubt belonged, but the shivering doe-like woman stirred my empathy.

Cadmus' voice broke my trance. "Let's get her out of the cold."

I turned and left her to my Obstinacies as I breathed in the serenity of the frozen forest. Ferah made her way to me, her dark eyebrow raised, and her mouth twisted into a pleased smile. "Well?" she said, her gaze sweeping over my face.

"We shall see."

A slight movement in the corner of my eye made my ears twitch, but the snow-white terrain remained unblemished. "Stay with the Obstinacy. I'll be right back."

I walked through the forest and closed my eyes, focusing on the hushed whispers of the woods. I tuned out the Obstinacies as they began to march the girl back to the greenhouse and the creak of the trees as they pushed against the wind. Then I heard the sound I was listening for, the sound of retreating waves that rose and crashed on the shore. The steady unmistakable rhythm of wolfish lungs. I opened my eyes, and several snow-white masses rose from the snow. Their beady eyes glared and the white of their canine teeth shone in the wintery moonlight.

I held my ground as one of the wolves began to shift. I always hated being present for a shift. It was an unnatural abomination of snapping ligaments and bone as the snow-white wolf morphed into a man. I cleared my throat. "Herod."

His chest was covered in blue markings as he began to circle me, like he forgot he was no longer in wolf form. "What's going on here?"

"I need you and your mutts to leave now."

A wolf growled and snapped at the air beside me.

Herod smiled brightly. "I'm not leaving shit."

The last thing we needed was to draw more attention to what we were doing. I nodded to the wolves at his side. "Call them off, and I'll tell you."

Herod crossed his arms and glared at me. Finally, he nodded, and without a word the wolves headed back through the woods.

"Now," he said, "tell me what's going on here."

I looked around the empty forest, heard the retreating footsteps of the Obstinacies in the deep snow, the girl, and the wolves as they raced through the dense forest.

"I found Maddox's mate."

He studied my face. "You seem very certain of that."

"I had a lead and I wanted to check it out before I came to you."

"And?"

"It's her."

He nodded but his muted reaction suggested he wasn't convinced. "I'd like to see her for myself."

"You're putting us more at risk by being here."

His breath released a cloud of dewy, white air. "You expect me to believe you without proof?"

"Tomorrow I will present the girl to Maddox along with other tributes. If he keeps her around, you'll have your proof, but I suggest you prepare for a battle. Once the King's immortality is compromised, we will only have a small window to take him down, and the rest of his court won't go down easily."

His nose twitched. "This doesn't smell right. What aren't you telling me?"

I'd hoped to keep my deal with Ferah a secret, but Herod was right to question this. Outside of the Shadow Court, there was no way to find an immortal's mate aside from dumb luck. Herod was always suspicious, and he certainly wasn't going to like how we'd ended up in business with Ferah.

"We kept a prisoner from the war. A shade. She agreed to divine Maddox's mate and retrieve her, in exchange for sanctuary in our court."

Herod's blue eyes lit as my story began to take root in his head.

"I want to see the girl."

"In due time," I said, looking over my shoulder. "Don't you think it'll raise suspicions for Mad if she knows us both? Give it some time, visit the Blood King and if she is what we think, I'm sure he will be eager to show her off."

With a twitch of his nose, he turned away, his body contorting as the white, wolfish fur pierced his skin like tiny needles through dark brown fabric. I hurried after the Obstinacies and their mysterious prisoner. If we were going to use her to catch Maddox's eye, she'd need a lot of work before I presented her to the Blood Court tomorrow morning.

SIXTEEN

— S I N N A —

Whe trudged through the snowy terrain, the crunch of the snow beneath my boots was unfamiliar in the way my foot sunk into it. The air was crisp and dry, as the Fae King's Obstinacies marched me through the woods. Each court had their own version of Hunters, the military force that kept them in power. I had to admit that the Obstinacy was pretty cool with their pointed ears and earthy uniforms. I had hoped they'd take me through the town, so that I could glimpse the warm buildings, all nestled together, and perhaps the mortal faces that reminded me of my mother, but the Fae stayed in the woods, unwilling to risk me being seen by The Blood King until I was ready to be presented. The moonlight glittered over the unmarred snow like luminescent crystals. Winter was shaping up to be my favorite season. Finn had described the season as a barren wasteland, but all I saw in the shimmering branches was a crystalline wonderland.

Those who favor warm climates are foolish. I'd no sooner thought the words when I caught my first glimpse of the Fae Greenhouse, stretching up above the tree-line. It was a lush, tropical world, green and vast, trapped behind foggy windows. It was obstinate both in its grand dome-like structure and defiance of the season, like a reverse snow globe. The vibrant greens pressed against the glass panes, beckoning us out of the cold, as the strange sight rose from the forest like a mirage in the desert.

My steps became labored. There was a weight pressing in on my chest, harder with each step. I couldn't possibly be fatigued already. I lifted my hand and placed it on my chest, and my heart raced against it. Each step farther from the caves drained my energy, like this world knew I didn't belong. But why? My legs felt strong, my lungs were unencumbered from the journey, unless... was it the tether? I let my gaze wander until it came to rest on an unremarkable section of the woods.

"Are you alright?" King Delton asked, tearing me from my reverie.

This was no time to show my hand. "I need to rest," I muttered.

He gestured to the dome-shaped greenhouse. "We're nearly there."

I nodded, but his gaze moved to the direction I'd traced the tether and his wild, green eyes narrowed. He moved ahead of me, the fletching and nock of his arrow peeking out over the top of his quiver, but they didn't jostle, not even with the Fae King's powerful and uneven gate. Ezra had told me of the powerful poisons that tipped all arrows of the Fae. If the stories were true, they couldn't be handled lightly, so it shouldn't have surprised me that the quivers had a system to lock arrows in place. My curiosity began to take hold as I wondered about the intricacies of the other courts. We all lived so differently.

I'd been in their company for such a short time, but it was hard not to be seduced by the beauty of the Fae, and certainly the grace and nuances of their chosen method of killing. I was drawn to the idea of poison more than I cared to admit, and I hoped I'd get a chance to see it before they shipped me off to the blood court.

Up close the greenhouse looked like the emeralds that sometimes glittered along the walls of my home. The green of the plants inside shone through the glass panes, which scattered the moonlight like a large gemstone atop the snow.

An Obstinacy opened the door and I held my breath in anticipation as the other Fae, and Ferah, herded me through the doors. A blanket of warmth and moisture clung to my face, and my extremities tingled from the change in temperature. The room was a jungle, with trees and vegetation sprawling across all but a narrow path that wove throughout it. The air was filled with the rustle and chatter of life hidden in the greenery, and I strained to catch a glimpse of whatever hidden creatures peered at us as we passed through the moonlit forest.

The path opened up, and at the far end of the room was a wooden throne carved into a massive tree. A deer froze as its eyes met mine, before it skidded into the depths of the forest. With the Obstinacy lined up, their bows at the ready, with arrows still secure in their quivers, it was easier to see their similarities and differences. Their facial features were kissed with the versatility of nature, but they all had the same shade of snow-white hair, and the same long pointed ears. I drank in the strange atmosphere, more certain than ever that if I had my choice of courts, I would have had no difficulty choosing the Arrow Court.

I was sure it wasn't only because I was experiencing something new. Anyone would have felt the same way. The essence of nature lives in all of us. Ferah slid into my field of vision across the room. As planned, she'd kept her distance, unwilling to give away our previous connection, and only now was her usual grimace replaced with a pleased smirk. My gaze moved to King Delton, whose eyes watched me with a softened gaze and a raised eyebrow. My wonderment was unintentional, but I could see how that might stroke the ego of an immortal king.

"Your Majesty," an Obstinacy said, "time is short."

The King's gaze dropped away. He flicked his wrist, a gesture I didn't understand, and two of the female Obstinacies, took me by the arms and led me out of the throne room. The rest of the manor was what I'd expected of the Fae court. It was elegant, if not a little plain. The corridors were made up of wood and stone, with small waterfalls trickling into black pools that reminded me of home.

"Where are you taking me?"

The Obstinacies exchanged a glance, a wordless deliberation on whether to respond, but ultimately they held their silence, choosing instead to nod toward a wooden door. Not wanting to appear too eager, I slowed my pace as I approached, looking back at the Obstinacies as they watched to make sure I'd enter. I pulled on the door handle and needed to use my body weight to yank it open. Thick white plumes of mist poured through the opening, and I peered through to the glimmering pools. A Fae woman approached me, nude as the day she was born, with her long silvery hair tucked behind her pointed ears.

The basins were rocky and similar in shape to what we used

in the Shadow Court. In fact, there were more similarities than differences. It wasn't uncommon for our washers to be naked, but I'd known them all of my life.

The Fae woman reached for me, and I instinctively drew back.

"I'm Ava. I need to get you clean and to bed with the rest of the tributes."

Her gaze was soft, but her voice was full of urgency. I nodded and she carefully stripped off my clothing, took my hand, and led me down to the water. The black soot from the caves where I'd spent all my life was practically a second skin, but the woman scrubbed it until the rich brown color of my natural skin tone showed through.

The woman worked quickly and thoroughly, and I admired her beauty, both the ethereal lines of her profile, and the sheen of her glossy hair as it floated on the surface of the water. The corners of her mouth tipped up and I felt scorched by her green eyes as they flitted to me for the smallest moment.

"Are you not allowed to speak with me?"

She rose from the water, the translucent beads slipping down her torso as she ascended the stairs.

"Am I not allowed to speak with you?" I pushed as she disappeared into the mist, returning a moment later with a bottle.

"If you wish," she said softly.

She poured the bottle rather than squeezed it and when she placed it on a stone, I realized it was made of glass. She rubbed her hands together, and bubbles oozed through her fingers.

She sunk back into the water, the floral aroma filling my nose and making my eyes roll back as I breathed it in. The woman's touch was stronger now, her fingers digging into my muscles as she rubbed the scented oils deep into my skin. She grew more bold, teasing at my nipples, her expression warming and her lips playfully pursed as my breath skipped.

I felt a tug on my shadow which lay just on the surface of the water around my shoulder. *Finn.* I'd been so overwhelmed by the Arrow Court that I'd almost forgotten about him. Was he warning me of a danger I couldn't see? Then I felt my shadow slide down my back and shortly after the press of Finn's shadowy fingertips on my thighs as he pried them open. The Fae women's eyebrows rose, as heat burned my face. What was Finn doing? He was going to get us caught. The woman eased me back against the rock with a smile. "You're different," she said, teasing her fingers down my body.

Heat radiated up my neck as desire began to flare along with curiosity. "How so?"

"Most of the tributes are terrified on their last night. I've always wondered why they don't-" she slipped her fingers between my legs, "-relax and enjoy their last night, since most of them don't survive a day in the Blood Court."

I forced myself through the pleasure and her warning to keep my eyes open, to watch the beautiful Fae girl, as I knew this would be my last chance to experience intimacy with a Fae. I knew there was truth to the danger she spoke of, but my body couldn't hear it, not with the pleasure building as I writhed against the cold stone.

"You'll meet the others tonight," she said softly.

My body jolted with delight, the motion sending glitter through her eyes and eagerness to her touch. But the Fae girl didn't know that she and I were not alone, that my shadow's hands were practiced, relentless, and knew exactly where to touch me to make me forget she was even there.

SEVENTEEN

SINNA

I heard the faint whispers of the other tributes lilting down the hallway as Ava led me toward my room. Exhaustion settled into my muscles from the brutal climb to the surface, after I had calmed down from the wonder of seeing the fabled Arrow Court with my own eyes. I'd imagined the mortal town above so many times, piecing together Finn's stories and adding in my own daydreams, but I hadn't even glimpsed it. Instead I was given the rarest of opportunities to see an immortal court outside my own, an honor that only the crown King or Queen could possibly hope for, unless of course they were hidden away underground. Ava reached for the wooden door, and when it cracked open, the voices hushed.

I stepped through into a room that resembled a grassy field. Moon and starlight beamed down through glass panes on the vaulted ceiling. Several women lay on blankets on the soft plane.

Ava gave me a moment to take in the splendorous view before returning with a blanket. "Big day tomorrow. Best get some rest, if you can."

I smiled my thanks and she closed the door behind her, locking it with a resounding click. I looked around at the motionless tributes, who appeared to be asleep, but I could practically feel their energy as I searched for an open place. I saw the first stirs of movement as curious eyes peeked at me through the dark.

I found an empty patch of grass between two women and lay down my blanket between them. I climbed onto it, surprised to find the blades of grass to be both soft and supportive beneath it. The day's physical and emotional weight threatened to pull me instantly to sleep, but I heard a faint voice whisper behind me.

"You're very beautiful."

I rolled to face the girl who had spoken. She peeked at me through glossy red hair. She had mortal eyes, just like my mother. The vibrant, hopeful eyes of someone who didn't know what would come next. I wondered if mine looked that way, now that I'd been thrust into new territory and would possibly face my own mortality in the near future.

"You're very beautiful, too," I said, remembering myself. "I'm Sinna."

"My name is Celine."

I offered a smile before I rolled onto my back. I didn't mind the conversation. It was a welcome distraction, and I'd been living off those since I had been given my mission. When I was idle, I felt overwhelmed by the tasks at hand. Don't get bitten. Stay in character. Seduce the King. Don't fall in love. I could feel the tension in the room, as if the other tributes were listening to my conversation with Celine, as if we were all clinging to the hope that tonight wouldn't be our last. I wanted to think the King would choose me and that my plan would go accordingly, but as I lay in the moonlight, I realized that every tribute there had that in common, and that like them, it could easily be me who died at the hands of the Vampire King.

I shuddered.

"Have you ever seen him?" Celine whispered.

My heartbeat stuttered as his pooled image rushed back. "No."

"My cousin saw him at the tavern once. She said he was divinely beautiful. Can you believe it? *Divinely.* She said she'd die, just for the chance to be his immortal queen."

Existence seemed too great to give up for beauty, even divine beauty. I reminded myself that I wasn't here for beauty but for the elevation and protection of my family and court.

"Is there any beauty worth dying for?"

She paused so long that I wondered if she'd fallen asleep, then she said, "I hope so. She volunteered a few years back and never returned. I like to think it was worth it."

I sat up, my voice stronger than I meant it to be. "Then, why are you here?"

She sat up, sending her wild, red curls bouncing around her head. "Believe me. Any alternative to the life I've been born into is an improvement. . .Why are you here?"

My answer stalled on my tongue when I caught the smallest shift of my shadow under the moonlight.

I covered my face with my hands, finding it all too easy to force weakness into my voice. "I was taken."

Celine sucked in a breath.

"For fuck's sake," a voice boomed from behind me. I turned

to see a girl with strikingly angular features snarling at me. "Firstly, you're both going to die within three seconds of entering the Blood Court."

"That's needlessly harsh, Mel," someone whispered from across the room.

She pointed her finger past me. "She's too frumpy to catch the King's eye and the second you start with that hostage nonsense, the King is going to lose his shit."

I raised an eyebrow. "And I suppose you think he's going to choose you to be his bride?"

"We'll never know because if you half-wits chatter on all night like this, I'm going to off myself long before we get to the Blood Court."

A smile tugged at my mouth, and my next words were practically involuntary. "I like you."

She had no shame, played no games, and spoke her truth.

Her eyebrows rose, before her face fell back into a scowl. "Whatever. Go the hell to sleep."

Celine shrugged but her eyes glistened with a touch of sadness, no doubt wounded from Mel's harsh appraisal. I lay between them, intrigued by their uniqueness. By comparison, immortals seemed to eventually fall into the same few attitudes, never evolving into anything other than lustfulness, arrogance, and hunger for power. Celine was gentle, kind, and hopeful. Mel was strong, opinionated, and optimistic. Who was I?

The more words rose up to answer me, like deceitful, conniving, and promiscuous, the more they came to resemble the traits I'd assigned all immortals. If for the first time in my life my immortality was on the line, perhaps, I thought as I drifted off to sleep, I could be something else.

EIGHTEEN

I awoke suddenly. The sky was bright outside the skylight, but the sun was not yet high enough to shine through the misty glass panes. A line of Obstinacies marched with their pointed ears peeking through their hair. They stood at attention, crossing their bows as I and the rest of the tributes scrambled to our feet, brushing the sleep from our eyes.

Celine's gaze met mine, but in the morning light, her eyes were less hopeful than the night before, and instead, just beyond her neutral expression, there was a sheen of fearful despair. When I looked to Mel, her eyes were trained on the Fae Guards with the determined intensity that mirrored how I'd looked at the Hunters all my life.

The Obstinacies ushered us out of the meadow atrium where we'd spent the night, through the cramped wooden labyrinth that appeared to make up the bulk of the Fae Court, until the room opened to a new, heavily wooded greenhouse. The branches of the canopy were woven together so tightly that there were only small slivers of space where the sunlight slipped through it, spilling silvery, white light through the candlelit greenhouse.

The other tributes took their seats in elegantly carved chairs that were set around a long wooden table at the center of the room. Celine stuck behind me like my shadow, but I thought I'd have to jockey for a position beside Mel. Surprisingly, instead of making her way right to the table, she lagged back a bit, wrapping her sleek ponytail around her finger as she over-intently examined her surroundings, losing interest just as I came up behind her. We wordlessly took a seat at the table as trays of thinly sliced fruit and multicolored rice were set out in front of us. As I looked around the table at the other girls, I could practically taste the anxiety in the air, or maybe it was my own. We were all going to face an excruciating death, and worse than that, we were all going to face him. A shudder tore through me as my mind brought forth the image of his dark, cold eyes.

When I looked up again, many of the girls had already begun eating, some of the braver ones even chatting quietly on the far side of the table. I reached for my fork only to find the table completely without them. I eyed Mel, who smirked at me, giving a slight shrug of her shoulders before she popped a slice of yellow fruit into her mouth.

"How are we supposed to eat rice with our fingers?" I asked Celine.

Her curly red locks blocked most of her face, but her plate was already almost completely clear. I hadn't eaten in some time. Food wasn't necessary for my survival like it was for the mortals. It was more of a luxury. I reached for the rice, and to my surprise, it stuck together better than I'd anticipated and had a sweet buttery flavor.

When Celine finished her plate, she turned to me, her eyes moving to my plate ever so often as she made conversation. "You seem nervous today."

Her voice drew the attention of several of the other girls. I swallowed the rice I was chewing before I said, "I am."

"Are you more afraid to die, or that the Blood King won't choose you?"

I wasn't sure this was an appropriate breakfast conversation, but the rest of the tributes were listening intently now. I paused a moment to gather my thoughts. There was nothing about the situation that wasn't scary. If they discovered me, my whole court could be in danger. I could fail at my first task as a Hunter. What if the tether was too strong to resist? My neck stung as my mind played through the worst-case scenario.

The King biting into my neck.

If he did and I didn't bleed, my cover would be blown. Or worse, if he bit me and I did bleed, it would mean that I'd fallen in love with him and could no longer complete my task. Either way, I was sure being bitten was the worst. I couldn't reveal my other fears, but Celine and the rest of the girls would certainly buy this one.

"I'm afraid to be bitten."

There was a collective softening of the other girls as if the freely spoken words lifted some of their apprehension. Conversation swelled as the girls began sharing their hopes and fears.

"What about you, Celine?"

Her gaze moved to my plate before it snapped back to my eyeline. "I'm most afraid he won't love me."

Mel interjected. "What if you don't love him?"

A few of the girls giggled at that. Apparently, King Maddox didn't have the same reputation among the mortals. All my life, I'd heard nothing about the Blood Court other than their ruthlessness and cruelty.

Celine tripped over her words, so I took the opportunity to get to know a little about Mel. "Do you expect to fall in love with him?"

"I'm not here for love. I'm here for immortality. I don't have to be the King's true love. I just have to be interesting enough for him to want to keep me around."

I bit back a smile. *True love.* What an odd expression. Before I could inquire further, the Obstinacies barged in.

"Line up," one said, his voice echoing through the canopy.

I slid my plate to Celine, and with a few determined scoops, she polished it off, mouthing a 'Thank you,' before we were ushered into line with the others.

I was familiar with our next destination, the bathhouse. I was a little sad not to see the beautiful Fae girl from the night before, but instead, the Obstinacies stripped naked and stood in waist-deep water, ready to bathe us. Their steely bodies were beaded with water, as we were all ordered to strip and join them in the pools. None of us fussed much. The beautiful immortal Fae had a way of numbing the senses. They were surprisingly thorough, swift, and business-like in their movements, as each tribute was washed and then rotated out to the next room. The Fae didn't offer so much as a salacious glance at any of the tributes. Even the more confident ones that had strut around in hopes of drawing their attention. It was as if they thought all mortals were inferior. Had my mother not been mortal, I wondered if I would have felt the same.

I was wiped down with a towel and sent nude through the

hallway, where I was ushered to the next room. Some of the other girls were already there. Their wet hair was towel-wrapped on top of their heads like mine. The variation of skin tones, body types, and prominent features had me wondering if the King had any preference at all, but each girl had obvious beauty, even when stripped down and damp. Some of the girls were being measured, while others winced in the mirror as more Fae pulled their hair into styles that suited each girl, as if they were carefully planned and chosen.

The hours dragged. The activities were so tedious we could do nothing but fear the night ahead, and occasionally exchange those fears. When the first few girls slipped on their custom gowns, with white fabric cut flawlessly to complement their best features, they all could pass as immortals. It was odd to see the white fabric, so royal and elegant, but it was not worn by any of the courts. Arrow always wore green, Blood wore red, Moon wore blue, and the Shadow Court wore black. White felt like a blank slate, a statement of non-belonging. It wasn't until the Obstinacy zipped my dress as I caught a glimpse of myself in the mirror, that I felt naked for the first time. It was as if I no longer belonged to my court. My gaze trailed down the white fabric to my deep black shadow, and I felt the smallest bit of comfort. I was not alone. I was still a princess of the Shadow Court, and those were the thoughts I held onto all the way until I stepped foot in the Blood Court that night. After that, who I was, my mission, what I wanted, all slipped away from me like water through my fingers. After that, everything went to hell.

NINETEEN

—— M A D D O X ——

I stood under the full moon, my breath coming out in white plumes, briefly obscuring the simmering orb, before dissipating. There was something about it that drew me out on clear nights. Perhaps it was the way it waned and eventually died, bright and temporary like the shooting stars that framed it. I envied them. The cold air quenched the burning thirst in my throat, and I reached out as if I could feel the beams of moonlight brush against my fingertips. Something was amiss, something I couldn't wrap my head around yet. I'd completely forgotten that Delton was presenting tributes tonight, but his footsteps behind brought the memory back to the surface.

"Sire, they're here."

A pang of sadness hit my stomach. I didn't want to tear myself away from the moon's light and the peace that came with it, in exchange for a parade of women who would no doubt remind me of Nova.

"Sire?" Ronan said, his voice a little softer this time.

"Something is off," I said, turning to him. "Can you feel it?"

He pressed his lips together, and I could feel annoyance radiating from him, fueling me with a twinge of pleasure. It was enough to send me trudging through the cold, back to my stained glass prison. With every step toward the palace, my unease grew, until it felt like a weight resting on my chest. I could hear Ronan's footsteps behind me, so I squelched any visible signs of distress.

If this was something new, something that could shake me from the mundanity of eternal life, however abhorrent, it would be a welcomed change. When I stepped into the Blood Court, the sanguine aroma struck me so hard it could have knocked me off my feet. Instead, I went straight for the Throne room, where I knew the tributes would be waiting.

I pushed open the door as the weight on my chest threatened to crack my ribs. I pushed on to see Delton, sitting on the arm of my throne. Rage swelled, and I saw a glimmer of amusement in his swampy eyes.

I straightened and forced a smile. "If it isn't the King of the Fairies."

His jaw clenched as he stood. "It's Fae," he muttered.

"What do you have for me tonight?"

"A gesture of my respect and admiration of the Blood Court."

They were the same words as always, but tonight they had a bite to them that I couldn't place.

"Let's see them then," I said, walking down the small flight to the carpeted floor where the tributes waited to be appraised.

I strode past the first row, hardly glancing at the trembling tributes as I moved to the next row. When I stepped into the second row, the weight on my chest amplified. Was this a *tether*? My gaze moved to Delton whose mossy green eyes were locked on my every move. His eyebrow twitched, and a wave of shame slammed into me. Did he really think I'd be so easily killed? That I'd sacrifice my immortality for a sensation that literally felt like it was going to crack my ribs? It was simple; all I needed to do was walk by the tributes and order them all to be drained. I straightened and walked down the aisle, too afraid to look at the source of this feeling. I passed the tributes one by one until I could feel her beside me. My pace slowed, and my body refused to pass by. I forced myself forward but only made it a step before I stopped, my heartbeat throbbing in my chest. I turned to face the tribute standing next to the one with the tether, and promised myself to focus on her only. Her resemblance to Nova was uncanny. Dark straight hair, glossy blue eyes, and a stare that was equal parts cold and fearful.

"What's your name?"

"Melany," she said, but my focus was starting to drag away from her.

"Why are you here?"

"Immortality."

An honest answer, refreshing. I looked to Ronan, gesturing over my shoulder as words I never meant to speak slipped out. "I'll take these three. Have them in my chamber in an hour."

I turned to glare at Delton, who only bowed graciously and took his leave. Perhaps I'd given Delton too much credit. He didn't so much as snicker when I made my selection. I hadn't so much as looked at the girl, but that might've worked against me--feeding into my curiosity. If I would have looked, I was certain she wouldn't have been anything special, but it wasn't a risk I wanted to take so publicly.

I passed Ronan on my way out of the Throne room. "Drain the rest," I said, patting him on the back. "Let's eat."

I tried not to be preoccupied at dinner as I sipped fresh blood from the goblet, but my mind was occupied with what was waiting for me in my bed. Ronan seemed more at ease than usual, probably comforted that I had chosen three tributes instead of one, but the danger was greater than ever. I just needed to find out if it was greater than me. I took my time chatting with the other courtiers and some council members who all seemed in good spirits from our shared feast, and only when the numbers dwindled did I stand, and wish the straggling few a goodnight. I made my way to my chambers. I expected the intensity of the tether to shine when I got there, but the feeling was far less prominent than it had been in the Throne Room. It must've been all in my head. I swung open the door, and sure enough, Melany lay nude and strewn across my red satin sheets alongside an orange haired girl who shyly covered herself with her arms. I scanned the room, looking for the third tribute.

"Where is she?" I spat. "I asked for three of you."

Dread pooled in my stomach as I feared the worst, that some kind of mistake had been made and the woman from the throne room, the one with the tether, had been mistakenly drained.

A knock sounded at my door and I yanked the door open to see Ronan standing in the doorway.

"Where is she?" I asked between clenched teeth. "If you drained her—"

"The tribute is in her bedroom. She refuses to join you tonight."

"Where?"

"The east—"

Before he could finish, I barreled down the hallway to the east wing. Anger and excitement was a deadly cocktail in my blood as the weight on my chest increased with each step. I threw open the double doors and rushed to the woman in the white ballgown who was standing at the center of the room like she was expecting me. I rushed forward and cornered her, my fangs hovering less than an inch from her flesh.

"Why do you refuse to join me?"

Her bottom lip trembled, but she didn't look away. "I was taken from my home. I didn't volunteer. I was told that you don't accept hostages, now let me go."

She was right, I never took anyone underage nor anyone who didn't volunteer, but now, now that this new possibility was here, this new force, I couldn't just let her go. I stepped closer. The tether pressed in on me when I saw her hand rise to her chest. I froze. *So this is a tether. . . and she can feel it, too.*

I straightened and took several steps back. "I apologize for the misunderstanding. How about you stay the night, and tomorrow I will try to make amends."

She looked unsure but nodded slightly, so I took my leave before she could change her mind, and stationed two guards outside her door, just in case.

"Ronan," I barked as I reached my door. "Send the other tributes back to their rooms. I'm tired."

Despite my words, I didn't sleep for a second. My heartbeat never slowed.

I ran through the image of the girl who refused my bed and wondered, what terrors did she have in store for me?

TWENTY

— S I N N A —

I stood at the center of my bed-chamber; my heart still racing from my encounter with the Blood King. The tether had been much more crippling than I imagined, weighing on my chest and blurring my senses to the point where I could scarcely observe him when he was standing right in front of me. In fact, my memory of our conversation was nothing but a black empty space in my mind, save for one crucial detail that remained, churning my nerves.

He too felt the tether.

This was both a danger and undoubtedly what had saved me from his brutality. Either way, from this point on, he'd be wary of me.

Just when I thought he was about to show the cruel, angry tyrant that made up his reputation, he softened, and there was no possible explanation except for the tether. If I were to keep my wits about me long enough to seduce him, I'd have to find some way to overcome the tether myself. He might've had a moment of softness, but that didn't excuse a lifetime of wickedness.

He was a blood drinker. The bulk of the girls I'd gotten to know in the Arrow Court had already been reduced to pale corpses. If I hadn't whispered that small incantation, Mel and Celine might have been dead as well. It had been only a small bit of suggestion magic, I couldn't have risked more, but I suspected the tether might've made the incantation more effective.

Thus far, Ezra's plan was right on track. It seemed I'd be able to bargain with the King on my terms and hopefully take away the possibility of being bitten, which would surely give me away before I could complete my task. I wondered if I'd have enough sway to save my new companions as well. Though I knew I had Finn hidden away in my shadow, he could not risk leaving his shadow form, and therefore was of little comfort in a court that felt like it was drenched in blood.

I began to undress, peeling away the white fabric that labeled me as an outcast and took in a deep breath as I explored my bedroom. It was decorated much like the rest of the Blood Court. It was overly ornate, and dripping with red velvet fabric. Candelabras and decorative vases were studded with rubies and rimmed with gold accents. It felt like a natural opposite to the Arrow Court with its organic growth and wildlife. Here, everything was hand-chosen, gaudy, and dripping with the impersonal, judgmental feeling that all places of warship seemed to inherently carry. How fitting then that the Blood Court made their home in a refurbished cathedral. The absence of natural light should have reminded me of my home under the ground, but the stone-carved caves that made up my life were natural. Natural, like the winding branches of the Arrow Court.

I slipped into bed. The silky fabric was smoother and softer than it looked. I closed my eyes, and the blackness behind them brought a welcome piece of home. After many lifetimes of wishing to leave the shadows of my home, I missed it, and I wondered if I should have paused to enjoy it one last time, just in case I never made it back home.

I awoke feeling refreshed and well-rested, but despair quickly set in. I got up slowly and walked to the wardrobe, pulling it open to find an array of clothing, all in the exact same, empty white color as the ball gown that was still sprawled across the floor from last night. I grabbed a pair of white stretchy pants and a flowy top and threw it on the bed. A door at the side of the room caught my eye. I'd noticed it the night before but I'd been too tired to investigate. I tiptoed over to it and cracked it open to peek through, just in case someone was on the other side.

Relief rushed through me as I took a look around the private bathroom. Every surface was made of pristine, white marble, with the notable exception of the golden faucets and accents, which were a welcomed break from the red fabric. There was a large, oval shaped tub, big enough for several people at once and a vanity that was stocked with makeup, creams, hygiene items, cotton swabs, soaps, and anything else I could have imagined, down to multiple types of toothbrushes. We used magic to accomplish most matters of hygiene in the Shadow Court, and many of the items were new to me.

I was tempted to fill the tub with blankets and pillows and make this my new home, as the environment felt more welcoming than my stuffy bedroom, but I wasn't totally committed to the idea. I washed quickly, making use of a new toothbrush but giving the makeup a pass. I slipped on my new clothes and contemplated waiting until someone came to fetch me. My patience didn't hold out. I made my way to the door and peeked through. The guards on either side straightened to attention when they saw me.

"Good morning," I said, stretching my arms over my head and patting one of the guards on the back.

"Miss," he said, suddenly. "We are to escort you to the dining room for breakfast."

"Escort away."

I'd half expected him to hold his arm out and lead me to our destination, as we did in my obviously more civilized court. Instead, he stepped in front of me to lead the way while the second guard marched closely behind me.

For as ornate as the cathedral was, it felt like once you'd seen one gaudy red room, you'd sort of seen them all. It wasn't much to look at, so I thought I'd entertain myself with a little conversation. If I'm lucky, I might be able to pry some information out of them.

"I'm Sinna. What's your name?" I said, leaning forward to the guard.

He glanced back over his shoulder, but didn't speak. I was going to attempt again with another question, but the guard behind me spoke before I did.

"I'm Callum."

I grinned. "Callum, excellent. It's nice to meet you."

The guard turned back, rolling his eyes.

"See? That wasn't so hard, was it?" I teased. He turned away.

"If you don't tell me your name, I'll be forced to make one

up." He stopped short in front of tall double doors, gesturing to the guards stationed in front to open them.

He narrowed his eyes, so I stepped through, looking back at him over my shoulder. "I think I'll go with. . . Grumpy."

There were more than a few guards standing around a long, redwood table and once I got a little closer to it my heart leapt with excitement. Seated at the far side of the room were Mel and Celine. Mel's mouth dropped open and Celine's eyes widened when they met mine. I hastened over and took a seat beside them, bursting with relief . They were practically strangers and yet I felt responsible for them somehow, and a little less alone. I wanted to talk to them, to ask them a million questions about their first night or their impression of the Blood King, but the number of guards hovering around us kept us silent.

The second I took my seat, a plate with a golden cover was placed in front of me.

A guard removed the lid, exposing a plate of steaming red soup. My stomach churned. Is it blood? Mel caught my eye and she lifted her spoon, picked up a scoop of white rice from a side dish, and dipped the loaded spoon into the soup before bringing it to her lips. I leaned a little closer, breathing in the scent. It smelled spicy and a little fermented. I wasn't sure what kind of soup it was, but I doubted it was made of blood. Following Mel's lead, I got a scoop of rice, and dipped it into the bowl, letting the red soup coat the white grains.

There was a loud creak behind me, which set my nerves on edge. The sound of a man's heavy footsteps grew louder, until a man with a scruffy beard walked up next to me.

"Hello, miss. My name is Ronan."

"I'm Sinna," I said, my spoon hanging in the balance.

I snuck a glance at Mel and Celine whose faces seemed to drain of color. Why did they look worried? Did they know something about this man that I did not? Did he know something about me he shouldn't?

His next words sent a pang of fear racing through me. "I need you to come with me."

TWENTY-ONE

— M A D D O X —

The light that filtered through the parlor window looked more like light from the setting sun than the blood-red of the other stained glass windows in our court. It was slightly less comfortable than rooms that more proudly displayed my court's signature color, but that was why I had chosen it for the meeting. It was the most neutral place in the east wing. I could only sit for a short time before needing to stand up and pace a bit around the room. *So, she's my tether.* The very thing that could destroy my existence and topple my reign. Why, then, did I allow her to stay overnight, and what was I hoping to accomplish with this meeting? Was it just curiosity? A test of wills greater than any other, for me to prove my dominance? Had the tether already taken hold of me?

A knock rapped at the door, and I bounded across the room to have a seat by the window.

I took a calming breath, then said, "Come in."

The door swung open, and I felt the tether tighten against my chest. I turned toward the window and felt her presence as she crossed the room. The doors clicked shut, and I gestured to the chair on the far side of the window, hoping that the distance would ease the intensity of the tether. "Please have a seat."

She obeyed, and I ventured a peek at her only to find her already staring out the window, no doubt feeling the crippling effects of the pull as much as I was.

After several seconds of silence, I forced myself to break through. "What is your name?"

"Sinna, Your Highness."

Her presence choked me. "Do you know who I am?"

"Yes, Your Highness." Her gaze moved to me, her eyes a soft brown color that was rimmed in darkness.

"And you were brought here by force?"

"Yes, Your Highness."

I exhaled my frustration. Both at the situation and my inability to feel like myself. What did I have to be nervous about? She was nothing. Just a tether, which most likely had some kind of workaround. "I don't take hostages. You're free to go, but I wonder if there was something I could tempt you with to stay."

"Why?"

I must've stared with a blank expression, because after a moment she continued. "Why do you want me to stay here? What do you want with me?"

I wasn't sure why, but I felt like the question put me at a disadvantage. "I wanted three companions to entertain me for the next few weeks, and I've gone and drained all the rest of the tributes already. So you see, you'll have to do."

She nodded thoughtfully and I felt a twinge of relief that she bought such a weak reply. "So tell me, Sinna. What is it that you want?"

"I want you to give your word that I won't be bitten by you or anyone else."

I clenched my jaw. It wasn't unreasonable, but I didn't like being denied something I so dearly wanted to sample.

She leaned forward and the tether tugged. "I'd like not to be escorted everywhere by guards."

I ran my hand through my hair. "How will I know you won't run away?"

"You don't, but as you said, I'm not a hostage."

I clicked my tongue. "That won't do. Once you volunteer to be here, I can do with you what I want. How about you exchange your vow for mine. I'll promise you won't be bitten, and you won't be followed by my guards, and you'll promise not to leave."

She leaned back in her chair, crossing her arms over her chest. "Fine, but I have one more request."

She piqued my interest. "Oh? And what is that?"

"Immortality."

Disappointment was a silver stake through my chest. How boring. She was the same as all the others.

She turned to the window, allowing me to observe her face more closely without suffering under the weight of her gaze.

"Not for me. For the other two girls, Melany and Celine."

"You don't want immortality?"

She turned to me and lanced me with her next words. "Why would anyone want that?"

I bit my tongue to avoid hurling reasons at her. It was the ultimate prize, sought out by the world, and desired by all.

Wasn't she begging me to make her little friends immortal? Immortality was mine, and mine alone to give and yet, no one had ever asked me that question before.

The tether tightened, so I stood quickly, pacing to the far side of the room in hopes of relief.

"I will not guarantee immortality to anyone. But I can offer them relative safety as long as they obey the rules of my manor."

She stood, closing the gap between us, tightening the tether with each brazen step. "Do we have a deal?"

My eyes narrowed. "Answer one more question for me, and we'll consider our business finished."

She bit on her bottom lip before her face brightened. "Excellent. I have a question of my own. Yours first, of course, Your Highness."

I eyed her. She was an obvious beauty, but many of the tributes were. It was a trait I felt nearly numb to, but unlike the others, her arms and hands were free of the scars and burns of the brutal labor that drove the mortals to my door. If not for immortality, what reason other than desperation or stupidity would tempt her to stay? Could it be the tether?

Rather than show her all of my cards, I asked simply, "Why stay?"

She held my gaze, and when she spoke, it was barely a whisper. "Curiosity."

I understood. That was the force that drove me as well.

She looked into my eyes like my thoughts were hers to read, and several moments passed in weighted silence before I found my voice. "And your question?"

"When are you going to let me leave?"

The thought of this new and interesting challenge walking

out of my life left a bad taste in my mouth, but she wouldn't be new or interesting forever. I'd lose interest just as I had with the others before her.

"When the time comes."

TWENTY-TWO

— S I N N A —

I was more than eager to leave the King's presence, partly because of the tether and the grueling physical symptoms it always manifested, but also because of the King's frightening attractiveness. It was worrisome that I'd only been in the Blood Court for a single day, and I already struggled to look away. His sharp jawline, pale skin, blood-stained lips, and piercing white fangs were one thing, a jumble of features that came together in a ruthlessly seductive combination, but his eyes were what captured my interest the most.

When I first saw him, I would have said with certainty that they were black, but now that I'd seen them closer, they flared red without warning like hot coals in the wind. He seemed wary to get too close, and I couldn't blame him. The tether was brutal, painful even, but that did nothing to stop my imagination from running wild, imagining all the ways his eternity of lust could satisfy me.

But even if the tether wasn't an issue, my orders were clear. I was to avoid sleeping with the Blood King as long as possible in order to fuel his frustration. Thus far, Ezra's plan hadn't failed me. I'd been able to negotiate away my worst fear and although I couldn't save Mel and Celine absolutely, I was sure they were safe for a while at least. As I roamed through the carpeted halls, I realized I was more than a little aimless. I'd asked for more freedom and privacy, and in turn, the King had called off his guards. I wasn't very familiar with the court's layout, so I retraced my steps to the dining room with hopes that Mel and Celine would still be there. The guards opened the door, and I headed inside to find Celine polishing off the last of my soup. The room was still filled with guards, and I wished they'd clear out so I could chat freely with the girls for the first time since we had arrived. We were forced to sit beside each other, too afraid to reveal anything in the presence of the enemy. A few minutes later a bearded guard that I recognized from earlier, entered. "The King has reassigned the guards to concentrate their efforts on the perimeters of the court."

"Yes, Ronan," they said in unison, as they made their way out of the room.

Ronan approached the table, drawing our full attention. "The King is granting you all free roam of the Blood Court. You are welcome to explore, but you may not leave the cathedral unescorted. I suggest you avoid the kitchen, both to stay out of the servants' way, and also to spare yourself a potentially gruesome shock. Otherwise any forbidden areas or rooms will remain locked or heavily guarded for your protection, of course. Meals will be served three times a day in this very room. You need only to enter and ask a guard to have something made for you, and you are at the King's beck and call, no matter what time of night he requires your entertainment. I'm sure I needn't explain the consequences for violating any of these rules."

He smirked at our blank stares as if pleased with his speech, then he took his leave. We waited several minutes before any of us dared to look around and make sure we were really alone. Celine squealed with delight. "He picked us!" she said, beaming, her hand tightly gripping my wrist.

"I'm so glad you're both okay."

"Us?" Mel asked. "You refused the Blood King. We were terrified that he killed you."

I suppressed a smile. "You do care."

Her mouth straightened to a hard line. My mind was wracked with curiosity. If I couldn't touch the King myself, I could at least get some insight on whether I should be torturing myself by imagining it. "So, what happened last night? Did you guys sleep with the King?"

Mel leaned back in her chair.

"No, we were both in his bed but he got angry when you didn't come and we were asked to return to our rooms." Her orange curls bounced with every move of her head. "He's gorgeous, right? Mel won't admit it, but she was as excited to be with him as I was." She sighed, resting her head on her hand. "To think we almost slept with an immortal king."

Celine was sweet, endearing me to her with her little mortal point of view, but Mel was much more guarded. Both Mel and Celine had made full use of their makeup supply but it almost made me miss the quirks of their mortal faces.

I eyed Mel. "So is it true? You were excited to sleep with the King?"

The corners of her mouth tipped up. "I want to know what happened when you went to see him and why he pulled you away from breakfast. Are you sleeping with him?"

Her jealous tone caught me off guard and I felt the smallest tug on my shadow from Finn reminding me to stick to my plan. "No. Actually, I. . . I've never actually done that before."

I half expected them both to burst out laughing, because the lie was so severe, I was certain no one would buy it.

Celine's eyes bulged. "You're a virgin?"

I chewed on my tongue to stop from laughing. Virginity was such a mortal concept, so arbitrary and bizarre. I was glad to have Celine around to feed me the mortal perspective before I had to convincingly feed the lie to the King.

Mel smirked. "He's going to be so angry. I've heard that's a major turn off for him."

She was right. There wasn't an immortal on earth who didn't prefer someone with experience, but it might help me avoid sleeping with the King even if just for a short time.

I didn't appreciate Mel's smugness. She had her eye on the prize, seemingly rooting for Celine and I to fail so she could have a greater chance to win over the King, but that might work to my advantage. She smirked at her soup, as if basking in her sexual prowess, when I'd likely slept with more people than she'd ever come in contact with.

"Yeah," I said. "I'm hoping to keep it a secret."

"I promise not to tell," Celine said.

We both looked at Mel who nodded, but didn't make eye contact. We spent the rest of the day attempting to explore the Blood Court, but it felt like every door was locked. The hallways were clear except for an occasional stranger, who always ducked into the nearest room and locked it before we passed. We returned to the dining hall for lunch and dinner, and I found it interesting when Celine compared our day's activities to her experience as a child in summer camp. I had assumed we'd see more of the King during the day, but after I left the parlor, I didn't see him again. There were still many hallways to explore and more locked doors to test. We hadn't even stumbled across the forbidden kitchen, but we felt more at ease chatting when we knew for sure we were alone, so after dinner we returned to our rooms.

When we returned, we discovered that our bedrooms were in the same hallway and no longer had guards stationed out front. The rooms were identical, but the clothing choices varied. They all were made of the same, empty, white color but were drastically different in style. We lay them all out and traded for the styles that suited us best. Celine went for the more flowy garments, Mel chose the sexiest, while I made sure to get the least remarkable options.

We were all in my room chatting to pass the time, when someone rapped at the door.

I jumped, startled. "Come in."

Ronan opened the door. "The King has requested all of you to his bedchamber. You have five minutes to ready yourself."

TWENTY-THREE

— MADDOX —

After my negotiations with Sinna, I spent the afternoon hidden away in the library. I knew the council would be annoyed that I wasn't there to approve any new immortals. Even my least despised council member, Aiko had messaged her annoyance that I hadn't been more involved, but I had a more pressing matter at hand.

The tether.

Since it was a natural immortal occurrence, it had to have some countermeasure, as was the nature of all things. Normally I'd delegate such a time-consuming task, but if anyone found out that I had a tether to Sinna, she'd be killed on the spot. It wasn't like I was going to fall in love with her, there was no risk of that. My fascination was with testing my limits, which was more than a little unsettling to Ronan, and whoever started the treasonous whisperings that had become rampant among our kind. The library was endless, centuries of information stored under the Blood Court's protection.

It had been many years since I'd stepped foot in that room, and based on the amount of dust that rose into the air each time I pulled a tome from the shelf, it had been a while since anyone else had either. Occasionally, I stumbled across a book which triggered nostalgia from a past read, and I'd set it aside.Over the course of the day that stack grew. Book after book, hour after hour, and there was scarcely a mention of the tether in anything. I was starting to lose hope when I came across a historical book we'd stolen from the Moon Court. It spoke of a jeweled necklace that the Moon Court's mortal queen wore until her death. I abandoned my search for mentions of the tether, focusing on the necklace, and the more I looked into it, the more convinced I grew that that necklace could suppress the tether.

I sat down at the table, exhausted but satisfied when Ronan busted in.

He eyed me suspiciously. "What are you doing, Sire?"

The books in front of me were the harmless ones I'd stumbled across, and the ones I used for research were already tucked back onto the shelves. "I was gathering some reading material."

"Bored with your tributes already?"

"Shouldn't that be a relief to you?"

He crossed his arms and took a seat at the chair across from me. "I'm not worried. You may as well have said, 'I'll take any three.'"

I smiled at his dimwitted appraisal. "And how do you find them?"

"Unremarkable. I doubt they'll survive the week. You didn't even care to station guards outside their bedrooms."

I shrugged. "It seemed like a waste of resources."

He sighed, so relieved with the tributes he assumed were failures, that he didn't badger me about skipping the council meeting.

I thumbed through the book in front of me, and Ronan eyed in only to settle quickly back into his peace.

"Ro, I was thinking of inviting Herod over for dinner. Can that be arranged?"

He straightened. "Sire, revenge will only lead to—"

"It's not for revenge. Just a gesture of peace."

His eyes narrowed. "Will your tributes be dining with you as well?"

"Of course not. Just me and the Moon King."

He stood. "Yes, Sire. I'll have him informed of your invitation."

"Have the tributes ready in my bed chamber when I'm finished."

"Yes, Sire."

He bowed and left me with my dusty stack of books. I had a few hours to come up with a plan to get into the Moon Court and snoop around. I'd be watched closely from the moment I stepped foot there, and it wasn't like I could ask around about the necklace without revealing my extremely dangerous and complicated plan with Sinna. The wolves would literally descend on my court.

I needed chaos. Herod could be nudged into action. I just needed to be cautious about which action to take.

A few hours later I had a decent plan in place. Herod arrived and I met him in the guest dining room for dinner.

"Still no shirt, I see."

"How would you know what a real man looks like if I didn't

show you one every now and then? Besides, I wore my finest paint."

I smirked at him, but I could tell that a lot of the tension was genuine. We took a seat at the table.

"Relax, I wish you no harm."

"I heard you got sick after draining my tributes. I assure you I had nothing to do wi—"

"Water under the bridge. I invite you here to mend any discourse between us."

Our servants entered, carrying trays of raw, partially bloody steak. Herod couldn't hide the smile that crept onto his face. We ate, and each bite seemed to dull our tension.

He chewed happily, chatting to me between bites. "I hear you have some new favorites."

"Three new guests."

"Anyone special?"

I shrugged. "Are you jealous I kept some of Delton's tributes and not yours?"

He grinned.

I saw my opening and went for it, but it was an offer I'd never made as it slightly shifted the power dynamic, even if just for an evening. "I was thinking that it's been some time since you've held a ball at the Moon Court."

He slowly lowered his fork. "It would be my honor, if it pleases you."

"It would, and I'm certain Delton would also appreciate an invitation."

He perked up and I took it as a sign that when it came down to it, Delton would side with Herod and not with me. It would be an interesting tidbit to share with Ronan later. Herod nodded. "You shall name the day."

"Tomorrow night."

He stared at me, but I challenged his gaze with my own. Surely it would be an excellent opportunity for him to show the wealth and stability of his court as well as network, all while on his own grounds. It might've slightly put me out, but with so much going on, it could've opened an opportunity to seek out the necklace. Of course, one night didn't give Herod much time to plan a large event, but he wasn't the type of man to back down from a challenge.

We finished our meal shortly after. I invited the Wolf King to a nightcap, but he refused, stating politely that he needed to go make preparations for the ball the next night. I was happy to wish him adieu, because I knew my tributes were waiting. Tether or not, tonight I'd test my limit and tomorrow I'd get that necklace and that limit would be no more.

TWENTY-FOUR

—— SINNA ——

The tether tugged as the King drew closer to his bedroom, sending my heartbeat racing. Celine had chosen a white baby doll with furry panties for tonight, while Mel went for a lacy corset complete with garters and heels. I chose a modest silk nightgown that stopped just above the knee. *Think Sin, what would a virgin do?*

I took a seat on a bench by the window while the other girls lay across the bed like treats on a tray of desserts. I felt silly and out of my element, hidden in my lie. Unlike the Hunters, creeping through the shadows to take out their targets, I had to wilt when I was born to take control. Not to mention pass up a night with the Blood King.

I wasn't used to denying myself things I wanted, or forgoing pleasure for any reason. When I'd first heard my sister's plan it had sounded counterproductive. If my ultimate goal was to seduce the Blood King, why did I have to refrain from sex as long as he'd allow? But I was in the habit of trusting my sister and she had never steered me wrong before.

The King pushed through the doors, startling us all. The guards promptly closed them behind him. His gaze met mine immediately, and in one smooth motion he pulled off his shirt, revealing a chiseled body that made my mouth drop open involuntarily. He marched straight toward me, the tether throbbing in my chest as I swallowed a mouthful of lust, that manifested as a lump in my throat.

"Get in the bed," he said, his eyes flaring a deep red.

I stood, inching toward the bed while keeping my distance, anything to lessen the intensity of the pull on my chest toward him. I sat on the edge. I glanced at Celine and Mel. Celine was mesmerized by the King's bare chest, but Mel's face caught my attention. Her lips were pursed, and her eyes were rolled back in pure annoyance. I remembered our conversation earlier, it didn't seem like it would take long for Mel to spill about my supposed virginity. The King walked over and sat on the bed, the silky fabric beneath me tugging from his weight.

He reached for Celine, pulling her in for a kiss, while Mel's hands slid over the King's pants, making their way to the strings around his waist. A blush washed over me as I watched them, enamored by the sight. His hand rose, reaching out to me. I wanted to take it, to surrender to the tether and take my share in the delight to come, but I couldn't. I'd taken this mission with a promise to my sister that I would stick to her plan at all costs. I needed to prove I was still in control. I let his hand hang there, as he worked Celine's strap off her shoulder and kissed down her neck.

He pulled away, his black eyes glaring at me, rage flaring behind them. "What is your problem?"

Mel sighed loudly. "She's a *virgin.*"

I stared at her wide-eyed and betrayed, though she'd filled her role perfectly.

"What?" she said. "You were making it so obvious."

The King stood, rubbing his palm across his face, his silk pajama pants bulging. When he dropped his hand, I could see that everything that Mel said was true. He really did hate virgins. I knew exactly how this was going to go. I would be banished back to my room and have to beg Celine and Mel for details tomorrow, but the King looked ready to strangle me.

When he finally spoke, it was through his teeth. "Is it true?"

I swallowed hard. "Yes, but it's not a big deal. If you just tell me what to do—"

"Not a big deal? Tell you? What can a novice possibly offer me? I'll settle for nothing less than a competent lover." He marched over to me and I winced from the tether, half expecting him to strike me. He lifted me, cradling me in his arms as he carried me across the room before dropping me onto a chair. He yanked the tie off the nearby curtain and used it to bind my arms behind me. Then he proceeded to drag the chair to the side of the bed.

He took a deep breath through his nose, and I could practically feel his frustration in his exhale. "Watch and learn."

"Why are my hands tied?"

He turned away. "Just in case."

What might've been meant as a punishment was anything but. Sure, it was a little hard to watch without hope of release, but I could take care of that when I got back to my own room.

Then he started. Fuck. *I might not be as in control as I thought.*

Once again, he started with Celine, pulling her top off over her head. She radiated with pleasure as he tasted her one lick at a time, but Mel wasn't going to give up so easily. She slid her hands under the waistband of his pants and began to work him. His head turned to her, his hands dropping from Celine and moving to Mel. He pulled off his pants and Mel's stringy thong at the same time. I strained to get a look at his equipment, but Celine was in the way. She crawled over to them, searching for something to do, but she'd already lost the King's interest. Before I could get a good look, he thrust into Mel, her pleasure ringing out through the room, as desire blared between my legs.

I felt wetness seep between my legs as he wrapped her pony-tail around his wrist and drove into her. Harder and harder until she was pressed against the headboard. Celine's face was wrought with despair, but she didn't matter. Nothing mattered but the sounds ringing in my head, and the sweat that slipped down the Blood King's face as he brought Mel to ecstasy and, without pause, repeated the process. I pulled on my binding, begging myself not to give in to the temptation to join, and breathed through the flimsy tie.

That's when I felt the shadow between my legs move. *No Finn. He'll catch us.* Finn's fingers slipped into me. I remained perfectly still as Finn synced with the King's rhythm. I imagined he had me pressed against his headboard, filling my body with waves of pleasure. I didn't make a sound and instead imagined that my voice echoed through the King's chamber. The King sped up, with Mel bucking as she came to her third orgasm.

Finn's fingers challenged my body not to grind against him. Then the King's attention snapped to me, my eyes widening as my body exploded into orgasm. His body jerked, his eyes clamping shut as he hunched over Mel. The spasms between my legs slowed, but I didn't dare move a fraction. After a few moments, the King got up and walked towards me, his penis in full view-- still pulsing as the last bits of cum dripped from the tip. My mouth dropped open as I sat balanced perfectly between the fear of being caught and the desire to participate.

His eyes narrowed as he leaned over me. "Get the fuck out," he said, then he turned to Celine. "You too."

Mel sat up straight as Celine untied me, tears already streaming down her face, as we scrambled toward the door.

"Compose yourself," we heard him say. "We're going again."

I felt my first bite of jealousy as Celine and I walked to our rooms. No matter, my shadow was going to fuck me until the sun came up.

TWENTY-FIVE

— S I N N A —

I closed my eyes and listened for footsteps outside my bedroom, but I hadn't heard anyone pass in hours. I might've been entertaining a bit of risky behavior but that didn't mean I wanted to blow the whole operation.

"What's with you tonight, Sin?" Finn whispered, through the darkness.

"Get up, we're fucking again."

"I'm serious. Talk to me. Is that guy getting to you already?"

I sat up. "What? No. He strapped me to a chair and made me watch. Of course I'm horny."

"That's why I helped you along. I've never seen you like this. I've never seen you rally this quickly or go so many times in a row."

I groaned and straddled him, as I started slowly grinding against him.

"I'm fine," I said. "I just can't get enough of you tonight."

I felt him start to harden between my thighs, so I slipped him inside me and began to ride. He slowly worked his way back into it, but I knew he was right to be concerned. It wasn't him I couldn't get enough of. I was chasing something. A feeling I couldn't find no matter how many times I came. I forced him back into shadow form before first light, as the possibility of anyone casually strolling by my room grew the longer I allowed it to continue, but I couldn't get to sleep. I took a long bath, dozing off for a few minutes before I pulled my pruney body out of the tub, and got ready for the day. I decided to head to break-fast, if for nothing else, to take a break from my own thoughts, only to find Celine already seated at the table. I took a seat beside her, and her somber mood seemed to match mine.

I'd barely thought of her all night, but I was sure she was equally frustrated by the night's events. The King seemed to go for her right away, but Mel had completely edged her out of the picture. At least I had the excuse of being tied to a chair. We sat in silence for a full hour, pushing things around on our plate, letting the mood overtake us until the doors swung open and Mel limped in.

She wasn't moving well and she winced when she sat down at the table. I pretended not to notice even though all I could do was notice every micro movement. Her eyes flared with smug-ness but she matched our somber mood as best as she could with the rest of her face.

"Sorry I outed you as a virgin," she said. "And Celine, I didn't see where you went. I got so caught up."

The words shot out of me before I could stop them. "How was your night?"

Her face brightened. "I know you both are upset with me, but you don't understand."

A servant entered, and we all went quiet while he placed a plate of food in front of her. *Oh I can't wait for this explanation.*

"There's this like. . . cosmic connection between us. I was wrong about him, and I think he's found what he's looking for. I just hope you two can find a way to be happy for us."

I faked a cough to muffle a laugh. Suddenly draining mortal tributes for their blood seemed pretty victimless. I didn't care that she got to spend the night with the King. That was my plan. In fact, if I was lucky, she'd spend many more nights with him before I ever saw his bedroom. I might've considered the entire situation as amusing, but Celine looked like she was going to burst into tears at any moment. Luckily someone knocked, stealing the moment, and we turned to see Ronan stride in.

"Good morning, ladies. The King has requested that you all attend a ball tonight at the Moon Court."

I gasped. The Moon Court? I was seriously going to go three for three on this mission?

I snuck a glance at Mel and Celine who both looked a little confused, so I mirrored their expression but Ronan didn't pause to elaborate.

"You will be measured and styled, commencing after you finish eating. It should go without saying, but you are expected to only speak highly of the King and anything regarding the Blood Court."

"You don't have to worry about that," Mel said, flashing a smile.

"Indeed," he said warily. "I too will be in attendance and will be keeping an eye on all of you. If anyone crosses the line of what I consider acceptable behavior, the consequences will be dire. Do you understand?"

I nodded but inside I was practically screaming with excitement. I was the greatest Hunter on earth. In a matter of days, I'd infiltrated all of the immortal courts. Oh, if Ferah could see me now.

All day I imagined what the Moon Court might be like, barely present as the servants spent the day preparing me for the party. My body was stuffed into a white, floor-length ball gown and I was given gloves that went nearly up to my shoulders, along with a fur wrap, but my mind was already in the Moon Court.

I paced around my room, waiting for someone to come collect me, when Finn slithered out of shadow form.

"What are you doing?" I whispered. "Get back. They'll be here any minute."

"I can't go with you."

"What? Why?"

"There's a small possibility one of the wolves could smell me. We can't risk it. I'm going to stay here and shadow your bed until you get back."

"But—"

"We don't have time to discuss this. Just stay out of trouble at the ball and get back safely, no matter what."

Before I could respond, I felt his weight lift from me and saw a flash of darkness slip under my bed. My excitement drained as fear filled its place. I was alone, and somehow for the first time since I'd arrived, the danger felt real.

TWENTY-SIX

The sun was already peeking over the tree line and through the stained glass window as Melany snored loudly on the far side of my bed. All night I had chased the satisfaction of that first release, but none had come close. I could only assume that looking at Sinna had pushed me over. But how could it? I certainly wasn't interested in wasting my time with a virgin. But all night I pictured her blushing face as I asked her to leave. All night, I'd replaced Melany in my mind with Sinna, chasing that feeling to no avail. To Melany's credit, she knew what she was doing, and for a mortal, her endurance had held out longer than I'd anticipated. It was clear by morning that she couldn't satisfy me, not anymore.

The day moved at a glacial pace as I visualized every possible scenario at the ball, none of which ended with me finding the necklace. It was a small object and there was no guarantee it even still existed. Even worse, the entire Moon Court would be swarming with wolves and I doubted they let anyone have free roam of their court, especially not their natural enemy--but after last night, I was desperate to dull the effects of the tether without killing Sinna. For the time being, she still intrigued me and that warranted a little more time. Then I saw her standing in the hallway, dressed in white. Her hair was pinned back out of her face so she couldn't hide behind it as she so often did. The tether tugged on my chest and took me several moments to realize she was standing with the other two girls. The tether choked my air supply, and I forced the struggle away from my expression as I walked to the ladies, offering Celine and Melany each an arm.

They took them eagerly, and I turned before I could see Sinna's reaction. I felt her follow behind as we walked out into the frigid winter night. We traipsed a short distance to the forest edge where an elegant dog sled sat, with two massive wolves harnessed to the front. We climbed in, and the girls huddled against my arms while Sinna took a seat across from us. Face to face, she was in my direct line of sight, and I didn't dare look away. Her gaze bore into me, but I held it.

The dog sleds were limited, usually only offered to me and Delton. They kept the trail to the woods, which stretched almost thirty minutes from my court to theirs and forty five from Delton's. I was sure Herod's pack had better things to do than chauffeur us around; still, I always appreciated the gesture. I figured that Herod insisted on keeping the tradition alive because one of the privileges of holding a ball was to show off the unique abilities and uses that our courts possessed, with the hopes of conjuring envy from our honored guests.

The dog sled bobbed between the moonlit trees, gliding

across the glittering snow. The strength of the wolves was evident in each powerful stride. It was not a smooth ride, jerking with the movement of the wolves as they waded through the snow. Sinna said nothing, but her eyes were lit with excitement, as a smile played at the corners of her mouth so incessantly that I wondered if the ride was more exciting moving backward. I got my enjoyment from watching her, vibrant in the moonlight as the cold brought a pink tint to her cheeks and nose. Melany nuzzled into my arm, drawing my attention. I needed to be more careful with the slight preference I'd developed for Sinna, at least until I got the tether situation sorted out. The wolves grew winded, clouds of breath rising above their thick coats until finally, they halted outside the Moon Court.

The stone structure that made up the court hadn't changed much since I'd last seen it, but it always looked much grander in the moonlight. The wolves shifted back to their human forms and helped us out of the sled, and I wasn't sure whether the shift or the court itself intrigued Sinna more. On the outside, her expression stayed almost neutral, but the way her eyes glittered betrayed her.

The architecture of the Moon Court was a bit unusual, an eyesore during the daytime, but at night, a series of mirrors reflected the moonlight into every inch of the space, shifting to follow it as it moved through the sky. We stepped onto a midnight blue carpet and made our way up the path. I held tight to Melany and Celine, but slowed so Sinna could walk beside us. The doors opened, and two snow-white wolves flanked King Herod as he welcomed us with open arms. He wore his typical paint but had a fur cape draped over his shoulders, and a silver crown on his head.

I suppressed a groan.

One ball and he thinks he's King of the world. *The nerve.* I snuck a glance at Sinna and her chest was puffed out as if she was holding her breath. A pang of jealousy threatened to run through me, but I quickly got the better of it, as I remembered the reason I'd gone through the trouble.

Herod grinned. "Welcome, Your Majesty. These must be your new favorites."

I tried to match the kindness in his tone, but I hardly sounded genuine. "This is Melany, Celine, and that's Sinna."

His eyes lingered on Sinna for a few seconds too long before he caught himself. "Well, come in and enjoy the party. King Delton arrived not five minutes before you."

Herod looked down at one of his wolves, and the creature twisted into a man in a matter of seconds. He walked over and took Sinna's arm and began to lead her into the party. Sinna tossed me a look over her shoulder as if to ask permission to enter, but I couldn't muster a smile.

TWENTY-SEVEN

— S I N N A —

All the frustration and fear I'd felt all day melted away the moment I stepped into the ballroom. At the center of the high ceilings was a crystal chandelier that seemed to amplify the moon light and scatter it across the room like snow, or fallen stars. The room was filled with attendees chatting with drinks in their hands, and swaying to music which was played by an orchestra tucked away in a dark corner.

The members of the Moon Court were mostly shirtless, their skin decorated with elegant blue paint. The Arrow Court members all wore shades of green, their signature white hair and pointed ears proudly displayed with ornaments and hanging jewelry. The Blood Court members all wore suits and gowns in their specific shade of crimson. I was in awe of how easily everyone interacted. I wasn't sure if it was because of the occasion, or if the Moon Court just had a more relaxed environment compared to the uptight Blood Court and the elitist Arrow Court. Now that I'd seen all of the immortal courts, I firmly put the Moon Court as my top choice.

My escort bowed once we reached the center of the room and disappeared into the crowd. It was a shame as I'd gotten more attention from that silent stranger than the Blood King since I arrived in his court. Whatever the plan had been, I needed to start deviating, and gaining his favor. He didn't seem remotely interested, and if I didn't do something, Mel would have me tossed out before I could fulfill my purpose. I was surprised to see a familiar face among the crowd, the intense green eyes met mine from across the way and I froze in place as King Delton made his way to me. He handed me a flute of sparkling wine.

"Hello again."

I bowed. "Your Highness. I hope you're well."

"Quite well, thank you. Where has your Sire run off to tonight?"

I shrugged. "I'm sure he's around here somewhere." It was a vague answer considering I knew exactly where he was at all times. The tether made sure of that.

"How do you find the Moon Court?"

I took a sip of the wine, feeling more than a little out of my element. "Enchanting."

"Do you prefer it to the Arrow Court?"

The egos of immortal kings never ceased to amaze. Of course, I preferred the Moon Court. "That's impossible, Your Majesty."

His pleased smile almost made me laugh, and I hoped I'd have the opportunity to converse a little with the Moon King as well. I'd been struck silent by his blue eyes, dark skin, and bulging muscles. I never thought I'd enjoy this part of my mission so much. I would have saved dancing with immortal kings to the type of girl I was pretending to be, but at present I was taking immense pleasure in the night's festivities.

Mel draped her arm over my shoulder. "There you are, Sinna," she said with a forced smile. Her gaze moved to my glass. "And uhm, where did you get a drink?"

Celine joined us a moment later, looking dejected.

"Allow me," King Delton offered before he hurried away in search of a servant with a drink tray.

"You look beautiful tonight, Celine. "

The comment made her stand a little straighter. "Thanks, Sinna. This place is magical."

Mel scoured the crowd. "I wonder where Maddox snuck away to."

She wasn't going to find him here as he was in the next room, walking very slowly from the feel of it. I wasn't sure how long I'd have before Mel found him and clung to him for the rest of the night, so I had to find a chance to slip away. All I needed was a minute with the Blood King to try to get back on his good side. When King Delton returned, Mel took the glass from him and resumed her search without so much as a second glance.

"Mel, Celine, have you met King Delton of the Arrow Court?"

Mel whirled back to the group. "*King* Delton? Your Majesty. I had no idea we had the honor."

"I knew." Celine chimed in. "I saw you once when I arrived at the Arrow Court."

I slipped away as the two girls found a new King to fawn over, and when I was out of sight, I headed out of the ballroom towards the pull of the tether. I ducked into the hallway and into the next room. The walls were covered with bookshelves with the occasional space for a gold-trimmed family portrait. The midnight blue curtains were open, allowing the moonlight to spill across the floor. On the far side of the room, the Blood King stared into a glass box, his arms crossed over his chest, his focus completely locked in on whatever was inside that case.

The music from the orchestra wafted through the open door, but I expected him to look up when he heard my footsteps approaching. He didn't and then I remembered that, like me, he probably knew exactly where I was at all times. As I neared, I looked into the glass case where a headless bust displayed a diamond necklace.

"Alone at last," he said, without looking away.

A pang of anxiety shot through me. Did he mean because Finn wasn't here? Did he know who I was? The calmness in his demeanor assured me that he only meant that Celine and Mel weren't with me as they always seemed to be.

"Your Highness, I want to apologize. I feel like we've gotten off to an interesting start."

He kept his gaze on the necklace. "Interesting, indeed."

"May I ask why you're out here by yourself."

His gaze moved to me, and the tether tightened in my chest.

"May I ask how you found me?" He smirked and I saw a devious glint in his eyes as he watched me wrestle with whether or not to answer.

"What's with the necklace?"

"I don't know." He closed the gap between us. "I suppose I like it." The tether strained against me, and I swallowed a lump in my throat as I held my ground.

He stared down at me, his charcoal gaze sweeping over my face. "When I like something, I have to have it."

"So, take it," I whispered.

His eyes flared red and cooled back to black as he smiled down at me. Then he turned back to the case. "Alas, it's protected by something."

He reached for the case and the moonlight flared in front of his hand, like light bouncing off an iron shield.

He crossed his hands behind his back and strolled past me. "We better get back to the party before we're missed."

He didn't wait for me to follow and instead left me with my thoughts as I felt the tether ease one step at a time. His aloofness was grating on me, especially after I'd seen him be affectionate with Mel all night. The way he crossed his hands behind his back like that, it was like the thought of touching me repulsed him. I thought if I apologized, spoke to him one on one, he'd warm up a little, but if anything, he seemed less interested than when I had first arrived at the Blood Court.

I turned back to the case with the necklace, tracing my fingers over the glass. The moonlight shone off the case and the shield protecting it showed itself once more. Interesting. A shield of light. Certainly, taking the necklace would be a risk, but it might be my only chance to turn the head of the Blood King.

The shield felt strong. It would have drawn a lot of attention if the King had tried to smash through. But the thing about light was, the stronger it was, so too was the shadow.

Before I lost my nerve, I focused my attention on the shadow. It deepened the closer I reached to the shield. I let my fingertips slip into the shadow, moving through both the shield and glass. I heard something move outside the door so I yanked the necklace into the shadow and pulled it back through the glass searching for a place to stash it.

"There you are," a voice said from behind me.

I turned to see Ronan standing in the doorway. "It's not polite to snoop. I must insist you return to the ballroom immediately."

I squeezed the necklace so tightly in my hand that I felt it dig into my skin, I took several steps toward Ronan, with the hopes he wouldn't see the empty display case and get suspicious. "Sorry, I just love libraries."

His blank expression gave me the impression he wasn't amused. I rushed by him, but he caught my wrist squeezing so tightly a yelp escaped my lips. I opened my hand and the necklace slipped out into his hand.

"What's this?"

Straining from the pain of his grip, I said, "It fell off, I was going to ask Celine to help me put it back on."

"Allow me," he said, dropping my wrist.

I rubbed at the lingering pain, and contemplated cursing him as he clasped the necklace at the back of my neck. I nearly gasped as a weight lifted off my chest. The tether was completely stripped away in an instant.

"All better, now back to the party."

Before I could move the Blood King bounded around the corner, his eyes wide, his dark hair disheveled.

"What happened?" he said, his chest heaving.

Ronan's brow furrowed. "I found this one wandering around alone, but she'll be joining the party immediately."

The King's gaze moved to my wrist, alerting me that I was still rubbing it. I dropped my hands to my side.

He glared at me. "This is unacceptable behavior. Ronan, join the others in the ballroom, I'll handle this."

Ronan smiled, as he slipped out of the room, shutting the

door behind him. I turned frightened by the King's sudden intensity.

"Where were you?" he said, his voice much harsher than before. I stumbled back until my back pressed against the bookshelf.

"I was—"

His gaze moved to the necklace and all at once the color seemed to return to his face. "How did you get that?" His tone was filled with relief.

"You said you wanted it."

His head dropped, tension draining from his shoulders.

His next words came out as a whisper. "I thought I lost you."

He could have only meant the tether, but I wasn't sure what caused it to stop. He was inches away from me and I could barely feel it. "I-I'm sorry."

His gaze met mine and he moved closer, resting his forehead on mine, as his breaths slowed. My heart slammed into my chest. What was this? Or rather, who was this? His hand closed around mine and he lifted it up to the side of his cheek.

"Did he hurt you?"

"I-I'm fine."

He sighed. "I'll talk to him." He released my hand and reached around to the back of my neck. "I have to take this. I wouldn't want you to get in trouble."

His lips were so close I could feel the warmth of his breath on them. He paused, his gaze lowering to my lips. He ran his thumb over the bottom lip, but shook the thought away.

"Please," I whispered, the word escaping against my will.

He smiled, reached around, unhooked the clasp and stepped away with the necklace. The tether slammed into my chest, knocking the wind out of me. I put my palm on my stomach to settle myself as the Blood King made his way to the door.

"That's why you wanted it."

He smirked at me over his shoulder then held a finger to his plump lips, before returning to the rest of the party.

TWENTY-EIGHT

— H E R O D —

I 'd been on edge since Maddox first invited me to dinner. I knew he was still furious that an underage tribute snuck into my last batch, but when rumors circulated that the Blood King got sick after he'd drank the blood of my offerings, I was prepared for the worst. I'd expected a duel, or at the very least a cruel act of revenge, but as I sat down to dine with him, he was more at ease than I'd seen him in a hundred years.

The only wrench he threw at me was the insistence that I hold a ball on short notice which at the end of the day was more of an opportunity than a punishment. I couldn't help but wonder if Delton's supposed match had somewhat tempered his cruelty. I'd heard the King had chosen three tributes to keep him company, and I hoped he'd bring them to our dinner, but I wasn't so lucky.

The night of the ball, Maddox arrived with his three trophies at his side but I knew in an instant which he favored. Two of the women were draped on his arms, and the third, he could hardly look at her. Arranging the event hadn't been much of a challenge, when I informed my pack of the Blood King's request they were eager to show our improved numbers and wealth to the other courts.

Everything got started without a hitch, with the members of each court mingling and enjoying the ambiance we'd worked to perfect, until an hour into the festivities when a foul smell set my entire back on edge. It was only there for a moment, but my people knew the salty unmistakable scent of a Shadow Mage's spell, ever since the last war. There was only one possible explanation.

The Shadow Mage Delton used to find the Blood King's mate was somewhere in the Moon Court.

I scanned the crowd for Delton, anger bringing my blood to a boil. *How dare he bring that witch here?*

I heard his boisterous laughter before I spotted him chatting with some bloodsuckers by the orchestra, a surefire way to tell he was already drunk. He met my gaze before I made it to him, his smile dying in an instant. He excused himself politely and met me a few strides away from his group.

"What is it, Herod? You look perturbed."

"How dare you bring that disgusting rodent here."

His brow furrowed and he looked around the room, before shaking his head. "I don't know what you mean."

My canines sharpened, jutting past my bottom lip. "The witch," I hissed under my breath.

He looked around nervously, taking me by the arm and leading out of earshot of the other guests. "I told you that in the strictest confidence. It is not safe to discuss such things here. It seems you are mistaken. That which you fear is under guard in the Arrow Court and I'll thank you not to mention it again."

His green eyes had a hint of anger behind them, but were otherwise full of absolute certainty. The scent still lingered in the ballroom, and several pack members exchanged glances with me, but it was Tren that approached me.

I bowed my head to Delton. "I apologize," I said with a laugh, patting him on his shoulder. "I suppose I've had too much to drink."

Delton glared at me, so I nicked a champagne flute from a passing tray and handed it to him. He sipped it and turned back to join the party.

Tren waited until Delton was long gone before he approached.

"We've tracked the smell to the study," he said, already leading the way. I'd maintain my human form as long as possible but I couldn't help the horrors of the war from slipping into my head. What awaited me in the study wasn't what I expected, though equally dangerous.

I stopped short. Ronan stood staring into the display case for one of the Moon Court heirlooms. The smell was weaker but the study was definitely its place of origin, right around where Ronan was standing. However, I knew for sure Ronan wasn't a Shadow Mage. He was one of the most famous Vampires to fight in the war.

He smiled when he saw me, seemingly unaware of whatever had transpired in this room a few minutes before, but then again, he was a born liar.

"I didn't mean to snoop, I just needed a break from the crowd. What a lovely collection of books you have here."

I walked over to him, smelling for salt, but he smelled just like all the other bloodsuckers. Like iron. He didn't seem to mind my obvious appraisal, and instead turned back to the display case. "I must ask, though, if this case is meant to be empty."

I exchanged a loaded look with Tren, but before I could sound an alarm, I heard the shuffle of a new presence in the room.

Gigi hobbled into the room, her frail frame supported by a bejeweled walker. She was a curious case in any immortal court as immortals never aged after they reached full maturity. But Gigi had chosen a different path. She'd decided to give up her immortal life to be with her mate, and she'd lost her immortality and aged just like an ordinary mortal. Around her ninetieth birthday, she was struck with a disease that made her forget much of her life, including her mate that had been long since dead. Once the last of the memories of him faded away, her immortality resumed and she was locked in an elderly body for eternity. Though she was practically useless, too frail to shift or hunt, and too forgetful to be of use politically, she was beloved in our court for her innocence and sincerity.

"Gigi," I said quickly. "What are you doing out of bed?"

"There's a party," she said, flashing a toothless smile.

Ronan cleared his throat.

I nodded to Tren to have him escort her. "Why don't you head to it then, while I sort out a few things in here?"

"I hope this isn't about that heirloom," she said quickly.

"What do you know about that?"

She smiled coyly, delaying her response to relish in our attention. "I had it cleaned but didn't get it back into its place before the party." She took Ronan by the hand, as if they were old friends, and he slouched to meet her height. She patted him on the cheek. "We were in quite a rush you know."

This reply seemed to ease Ronan's concerns and he straightened, shaking loose Gigi's grip on his arm. "I'd better return as well, before someone notices my absence." He hurried out of the room, and Gigi's playful demeanor instantly darkened.

She waved me over like she intended to whisper, so I leaned in. She grabbed my ear and a whine slipped through my nose, prompting a laugh from Tren.

"You make a foolish king," she said bitterly. "Tren, close the door."

"What's going on, Gi?"

"Our court has the unique ability to smell shadow magic. We don't give into impulses and squander information that precious to our enemies. The heirloom was stolen using shadow magic."

I wiggled out of her grip but could not break my attention free. I rubbed my ear, my pride wounded, but unable to guess what she'd say next.

"We know that Delton has found Maddox's mate. Few know the true purpose of the heirloom, as it's been a secret kept by the Moon Court since it came into our possession, but it sheds some light on what occurred here."

"What does it do?" asked Tren.

"It dims a tether."

"You think Maddox stole it to keep himself from falling in love with his mate?" I asked her.

"I think his mate is of the Shadow Court and if there are two Shadow Mages after all this time, there may be many more."

"What are you suggesting?"

She chewed on her bottom lip before answering. "We keep everything that occurred here tonight between the three of us."

"But the last thing we want is for Maddox to dim the tether."

"It's a dangerous game to play, one he'll eventually lose. If the Shadow Court is manipulating Delton to get to Maddox, all we have to do is wait for things to play out and when the girl's plan comes to pass, and Maddox is vulnerable enough to die, we'll be ready to swoop in and finish him off while Delton deals with the consequences of letting a traitor into his court. A shift in power is coming. I suggest you put on a smile and escort me to the party."

My head spun with everything I'd learned.

How did Gigi with her scrambled memory, put together so much while I ran around impulsively accusing Delton? Gigi returned to her cheerful self, especially once we made it into the crowded ballroom. My gaze landed heavily on the woman in white at the center of the dance floor. After all this time, a Shadow Mage was Maddox's mate as well. She was as rare as she was beautiful, and I struggled to pull my attention away.

Gigi tugged on my arm and I bent down to hear her.

She whispered, "Why don't you ask that lovely girl there to dance?"

TWENTY-NINE

Sinna was special, there was no doubt about that. I wished I had stuck around to see how she managed to free the necklace from the display case with that shield in place, but like so much about her, that was a mystery that would have to remain unsolved.

I was cheerful that because of her, I'd easily completed my objective, and could spend the night enjoying the festivities. After that encounter with Ronan, the last thing I needed was him getting suspicious about the amount of time I spent with Sinna. He was just ruthless enough to take matters into his own hands if he thought my life was on the line. I had no choice but to shower Celine and Melany with my attention throughout the party, but I wasn't expecting the consequences to affect me so severely.

With the tether still in place, I could feel Sinna's every move.

It was impossible to ignore when Herod stepped in to escort her. I was sure, from what I knew of him and his eagerness to get back in my good graces, that it wasn't intentional. He probably chose to entertain her as she was left on her own for the entirety of the ball, but I still didn't like it.

Not when they danced, not when she smiled or laughed in his arms.

Melany grew bolder as the night went on, which I accredited to her alcohol consumption. Her attempts at kissing my neck or whispering in my ear made my annoyance flare, which drew pleased smirks from members of both the Arrow and Moon Courts. Eventually, I took her to a dark corner and asked her not to approach me for the rest of the night while I shifted my attention to the more reserved Celine.

With Melany pouting in the corner and Herod charming Sinna, I couldn't wait to get out of there. I stayed until a large portion of the guests had begun to head home. I said my good-byes, thanked Herod for the ball and gathered my tributes to go.

"Stay a little longer," he insisted.

"Next time."

He seemed pleased with himself, and I had to admit, the occasion had gone without a hitch. Even Delton seemed reluctant to leave the ever-flowing trays of champagne. I wondered if I'd unintentionally altered the culture of our community by bringing back joint celebrations. I would no doubt receive a similar invitation to the Arrow Court in less than a month.

As Herod's wolves pulled the sleigh away from the Moon Court, back through the forest the way we came, Sinna shivered. I wanted to sit beside her and pull her into my arms to keep her warm, but I didn't. Instead, I wondered what passed through her thoughts as her dreamlike expression moved to the starry night sky. Melany was asleep when we arrived back at the Blood Court, so I had Ronan carry her to my chamber for the night. I figured having her there would both cause Ronan to assume I was in there and start to make him nervous enough to insist I spend time with one of the other tributes, but he was a little too drunk from the party to want to lecture me. Sinna and Celine went straight to bed, and I waited in my room until I was sure that Ronan had gone to bed. Then I headed to the drawing-room to start my preparations.

I clutched the necklace Sinna had stolen in my hand, too afraid to set it down.

It promised everything.

I was eager to see her and put it to use; to finally feel like myself in her presence. How much of the tether would remain intact? How far could I push things before I was in any real danger? They were questions I didn't know the answers to. After centuries of the same old conversations, scheming, and patterns, there was finally something new. Someone new.

I paused, my closed hand hovering an inch outside of Sinna's door.

Before I could gather myself, the door swung open and Sinna stepped into the frame. "Having trouble sleeping?"

"I'll sleep when I'm dead."

"Shouldn't be long now. At least two-thirds of the people at that party wanted you dead."

"That's quite an optimistic estimate. I was thinking of going for a walk. Would you like to accompany me?"

Her eyes brightened. "I should probably change into something."

I looked down at her sheer nightgown and quickly turned my face away before the tether strangled me to death. "Nonsense, we're not going to leave the grounds. Just put on your shoes.

She hustled into her room to retrieve them and came back quickly. I suppressed the urge to offer her my arm and crossed my arms behind my back as she fell into stride behind me. I unlocked the southern corridor and then locked it behind us, just to be sure we were alone.

She gasped. The glass windows and doors on the right side of the hallway offered a moonlit view of the atrium, complete with fully bloomed, snow-white roses which were covered in snow and doused in moonlight. She pressed her hands against the window and looked out at the motionless garden as soft white flakes began to fall. She turned to me, pleading with her eyes to go out like a puppy due for a walk.

I rolled my eyes and began pulling off my jacket before I draped it around her shoulders.

She grinned up at me.

"Don't get excited. I'm just curious about what you'd look like in red."

She bundled herself in the jacket and then said, "I've been meaning to ask you about that. You all know there are other colors, right? Yellow, orange, purple. Why are all the courts so dedicated to one color?"

I pushed open the door, and we stepped out into the frosty night air, prompting me to slip my hands into my pockets. "Tradition, I suppose. Besides, have you ever tried to wash blood out of something? It's just easier to wear red."

She flashed a smirk over her shoulder before she began to investigate the roses. "Then why are these white? Why not red roses. . . and how are they still alive in winter?"

I walked over to one and picked it. Sinna's lips parted as the white petals turned a deep crimson. When the change was complete, I handed her the flower and said, "They're blood thorns. They bloom in late fall and then freeze that way, only to die in early spring. They're as old and as rare as the members of my court."

She rubbed her shoulder with her free hand, and I couldn't move to warm her, not with the tether still in place.

"How about we get out of the cold." She nodded, and we left the way we came. She looked back at the flowers for a moment with sadness in her eyes, then clutched the rose I'd given her to her chest.

I led her to the drawing-room, where earlier in the night, I'd stocked a fire and laid out pillows across a furry rug. I felt a pang of uneasiness about giving her the necklace because once the tether wasn't stopping me from touching her, I wasn't sure I'd be able to stop.

THIRTY

─ S I N N A ─

I t wasn't easy convincing Finn not to return to my shadow after the ball, but after I explained my close encounter with Ronan and urged him to keep an eye on him instead, he reluctantly agreed--and I was glad for it. Because at the ball, the King showed me a side of him I hadn't seen before, and I was eager to see more. My task was challenging enough without having to worry about Finn constantly asking if I'd been compromised.

I had, thus far, followed the plan to a tee, with the small exception of stealing the necklace. Based on the King's strange reaction, I'd say it was worth the gamble. Even more unusual than the King's behavior was the necklace itself. The moment Ronan put it on me, I felt the tether weaken, almost to nothing, and not a minute later did the King rush in. I'd hoped he'd let me keep it so that, at the very least, I could compose myself enough to win him over. After the King took the necklace back, I noticed a subtle change in the tether itself that I purposely didn't mention to Finn.

The tether was like gravity, pulling the King and me together. The more I fought against the sensation, the more crippling it felt, scaling up with close proximity. However if I allowed my intrigue or attraction to the King to flow freely, the tether almost felt bearable. Even as he had me pinned against a bookshelf.

When the King ordered Ronan to bring Mel to his bedchamber, I was sure I'd seen the last of him for a while, but an hour later, he arrived outside my bedroom. My mother used to tell me stories about the Blood Thorns, but I couldn't have believed their beauty until the King showed me. He had picked one and handed it to me, and I had watched with amazement as the magic took hold. On our way back inside, as I had turned to take one last look at the fabled flowers, I mistakenly pricked my thumb on a thorn. The King turned away, and I checked my thumb for blood.

My heart raced as Finn's fears echoed through my head. Immortals couldn't bleed, not unless their immortality was compromised. As expected, there wasn't a drop on my finger, and I felt myself relax as the King led me into another locked room.

When the door opened, I walked into a wall of heat, the fireplace ablaze. My fingers were numb, and I looked at the King whose mouth curved up, granting permission. I rushed over and took a seat on the rug next to the fire, rubbing my hands in front of the flickering heat. The King took a seat beside me and stared into the flames.

"Come here," he said a few minutes later, the necklace dangling between his hands.

The tether didn't bother me as much, but I could tell by how far he chose to sit that it was still a struggle for him. I crawled over, turning my back to him and lifting my hair. His hands swept over my neck, sending a chill through my body and leaving my nipples erect.

"I want you to give this back to me at the end of tonight."

"May I ask why?"

He tilted his head to the side. *Ah. So you know where I am.*
"Your Highness-" I started.

"Maddox, please."

His use of please struck me, but I didn't question it. Everything about tonight felt informal. "Maddox." I closed my eyes, the deliciousness of his name in my mouth catching me off guard. "You seem different tonight."

He adjusted some pillows and lay across them, staring into the fire. "I'm expected to be a lot of things," he sighed. "We all are really. Sometimes I get so tired of the mundane tasks that make up each day that I can't stand the thought of tomorrow."

I shifted. "I wasn't expecting an honest answer."

"How about you give me one as well?"

My heartbeat raced. Well, whatever he wanted to know, I couldn't tell him. I'm sure no truth of mine would go over well.

I'm a spy. I'm here to kill you. I've snuck another member of my court in here.

His next words surprised me,."Tell me something true. Anything but a lie."

I thought for a moment and was sure the truest thing about me could do no harm. "I have a sister." My smile was involuntary, and his face brightened in response. I tucked a strand of hair behind my ear. "She's my favorite person."

"And your parents?"

"They died, but they were pretty great, too. I suppose your parents are still alive, since your people are immortal."

"Actually, they died. Having children is a mortal privilege. One only reserved for someone foolish enough to fall in love."

I bent my knees and pulled them to my chest. *Well, this is awkward. I need you to fall in love with me so I can kill you.*

"I've lived a pretty sheltered life," I said, finally. "I think if I was immortal, I'd use that time to see the whole world."

"So immortality does interest you?"

I lay back, propping a pillow under my head. "I mean, you're doing such a great job selling it."

He laughed, a musical sound that I didn't know he was capable of. "I suppose not. I traveled a lot many years ago."

"And? Where's the greatest place in the world?"

"Here."

I wasn't sure if he meant his court or if there was another meaning locked away there, but I didn't have the nerve to ask. I was fairly certain he'd taken me here and gone through the trouble of getting the necklace so he could have sex with me, but he never moved closer. Instead he used the release of the tether to talk general nonsense.

The hours blurred together.

"Where would you go, Sinna, if you could travel?"

"Just Sin, please."

"Sin? As in, innocent? I'm not sure that fits."

I laughed. "Hey, I get in trouble all the time. I used to—" I stopped myself. *I used to what Sinna? Curse the servants?*

I scrambled to fill the silence with a lie, but when I looked back at Maddox, he didn't seem interested in whatever came next. He nodded, his smile dimming as if he preferred to fill in the rest himself.

Finally he sighed. "I should let you go," he said sitting up, "before anyone notices we're gone."

The bitter taste of disappointment filled my mouth. I nodded and we both stood, the last of the embers glowing beside us. I held my breath as he reached around and unhooked the necklace.

Before he walked me back to my door, before he left, he leaned in. "Speak of this to no one, and I shall come again tomorrow."

The tether tugged as I internally scolded myself for the blush that slipped onto my cheeks and the way his dark eyes made my legs jelly. It might take more than I thought to seduce Maddox, but it seemed as if I'd have another chance tomorrow. I sunk into my bed. With the morning light seeping through the tinted windows, I knew in all of my immortal days where the time seemed to drag on, none would compare to how anxiously I'd wait for tomorrow night to come.

Perhaps I'd be a Hunter yet.

THIRTY-ONE

— MADDOX —

For the next thirty days, when I was sure Ronan was asleep, I showed up to Sinna's room and took her somewhere we could be alone. It was a hassle to invite Melany to my room several times a week, but it kept Ronan's suspicions on the wrong girl. Meanwhile, Sin and I were free to sneak away until the sun broke the horizon.

I brought the necklace to all of our secret meetings, but for some reason, I was afraid to touch her. What would happen when we crossed that line? Would the necklace be able to dull the tether enough? Would we feel differently after? Instead, we talked about everything we were able to. There were notable gaps in the stories she shared as there were with mine, things too precious to disclose to a stranger, but those secrets got more difficult to lock away. One of our favorite topics to discuss was why vampires like blood.

One night while we were strolling through the gallery, Sinna asked, "It can't taste very good. Why do you even like it?"

It took some time to compose a thought. "You know how the mortals say dying makes your whole life flash before your eyes?"

She nodded.

"Well, it's almost like we can taste it. Every feeling, every truth, every memory. Not just at the end but with every drop. It's a reminder of why we should keep living."

I was satisfied with my answer, but it only prompted more questions.

"It doesn't really sound like you want to live."

I shrugged. "If I were to die, this court would fall to infighting and probably an attack from one of the other courts. All immortal courts work this way. The safest way to pass on the throne is to appoint someone, but immortal kings and queens rarely do this. Sometimes if they find their mate, they choose to die and be together. In that case, with their immortality corrupted, they can produce an heir, but both the monarchs and their heir are extremely vulnerable to attack during this time. They rarely survive the transition."

"You did," Sinna said, looking up at me.

"Yes, but that choice started the war. My parents didn't survive, and I grew to maturity and into the full strength of my immortality without them. I was lucky that Ronan chose to protect me, instead of taking the throne for himself."

"He probably didn't want to live forever with a target on his back."

I smiled. "That's a good point."

She turned away, the way she always did when she asked a difficult question. "What do you plan on doing?"

I usually leaned toward silence before I'd resort to lying to her, but I thought she'd appreciate this particular lie. "I plan on living forever as King."

Some nights we'd go to the library, and I read some of my favorite passages to her. Her questions always surprised and entertained me. She had a strange mind. We often spoke of immortality, the sorrows of it, and I was curious about how knowingly she spoke on the topic.

We shared the unique opinion that immortality was as much a burden as a gift, and she suggested that was perhaps the reason I was hesitant when turning new subjects to join the Blood Court.

The council had been remarkably quiet the last few weeks as if they were standing in the wings waiting for my immortality to give way so they could bleed me dry, but I was used to their treachery. I was used to them underestimating my will.

One night I instructed Ronan to send Melany to my chamber, and his face grew deadly serious. "Sire. . . the council sees you giving Miss Melany preferential treatment. They're starting to talk. I must insist you choose another tribute to accompany you for the time being. At least for a while."

I paused, as if thinking hard on the matter when I was practically bursting at the seams that this moment had finally come. "I will not be bullied, Ronan."

"Sire, I too am beginning to question whether. . . I just want to protect you. That's my job."

I put my hand on his shoulder and let out a slow breath. "Fine, send one of the other ones. Maybe Sinna."

He bowed, his demeanor immediately more cheerful. "Yes, Sire."

I closed my door and sat in my bedroom, waiting for the

door to open. I wasn't sure if it was because we were meeting in my bedroom, or if it was because the tether was still firmly in place as she walked down the hall toward me, but nerves flooded my system. There was an energy in the air, a shift, and a hunger in me that wrestled my will before she'd even entered my chamber.

A soft knock sounded at my door, and I stood so fast that I knocked over the chair I was sitting in. I opened the door, and Sinna bowed. "Your Highness, I was told you requested my presence tonight."

I opened the door, and she stepped through, falling instantly into the more casual version of her that I'd gotten to know this past month. She walked around my room, picking things up and observing them, and I closed the door and locked it behind me.

"What happened?" she said finally. "Did Mel tire out early tonight?"

She was teasing me as I often complained about Melany and the show I put on for Ronan's sake, but tonight I didn't feel like joking. I was mesmerized by her presence and struck silent by how badly I wanted to touch her. She picked up the necklace off my vanity and brought it over for me to fasten.

"Wait," I said. "Let me try one thing." I turned her by her waist and slid to the back of her neck, pulling her lips almost to mine.

The tether writhed inside me and I pulled away, grinding my teeth together in frustration.

"How?" I asked half out of breath. "How can you stand it?"

We'd spoken of many things, shared secrets that were best left unsaid, but I'd never addressed the tether so directly. She watched me carefully, and I could see in her clouded eyes the debate she was having about what she should disclose.

"Please," I urged.

She set the necklace down on the table and closed the gap between us taking my hands in hers. "It only hurts when you fight against it. Try giving in."

"I'm afraid." The words slipped out so quickly and I immediately wished I could take them back.

"Me too."

I slipped my hand to the back of her neck and felt my instincts pull away from the tether, the pain rising up, then I let go.

I pulled her lips to mine, letting the tether rush through me, exploding into a fierce sensation that jolted my body to life. Her arms wrapped around my neck, and I pulled her to my body by her waist. The kiss deepened, and I pushed her back onto my bed before I willed myself to break the kiss.

Hunched over, we fought to catch our breath, her eyes were wide, and her lips trembled. I took a step back, and she sat up quickly, covering her nightgown with her arm like a shield like it wasn't the same one she wore on all of our secret meetings.

My heartbeat slowed. "Put the necklace on," I demanded, fear echoing in my voice.

She scrambled for it, and I let her struggle with the clasp rather than help her, too afraid to get any closer. The tether dimmed, and I took a seat beside her on the bed.

"I don't know how you stopped us. If you're as strong-willed as they say. . . I don't think I could've. . ."

My body still pulsed with desire, even with the tether dulled. I needed to have her tonight. I reasoned with myself that this was the whole reason that I sought the necklace to begin with, so that I could safely have my way with her, without damaging my immortality.

What I felt when I kissed her without the tether concerned me. The sensation was more intense than the need to feed on blood. For the first time since we'd started our secret meetings, I doubted my will to resist her.

Luckily tonight I didn't have to.

THIRTY-TWO

— SINNA —

I'd been warned with every kind of rhetoric about how dangerous the tether was. I'd even been practicing giving in so I could build up my tolerance, but when Maddox kissed me, and we had both given in at the same time, it was as if nothing else existed but him. For those precious few moments, there was no assassination, no courts, and no immortality.

That scared me.

I wanted nothing more than to stand up and run back to my room, but as much as I was struggling to compose myself, Maddox seemed equally vexed. I'd rushed to put on the necklace, desperate to dull the tether, but even after I put it on, something lingered.

Maddox's hair was tossed, his eyes red, his body tight with tension. If there was ever a time to coax him into sex, this was it. In all our time together, he hadn't laid a finger on me, and now he looked as if he was struggling not to devour me. I wanted it. I wanted it so bad that I was practically squirming out of my nightgown. This was just the plan. I promised I could keep myself from feeling longer than he could. It was time to prove it. I let my nightgown slip off my shoulder, and Maddox's eyes moved to it before he squeezed them shut, a pained look on his face. When his eyes opened again, they were filled with anger, his brow furrowed as he turned to me. I held my ground, challenging him to push it further with my eyes.

As long as the necklace was on me, it couldn't possibly be as dangerous as that kiss was.

He pushed me back onto the bed, grabbing the collar of my nightgown and tearing it down the middle. He pulled off his silky shirt and pants, his erection pulsing as he crawled over me. I sat up, startled by the suddenness, forgetting my supposed virginity as my body begged for his. He got to his knees, and he stole a kiss before he pulled my body to his. Losing myself, I wrapped my legs around him, and he pushed into me, sending a moan of pleasure echoing through his bedroom. My head rolled back as the pleasure overtook me, and he slid his hand up the back of my neck until my gaze met his. His white fangs glistened with hunger, the need reflected in his ember-glowing eyes.

As his dark tousled hair fell across one of his eyes, I couldn't see the monster. I could only see my mate. He only moved a fraction and the pleasure stacked, so I rolled my hips to push him deeper. He began to drive into me slowly, one godly thrust at a time, pulling an involuntary sound from my lips on each one. Chest to chest, his lips brushed mine. He ran his fangs gently across my neck, sending a chill through my body, and then he kissed me, driving harder into me.

The tether strained for release, fighting to break through the suppression of the necklace. Behind Maddox's eyes, I saw something I couldn't understand. Frustration, maybe? But what he did next made everything clear.

He kissed me as if in search of that feeling; The one that the necklace kept at bay.

He kissed me harder, timing it with a powerful push that started a frenzy in me. Without warning, he reached up and tore the necklace off of me, and the jewels scattered across his marble floors. We froze, my heartbeat synching with his as all the fear I should have felt blurred by desire.

The tether ignited, and I leaned forward and whispered against his lips, "Please."

He watched me so carefully I was afraid to breathe, then thrust into me. This time the necklace wasn't there to dull the pleasure from tearing through me. I lost control, my voice carrying, my hips driving him deeper. I burst into orgasm in seconds, my body shaking, with tears streaming down my face, but Maddox didn't stop. He held me, watching closely, driving into me again and again, until finally his body jerked and I felt his release explode inside me.

He buried his face into my chest and pulled me close. We collapsed, straining for air until we caught our breath. Then, with only a glance to acknowledge the line we'd crossed, we started again.

I awoke to the red-filtered light pouring through the window onto my face. Maddox's arms were wrapped around me, his breaths even and slow behind me. The tether flowed, and I felt the warmth of something new present in my chest. I was too afraid to move, too afraid to wake Maddox and put a permanent end to the loveliest night I'd ever had.

"You're awake," he said softly.

I sat up, turning to look at him, only to realize that he'd already been awake. He had already showered and changed into his day clothes. I rubbed my face. "Good morning."

He looked somber, his expression full of the same hard lines that were a permanent fixture on the Blood King, but rarely graced Maddox's face when we were alone. He lifted me and carried me to his bathroom, where a bath was already drawn. He lowered me into it, with no regard for his clothes getting wet. He sat on the edge of the tub then sighed. "I think we should stop this. We should take some time apart."

I wanted to tell him no, to pull him into the tub with me. I wanted to tell him we could endure it a little longer, but I was his assassin. The Hunter who would take his life. I didn't know how things had changed overnight. I held my tongue. When I didn't reply, he rubbed his hands together and stood, leaving me to soak with my thoughts.

I sank into the tub, my thoughts racing as the doubts about my mission crept in. Was I compromised? Was that why I insisted Finn to follow Ronan instead of me? What would Ezra say if she could see me now?

What was I thinking? Maddox drank the blood of innocents who were just trying to escape poverty. He lorded his court's strength over all the others, and his court nearly succeeded in wiping my court out completely--driving them into a hundred years of living underground. He was the devil, and yet, each time I closed my eyes, I could taste his lips and feel the threat of his fangs sweeping over my neck. My body perked with the memory.

If I was compromised, did that mean he was too? I splashed my face with water. If there's a Hunter in me, it was time for her to emerge.

I was in daze as I walked somberly to the dining room for breakfast. The other girls were already seated. It wasn't until the servants placed the dinner trays in front of me that I noticed Mel's scowl. But it was Celine's face that struck me.

Her eyes were dim and rimmed with darkness, her cheeks were sunken in and although she had a plate in front of her, she only pushed the food around with her chopsticks.

Before I could ask her what was wrong, Mel blurted, "You were with the King last night, weren't you?"

I exhaled before taking a bite of spicy cabbage. "Ronan was concerned the King was spending too much time with one tribute. If anything, it's a compliment."

Celine's mouth dropped open. "And he picked YOU instead? He likes me the least?" Her eyes welled, and she began to cry.

"W-we don't know that. I think he just told Ronan to pick anyone else."

She shook her head, burying her face in her hands. "No," her breath skipped. "He hardly looks at me at all."

I wasn't sure if my words had eased Mel's worries or if she was reacting purely to help Celine feel better, but we both sprung into comfort mode. Even after Celine fell asleep with Mel and me stroking her hair, Mel's intensity never returned.

"Sorry," she said, her voice low as to not wake Celine. "I think all of this is making me crazy."

I nodded, my gaze moving back to Celine. "I think it's making us all crazy."

"You just don't understand," she said. "I love him."

I did understand. I understood more than I wanted to. Her words stung me, but instead of turning away, I needed to know more. "How do you know?"

She sighed and stared up at nothing in particular, her eyes

distant. "I can't stop thinking about him. It's like. . . my body craves him or something. And immortality, that eternal gift that I'd come here seeking, it wouldn't matter unless he chose me. Does that make sense?"

All I could offer her was a nod. I stood and headed towards the door. "I'm going to get some rest. I'll be right next door if either of you needs me."

She smiled, her thoughts still adrift in her feelings for Maddox-- feelings she could embrace while I was forced to swallow them. I left the room feeling sorry for myself--turning my back on someone who truly needed me. Now I wondered if I could have endured Mel's feelings for Maddox for a few more hours, if Celine would have survived.

THIRTY-THREE

—— MADDOX ——

I spent the morning in the atrium among the blood thorns, the slow falling snowflakes punctuating my thoughts as I replayed the night before in my head and scolded myself for losing control. I'd known what Sinna was since she entered my court. I just planned to resist her longer. I wanted more of these perfect, beautiful moments. We'd only just begun, but the pull of a destined mate was far greater than I'd anticipated. Now the danger was real. I could feel it in my body, the rush of blood in my veins, my mortality looming. I'd lived too long to believe I could hide it. I'd seen immortal monarchs fall before. The moment a King's immortality fails, the sharks smell blood in the water. Would I have a week? A day? Or less? Would Sinna?

I wanted more time with her than I had counted on, the only loose end to an otherwise perfect plan.

If I spent time away from her, would my feelings dim? Was

there any way to reset what had already been done? For once in my existence, my time was up, only it didn't bring me the comfort I thought it would. I picked a flower just as I had the night things started to change. I stared at it as the petals turned crimson. How had she bewitched me so completely, that for the first time in centuries I had the will to live? I should've sent her away before it was too late for her to escape.

A bone-rattling scream tore through the Blood Court. My skin felt on fire when I recognized the voice as Sinna's. I tore through the cathedral towards the sound and burst into the hallway where Ronan stared wide-eyed into Celine's bedroom. Before I reached him, I tasted Celine's blood in the air and saw the veins protruding from Ronan's neck as he restrained his urge to feed.

I turned to him, but his eyes looked through me. Several courtiers wandered into the hall, drawn to the scent of blood like flowers to sunlight.

"Don't let anyone in," I said, rushing in.

Melany sat at the foot of her bed, her gaze hollow, her face pale and clammy. She stammered and gave up on whatever she was trying to say, dropping her head and staring at the floor. The sound of running water drew my attention towards the bathroom, where blood mixed with water seeped onto the bedroom floor. The smell threatened to put my head in a fog, but fear for Sinna kept me alert.

I stepped into the bathroom, my eyes widening as the tub overflowed with Celine's blood, the tap still running over. Sinna held Celine's body to her chest, squeezing a blood-soaked towel around Celine's limp wrists.

She turned to me suddenly, her eyes widening.

"Help her, Maddox!" she screamed, her voice cracking, tears streaming down her face.

There wasn't a member of the Blood Court who would have reacted so strongly to a bloody death. It was practically built into our culture, but it was obvious Sinna had never witnessed anything quite so gruesome. I'd forgotten long ago that these were people, worth more than their blood or their company. Sinna's agony reminded me of that.

"What happened?" I said, finally.

"Bite her, Maddox! Change her! Make her immortal!"

"What happened, Sin?"

"She-she cut herself. She's out of time. Save her Maddox! Please!" she begged.

I stumbled back. "I can't."

She began to rock with Celine in her arms. "Why can't you? Do this for me."

"If she wants to die. . . I can't make her immortal. I won't. I'm sorry, Sin."

Celine's body convulsed, but I hadn't heard a heartbeat, not even when I first came in.

Sinna wiped her tears, smearing blood on her face. She rested Celine down on the floor and stood.

"Sin, I'm sorry." I reached for her, "Immortality is—"

She slapped my hand away. "I know very well what immortality is." She stared up at me, her brown and black flecked eyes bearing into me. "I'll never forgive you for this."

She pushed past me.

"Sin, please!"

I stopped short when I saw Ronan's face as Sinna pushed by him. His eyes narrowed, then he turned and hurried away. A mortal king is a dead king. I was surprised Ronan didn't rip me to shreds right there. If Sinna didn't leave now, she was going to die, and I was dead either way.

How could she expect me to imbue someone who wanted to die with immortality? How, after I'd shared with her my own feelings on eternal life? It was a curse, an unnatural divinity given to those who deserve it least. The greedy, the power-hungry, and the envious. Mortals had loved ones to leave behind. Immortals were empty, and I was now somewhere between them. There was no time to make amends. I needed her to leave.

I went to her bedroom, knocking on the door and urging her to come out, but I heard nothing inside. The courtiers who usually avoided this part of the cathedral to avoid the temptation of the mortal tributes or to be beyond suspicion if one were to be found dead and drained, breezed casually through, their prying eyes all whispering the same thing, *time is up*.

I headed back to my room, hoping that Ronan might be able to coax her out, as long as I could convince him that he'd misinterpreted what he saw. I stopped short when I saw Ronan pacing outside my door, no doubt waiting for a private moment to interrogate me. I'd been so swept up with Celine's death and Sinna's anger that I'd allowed her to speak informally, with no regard to who was listening.

Ronan was no idiot. I'd have to be resolute in my argument to convince him not to wipe Sinna out immediately, or if his loyalty was in any way compromised and he didn't believe my lie, he might kill me instead.

He opened the door, following me inside my quarters and closing the door behind me.

"She's your mate, isn't she?"

"No. She is as unremarkable as the others."

He stepped closer. "Don't lie to me. I heard what she said."

"Her friend died. She was in shock, and she'll be punished and killed immediately for her disobedience. Bring her to me at once."

His fangs jutted out of his mouth. "There's talk of an uprising. The whole court thinks you're compromised."

"Now that I've explained that I am not, you should know we have nothing to fear."

He rubbed his hands over his face. "If you're lying about this, I'll—"

"You'll what? If you don't fall back in line, your disobedience will be dealt with, just as I will deal with Sinna's and anyone else who would question their king. You may consider this an opportunity to prove your loyalty. Bring the girl here immediately, and I shall drain her just like I did with Nova."

I could see in the sudden slump of his shoulders that the mention of Nova had temporarily disarmed him. He'd had similar suspicions of her and confronted me in a similar manner, only to be proven wrong with a pale corpse.

His gaze filled with sadness. "Yes, Sire. I'll be right outside, just in case."

THIRTY-FOUR

— S I N N A —

I was all the way back to my room when I realized how covered in blood I was. I ran into my bathroom and tried to wash it off in the sink, while bile rose in the back of my throat. My throat was raw from screaming, my eyes red from crying. *Why, Celine?*

I'd never seen blood before. It was a terrifyingly bright substance that boisterously screamed how quickly a life was fading. In that desperate moment, I wanted to save her. I'd been so caught up in my own goals I wasn't there for her. If I had the power to save her, the power that Maddox was so hesitant to use, she'd still be alive. I stared at my blotchy face in the mirror, and no matter how long I looked, I didn't see a Hunter. Ferah was right. I'd gotten this far only to realize I didn't have what it took.

Movement behind me drew my attention. A dark shadow

slithered across the tiles, weaving through my bloody footprints. The color deepened then rose out of the ground in a black mass. The black mist cleared, and Finn stood in front of me, his eyes filled with sorrow.

"She. . . she died."

He pulled me into his chest, and I let my legs go weak as he rubbed my back in circles. "I know."

He pulled back, his hands on both my shoulders and his jaw clenched. He exhaled through his nose, and then he said, "You need to make a choice Sinna. The vampires know you're the King's mate and the majority of them also believe the King is no longer immortal."

I stepped back, shaking his hands off me. "Are you sure?"

"Yes. They didn't know which of the tributes it was, since he spent a lot of time with Mel too, but after you yelled at the King, they were certain."

I wrung my hands. "Okay, so what do we do?"

"I think we should escape."

"W-what about the King? You just said he's mortal. I can kill him, and we can escape after."

He ran a hand through his hair. "Ferah hasn't responded to my correspondence. We don't have backup yet. Something's wrong. After everything with Celine. . . surely you're not considering trying to go through with the assassination."

I turned away, hoping to hide any pain that slipped onto my face.

"You've already done enough. It's too dangerous. I just heard the King say he was going to kill you himself. We don't have time. We have to go now."

I spun back around. "He said that?"

He nodded.

Why was I not surprised? I'd been told again and again how heartless the Blood King was. How did I allow myself to get so caught up in it and think I was somehow exempt from the slaughter? He hoarded immortality and slew anyone who sought it. He wouldn't even save my dying friend when I begged him. He let her die in my arms.

My blood boiled, my heart racing inside my chest. He thought he was going to kill me? He had another thing coming. "Let's finish the mission."

Finn licked his lips, his eyes never rising to meet me. "Is your immortality compromised, Sin?"

"No. Let's finish this. We kill him, and then we'll escape."

"I need to know the truth. If I go in there thinking you're safe and it turns out you are compromised, I might not be able to protect you. I need to know, Sin."

I crossed my arms over my chest. "I--I don't know for sure. I just know that if I don't do this, if I don't prove myself as a Hunter, I'll always regret it. This is my shot. Are you with me or not?"

His gaze struck me with intensity. "I've been with you the whole time."

The black mist rose up in his hand, dispersing to reveal his granite-hilted dagger- those used only by the Hunters.

I took it, steeling my nerves for whatever came next.

"We'll have to lay low for a little while. Hide in the woods until Ferah signals us that it's safe to return. Otherwise, we'll lead them right to our court, and we don't know how far along they are in their preparations."

"Got it." He placed his hand over the dagger and it dissolved into mist. "It'll be there when you need it," he said, brushing his thumb across my cheek. "As will I."

My heart hummed with anticipation as Finn melted into my shadow. I turned back to the sink and resumed washing the blood off my hands, only now my hands shook. A knock sounded at my door and my body tensed, as I slowly made my way to it. I pulled it open and Ronan glared at me, his formidable frame puffed up, and his nostrils flaring.

"The King has requested your presence immediately."

When he spoke, his fangs grew into sharp points. I bit down on the inside of my cheek to stop myself from cowering. I followed as he marched me to the King's bedroom, like a prison guard marching a prisoner to death row, but Ronan didn't know what I was.

I might be the King's mate, but I'm much more than that. I'm a Shadow Mage. I'm a Princess. I'm a sister. I'm a spy. And when the night is over, I'll be a Hunter too.

I am an executioner.

A King Killer, and no one will ever underestimate me again. I want Maddox to look me in the eye in his last moments and beg for his immortality while his life slips away. Only then will I be satisfied.

THIRTY-FIVE

—— M A D D O X ——

I knew she was coming, but I was still stunned when she stepped into my chamber. She'd pulled her hair back into a ponytail. Her eyes were focused on me, but they didn't look at me with the same deference that they had before. They were ablaze with anger. I knew my decision to let Celine die had hurt her, and that she might not ever understand it, but I wasn't meeting with her to make amends.

I walked to my dresser and tossed her a rose that was sitting there, the one I'd given her the night before. She caught it, then jerked her hand back, dropping the blood thorn to the ground. Then I smelled it for the first time. Her blood. I walked over to her and took her hand in mine, wiping the red bead and staring in disbelief.

She loves me.

Her blood was the sweetest, most intoxicating scent I'd ever known, and I stepped back, frightened that I might break my promise and give in to the powerful temptation to taste her. Her cheeks bulged from her clenched jaw. A black cloud engulfed her hand, then cleared, leaving a dagger in its place. I walked to the door and locked it.

I took a deep breath and turned to face her.

"You don't seem surprised."

I put my hands in my pockets. "Why would I be surprised?"

"That I'm a Shadow Mage."

I grinned. "You may have a mortal father, but you could never pass as mortal. Plus, you look a lot like your parents. I met them once."

Her brow furrowed.

"I knew from the second you stepped into my court who and what you were."

She gritted her teeth. "You're lying. If you knew what I was, why didn't you kill me right there?"

"You're my mate."

"That's more of a reason. Why did you spare me? Did you pity me? Did you really think the great and powerful Blood King could withstand the pull of the tether? You got cocky, and now you'll die for it."

I couldn't help but smile at her as she worked herself up. I knew she needed to in order to complete her mission. "It wasn't that."

She stepped close to me and placed the dagger against my neck.

"Why then?" Tears slipped from her eyes, rolling down her soft cheeks.

I wanted to reach out and wipe them away. To kiss her and to reassure her, to take away some of the pain I caused. But she needed that pain.

"I wanted to. . . " The words got stuck in the back of my throat, my fear making them grow thicker. I swallowed hard.

She lowered her knife. "You wanted to what?" Her eyes widened. "To die?"

"I wouldn't expect you to understand."

"That's right. I don't."

"You haven't been alive as long as I have. You weren't there for the war."

She dropped her head. "So, your plan was to just let me... " She bawled her fist. "Make a fool out myself?"

"You came here to seduce and kill me, right? I figured it wouldn't hurt to let you. We both were getting what we wanted."

Her voice came out soft like a whisper. "Wanted?"

"The tether was stronger than I thought. Much stronger. I didn't expect things to happen so quickly. I wound up kind of wishing for more time. But this is it. This is all we get."

"So it's true then. You're not immortal anymore?"

I unbuttoned my shirt, pulling my shirt open to my exposed chest. "There's only one way to know."

She cried softly, her gaze never leaving mine.

"Do it." I urged. "Or have your shadow do it. You both need to get out of here. You have a sister to go home to, remember? I don't have anyone."

The door handle rattled, and my heart jumped up to my throat.

Sinna stepped closer, and I could see her shaking. "I... I can't do it," She said, sinking her face into my chest.

I wrapped my arms around her. "Then listen. You have to get out of here. Quickly. Please, Sin. You'll die here."

"They're going to kill you. Your own people. . . they're going to kill you."

"It's okay, Sin. Go."

"I can't."

Fuck. She's going to die, and it's my fault. How can I make her leave?
Ronan pounded on the door.

Panic settled in. "Please, Sin, please go."

Sinna's shadow grew, growing darker and rising from the floor like a cloud of ash. Sinna's arms tightened around me, "I won't leave you."

The familiar sensation of steel pierced my chest, and sliced through only inches from Sinna's head. Only this time, I felt the warmth of my blood as it slipped down my chest. I collapsed to the floor, stunned as the pain ate away at the corners of my vision. *So this is it? This time it's real.* A man pulled Sinna away as she screamed and fought, her arms reaching for me.

Mine instinctively reached for her, but her voice was muffled and fading fast.

Black ash consumed them, and they were gone, seconds before the door crashed open, and Ronan rushed in.

In his eyes, I did not see the traitor I'd expected. I did not see a man vying for the throne. There was only desperation and sorrow as he fought to slow the bleeding. I guess I was wrong about him. I wonder what other things I was wrong about.

I closed my eyes, pulling the memory of Sinna back to me as I lost everything else, bit by bit. I wouldn't change a thing, Sinna. I'd fall in love with you all over again. It might've been selfish, knowing I'd corrupted your immortality as well. But you'll forget me and regain it in time. For now, at the moment of my death, you love me, and I wasn't wrong about how that might feel, except for one part.

I only wish we had more time.

THIRTY-SIX

— S I N N A —

A s soon as we made it out of the cathedral, we could hear footsteps behind us. My heart ached as Finn slipped us seamlessly through the shadows as only an expert Hunter could. Maddox was dead.

My mate.

Gone just like that.

I let my body go limp, relying fully on Finn's guidance to lead us to safety. I shuttered as I felt the tether waning, terrified that at any moment, I'd feel it go out completely. The sound of footsteps in the snow grew closer, and Finn's pace increased despite the fact that he already seemed winded. Was he scared of what he'd just done or what would happen to us if they caught us?

I didn't know. All I knew is there was still a tether. Maddox had known all along who I was. He fell willingly into love. I was no spy. I was no Hunter. I was nothing. I'd let down my sister, my people, and I lost my mate, trying to be something that I wasn't. Maddox might've been the things I accused him of.

He was careless with his life. . . with all life, and far too powerful for his own good. But, he knew who he was and what he wanted. My finger stung, so I popped in in my mouth, the iron taste of blood drawing my attention.

I loved him.

We'd hardly gotten any time at all, but it was more than most in the Shadow Court ever got.

Now that I knew what I was giving up, I no longer wanted to. I pressed my hand against my chest, hoping the tether wouldn't break. One more minute. Please, Maddox. One more minute.

Finn stopped short, interweaving us with the shadow of the nearest tree, and holding us completely still. A snow-white wolf crept through the moonlit forest, and we watched from the darkness where only Shadow Mages could dwell. The wolf moved closer, its nose twitching over the snow.

I held my breath. Could he smell us? We were dead. The wolf approached our shadow and started pawing at the darkened snow. We were undetectable to the naked eye, but if he could smell us, he could follow us until we came out of shadow form. A soft whine floated out of the beast. I looked closely, his icy blue eyes jogging a memory. The night of the Moon ball, I'd spent the night dancing with those eyes, but in human form.

"King Herod?" I whispered.

The wolf nuzzled the snow and let out a low whine.

"Finn, I think he wants us to go with him."

"It could be a trap."

"You said yourself we can't go home. This might be our best chance."

Finn paused for a moment then nodded to me.

I watched the snowy creature as its gaze stared at the nothingness of our shadow, pacing around as its breath came out in white clouds around its muzzle.

"Alright, Your Majesty. Show us the way."

The giant puppy started back through the woods, toward the Moon Court, with the full moon hanging over us all to witness what unfolded next.

I held my breath and counted down each minute, urging Maddox through the tether to hang on for just one more each time. The wind howled around us, filling the night air with an eerie gloom that said this was only the beginning of something I couldn't yet understand. I was glad for it.

I was not a Hunter--but maybe if I could be brave enough, I could find out what I am.

AUTHOR'S NOTE

Thank you for reading *Chaste Blood*! Stay up to date on the release of *Chaste Moon, Repressed Royals: Book 2* by signing up to my newsletter.

Need more NOW? I have two COMPLETE trilogies available now!
NA Paranormal Romance: *The Fae & The Fallen*
YA Fantasy Romance: *Kingdom Cold*

I specialize in multicultural romances with a ton of angst and my favorite trope is enemies to lovers.

Special Shout out to my amazing PATRONS!
Kisha Wilson
Shelly Wilson
Jeanette George
Kellie Rivera
Christopher J Canady
Sabrina Jacklin